A Star's Hidden Fire

K. Malady

Also By

For the stars that burn in hidden places, and the souls brave enough to chase them.

"It is that something in the soul which says, – Rage on, whirl on, I tread master here and everywhere; master of the spasms of the sky and of the shatter of the sea, master of nature and passion and death, and of all terror and all pain." -Walt Whitman

Chapter 1

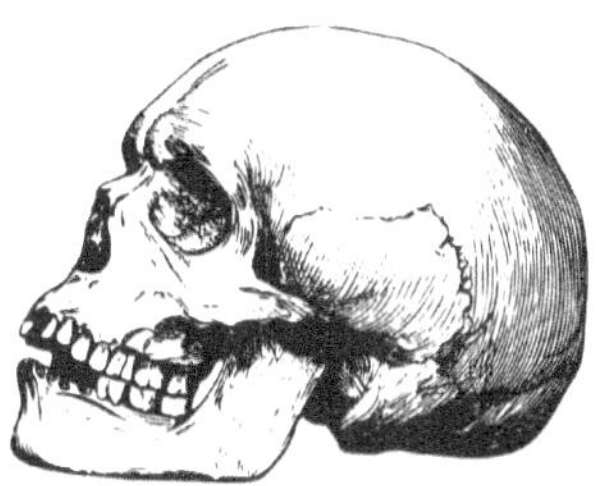

ALEC LEANS STIFFLY AGAINST the yellowed floral wallpaper, settling into the corner of the rundown house. Standing under six feet tall, his lean frame and deeply set blue eyes draw attention. Once an anomaly in his village—when he was a human eighteen-year-old—his tawny skin and slender build mark him as peculiar; now, in the twenty-first century, those same features are alluring.

He wears his standard black uniform, adapted for modern times: a black t-shirt and leather jacket replace the breeches and waistcoat of centuries past. The fabrics cling neatly to his form, immaculate from lack of wear. His raven-black hair, perpetually unruly, swoops into his vision until he shakes it aside. Attempts to trim it are futile—it always regrows by morning, just as his wiry physique remains unchanged by the years. Such are the curses of his immortal state.

But he isn't here for the shallow thrills of this gathering. Alec's purpose is singular: to hunt. In this sea of humanity, his senses are sharp, attuned to the presence of tainted souls. It's an art honed over centuries—finding prey among the masses, rooting out corruption to sustain his existence. He stays on the periphery, scanning, waiting.

The cloying scent of desire hangs thick in the air, making Alec wrinkle his nose. He has long avoided human indulgences—sex, romance, even casual connections with mortals—tools his kind wield for ulterior motives. Humans only real value lies in their souls, fuel for survival.

This gathering, however, is a disappointment. The room is thick with souls, but none carry the corruption he seeks. Alec pushes off the wall and heads toward the kitchen, the dim hope of finding better hunting grounds spurring his retreat. His time is running out—less than a month remains before his stolen soul fades, threatening to unmake him. Given his hunts take several weeks, he can't afford to linger here.

As he wanders past two dull-eyed men, someone shoves a young woman into the kitchen. She looks close to his age, or at least close to the age he was when the years stopped showing on his face. She stumbles, spins, and locks eyes with him. A flicker of amusement dances in her gaze before she turns toward the doorway.

A phantom pulse trembles in his chest. If he were a poetic being—if the romantic part of him survived his creation into a wraith and the trials his long life imposed on him—he might liken her presence to a lightning bolt cutting through a summer storm. But as he repeatedly reminds himself, he isn't.

She isn't the loveliest woman here, nor the best dressed. Loose, ripped trousers—a human invention, jeans—hang on her frame, and her olive shirt is crumpled as if she's arrived directly from bed. Stray locks of dark blonde hair escape a messy bun, framing a fawn-colored face. When she snarls at whoever pushed her, baring slightly crooked teeth peeking out from full lips, her brown eyes burn with defiance. She stomps past Alec, her presence a stark contrast to the room's cultivated revelry. The others recoil. He can't read their thoughts, as that isn't the immortal gift he received, but their sharp emotions reveal disdain.

That alone might draw him, as outcasts make worthy prey. Alec knows outcasts, having been one himself all those centuries ago. Though he tried, his village found him odd, with his unusual looks, his build too slender to work a metal forge, and his pacifist nature. His solitude made him easy prey for Michael, his sire, whose fateful decision spared Alec from death but condemned him to something far worse.

Alec sluices off the memories of his conversion to focus on the young woman. He exhales slowly, centering his mind to use his wraith gifts to discover the measure of her soul. His empathic ability skims the surface of her emotions. But instead of the barrage of foreign feelings he should find, he hits a wall.

The phantom pulse in his heart migrates uncomfortably to the pit of his stomach. His skills in reading humans are unmatched, and he's not had difficulty reading humans since Michael finished training him almost two millennia ago. Alec curls his hands into fists, using the bite of his fingernails against his palms to clear his thoughts. He tries a second time, gradually unfurling his hands until he *finally* locks in on her emotions.

A powerful burst of frustration hits him like a wave. Any other emotions stay hidden, muddled as if behind ice or at the bottom of a well. He frowns. There are only three reasons why her emotions would be shrouded: his exhaustion is dulling his gifts, she is something supernatural herself, or—most troubling—his abilities are somehow weakening. He immediately drowns the worry, instead reaching deeper to probe her soul.

But it isn't where it should be.

When he finally locates it, the discovery only deepens his unease. Her soul is nearly saintlike, its faint essence pristine but curiously diluted, like dye-tinted water instead of the ink thick color he'd expect. Still, what he can read is righteous and pure.

Alec exhales again, soft and resigned. As he only hunts tainted souls, the honorable shouldn't hold his focus, no matter that she is the brightest spot of goodness he's ever encountered. But she isn't prey.

He spins the amber ring on his finger absently, the ancient engraving cool against his skin. He *must* be tired, explaining both his interest in the woman and his inability to read her. Dismissing her from his thoughts, he turns back toward the kitchen, intent on finding his prey or leaving this cheap imitation of a bacchanal.

But then, a new presence brushes against his senses—a blond man by the sink, taking a slow drag from a long-necked bottle. He is a perfect example of androgynous allure, tall with tawny skin and strong, lean muscles, as if chiseled from marble. His allure masks the rot that festers beneath, his emotions a scuzzy mix of triumphant and entitled. Alec probes his soul and recoils. It's foul, a tangled web of deceit and depravity. It *also* seems half hidden, like the woman's, but her complete opposite—as if the burbling and clotting vileness on the surface conceals the greater infection below.

The only soul Alec has encountered that even came close belonged to a serial killer he investigated in London a century ago. The Council had feared the man was a rogue wraith whose killing spree might draw unwanted attention to the family. Yet even that murderer's soul, twisted and vile as it was, didn't compare to the festering corruption radiating from the man before him.

A slow grin spreads across Alec's lips. *Found you*.

The man now marked for Alec's consumption wanders toward the living room, and Alec follows with predatory focus. His steps falter as the man approaches the saintly blonde woman. Watching the pair, Alec's grin fades. The man places a hand on her waist, whispers something in her ear, and her emotions ripple faintly with familiarity and resentment.

His stomach turns.

This man, this odious human, not only knows the woman but claims her with an intimacy that twists Alec's stomach. He loves her—or at least, he believes he does—though Alec doubts the vile are capable of true love. A faint smile tugs at Alec's lips as he considers the unintended benefit of his hunt. His prey never dies when their souls are taken; they linger on, living out their natural lifespan as hollow shells, free from human desires or burdens. A husk is always preferable to a monster. She will never have to suffer that man's poison again.

Alec stalks toward them, their blond hair a beacon through the smoky haze. Somewhere, a music box whirs to life, smaller and sleeker than the clunky contraptions he remembered from decades ago. A terrible beat vibrates through the room, and the open space between him and the couple swarms with bodies writhing against each other. Alec's lips press into a thin line, his fists curling as a boy stumbles into him. The twit grins vacantly, holding out a hand-rolled cigarette that momentarily slows Alec's advance.

"I'm here," the woman mutters to Alec's prey, her voice smoky and rich, reminiscent of the lounge singers he once encountered in dimly lit clubs seventy years ago. Her figure, with its soft curves, could have graced the pinups of that same era. "Now what?"

Alec's prey tosses an arm over her shoulder. The woman flinches before schooling her face back to indifference. "Dear, sweet sister, you know the drill," the young man answers in a deep baritone.

Siblings. Alec should have realized it sooner. Centuries of practice have sharpened his ability to read human emotions, mapping their mannerisms to their experiences with ease. He can tell the drugged-out boy who bumped into him is studying something far beyond his grasp, his narcotic crutch reeking of self-doubt. He sees the bond between the men in the kitchen in their mirrored gestures and the faint ripple of affection they share. Desires, hopes, fears—Alec's senses lay them bare. But the siblings elude him, their emotions slipping through his grasp like water.

"Now? The semester doesn't start until Tuesday," the woman complains, throwing her brother's arm off her shoulder.

"As the saying goes: a wise man will make more opportunities than he finds," he says, smirking. The siren's mouth drops open before she clamps it shut.

"I can't believe you're using quotes on me. That's my thing," she complains with narrowed eyes. "How the hell do you remember that?"

"I went to high school, too, Az." He grabs her wrist as if afraid she will run off if he doesn't keep ahold of her. "Just look for someone who isn't a townie loser."

"*We're* townie losers," 'Az' says, pulling away.

"No, we're opportunists who happen to live in town."

She rolls her eyes as if this is an oft-repeated argument. "What about him?" She drags her eyes from Alec's hairline to his shoes, a move that would cause him to flush, if he'd been able to do so.

"He looks international," is the brother's terse reply.

"That's racist. Maybe he's been at the beach. Summer did just end."

"It's not racist, it's practical," he replies sharply. "How in the hell could I-"

Alec finally liberates himself from the crowd, interrupting the annoyed discussion between the siblings. He considers bowing, before remembering the action fell out of favor. "I am Alec Gravely," he announces.

The two stare silently for a moment, faces blank. He's about to peek back at their emotions to find out what he's done wrong when his prey finally speaks.

"I'm Eli, and this is Azalea," he says, jutting a thumb in Azalea's direction.

A dull flush appears on Azalea's cheeks. His eyes stray from her crooked smile to her bright eyes. "I go by Azzie," she says. "As my brother *should* know, I'm not a huge fan of my actual name."

"Azalea, meaning flower. A symbol of softness and feminine beauty," Alec murmurs. The name pulls him back to the Victorian era, when Michael had delighted in courting both eligible and ineligible women, using the language of flowers to send them risqué messages. Not once had he chosen an azalea for his swains. Alec had spent a month berating him for flouting the Rules, only for Michael to retaliate with a bouquet of withered leaves.

Her blush intensifies while Eli snorts, replying, "Right, when I think of softness and femininity, I think Az."

"I don't see why you wouldn't," Alec says sharply. In that moment, he vows to steal Eli's soul without delay and take him somewhere for the wraith-like justice normally reserved for the lesser orders. Though Alec rarely employs those tactics anymore, more concerned with Rule breaking than retribution, something about the siblings creates the craving. He wants to shield Azalea, to wrap her in silk and protect her from the monsters in human form—monsters like her brother.

Considering *he's* also a monster in human form, it's a confusing desire.

The siblings exchange a glance at Alec's remark, Azalea's lips curling into a grin. "So, where are you from?"

"Abroad."

Eli smirks and jabs an elbow at Azalea.

"My family has an old property here. I'll remain there for the few weeks I'm visiting Asheville," Alec adds.

"Which one?" Azalea asks, elbowing the brother back.

Alec's dark brows rise. "Rockton House."

Years ago, Alec had laid the groundwork for a long-term plan in Asheville. The 'Gravelys,' a reclusive family of his own invention, had purchased Rockton House and the surrounding land a century and a half earlier, back when Asheville was still known as 'Morristown.' Local history, carefully shaped by rumors and tales spread by Alec's servants, painted the house—a two-story, five-bay structure more fortress than home—as a Gravely family stronghold. Over the years, the whispered legends took root, elevating it to the status of a local landmark.

Azalea's eyes gleam while the brother's narrow. "No way," they say in tandem.

Alec nods, to cover his fumbling understanding of the phrasing. "Yes... way."

"Isn't that place haunted?" Azalea asks.

"Not that I've noticed," Alec says, one corner of his lips tilting upward. He is, after all, the only supernatural entity haunting Rockton. "But I will keep my eye out."

"You should have a party before you leave and show off the place," Eli says, an unsettling glint in his eye.

Alec considers that Eli's rotten core must be in his demeanor, as someone with a soul worse than a serial killer couldn't be freely roaming the streets of this small town. He doesn't seem clever enough to hide his crimes from the authorities.

"That would be cool," Azalea agrees, her eyes mirroring Eli's mischievous spark. There's no denying their familial bond now.

Alec has seen little of the human world this century, and for good reason. His time here must be focused on fulfilling obligations to his kind: capturing souls and preventing Rule breaking wraiths from corrupting the species. The wraiths who stray are as worthless as the lesser orders.

Yet, as Alec glances between Azalea and Eli, he weighs the risks. His past entanglements with mortals have cost him dearly, and the punishments from the Council were lessons he didn't dare forget. But if entertaining their suggestion for a 'party' brings him closer to his prey, perhaps it's worth considering.

"I might appreciate the chance to meet my neighbors," Alec finally replies.

"Eli, I bet Benji's lighting up in the backyard," Azalea says, her gaze still fixed on Alec. The glint in Eli's eye sharpens into something greedy, a scent that emanates from him, and he saunters off without a word.

When the two are alone, Azalea's gaze sharpens. "What brings you to Asheville?"

"It was time for a brief visit home," he lies. His eyes remain on Azalea, though they should follow Eli's departure. Azalea shouldn't to hold his interest, but she does. "Have you been in Asheville long?" he asks.

"All my life." Her eyes twitch. "Though technically, we're in Lonetree now."

"Your correction is appreciated."

"You talk like you're straight out of the 1800s," she says, laughing.

Alec's lip curls again in response to her smile. "Private tutors," he explains, hoping the lie covers any gaffe in his speech patterns. It's a smaller deception than she'll ever know, given his history with the language.

"Fair point," she says, her lips twisting in thought. "But why didn't you go to school here? I'm pretty sure you didn't, since I went to the fancy school in your neck of the woods until middle school." She studies him closely. "I'm sure I'd have remembered you."

Alec doesn't answer, instead running his eyes over the attendees once again. Her beguiling voice and innocent eyes make him *want*—and wanting is dangerous. The amber jewel in his ring flickers as if in agreement.

Azalea's voice draws his attention back to her. "You there, Alec? I'm not sure how it's done abroad, but here it's rude to ignore someone when they're talking to you."

Her words sound sharp, but her emotions ripple with amusement. He can't understand it—he's off-kilter, and it's her fault. To protect himself from pulling her to him and smelling her hair, he counters, "Is it not also rude to accost new acquaintances with questions?"

"Not when they're as secretive as you," she retorts with a smirk. "And 'rudeness' is the sauce to my wit."

"Shakespeare?" The word flies from his mouth against his will.

Her smirk changes to something less sharp. "Yeah, are you a fan?"

He can't admit he's met the man, much less saved him from a rogue wraith out of love for his work. That intervention cost Alec twenty years of penance for breaking the First Rule. "A bit," he says instead, the memory of his weakness souring his mood. "I have little time for reading," he adds gruffly—a lie, if ever there was one. He has nothing but time, counting his immortal life in months and years rather than hours and days, each year marking the never-ending creep toward oblivion.

"I have nothing but time," Azalea mutters with a sigh. Her emotions sour slightly, a smugness Alec finds oddly unpleasant. Perhaps even the brightest souls aren't as flawless as they seem.

Humanity can be so confusing.

"Almost no one I know reads," she tells him, explaining the smugness. "But it's the only way to escape the monotony of this place." She gestures around the room that serves as a physical example of the sleepiness of the town. Her demeanor shifts again, a giddy frisson of nervousness spiraling from her, smelling more like anticipation instead of fear. "Did you—do you want to dance?"

His sparking blue eyes reflect in the brown of hers. Another woman might run, probably should run, from the otherness so apparent in his gaze. But she leans closer, as if he wasn't a predator, as if she was something other than prey.

"I—I can't," Alec stammers, bowing curtly. As he rises, her face falls. Before she can respond, he stalks back to the kitchen, intent on leaving the party, refusing to turn and catch the look that matches the emotion of distressed surprise she throws at him.

He stops outside the shabby house, watching the fireflies flicker in time with the streetlamp on the corner. What would happen if he went back inside? He could pretend, just for a moment, to be human. He could dance with her, couldn't he? Others do before they take a soul—or worse.

He squeezes his fist, the press of his doubled-banded ring into his palm grounding him. He can almost feel the engraving on the inside, the Latin inscription declaring, *'When life is unchosen and death is unearned, emptiness cannot Rule.'* A stark reminder of the Rules that bind him. There are no choices, only duty.

Instead of turning back towards her, Alec walks into the darkness, vowing to ignore Azalea and focus his mind on the prey he leaves behind. Tomorrow, he will find Eli. The hunt begins.

Chapter 2

Everything sucks.

That's Azzie's general opinion of life in Lonetree, but especially after last night. She hadn't wanted to go to a party filled with people who wrote her off years ago, especially not one that ended with her alone, listening to former classmates mock her. After Alec left, she wasted two hours trying to convince Eli they should focus on the handsome, wealthy new guy in town instead of rehashing their half-baked long cons.

Eli liked Alec at first—with his fancy European accent and his talk of estates—but Eli likes schemes that are quick, easy, and untraceable. Targeting someone local is too risky. Strike one against him. Alec ditching Azzie at the party? Strike two. Eli doesn't wait for strike three; Alec's too much effort, and he doesn't want her getting close to him anyway. The possibility that Alec might end up liking her—and that she could like him back—isn't even on Eli's radar.

But Eli would never understand how important Alec could be to her. In middle school, Eli came into his own, reinventing himself after the family's bad luck forced them to move from Asheville. He skated through life on his All-American looks, with that hair and effortlessly straight smile, while Azzie was the opposite. He had the friends, the good grades, the squandered opportunities. She had Eli, and nothing else.

But after they graduated high school earlier in the year, Azzie realized it wasn't enough. She needed more; she needed to breathe and to leave Lonetree. During the summer, Eli started drinking as much as Dad, which *should* have worried her, but felt like an opportunity instead. Alec—handsome, wealthy, and worldly—is her chance to get out from under Eli's thumb. She doesn't need him for Eli's schemes, she needs Alec for her own. She needs to get out, but she can't do it alone.

She's never been alone, and she's not sure how to be. Azzie's mom died when Clara was barely walking, leaving their father a widow and six-year-old Azzie as the unofficial caretaker for her younger siblings. Being the caregiver and running the house landed on Azzie's shoulders as the eldest daughter. She learned responsibility, she had to, while her twin Eli ran screaming in the other direction.

He wasn't always her opposite. But the child who listened to her dreams of traveling and experiencing the world grew into a man who criticized her for suggesting it. It can't be because he'll miss her, but because he'd be responsible for Dad's health and their younger siblings. *That* would put a crimp in Eli's partying lifestyle.

Azzie's thoughts snap back to the present, where she sits next to a grumbling Eli, who drives her to downtown Asheville in the family's shared truck. It had taken hours of begging to get him to drop her downtown on his way to his "business." With five bucks in her pocket from cleaning the Simmons's pool last week, she can't afford much, but hopefully it buys her time enough to loiter inside one of the nicer shops and pretend she's someone different. She stood outside the stores constantly in high school but never attempted to go in, class and confidence both holding her back.

Confidence she can fake, but the residue of poverty stays on her no matter how she tries to scrub it out. It's something that permeates all her layers—her looks (gapped teeth because they couldn't afford braces), her clothing (thrift store finds), her *soul* (an ingrained 'otherness' she can't shake). Her only asset is her mind, having read everything she could—for pleasure, for escape, and for knowledge. Poverty can't steal that, but she can't shake the knowledge that others see right through her.

Alec belongs inside any of the Asheville shops, with his windblown hair, dark but well-made clothes, and trim body. He's made for the skinny jeans, ironic attitude and smirks the college boys love to don. A faint blush rises to her cheeks, and she ducks her head to keep Eli from noticing.

Boys, *nice attractive boys*, don't pay attention to her. And that 'Azalea means femininity and beauty' thing he said in his deep voice? She bites her lip around a smile.

The car rattles to a stop in the heart of downtown. Fueled by the memory of Alec's attention, Azzie slams the door without a backward glance and strides into *The Baroque Bibliophile*. The cheery door chime alerts the other patrons of her presence, and all eyes lock on her longer than is polite. In her thrift store clothes and her perpetual-looking bedhead, she stands out among the upscale clientele. Even the hipsters, with their faux-vintage style, look polished compared to her. Echoes of being the 'weird' kid haunt her steps, cracking the veneer of confidence she clings to. As the patrons' gazes rake over her, she isn't just out of place—she's sixteen again, buck-toothed and awkward, the girl who never quite fits in. She forces herself to swallow the knot in her throat and presses forward, even as the urge to flee tugs at her heels.

The store-cafe looks sumptuous, with bookshelves lining the walls and packed with leather-bound volumes—no dog-eared paperbacks or plastic-covered hardbacks in sight. Patrons recline in plush purple velvet sofas and rich brown leather armchairs, their conversations low and exclusive. Behind the counter, a refrigerated display glitters with slices of decadent cakes, vibrant macarons, and jewel-like chocolate truffles. A single truffle costs more than all the cash in her pocket, but the blackboard above the counter lists an espresso for $4.

Azzie tugs at her messy hair, pulling her knapsack higher on her shoulder. As the patrons' gazes drift back to their books and quiet conversations, she takes a steadying breath and shuffles toward the counter. The man perched on a stool glances at her with a sigh, his attention barely flickering away from the sleek iPhone in his hand before returning to the screen.

She clears her throat, but his eyes stay fixed on his phone. "Hi. I'd like an espresso, please."

"No, you don't," he replies without looking up.

"Ye—yes, I would. An espresso," she repeats louder, grip tightening on her bag.

His gaze finally lifts, lazily scanning her messy hair, oversized t-shirt, and pilled leggings. She wonders if he notices the small hole under her left armpit. "Your name's Buttercup or Lavender, right?" Even his tone sounds bored.

She presses her lips into a tight line. "Azalea."

"Right. Look, I've seen you trailing that brother of yours around at O-Rho date parties. You'd be better off somewhere else."

She can't even pinpoint what he's insulting—just that he is. "Look, I just want an espresso."

He drops the phone on the counter with a groan, rubbing his temples theatrically. "Listen, sweetheart. I'm trying to help you out. I remember you from Wretford." His nose wrinkles, his voice turning soft and patronizing. "And I know where you live now. This isn't your scene, Daisy. You'd just bring the place down. You get that, right? Our whole vibe would be... off."

Stunned and chastened, Azzie stumbles toward the door, her face burning. The patrons' judgmental stares feel like a weight on her back. The door chime, once cheerful, now sounds like mocking laughter, jeering at her escape. Outside, the hot summer air hits her like a slap, but it can't cover the sting of his words. She rubs her hands over her eyes, determined not to cry, and starts the long, sweaty walk back to Lonetree.

Her steps get heavier as she pads past the last Asheville business and hooks a right onto the one-lane highway that separates her dreams from her reality.

This is why she needs out. *This* is why she needs Alec. She's trash in Asheville, but too good for Lonetree. Alec doesn't know the history holding her back in both, of being Eli's awkward sister, of being from the sad family with the dead mom and alcoholic father. Unlike the other boys Eli tried to scam, Alec was her choice.

She trudges past the fading suburbs until the hardware store comes into view, its peeling yellow paint marking the entrance to the road that leads into Lonetree. Memories surface as she walks—of pre-school, when she and Eli were tasked with making a wind chime out of sticks and rocks. Mom had wanted to make the project special, so Dad stayed home with the younger girls while their heavily pregnant mother took Azzie and Eli to the nearby nature conservatory.

Mom was terrible with directions. Instead of veering left, she turned right, driving past the hardware store and into the heart of Lonetree. They ended up at a tiny nature preserve a mile south of what is now Azzie's neighborhood. The three of them spent the entire morning in the woods, gathering sticks and stones, enough for six wind chimes. It was one of those rare, magical days—one of the last.

Mom died a year later, and when Dad lost his job and they were forced to leave their comfortable Asheville home, the wind chimes were left behind too. By the time Azzie was ten, she'd lost everything: her friends, her school, and the version of her dad who still smiled. Lonetree became her cage, and she's never found a way out.

She storms past the hardware store, anger simmering just beneath the surface. As always, the perfect comebacks come too late. At least four sharp retorts flash through her mind, each one more satisfying than the silence she'd left behind. If she had even a fraction of Eli's brashness, self-assurance, or cocky charm, she'd still be at *The Baroque Bibliophile*—lounging on one of those plush purple sofas, sipping an espresso like she belonged there.

But she doesn't.

Her frustration takes her the rest of the walk until she hits the cracked pavement of downtown Lonetree, anger the only thing keeping her from slumping to the ground and wallowing in pity and foot pain. She heads into the library to lick her wounds around the best friends she has, her books.

Several hours later, with her feet no longer stinging but ego still chafing, she leaves the library, weighed down by more books than her bag can hold. Her thin knapsack digs into her shoulders. The worn thread is close to striping; she'll need to reinforce the seams tonight or try to find another one at a thrift store. With an audible grumble, she cups her arms under the heavy load as a shadow passes over her face.

"Do you need help?"

Alec stands with his hand outstretched, offering her a view of his defined muscles under his black t-shirt. His eyes appear to spark at her. Without a second thought, she hands over the bag, a smile dragging over her lips.

Chapter 3

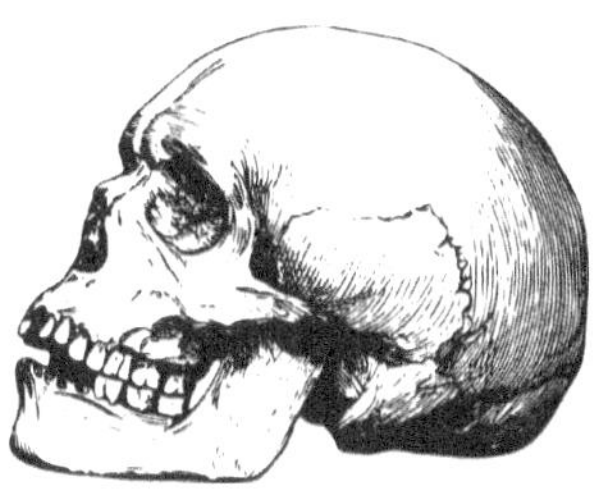

ALEC BEGINS THE EVENING after the party without thinking of Azalea—an effort that lasts only until sunrise. Then, she occupies his thoughts in a way that unsettles him. He rationalizes it as an occupational concern—she is, after all, the sibling of his prey and unusually difficult to read. If this preoccupation stems from fatigue, it is a manageable flaw, albeit inconvenient. The alternative—a weakness for a human—would be far graver, doubling any punishment the Council might impose should his focus stray from the Rules.

But prudence demands he understand his limitation. And as difficult as Michael is, his sire remains the one confidant Alec can trust to provide insight without exposing weakness.

At dawn when the first rays of sun struggle to peek through the heavy curtains of his dank library, Alec approaches the ornate mirror mounted on the wall. With a precise touch of the square jewel in his ring to the glass, ripples distort his reflection until Michael's face appears. Luck is with him; the call could have gone unanswered.

Alec takes in the sight of him with resigned familiarity. His sire looks unchanged from their last conversation seventy years prior. Tall and muscular, with broad shoulders that hint at the robust life he lived before becoming a wraith, Michael embodies an unsettling vitality. His long, curly hair, always dyed an unusual color, today a vivid shade of blue, is bound in a ribbon-tied bun.

Appearing not a day over twenty, Michael never looks in disarray, even when disrobed, a fact that Alec unfortunately knows firsthand after accidentally walking in on Michael before they went their separate ways on a more permanent basis. He's larger than life, both literally as his bulky frame spans the entire mirror opening, and metaphysically, apparent in how he lives his second life. As he explained to Alec centuries earlier—he was a wraith because there was too much life in him not to live twice.

Michael flashes that ever-present smirk at the corner of his mouth, looking like a cat that drank an entire pitcher of cream. With his over-the-top persona and recent penchant for wearing velvet brocade suits, he would stand out in a crowd, even without his massive frame, dyed blue hair, and emerald green eyes.

"Remember the Teachings," Michael says, his voice carrying the gravity of a ritual.

"Follow the Rules," Alec replies.

Michael grins, ruffling his dyed locks as if he sees his own reflection and not Alec's face, his many rings clacking against each other when he does. "With catechisms out of the way—what an unexpected pleasure, Alesandro."

"It's Alec."

Michael ignores the correction as usual, pouting instead. "You know I am doing my decade of exhaustion for the Council. Whyever you called, praise the Fates you have temporarily saved me from my duties."

Alec bristles at Michael's cavalier attitude. The Council, their governing body, assigned each wraith a decade of roving every five hundred years where they acted as enforcers and caught rogue wraiths. Unlike his sire, Alec has volunteered for centuries of service, finding solace in purpose. Michael treats his rare roving assignments as an inconvenience interrupting his hedonistic existence.

"I know what you do during your off hours while on assignment, Michael. I took a risk you'd be engaging in something less than productive. But I'll not be your excuse to shrink your responsibilities."

Michael chuckles as he peers behind him. Although Alec sees nothing but his friend's face, Michael is probably surrounded by all manner of debauchery. "You took a risk," Michael repeats, shaking his head. "I remember when you took *genuine* risks. How I long for the day when you remove the stick that made its home in your rear end."

"I'm content with the way I live," Alec replies.

This is a conversation they've had countless times over the centuries, one that began a millennium ago when Alec abandoned the indiscriminate lifestyle Michael still embraces. Michael's version of immortality prioritizes pleasure above all else, always skirting the edge of the Rules to avoid the Council's wrath. He operates without subtlety, seducing his prey before draining their souls, leaving them empty, soulless, and often with gaps in their memory. He's little better than the lesser creatures the Council has tamed and controlled. Alec is waiting for the painful day when the Council assigns him the inevitable task of hunting Michael down.

Michael narrows his eyes. "If that's true, then I can only be glad for you. That's all I want—you to be happy." He gazes behind him again. "And for physical pleasure of my own. But I ask again—why did you call?"

Alec falters. Michael is his only hope for information, his one link outside the Council, but appearing weak to anyone is dangerous. That's the First Rule, and one Alec had significant trouble over the centuries—Never show weakness. Azalea's brown eyes flash through his mind and his resolve firms.

"There is... a human here," he says.

"Your prey? Or have you found a human to turn?"

"No... absolutely not." Alec would never subject another human to the family. In a softer voice, he clarifies, "it's the sibling of my prey. The only thing of interest in my prey is that his soul is half gone."

Michael's expression glitters. "Why would you choose one that doesn't last? I would say it's ludicrous that you choose such meager morsels, but, of course, your continuous need to hunt is your only excuse for your frustrating fascination with hum—"

"I couldn't read the sibling of my prey," Alec says, interrupting what was sure to be another irritating lecture. "When I try, it's as if I hit a tall wall that has locked me out of her emotions. Unless they are overwhelming in their intensity, and then it's like a gale buffeting my mind. Even her soul took extra effort to uncover."

"The *sibling* of your prey locked you out. Fascinating," Michael murmurs to himself. "Is it affecting your hunt?"

"No." The answer comes too quickly for him to believe it's the truth. He wouldn't be calling Michael otherwise.

"Then I don't see the problem."

Alec clenches his fists. "I haven't been unable to read a human since my rebirth. Does that not seem cause for concern, a weakness to guard against?"

"Perhaps you need to relax. It isn't unheard of for our gifts to languish when overworked. We're like the humans we used to be in that way, unable to perform at our best." Michael offers him a surprisingly sincere expression. "You've taken no leisure time in centuries. Going straight from hunting to roving for the Council could dampen your gifts."

But Alec doesn't have the luxury of rest. If he cannot capture a soul within the month, he'll deteriorate into a near-death state—his rationality will falter, his impulse control will shatter, his wraith gifts will vanish, and his body will succumb to its true age. He should have accepted the Council's offer of respite years ago, but the thought of further solitude—and the risk of slipping back into old habits—kept him moving forward.

"Have you heard of that happening?" Alec asks, voice tight.

Michael ticks up a shoulder. "Not to my knowledge, though you know I abhor the histories. I suppose I *could* ask the current Historian what he knows."

Alec sighs. "Thank you, Michael. That is kind of you."

"It's hardly a favor. He is with me now." Michael peers behind him again and turns back with a leer. "Though I believe it may be some time before he answers you, as his mouth will be busy."

"Speaking of meager morsels," Alec mutters under his breath. Michael laughs before touching the mirror's face with his pocket watch, and the mirror returns to its normal state.

Alec's gaze pulls to the mirror. He looks human, except for his eyes. He has the same mannerisms, even ones he tried to remove. He has the same organs, though they don't work anymore. But he'll never *be* human. His stolen souls confirm that fact.

Perhaps he can afford a break from his duties. But he knows his own limitations, no matter Michael thinks he doesn't. He avoids regular hunting, keeping busy with roving and shunning the games Michael and other wraiths play not out of altruism—to allow more humans to keep their souls—but for survival. Alec's interest in humanity always starts small, a ripple that inevitably grows into a tidal wave, leaving devastation in its wake. He can't afford to backslide. Not again.

Determined to focus his mind before seeking Eli, Alec stalks to a large birch table near the back of the library. While Godfrey prepares his alchemy kit, Alec pulls a crumbling book from the shelves, flipping to one of the six well-worn pages he rereads obsessively. Godfrey slips away as Alec unpacks the vials.

Alchemy is the closest thing to a hobby Alec has, and the only allowable amusement that isn't inherently brutal. It's methodical, calming even, as long as he avoids the pages that promise darker results. For now, it's a simple process: grind eyebright and aster into a paste, sprinkle it over melted lead, and let heat bind the mixture. Alchemy feels like a reflection of what Alec wishes the Rules could be: clear, predictable, and precise.

He holds a tapered candle to the underside of the glass bottle, raising the heat until the ingredients meld. When the mixture reaches the texture of wet sand, he decants the liquid into a clay container he crafted centuries earlier. By noon, the gold has cooled into misshapen lumps. Alec straightens his back and inspects the results with a critical eye. The channels are uneven, making his gold coins rudimentary and misshapen, nothing like the metal his tribe's artisans made.

He sags over the table. Failure isn't relaxing.

Grumpily, he gathers his flawed creations and heads to downtown Asheville to dispose—deposit—them. One of his gifts is speed, and he takes less than a minute to arrive, his mood darkening with every step.

Asheville, though large enough to house a small university, isn't vast enough for Alec to discreetly offload thousands of dollars' worth of crude gold coins without attracting attention. Unlike Michael, Alec lacks the ability to confound humans, forcing him to rely on stealth and strategy. He spreads his deposits across the state under various aliases but staying too long in Asheville risks exposure. And if he lingers much longer without claiming Eli's soul, his gold won't be the only evidence of failure.

Alec leaves the bank with slumped shoulders, the reminders of his inadequacies everywhere. Even now, he swears he can hear Azalea's smoky voice murmuring in his mind, an unbidden distraction. Shaking his head sharply, he resolves to sprint back to Rockton and strategize how to isolate Eli—until her vision stops him in his tracks. Literally, as she stomps around the corner, heading straight towards him. He ducks into the bank's vestibule and waits while she passes him. She's grumbling under her breath, scuffing the pavement with worn shoes, her arms crossed tightly over her waist. Eli is nowhere in sight. Alec battles the weak, growing urge to step forward, to speak with her—an urge that is unrelated to his hunt.

It wouldn't be unreasonable to follow Azalea to her destination, Alec tells himself. With her brother absent, she might offer insights about his prey. This has nothing to do with her lingering in his thoughts from the night before or his inexplicable inability to read her as he does other humans.

He pinches his fingers harder against his nose until white spots dance behind his closed lids. He's never been a good liar, much less to himself.

With an inward groan, he trails her, his steps measured and silent. She walks the long route from Asheville back to the small town where the ill-fated party took place. Alec resists the urge to read her emotions again, knowing it will be fruitless, yet her desperation and melancholy seep into the surrounding air, spilling across the street like water from a broken vessel.

She pauses outside a ramshackle store, her posture shifting abruptly. Her head lifts, her hands clenching tight. The melancholy she radiates sharpens into fury so suddenly that Alec jolts, pressing a hand to his chest. The way some of her emotions strike him with visceral intensity while others remain faint and elusive creates an uncomfortable sensation in his stomach. Slowing his pace, he clenches his ringed hand, the metal biting into his palm, and watches as she approaches a worn-down building with chipped white paint peeling from its brick facade.

Alec can't summon a convincing lie to quiet his conscience, which knows following Azalea edges dangerously close to a Rule break. Human society has bewitched him before—with its literature, art, and social constructs—but only twice in two thousand years has a human captivated him in ways unrelated to sex or the seizure of a soul.

The first was Cassius, not long after Alec's conversion. Cassius had been a beautiful man with sparkling blue eyes, soft skin, and a high-pitched laugh that lingered in Alec's memory. Alec brushes his fingers against his lips, recalling the two fleeting kisses they shared, though the details have blurred with time. What remains vivid is the moment Alec naively asked Michael if he could ever return to being human—a foolish wish, driven by the desire to share an untainted life with Cassius. When Alec next visited him, Cassius lay dead in his insulae, trousers undone and an eternal smile frozen on his face. Michael claimed the death was accidental, that Cassius had died happily, and assured Alec that the man's feelings were never true, as *Cassius* had approached Michael's bed. "At least now you have no regrets about being a wraith," Michael had said. But the memory festered, driving Alec to burn the image away through centuries of distraction with every human and wraith he met.

The second was Lucia, a tenant farmer's daughter he encountered in the 12th century. By then, Alec had sworn off indiscriminate killing and coupling, determined to uphold the Rules and reform himself from within. Lucia was innocent and filled with wonder, her simplicity grounding him in a way nothing else had. But their connection ended before it began. She stumbled upon Alec mid-hunt, and the sight of him taking a soul drove her to hysterics. Alec had no choice but to summon Michael. To this day, Alec doesn't know if Michael killed her or erased her memories. He never asked, and Michael never volunteered the truth.

And now, for the third time, there is Azalea. Alec knows he might never forgive himself if he harms her as he did the others.

With a sigh, he turns to leave but then she appears, one shoulder hanging lower from the weight of her satchel. Before he realizes it, he slips across the street in the span of a blink.

"Do you need help?" Alec's voice comes out unsteady, a detail that would concern him if her smile weren't so distracting. He can run for hundreds of miles without tiring, yet the five-meter walk to her steals his breath.

She wears an oversized blue shirt emblazoned with *Raleigh Fun Run 2018* and tight gray pants that cling to her hips. The uncomfortable sensation in his gut flares again, bubbling like boiling water. He forces his gaze to the pavement.

"Thanks," she says, handing him her bag and directing him back across the street and down a cracked sidewalk. Her leaking emotions vanish abruptly. "I didn't expect to see you after you bolted last night."

"I had hoped to speak to your brother again." *There*, he reassures himself, *I stay fixated on the hunt*.

She frowns, a lock of hair falling into her face. "Aren't I special."

His fingers twitch to tuck the strand behind her ears, and he clutches her bag and the books within like they're his most prized possessions to avoid the desire. The words force themselves from his throat before he can stop himself.

"There can be more than one reason for a single action. I assumed, *hoped*, when I found him, I would come upon you, given you were together last night."

"So, you were hoping for a 'two birds with one stone' situation?" she asks flatly.

He nods, reaching out with his gift to read her, desperately hoping it had reset after his morning playing with alchemy. No such luck—her emotions remain shrouded, as dull and distant as her blank expression.

She tilts her head back with a sigh, staring up at the sky. "Isn't that the story of my life? Eli comes first, Azzie comes second. Here I thought we connected last night, but nope—I'm just the detour on your way to my brother."

Alec's grip tightens, the memory of Cassius and Lucia flooding his mind. Attraction has always been his undoing, even in his human life, where potential marriage candidates barely noticed his awkward overtures. Azalea's arched brows rise as his silence stretches, her expression edging toward exasperation.

Fates, he is *appalling* at this. He needs to return her bag and flee. Before he can formulate a response—or plan a quiet retreat—a wave of amusement sweeps over him, warm and disarming. Her crooked smile softens the moment.

"Sorry, that was mean. I didn't realize how easy you'd be to rile up. *That's* your punishment for ditching me last night." She bumps her shoulder into his, sending him staggering back in surprise. "It's true, though—I'm always second to Eli, but I'm—I'm used to it. Plus, I shouldn't tease you when you're holding my books. Saving my bag *and* my back definitely makes up for you running off."

Alec loosens his grip on her bag, hoping she won't notice the faint indentations left by his fingers. "I'm glad to help."

Azalea hums and fingers the loose piece of hair that captured his attention, pausing in front of an empty field. She takes the bag back and stares at the broken concrete. With a sudden intake of breath, she squares her shoulders, as if steeling herself up for something, but Alec can't guess what. "If you're desperate for Eli," she says, "there's another party tonight in Lonetree."

He almost sags to the ground at the excuse she provides him. His escorting her has meaning now. *This* can be the reason behind his preoccupation with her, the justification for the irrational draw he feels, one that furthers his hunting demands and ignores how much he wants to stroke her hair. Still, he can't help himself, and asks, almost shyly, "Will you be there?"

Hope floods from her like a spray from a ruptured hull, bright like oranges. "If you will," she murmurs, ducking her head. He spies a smile curling through her hair.

His thumb turns his ring absently, the amber jewel winking in the light. "That would be agreeable."

Azalea gives him the details before crossing the field alone. He watches her go, resisting the odd urge to follow. Instead, he turns back toward Rockton, reminding himself of the Rules, the Teachings, and the task at hand. He'll take Eli's soul tonight, leave this confusing place behind, and let Azalea's fleeting hope comfort him on his next roving assignment. Perhaps he'll return to Asheville when Azalea can't affect him, likely when she's an octogenarian.

Without another glance back, Alec heads home, determined to prepare and, above all, not think about her.

Chapter 4

Then

THE COUNCIL SUMMONED ALEC back from his roving assignment in the Kievan Rus before he could corner the wraith leaking secrets to the prince of Novgorod. He didn't mind; he would have needed Michael's mind manipulation to erase what the prince had already learned. All non-exiled wraiths were required to attend the Council's latest trial, and that meant seeing Michael again and seeking his aid in the matter.

The prospect of facing Michael brought a mixture of anticipation and dread. Alec hadn't crossed paths with him since Muscovy, where their reckless gameplay had led Alec to waste a soul. Michael had been unbothered, urging Alec—as he had for centuries—to carry a second or third ring for emergencies or upgrade his soul receptacle to one capable of holding more. Alec, a wraith of routine and discipline, had refused, but losing that soul had unsettled him deeply. He had taken a two-century roving stint to avoid Michael, burying that memory alongside countless others that made him feel... wrong. He'd told himself the unease was fear of discovery, that the family of the soulless husk might seek answers. But deep down, he knew there was more.

When he arrived in the wraith city of Satu, nestled in the realm directly beneath Kish—the Council's seat and the oldest city—Alec still hadn't been told the circumstances of the trial. The summons had called it the "trial of a millennium," and though vague, the phrase had carried enough gravity to compel his return.

The judgment chamber, where the Council would hear the trial and dole out punishment, teemed with wraiths when he slipped inside.

The Accuser—a wraith Alec had always disliked—stood beneath the seven-pedestal dais, his stance eager for spectacle.

Michael loitered near the copper stocks where the Accused hung by his wrists. Alec didn't recognize the bloodied wraith, his face obscured by black hair matted with blood. Michael caught Alec's eye and gestured to the space beside him, as if he'd saved Alec a seat, his manic grin fracturing under tension.

Bisa, the Head Councilmember, rose from her pedestal and demanded the Accuser begin. Alec listened at first but soon his attention drifted. He'd stood in this chamber as an Accuser over a hundred times; the process was rote. Before he expected, the trial ended. Bisa delivered the sentence: exile. Michael stiffened beside him, his green eyes briefly shutting before he masked his reaction with boredom.

The congregated wraiths hissed; trials with blood were always more popular. Most of the wraiths Alec brought before the Council were sentenced to death, and Alec was a swift executioner, ending the Rule breakers' lives with a single blow. Exile was rare.

Bisa raised her pale arms, silencing the room. "Rawi," she hissed, "has done the unthinkable, turning the skills we taught him to benefit humans, showing them preference, aiding their sick. Such weakness cannot be borne. Death is a mercy he has not earned. Instead, he shall live in pain, barred from our kind, denied the power he was made for."

The crowd jeered but Alec's attention shifted to Rawi in the stocks. The more recent converts believed being a wraith was an excuse to terrorize and destroy humans, and most recent trials came from Alec hunting them down for breaching the Second Rule. But trials on the First Rule were rare; wraiths avoided the softer sentiments. The most common First Rule breach was when a wraith failed to hunt and succumbed to soulsickness. If caught, they were punished and forced to find a soul without the use of their gifts.

Most of them withered away.

But this was different. This wasn't a wraith succumbing to idle weakness or losing themselves to soulsickness—this was a wraith deliberately seeking human pastimes, immersing himself in a world Alec had once yearned to explore before learning better. The temptation still surfaced occasionally, brief and fleeting, but Alec buried it beneath layers of discipline and distractions of the flesh.

He couldn't help but wonder how Rawi had been caught. Had someone betrayed him? How long had Rawi indulged in that sliver of humanity before the Council's punishment descended? And, more troublingly, what had driven him to take such a risk?

Rawi was older than Alec, an almost contemporary of Michael, and more devout than some of the Councilmembers Alec had served under. But Rawi was unrecognizable from the last time he saw him, his golden skin scratched and blackened not with dirt but with the burnt red of dried blood. Rawi had lifted his head and was glaring in Michael's direction, his eyes flashing even as blood dripped down the corners. After glancing around the room, Michael sidled closer, dragging Alec behind him, using the continued jeers of the wraiths as a distraction.

"Rawi, you're looking well," Michael said blandly.

Rawi spat blood onto Michael's leather slippers. "Find her," he rasped. "Find her and tell her."

Alec expected Michael to make a joke or saunter away, but Michael nodded silently. As soon as he did, Rawi slumped again, just in time for the seven Councilmembers to stand in unison and reach their hands out towards him. Rawi's screams echoed through the chamber before they were swallowed by the howls of the crowd.

"I need a favor, dearest," Michael said, leaning close. He slipped his hands inside Alec's vest and pulled out his journal. Alec's stomach tightened at what Michael might see in there, but the knowledge that they were being watched kept him from attempting to snatch it back. Michael didn't read it, instead ripping a page from the back, and jotting something down. "Go to this location, in Albion, and find this woman. Tell her of Rawi's fate. Whatever happens next is your choice."

"They don't call it Albion anymore," Alec said, blinking down at the address in his hand.

Michael smirked, but it was grim. "I'd not mention that knowledge, or your implied interest in the ever changing human civilizations too loudly in this room."

"That information helps me track—"

"Best be off," Michael said, rubbing flecks of Rawi's blood from his tunic.

Intrigued despite himself, Alec followed the instructions. The address led him to a small, thatched house near the sea—close to where his human home had once stood, though he swallowed that thought quickly. Inside, a woman stirred water over a fire, strips of linen drying above. She didn't look up as he entered.

"It's time then," she said, though it sounded like a question. She lifted her head and bared a weary face, wisps of black hair sticking to her pale but glistening cheeks. Her soul was clean, with faint marks of hardship.

"Rawi has been exiled," Alec said, stepping closer. She looked familiar, especially in how she held herself and the long black hair and dark eyes she displayed.

She smiled faintly. "Better than we thought. You're here to kill me?"

"I haven't decided," Alec admitted. He needed to alert the Council about her, but he had some freedom to make decisions on his own. And she reminded him of someone—a face with a crown of flowers—but the memory remained buried under centuries of suppression.

Alec lowered himself to her level to better stare at her eyes. He could almost place another face over hers. His Michael-mandated task was complete, he'd told her what happened to Rawi. But he couldn't leave yet, not when another possible Rule break had occurred. At least, that's what he told himself. "What led Rawi to you?"

"It started as a bit of a game. He had boasted to some men in town that he had the best tinctures. He'd been drinking, though not the alcohol I thought." She smiled in memory. "Some form of elixir just for your kind. But the innkeeper is my brother and started bragging that I was best healer in town. The only healer mind you, else I'd probably not be allowed to do as much as I did. But Rawi came and demanded I prove what I could do. It turned into a competition. Each time he visited, he'd have some new herb and whoever came up with the best tincture won. Rawi never enjoyed losing."

Alec remembered as much, from the games Rawi and Michael played before their disagreement. "How did you learn of us?"

"The town was annexed, and I could no longer work without a man's supervision. Rawi always came back quick when he lost, to renew the game. When he'd learned my ingredients and kit were slated for the male healer the next town over, he suggested the farce that he was the lead healer. That turned into him living here and telling me of his life."

"Were you…" For all his years, and all his experience, he couldn't speak the words to her.

"Lovers?" She laughed, a throaty sound. "No. We understood each other, and he was my partner in survival. But I could not love him. He did not possess what I needed," she finished ruefully.

Alec could delay no longer and stood. "I do not have manipulation magic to remove your knowledge of my kind from your mind. The Council was unaware of the depths of Rawi's descent when he was punished, else they would have surely done more, including come for you."

She dried her hands on her shift and stood. "I am prepared."

Alec pulled his dagger from its banded hilt by his ankle but hesitated. "Do you not have regrets?"

She smiled again, something soft and secretive, uncurling over her lips like a blooming flower. "I have walked this earth for five and forty years. I spent fifteen of it with Rawi by my side. And in that time, I learned of his hunger, that though he consumed souls for sustenance, he did so to feast on what he feared he could never taste, the experience of humanity. I ate my fill of life. I will welcome what comes next."

Alec shuddered, her words too similar to something he felt after Cass—after he made his early mistakes. As he stalked closer, she gazed upward. There was a wisdom in her eyes, something he'd sought for a time and banished from his mind. Suddenly, he realized who she reminded him of—his sister and he felt like he was drowning.

She cupped his cheek, and he shivered again. "There is still time for you. You need not look upon life in jealousy of what you cannot experience. Instead, you can find it yourself and taste that joy. There is space for both."

MICHAEL WAS WAITING FOR him in Satu. "It's done?" he asked idly.

Alec nodded.

"And you are well?"

Alec stared back at Michael, who held an intensity in his green eyes Alec didn't like. "I have the Rules to guide me," Alec said, "and my skills to keep me. I am always well."

Michael's face contorted to a frown before quickly returning to its usual leering display. "Indeed. Though it has been too long since we've convalesced together. Shall we hunt? Damascus is lovely this time of year."

Alec tapped the journal resting beside his breast, where he'd written of what occurred with the woman. "I must return to Novgorod." He paused and considered his next words. "Why did you have me find her instead of seeking her yourself?"

Michael lifted one shoulder in an elegant shrug. "I owed Rawi a debt and it is too frigid in Albion this time of year. You know how furs cover my physique."

Alec nodded, hiding his scowl under the stillness of his expression. That did sound like Michael, who only thought of himself. He considered asking whether Michael had met her and seen the resemblance to his sister but knew it wouldn't matter. That it shouldn't matter. "Then I suppose you won't be joining me in Novgorod to manipulate the prince."

Michael bared his teeth. "No, I shall. One must make sacrifices for the good of the family and its esteemed Council. Perhaps we can hunt on the way."

Alec stared down at his ring. "No, I—I believe I'm sated."

But he would never be sated from the hunger she described. No succor would be found with the wraiths, or within himself.

Chapter 5

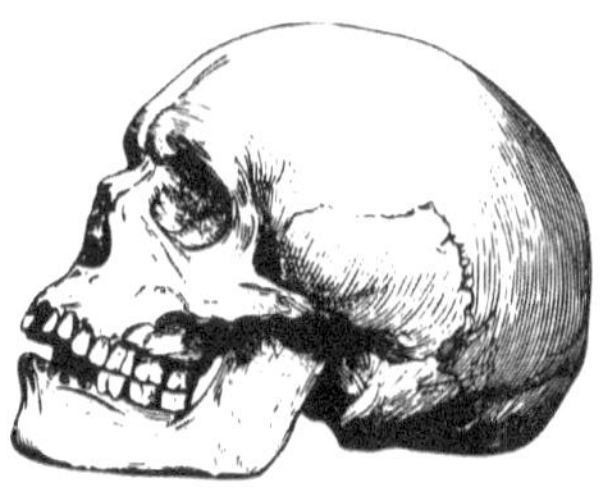

THE EMOTIONS OF HIS prey poison the air, guiding Alec to a run-down home on the outskirts of town. Trees and overgrown shrubbery bracket the building, their tangled forms cloaking it in shadow. No streetlamps or nearby lights disturb the darkness. If Alec had chosen the location himself, it couldn't have been more ideal. With his preternatural speed, he can seize the soul and disappear before anyone notices anything amiss. And, most importantly, without encountering her.

Scent and sound accost him the minute Alec prowls inside the house. It looks no smaller from the earlier party as the attendees still pack together in a small living area while an ear-splitting tune roars around them. Several partygoers share a single cigarette while another clump passes around a glass pipe. Alec locates Eli in the latter group.

"No, no man," Eli gurgles, his voice sluggish. "I got the best one yet. Kid's named James and his parents have a house in Hilton Head."

"How'd you know about that already?" another man asks, snatching the pipe and lighting it.

"Some magazine interviewed them." Eli snorts. "It's like they're just asking for it!"

"Good evening," Alec drawls, causing the three men to shake in surprise and a bolt of fear seep into the air. "Eli, you're just the man I've been looking for."

"Not into dudes," Eli says, straightening his back with a forced air of confidence. He motions to one of the other men in the room. "Give Benji here another hit or two, and he'd take you. We don't call him Bend-Over Ben for nothing!" Eli finishes with a nervous chuckle, shoving the reddening man beside him.

Alec's eyes narrow, catching the sour tang of anger and the damp stench of shame radiating from Eli. The emotions are vile and unmistakable, fitting the corruption Alec sensed. But something about it doesn't align. A man with such a deeply tainted soul shouldn't just be sitting here, laughing and mocking. He should be murdering, pillaging—at the *very* least, committing some form of sacrilege.

Suspicion prickles at Alec's thoughts. With a frown, he probes deeper, preparing to complete a second read of Eli's soul and—

"Alec! There you are!" Azalea's smoky voice slithers over the din on the music box. A warmth presses on his arm and refrains from jolting, flexing his fingers as the only outward manifestation of his surprise. It's been centuries since he experienced the touch of another borne not from obligation or to cause pain.

"Don't you fit in well," she teases, eyeing his shirt.

Although the black shirt, emblazoned with a rough smiling face and crossed out eyes, isn't his normal style, it had a symbolism he appreciated when Godfrey offered it to him. She saunters away from her brother, and like a dog on a lead, Alec follows.

"I was worried you weren't coming," she says with her back to him. "Eli and his friends have been here for like an hour. I've been hiding in the kitchen." She hooks her thumb towards another room ahead of them, and her voice takes on a hopeful quality. "It's quieter in there, if you wanted to hang out?"

Alec stares at her bright brown eyes and back at her worthless brother. Desire and duty war within him. "I must first speak with your brother."

Determination in her face, Azalea grabs his arm. "He's trashed. You'll have to try again later, either when he dries out tonight, *if* he dries out, or tomorrow. Come on." She pulls him towards the kitchen.

Letting his duty rest for the moment, he complies.

Chapter 6

When Azzie crosses the threshold, Alec withdraws from her touch like she has lice. With an internal sigh of frustration, she snags them both a soda from the buzzing fridge and leans against the stained Formica countertop.

"He won't date you," Azzie says, her hopes of leaving North Carolina slipping further with each word. She pries open the can in her hands with more force than necessary. Alec seemed perfect—too perfect—but she knows what his fixation on her brother really means. This isn't the first time she's seen this play out with boys from out of town.

Alec's brows lift, his confusion apparent. "Who?"

She huffs, slamming the can onto the counter. "My brother. He won't date you." His masculinity and image were too important to him to come out in Lonetree. That's why she's surprised that he wants to *stay* in their backwater town—if he'd left, like she wanted, he could be open about his identity. Not that it was her decision to make, and not that she can be as direct with Alec as she'd like to let him down easy when it's Eli's secret.

Instead, she tries again, her tone deliberately light. "Anyway, just... don't hit on him, okay? He'll probably try to punch you, and I know you could take him, but he'd be really irritating about it."

When Alec continues to stare at her with that unreadable expression, Azzie sighs. A small, frustrated part of her wants to flounce off the way Eli would, but a larger, more persistent part of her feels compelled to help. an inaudible groan. Of course, the nice new boy didn't want to broadcast his drug-seeking aims. But he seems too good for something as plebeian as what Eli sells.

Gently, she offers, "There's an inclusive bar in Hendersonville if you're looking. I can get you the address." She tries to keep her voice light, but the memory of suggesting the same to Eli lingers. He had sneered at the idea, snapping that he didn't need his sister to help him hook up. That moment marked the beginning of her pulling away from him, a slow realization that they weren't on the same path anymore.

"He only sells weed now," she offers, opening her eyes as her opportunity reappears, but at the expense of dealing with another addict. Everyone has vices, but drugs and drinks are her least favorite. "He stopped selling the harder stuff a few weeks ago. Using it, however..."

"I am not—" he starts, eyes like a flashing candle in the artificial light, before Eli's voice echoes into the small kitchen.

"Sister-of-mine, I need to tell you about James." Eli stumbles into the kitchen, his two lackeys in tow. He lands next to Azzie, leaning his head on her shoulder.

"Who is James?" Alec asks, his tone dark. A shiver trickles down Azzie's back at the sound.

"Good question. Eli, who *is* James?" Azzie shoves Eli off her. Every time he acts affectionate with her, she feels like her five-year-old self, the one who thought touching her brother would give her cooties. That reaction began with Eli's drinking. Maybe her subconscious doesn't want her dealing with a younger version of their dad. That didn't bode well for her Alec aspirations if he kept after Eli for drugs.

"James is a legacy from Zeta. He is 'ever so excited' to meet you at the open house next week." Eli's voice is teasing, presumably mimicking the boy he wants Azzie to meet.

"I think I'll be too busy to hang out with James," Azzie says meaningfully, flicking her eyes to Alec and back.

"Don't think so," he counters, reaching up and grabbing a lock of her hair. It takes two tries before he yanks the strand tight. To an outsider, it looks like he's teasing, but the dull pain in her scalp tells Azzie otherwise.

"Good question. Eli, who is James?" Azzie shoves Eli off her, irritation bubbling to the surface. Every time he acts affectionate, it takes her back to when she was five, convinced that touching her brother would give her cooties. The feeling had started when Eli began drinking. Maybe her subconscious was trying to protect her, warning her away from dealing with a younger version of their dad.

That thought twists her gut, especially when it ties into her Alec aspirations. If Alec is chasing Eli for drugs, what does that say about her own judgment?

Eli narrows his eyes, glancing at his lackeys, who fidget uncomfortably. "Now look, Azalea—"

"It's Azzie," she warns. Eli grabs her shoulder to jerk her forward, doubtless to yell directly in her face. Before he can so much as hiss out another breath, he's wrenched backward, his golden face paling. The lackeys stay silent, now their only movement found in their wide and shifting eyes.

Alec spins Eli as Eli wraps one hand around his throat, lifting him into the air until Eli's feet only skim the ground. Rage pierces his gaze, his face set in a snarl. The man who seemed docile and mild-mannered now looks like he could kill Eli without a second thought.

"If you touch her again, you'll lose that hand," Alec hisses. Azzie rubs his shoulder, the muscle tensing as he holds Eli aloft. Eli has three inches and about fifty pounds on Alec, but Alec has all the control.

"Alec, it's fine. Let Eli go," she says. Alec startles at the sound of her voice, like he forgot she was there. She presses on his shoulder, and he loosens his grip, dropping Eli to the floor but keeping his hands circled around Eli's neck. The lackeys sidle to the fridge, out of Alec's reach.

"He appeared ready to harm you." Alec sounds confused, his eyes distant and unseeing, like he's not standing ramrod straight in the kitchen of Nate's house holding Eli in place but somewhere far from here.

"He's high. Eli gets mean when he's high. He forgets to reign in his jerk impulses," she explains. Eli struggles to look nonchalant, running trembling fingers through his hair as though Alec doesn't have a handmade collar around his neck. "Let him go and let me talk to him alone."

Conflict skitters across Alec's handsome face before he releases Eli with a push.

Eli strokes shaking hands over his neck, stopping only to cough as he leans over the counter. "That's what I thought," Eli says between coughs.

Alec snarls and stalks towards him again but stops when Azzie steps between them. She gives him a strained smile before hauling Eli outside, refusing to look back at whatever expression might be on Alec's face.

"Foolish, self-centered jerk, should have let him pound you," she mutters when they cross the lawn. Darkness covers the gravel driveway but light from the door reflects on Eli's dazed face. The outline of Alec's hand remains a red mark against Eli's golden skin. Anger fills her and, for the first time in months, Azzie's first impulse isn't to kowtow to him.

"What just happened?" Eli looks dazed, forcing Azzie to reign in her impulse to smack him. Either shock sobered him, or he moved past the 'asshole with no sense of repercussions' stage of the drugs and made it to the childlike 'is that what my fingers look like?' stage.

"You were a dick," she says flatly. Eli passes a no-longer-shaking hand through his blond hair and lifts one shoulder as if resigned to his behavior. "And he looked like he wanted to murder you, so you're welcome for my help," she adds.

"I don't like him," Eli slurs, frowning. Azzie growls. "Of course, you don't. He's classier, smarter, *and* could wipe the floor with you."

"I could take him in a fight," Eli says, turning towards the door as if to do just that. "*That's* what you disagree with in that sentence? And no, you couldn't. Drugged-out Eli may have a mediocre memory and low reflexes, but regular Eli isn't much better."

Anger rises within her, sharp and unrelenting. For the first time in months, her first instinct isn't to appease him, to bend under his moods. Instead, she lets the fury settle, steady and empowering. spins back towards her, losing his balance on the turn and stumbling into her shoulder. Azzie refuses to catch him, and he drops to the ground. Sitting on his knees, he grabs her legs and peers up at her with big doe eyes. "Come *on*, talk to James for me. It'll be the last one. I've got something else cooking for us but until then..." He smiles innocently as she struggles to remind herself that this is the jerk who drinks and knows how to push her around, not the sweet brother she grew up with. That Eli disappeared when they turned sixteen.

She kicks at him until he releases her. "I've got my own plan," she snaps. *And it involves getting far away from you*, she adds silently. "No," she says before she stomps back inside.

She finds Alec where she left him, with the same dangerous expression on his face, his fingers clenched on the stained Formica. Eli's two lackeys vanished during her absence, either back to getting high and waiting for Eli to tell them, her tone sharp.

"'What unusual creatures brothers are,' and all that," she jokes, the backbone she showed outside cracking. She desperately hopes Alec will overlook the mess that is her brother, or why she continues to condone his behavior.

"I almost lost control. That hasn't happened since the last time I—" He blinks, a horrified expression on his face. "I could have killed him."

She winces. "I'm glad you didn't. Jerk or not, he's important to me."

He makes a thoughtful noise. "Why do you not care for your name?" Alec has that puzzled look again.

Azzie lets out a breath now that the ghost of Eli no longer floats between them. She doesn't need to think about it, it's been a buzz in the back of her head for months now.

"Flowers are delicate. I'm not anymore." she says. Alec looks like he plans to protest but she holds up a hand. "That's a *good* thing. I didn't fit in when we lived in Asheville, and it got worse when we moved to Lonetree. I've always been a weird and slightly chubby wallflower who followed her popular brother. When I turned 18, I told myself I wasn't living that way anymore. I'm trying to make myself harder, so I can have the guts to do something for myself."

She needs to be hard to do what's best for her and get out of this godforsaken town. That's what Eli would do, if his goals weren't to be the whale in their small pond. Azzie doesn't care if she's a small fish, she just wants to see the ocean.

Her voice falters for a moment before she presses on, the words spilling from her as if admitting them out loud gives them weight. "A sweet-sounding name like Azalea? Something that wilts and gets crushed? That doesn't fit anymore. And I don't want it to."

Azzie pauses, her thoughts swirling. She's laid herself bare, her insecurities raw and exposed. For a moment, she wonders if Alec will say anything at all—or if this, too, will crumble into silence like so many of her dreams.

"Flowers aren't simply delicate," Alec says, staring at the counter. "They must fight for resources, bursting through the dirt and staying alive through the ravages of weather and time, while keeping their petals from breaking and offering other mortals something beautiful to gaze upon." He lifts his sparkling eyes and studies her face. "You should be proud of such a name."

Chapter 7

Eli bounces his knee against the white-veined marble flooring, his nerves thrumming as he waits in the steel-and-glass high-rise in downtown Raleigh. The lobby is the nicest room he's ever been in, with dark wood bookshelves flanking the space and a buttery black leather couch beneath him. Everything gleams—especially the windows, which throw blinding reflections of light and distort his own mirror image.

For the first time in weeks, Eli is sober, but the pallor of his drinking clings to his face like a stubborn shadow. He rubs his hands down the front of his button-down shirt, attempting to smooth wrinkles that might not even be there. His reflection doesn't reassure him.

He doesn't know what this meeting is about, but the woman who approached him was sophisticated and smelled like money. That alone was enough to pique his interest. He'd show up to this meeting naked and toasted if it meant the chance to ride whatever opportunity she offered.

He needs it to keep Az from leaving him. For whatever reason, he can't convince her to stay. The more he brings it up, the harder she rails against him. It wasn't always this way, but when they turned sixteen, their once-synchronized personalities careened in opposite directions. Every time she pushed, he felt compelled to lean the other way. When he pulled, she planted her feet and twisted against him.

It wasn't just their dynamic that shifted. Around that age, he started experiencing wild emotional swings, like he had freaking menopause. Az only made it worse. Something about her presence sharpens the edges—when she's angry at him, he feels like collapsing at her feet. When she's sad, he ends up yelling at her and making everything worse. But nothing compares to when she talks about leaving. Those fights are awful, the moments when they seem so far apart he'd swear they weren't even related, let alone twins. Then he clings to her like a kid on his mom's skirts. And the more she pulls from him, the more he hangs on. The thought of her leaving makes his chest hurt, like something might rip him in half. He presses a hand to his chest, almost feeling the phantom pain.

School counselors tried to explain it—'sibling rivalry,' 'seeking individuality,' 'growing pains.' He doesn't care what they called it. All he knows is that something inside him hates it. That's why the drinking started. Alcohol dulls his senses, makes him feel more like himself. The tradeoff—a shortened life span and the risk of turning into their father—is worth it for the relief. It steadies him, stops him from being pulled in opposite directions.

What he can remember of the party last night with Az was a train wreck. The drugs dulled his normally roaring emotions, but not enough. He needs to stick to alcohol in the future; it's the only thing that works. There's a sweet spot where he feels normal—not manic, not wasted—but it's harder to find lately. He has to drink more to get there, and sometimes he overshoots, which swings him back around to being a mess.

Eli rubs the back of his neck before running his hands through his blond hair, petting it into the 'effortlessly tousled' look he perfected. If only he'd snuck a flask into this interview to take the edge off his nerves. This job, whatever it is, is his chance to gain some respectability. It's for him and Azzie, who's close to not putting up with his crap anymore, and to a lesser extent, for the girls. He'll do this and then they won't have to run any more schemes. They'll have it made and Az won't want to leave.

It's perfect. He'll make it perfect.

Footsteps echo on the marble floor, crisp and deliberate, until a man steps into the doorway. He's tall and broad-shouldered, built like a linebacker, and dressed in the kind of suit Eli's only seen in glossy magazines—tailored so perfectly it hugs his muscular chest and shoulders like a second skin. The man looks only a year or two older than Eli, but his long, stark-white hair skims his shoulders, an unusual contrast to his caramel complexion. When the man smiles, Eli's stomach twists. For a split second, his teeth seem jagged, like the sharp canines of a predator ready to tear out its prey's throat. Eli blinks hard, and the vision is gone. The teeth are perfect now—gleaming white, even, and orderly, shining against his smooth skin.

Eli shakes his head sharply, the unsettling image lingering on the edges of his mind. He scrubs a hand over his face. *No more hard drugs*, he vows.

"Hello, Eli," the man purrs, dragging out his name in a soft European accent. Eli reigns in the shiver that threatens to trail downward. "You cannot imagine how delighted I am to meet you. I've heard much about you and am eager to learn more." He motions to the door he's come through, showing off stacked golden rings on every finger. "Come in, let's talk."

Chapter 8

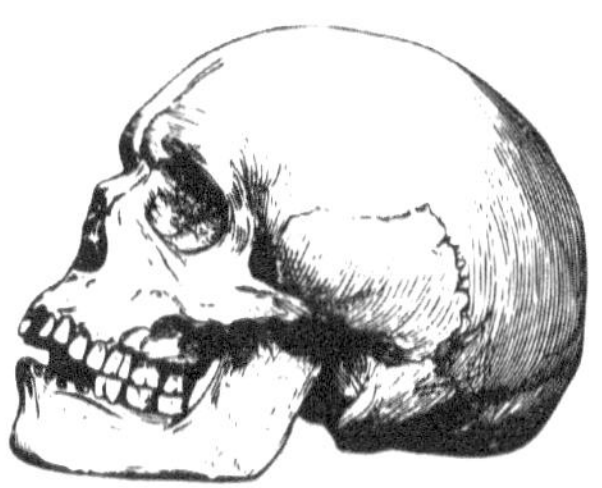

ALEC SPENDS TWO WEEKS avoiding all thoughts of Azalea, telling himself the distance will break the tether she has unknowingly tied around him and sharpen his focus on her brother. Hunger gnaws at him, body and spirit weakened by the delay. He isn't rational anymore—if he were, he wouldn't have nearly exposed his gifts by attempting to strike his prey in public. He wouldn't have let violence replace the careful subterfuge that defined his hunts. He wouldn't be thinking of Azalea as anything other than prey.

He finds himself standing outside a shop selling gaudy confections. He had half-heartedly sought Eli around town but without success. The time left before his ring turns black grows dangerously short, yet the urgency refuses to grip him. His rationality is surely fraying, but he can't hold the thought long enough to care.

The store's bright colors and the effervescence radiating from the patrons had drawn him to the window, a rare moment of distraction. Children and adults alike indulge in the globs of spun sugar, their laughter light and unburdened. Alec stares, unable to remember the last time he found joy in something so simple. Alchemy, perhaps, but even that has long since lost its spark. With a last glance at the carefree humans, he turns to leave, prepared to spend the rest of the day pacing the empty halls of his estate. There is no sign of Eli—and he tells himself it is only Eli he is looking for.

Then her voice, rich and smoky, cuts through the din of the street. He freezes. Azalea stomps toward him, trailing three black-haired girls. His body tenses, ready to flee, but he doesn't move. He convinces himself it's too late; she's already seen him. She beams at him, her emotions bright and unchecked as they sweep over him in waves of giddy lightness. The youngest girl clings to her arm, while the other two follow, their matching frowns casting shadows over their otherwise almost identical faces.

Azalea wears those tight trousers again, the sight of her stirring an inexplicable need. Not lust—he has long since learned to suppress that—but something deeper. He imagines that touching her might fill the hollow spaces of his second life, might grant him even a moment's reprieve from the cold emptiness that has consumed him for centuries.

He drowns the thought before it can fully form. He cannot afford such weaknesses. Not now. Not ever.

"I thought you might have left town already," she says, ushering the youngest dark-haired girl past him and into the store. The bell chimes when it opens, and the littlest girl makes a pleased sound as the other two children trudge in behind her, grumbling inaudibly.

"Something has convinced me to stay longer." He speaks to the glass window to avoid looking at her and those trousers.

"I'm glad," she says, grinning, hope pulsing from her along with—is that affection? Fates, how he wishes it was. He swallows the ache rising in his chest, saying nothing, the weight of his reasons for distance pressing heavily upon him.

Azalea's gaze flits from the bright window display to his stiff, unyielding stance. Her grin softens into something teasing, almost coaxing. "Are you coming in for ice cream, or are you just going to stand there staring all day?"

Alec shakes his head, still silent. That must be what the globs are, but the vats of sugar look nothing like the iced cream he saw on one of his prior journeys to human civilizations. He opts for a half-truth he hopes will appease her and then she can be on her way, and he can be alone. Again. "I've not had it before."

But instead of leaving him, Azalea grabs his arm with a gleam in her eye and ushers him into the store. "Well, that changes today."

Chapter 9

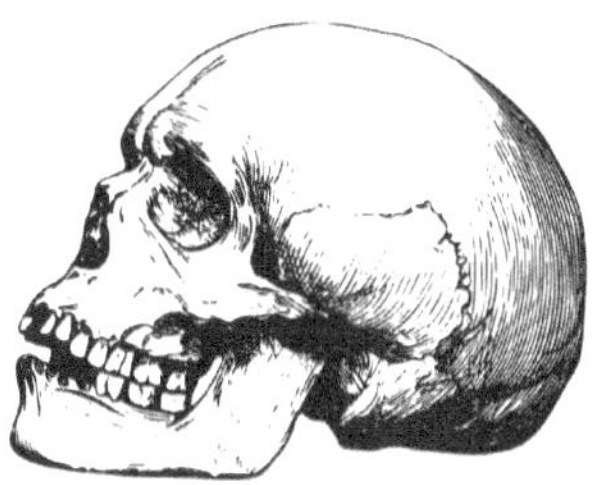

"Thanks for the ice cream," Azalea says when the bowl Alec purchased is half-empty. "I always think clearer on a full stomach. The girls would thank you too, but they're basically half-feral."

"Nonsense." The word is short but his tone mild.

Another minute passes in silence before Azalea's fingers drum on the table, breaking his concentration and internal rant. "You're a man of few words. I get it. But I've been dealing with teenage drama for the last week and I could really use some adult conversation."

Alec shakes himself. The 'drama' of his own mind is nigh on unbearable. He'll appease her with light conversation, *then* find Eli and hide. The memory of today will be enough to sustain him until the Council finally gives him his assignments back.

"I apologize. Let us speak pleasantries then. How is your family?" He can pretend he's focusing on the hunt. He hasn't outright mentioned her brother, but her family includes Eli. It counts.

Azalea rolls her head back and lets it drop behind her. The line of her neck, trailing down to the wide scoop neck of her shirt draws his eye. He keeps his gaze focused on the table.

"No," she says. "Family talk is off limits because it's teenage drama central right now. Keeping those two," her fingers hook to point at the older girls she dragged into the shop, "from becoming statistics on teen pregnancy is taking up all my energy. You'd think school would distract them, what with all the homework, but nope."

A benign conversation, to be sure, but he has nothing to add. He grasps the only topic he has. "What—what do you do whilst your siblings are in school?"

"Not much," she says, lifting her head as a hint of resentment flashes over her eyes. "I do odd jobs here and there, like cleaning or lawn care since no one in Lonetree's hiring full time and I can't walk to Asheville every day. I volunteer at the library and read a lot."

Her preoccupation with reading isn't a surprise as he committed their few discussions to memory. She quoted Shakespeare and wanted to dance with him, two encounters that will live within him long after her death. "Do—do you have a favorite author?"

Azalea plays with a loose lock of blonde hair, twisting it between her fingers. "The Lonetree library is pretty lacking. Most of what I get are the big hits, classics written before the 1950s. Mostly Shakespeare and the like." Her eyes drift far away, as if she's scanning the shelves of the library in her mind rather than sitting across from him. "I love fantasy, though. There's just something about the wonder and otherworldliness that always draws me in. I've gone through all the H.G. Wells, C.S. Lewis, and J.R.R. Tolkien they had. I've even put in some inter-library loan requests for more Le Guin. The Asheville library only has one of hers, but it stays with me." She bites her lip, lowering her head to stare at the melted bowl of ice cream between them. "Sorry, I can get carried away."

"No." The word comes out too quickly, an impulsive reassurance he can't recall ever giving anyone else. He pushes aside the nagging thought that follows—he is otherworldly; perhaps that same wonder she loves draws her to him. "Your interest is commendable."

Her head stays bowed, and she traces shapes in the stained plastic tabletop. "You're one of the few people who think that, aside from my old teachers. Most people get annoyed by the quoting or don't understand what I'm talking about."

"I haven't noticed that you quote incessantly."

"You don't know me that well," she says with a small, wry smile. "I memorize my favorite quotes from everything I read and try to apply them to my daily life. It's my best chance to experience something bigger and better than what I've got. Maybe if I ever get out of North

Carolina, my life will be interesting enough that I won't need to do it anymore."

"Why do you stay?"

She snorts, her eyes flicking to the girls still enjoying their treat a few tables away. "Do you have any siblings?"

Alec shakes his head, although he has an inkling he had one, but that was long ago. He hasn't thought about his original family in years. Michael became all he had, and Michael doesn't count.

"Eli and I are the same age, twins. But I have the responsibility while he makes the decisions. Plus, I'm the little mother, but it's not a gender thing," she says, resentment bubbling from her. "It's because I'm the meek one, the tagalong. Everything I do here is with him or for my family while he gets to be off living life however he wants. I've done nothing just for myself. Like, I wanted to go away for college when I graduated high school last May. I'd gotten a great scholarship that would have covered my expenses." She slumps further in her chair. "But I couldn't leave Eli."

"Why not?" He asks, but he can guess the answer. Expectation and duty are burdens for humans and wraiths.

"I've never been on my own. It was always us and the girls, so for years the idea terrified me. When the time finally came a few months ago, Eli started acting incredibly unreliable. I felt guilty at the idea of leaving them when they needed me." She shuffles in her seat. "But I can't remember why anymore—the girls don't need me anymore. And Eli's gotten weird and missing half the time on these mysterious trips." She eats a few more bites of iced cream. With a cream covered mouth, she grins. "I guess you're right. If Eli can have a life away, so can I. Are you in the market for a traveling partner when you leave?"

Alec's mind shutters at her blatant invitation to stay with him, the thrill of her words rushing through him like a spark. When he repeats the moment inwardly, dissecting it for a sense of control, he realizes the insight she unintentionally provided about Eli. Her comments weren't meaningless chatter—they revealed valuable information about his prey.

Relief floods him as the pieces align. His preoccupation with Azalea, the small talk, the fixation—it all makes sense now. It's not about her; it's about Eli. Every interaction, every moment spent in her company, is just another calculated step in his hunt, surely. He isn't *obsessed* with her. He's simply exhausting every available avenue to achieve his goal, planning his strike with the precision he prides himself on.

His mind seizes the conclusion like a lifeline, clinging to it with desperate certainty. It avoids the treacherous path of introspection, the path that could (*would, will*) unravel the careful narrative he's constructed. Instead, he stands firm, the comforting lie held close to his chest like armor.

"What trips does Eli take?" he asks.

"I'm not sure," Azalea says, her voice tinged with frustration and a hint of concern. "He's gone to Raleigh at least daily to work on something big that he says, 'will change everything for us,' but he won't tell me what. He's been going to Hendersonville pretty regularly since our eighteenth, too."

Alec files away the information, his mind clicking through the possibilities. "Do you know if he's been meeting with someone at either place?" Alec can track them and be done with the entire affair. The very idea rouses a regret he wished was a surprise, but the lies he tells himself are never convincing.

"No," Azalea scoffs, tugging at her hair again and letting a few strands fall loose. "He doesn't tell me anything anymore. I guess he has his reasons for keeping things from me. Everyone has a few secrets. You of all people would understand that." His mind shutters for a second time. *Has she figured him out?* He committed a Rule break and didn't even get to enjoy it. "Me of all people? What do you mean?"

The melancholy fades and a mischievousness overtakes it. "Don't pretend to be oblivious about it. Your entire personality is mysterious. I'm going to figure you out," she teases.

Against his better judgment, he smiles in response. His secret remains safe, but Fates, if she doesn't make him want to offer himself to her.

"Give me your phone so I can put my number in it. Then I'll text you. Or call you, if you're lucky because I hate talking on the phone," she says, holding out an expectant hand.

Alec leans back against the rigid plastic chair, his brows furrowing. Her demand and her sudden shift from melancholy to flirtation to casual friendliness bewilder him.

No matter how long he lives, he'll never understand how emotions can slip through humans' minds like wet sand.

At his twisted expression, Azalea withdraws a block of plastic from between her breasts and under her shirt, waving it in front of his face.

"Do you not have a phone?" she asks, snapping the device open to reveal a bright square displaying a photograph of herself and another dark-haired girl seated in a silver chair. Numbers and icons frame the glowing image.

"I don't," he says, peering closer to look at the shining photograph. The proximity to the plastic creates an uncomfortable buzzing sensation under his skin. He's seen humans in the area speaking into plastic squares but hasn't seen one that opened nor been close. He leans away, and the buzzing diminishes. "Who is that?"

She turns the phone towards herself and clucks. "That's my friend, Sarah. She got out of this place a few years ago. Lucky brat," she finishes in a sotto voice. A sadness wafts from her, colored by a tint of jealousy.

Another emotion switch, so sudden he can barely catch them. He studies her carefully, wondering how much of her drive to leave is about herself and how much is about chasing the freedom she sees in others. Yet even as her emotions shift, he finds himself drawn to her determination, even the fragile sadness in her tone. It stirs something he hasn't felt in centuries, something he'd thought long buried.

"How do you not have a phone?" she asks, her tone incredulous. "Mine may be a piece of crap, but I still have one."

"I—I haven't needed one. I've few people to talk to," Alec stutters, fumbling for an explanation.

"Well, you do now. Otherwise, I'll have to wait another two weeks to see you again."

Only centuries of discipline and his carefully controlled persona keep Alec from jolting at her words. She missed him. "You—you wanted to see me again?"

"Of course, I did. You're the most interesting thing in town right now." She laughs, standing to clear her now-empty glass dish. As she maneuvers behind him, her foot catches, sending her stumbling into him. The dish clatters against his cheek before hitting the floor.

"Oh my god, I'm so sorry! Are you okay?" Shame, fear, and other unknown emotions jumble together, swirling towards him like a thunderous maelstrom. He pats his cheek where the glass struck. It didn't hurt—only something with magical force could harm him—but she dabs at the spot with a napkin, cleaning up a smear of melted ice cream.

"I'm fine," Alec swears, but the intensity of her emotions lingers.

"Seriously, I can't believe it! My one shot with a cute boy and I brain—" Her words cut off abruptly, her eyes darting from his cheek to his lips, then flickering toward his ear. She closes her eyes, visibly cringing. "Any chance you'll forget I just vomited that out on you?"

Her nearness is intoxicating, and Alec licks his lips, grasping for clarity. "You what?"

She opens her eyes again, a blush spreading across her sun-kissed cheeks. "Never mind," she mutters, raising a hand toward him. He freezes as her fingers brush through his hair, the light touch sending a shiver down his spine. His gaze locks on her flushed face, his senses hyperaware as her hand lingers, then withdraws.

"Sorry, there was ice cream in your hair," she mumbles.

"I didn't mind it. I—I like your touch," Alec says before he can stop himself. His hand trembles as he reaches for hers, his thumb making small circles on her wrist. A craving builds deep in his stomach, a hunger that feels both unbearable and forbidden. It feels as though her skin burns his fingers.

She hums quietly, her attention fixed on his hand on her wrist. "It's like I'm in one of my fantasies. You're like this perfect Roman god who's met my brother, slummed it in Lonetree twice, and still sat here with me." Her gaze dips lower as she leans forward, her oversized shirt slipping just enough to expose more of her collarbone.

"Why wouldn't I want your company? You're fascinating," Alec murmurs, his voice low. This feeling, this heat spiraling through him, is familiar yet unsettling. Lust is simpler—a path he understands, even if he abandoned it along with the wraith games long ago. But the temptation to kiss her feels stifling, dangerous.

Azalea doesn't respond with words. Instead, her free hand weaves into his hair again. Alec's grip tightens on her wrist as his other hand moves to rest on her knee, the soft fabric of her trousers warm beneath his fingers. He wants to explore further, his restraint slipping as the scent of her cranberry-sweetened desire fills the air. Her fingers stroke his scalp, her dark pupils mirroring the spark in his glowing eyes. Her lips part, and he leans in closer.

"Azzie! Phoebe got ice cream all over my shirt!"

The spell breaks. Alec jerks his head back guiltily as Azalea drops her hands and blinks rapidly, her gaze narrowing in irritation.

"Phoebe, don't be a brat," she shouts, standing abruptly and stomping toward the source of the interruption. "I'll see you later, Alec," she calls over her shoulder, her cheeks flushed as she herds the three girls toward the exit. Just before the door closes behind them, her blonde head pops back in. "Hopefully soon," she adds with a grin before disappearing down the street.

Alone again, Alec pinches his eyes shut, gripping the edge of the table until his knuckles whiten.

This is getting worse.

Chapter 10

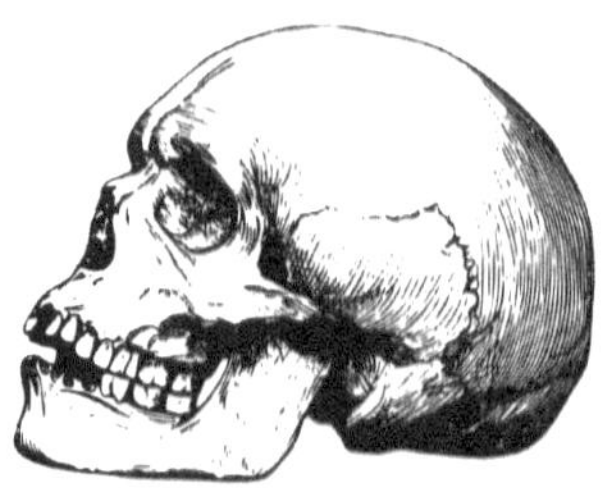

ALEC BROODS UNTIL THE small hours. It isn't a new pastime, given he's done so every evening since meeting Azalea *and* before, but the stakes are different now. Alone in the library as Godfrey scurries around somewhere else in the derelict mansion, Alec twirls his ring around his finger. The jewel catches on his knuckles, its cold weight a constant reminder of what binds him.

Her touch distracts him. There were others after Cassius—humans and wraiths alike—until the sight of his reflection made him feel as though he were drowning. He abandoned all intimacy, allowing only Lucia to tempt him in the centuries that followed. He held her hand before she fled, her screams haunting him even now. That was nearly a millennium ago. Azalea's touch is different—it relaxes something inside him, something sharp and thorny that he thought long dead.

Despite his two prior lapses, Alec has never needed true companionship. The Council and Michael provided all he required. The Council gave him money, status, and, above all, purpose—though at the cost of his unconditional fealty. Michael, though almost like a brother, offers no solace, no genuine support. He is a creature of impulse and insolence, seeking attention rather than connection. Azalea's presence is something else entirely—softer, less jagged and demanding. She stirs a yearning in Alec he thought extinguished: the human desire for friendship, for love freely given and returned. Her goodness feels like a balm, one that might even overlook the rot in *his* soul.

Alec stands abruptly, the chair scraping against the floor. He seizes a candlestick from the low-burning fireplace and hurls it at a curtain-covered window. Glass shatters, and moonlight spills through the crack, cool air following in its wake.

Alec isn't a human, and their wants must be weaknesses.

He's spent too long interacting in the human world. If he used the time to track Eli, that would be one thing. If he hadn't tried to glimpse Azalea in the field or at the library. If he took her and abandoned her, like his brethren would, instead of mooning over her like a human—

But he spoke with her, touched her, let her touch him. He can convince himself that it was helpful to speak to her at first, but he isn't delusional enough to keep up the lie.

His fists clench, the ring biting into his palm, the prongs of the amber jewel digging into his skin. The pain grounds him. The ring is a manifestation of who and what he is: the twin bands, a reminder of his second life; the engraving, a declaration he cannot escape his nature; the jewel's amber glow, a display of the souls he holds captive.

Alec has seen what happens to wraiths who break the Rules or attract the Council's ire. As a rover, he has hunted and punished them himself. He's received censure once or twice—nothing more than taps on his wrists—but the memory of harsher punishments lingers. Michael has never betrayed Alec's earlier interest in humans, though some in their circle might harbor suspicions. If anyone discovers his feelings for Azalea—feelings that teeter dangerously close to *honorable*—or his prioritization of her over the hunt, there will be no mercy. Certain destruction, and agony beyond imagining, await him.

He stalks to the bookcase behind the mirror, letting the frigid air from the shattered window seep into his pores. With shaking hands, he pulls a leather-bound journal from the shelf, its gilded "A" catching the pale light. Michael had gifted him the journal centuries ago to replace the loose parchment Alec once used to chronicle his life: his meticulous notes on the Teachings, the Rules, and the Rule breakers he was ordered to capture by the Council.

His own handwriting glares back at him from the pages.

> *The First Rule: Never show weakness.*
> *-of mind, of body, of soul.*

The Second Rule: Protect the secrecy of our kind.
-there are no exceptions.
The Third Rule: Never betray one of the family.
-there can be no others.

He flips through the subsequent pages, each inked line detailing his second life with ruthless precision. Every word feels like an accusation, a mockery of his recent failures. When he reaches the last entry—the one cementing his choice of Eli as prey—he pauses. The ink is black, the decision unchangeable, as immutable as the Rules themselves. As immutable as he is supposed to be.

Alec shakes his head, his feathery hair clawing at his vision. He snaps the journal shut and slides it back onto the shelf. Running his fingers over the twin bands of his ring, he breathes deeply, forcing his scattered thoughts into order. He needs a reminder of what he is—of who he is. And though it galls him to ask for help, there is only one person who can provide that clarity.

Facing the mirror, Alec touches the ring's square jewel to its cold, reflective surface. The glass ripples like mercury, but he doesn't step through. To visit Michael directly would be unwise, not when Michael could be anywhere and embroiled in any number of his indulgences. Instead, Alec tosses a folded note through the shimmering portal, the paper vanishing with a ripple as it hits the other side. His message is simple: *Come soon.*

He retreats to the damp chair near the fireplace, where the last embers of the fire glow faintly. Hours stretch into a slow crawl as Alec stares at his reflection in the cracked windowpane, the weight of his thoughts pressing heavily on him. Likely, Michael is preoccupied with his Historian or some other distraction. Still, Alec hopes the urgency in his message will compel his sire to come quickly.

When the mirror finally shudders, Alec rises. The surface ripples violently before a hand claws through, gripping the edge like a lifeline. Michael's foot emerges next, followed by the rest of his imposing frame. He steps out with theatrical flair, as though the mere act of passing through dimensions demands an audience.

Alec steps forward, offering a steadying hand. "Michael," he says, his voice even, though tension hums beneath it.

"Alesandro. Remember the Teachings." Michael leans down to cup Alec's face, crushing Alec's cheeks with his large hands.

"Follow the Rules," Alec says through clenched teeth. Michael laughs and releases him.

"It gives me such pleasure to see you again. You and your prey have been on my mind since our last chat."

Straight to business, just what Alec needs. "Thank you for your prompt visit, Michael. I hope I didn't take you from your duties for the Council."

Michael tosses himself into a dusty upholstered chair near the dark fireplace. "Your letter made you sound desperate to see me. Not that you shouldn't be. Lucky for you, I'm now between tasks and playing with a human nearby. I obtained a small leave through my dalliance with the Historian, although I believe he assumed we would spend it together." He motions to himself, as if to say, 'can you blame him?'

"I don't have any information I'm willing to share on the unreadable human, so I *do* hope this isn't about her," Michael finishes.

Alec grimaces. He forgot he had mentioned Azalea to Michael after their first meeting. His worries from two weeks ago—that he couldn't read her—seem almost laughable now. That's no longer the problem. Obsessing over her is. But he can't admit it to Michael. Not only is concealing his weaknesses a reflex, hammered into him over centuries, but revealing them would invite Michael to 'fix' the issue in his own chaotic and unsolicited way.

The memory of Michael and Cassius still claws at Alec in his darkest moments. He spent centuries afterward trying to burn out the guilt, burying himself in the most wraith-like behavior he could muster. All it achieved was igniting his insatiable need for penance, driving him to centuries of self-imposed exile and rigid adherence to the Rules. That he can't even ask Michael what happened to Lucia—whether she lived, whether Michael destroyed her memory or her life—tells him all he needs to know: Michael can never learn about his feelings for Azalea.

Alec forces his face into a practiced calm, tilting his head in feigned curiosity. "Can I not wish to see my oldest friend and relive the old days?"

Michael raises his dark, undyed, eyebrows, suspicion flickering across his vibrant green eyes. "Alright. Keep your secrets. But I'm bored, dearest. I've avoided fomenting chaos for at least six hours." He pulls a tarnished pocket watch from inside his coat. It appears broken, as the dials spin faster than they should, but Alec knows better. "How long has it been since we hunted together, dearest? Truly hunted and played?"

"Muscovy, twelve hundred years ago," spits Alec. It isn't a memory Alec wants to relive.

Michael laughs as he rubs the face of his watch. "We had fun then, didn't we?"

"You had fun, Michael. I only recall cleaning up your messes and stopping several near Rule breaks."

"Bah, the Rules. Did you know the Council has come up with another Teaching just for me? Apparently starting a gambling ring with the hawkers is a weakness, which ignores that—"

"Michael," Alec hisses to halt the possible confession.

Michael reaches for Alec's amber ring, the color now a dull yellow. Alec draws it towards his chest, hiding it from Michael's sight. "You know, if you loosened your pseudo-morals a little, you'd surely enjoy this life more," Michael says.

"You know my thoughts on the matter."

Michael stares at him with blank eyes. If Alec didn't know better, he'd assume Michael was plotting something. But he knows him, and it was more likely that Michael was thinking about how to set something on fire to liven up Alec's evening. Michael blinks twice before twisting his lips into another grin. "Your last soul runs out in a week or less, does it not?"

Alec nods. He has at most a week before his mind betrays him, one of the first side effects of soul sickness, where erratic and irrational thoughts will plague him before his body breaks down. It's likely already happening, but he can't admit it to Michael.

"Then perhaps we should make progress," Michael suggests. "We can still hunt together, even if our methods differ."

Alec eyes the pocket watch and stares at his sire pointedly. From the speed of the dials, Michael would need to hunt at the turn of the next millennia. "I can always hunt for more than just souls," Michael says, slipping the watch back into his coat.

Chapter 11

"WE'RE GOING OUT TONIGHT," Eli announces, tossing something onto Azzie's stomach. "Wear that. It'll make you look like a girl."

Azzie groans, pulling her head out from under the threadbare pillow on the bed she shares with Clara. Eli stands above her, framed by the harsh light from the broken ceiling fan. The glow around his blond hair gives him an unearthly aura that makes her snort. Angelic, her ass. If Eli were any celestial being, it'd be Lucifer.

She grabs the offending garment—a tight, shimmering red dress that practically screams *trouble*. Even on her short frame, it'll hit mid-thigh, showing off her chest and thick thighs. "Where did you get this? It looks like something a hooker would wear."

Eli smirks, his eyes drifting theatrically to the side. "Maybe one did."

She hurls the dress back at him, her face hot with frustration. "I'm not going. You can't say crap like that and expect me to just go along with it."

He catches the dress with one hand and snaps it back at her, the sequins scratching her cheek. Azzie yelps, glaring as the dress flutters to the floor.

"That could have hurt!" she growls.

"Then don't sass me," Eli retorts, leaning lazily against the wall. His nonchalance makes her blood boil. "James is expecting you, and," he points at the dress, "he'll be expecting you in that."

Her mouth dries. That's a new variable to the game. She only *be-friends* the wealthy new kids, ones who probably wanted Eli's atten-tion but settled for Azzie's. "Did you tell him what I was wearing? I'm—that's not how this goes. I'm just supposed to get information!"

Eli runs a hand through his tousled hair, his confidence infuriat-ingly intact. "No, but you need to entice him. He seems like the type that'd be into you. But he'll lose interest as soon as you open your big mouth, so hopefully, your dress will distract him."

"Rude." Azzie crosses her arms, her voice dropping to a low, sharp hiss. "It's not my fault you can't keep up when anything remotely intelligent comes up, sober or not. And I'm *not* a whore, Eli. That's never been what we've done."

Eli might tease about setting her up with his targets, but it's never been more than friendship once they figure out she's not the gate-keeper to Eli's pants. Her role is simple: she gets to know them, listens carefully, and gathers enough information for Eli to take the truck cross-country and rob their parents' vacation homes. Afterward, she scrubs the guilt off herself as best she can, though it never fully fades. The residue of deceit clings to her, a shame that feels like a permanent stain etched into her skin.

The money Eli gets from pawning their stolen goods in Raleigh and beyond is far better than the meager income Azzie scrapes together from her odd jobs. That's the only reason she goes along with it. If there were another way to keep their family afloat, she'd take it in a heartbeat. But there isn't. Not yet. So, for now, she plays her part, no matter how much it eats at her.

"Things are changing, Az. We need the money until I get this other thing settled. And if that means showing a little skin—"

"No. Never." She isn't worth much, but she's better than that.

"It's just sex. I'm doing it with the Raleigh guy. I never knew you were such a prude."

Azzie crosses the room to hit him hard on the shoulder. His body knocks into the wall. Eli may be taller than her, but she has pounds on him. "Shut up. It's called having standards, morals."

He snorts. "Someone with morals wouldn't *do* what we do."

"Don't lump me in with you, Eli. That's the difference between you and me." She waves her hands around the room. "I'm better than this whole place. As soon as I'm out of here, I'll prove it."

"You're not going to leave me, Az. Don't talk like that." Eli's expression is soft and confused, like he's never considered Az has plans of her own, like he hasn't realized just how far apart they drifted.

"Maybe I am, maybe I'm not," she says. "Stop trying to pimp me out and I'll think about telling you."

"Fine." He drags out the word. "Just no leaving. Not until I work through some options for us."

"With your Raleigh guy?"

For a moment, Eli looks almost chastened, but then the smirk returns, weaker but still there. "You're overthinking it. Just wear the damn dress and charm him. It's not that hard." He slips past her to pick up the discarded garment.

Azzie slumps back on her bed. She has no interest in going to a fraternity open house and meeting whoever Eli thinks is wealthy enough for his attention. Alec's ice blue gaze flashes in front of her face. Alec is wealthy, though she never intends for Eli to mess up her chances with him. He also seems interested in her, rather than Eli for once. He called her enthralling and let her fondle his hair, for God sakes, because in a fit of lunacy she felt like a bubble headed girl who wanted to flirt with the handsome guy. Only seeing Eli wasted on the couch when they arrived home forced her energies away from her spiral of self-consciousness.

"You're forgetting the *best* option." She makes her tone as casual as she can. Eli doesn't need to know of her duplicity; she just needs time.

"Winning the lottery?"

"No," she huffs. "Alec."

"The foreign kid that kept running away from you?"

"You mean the one who almost strangled you? The one with the massive house and family money? Yes, him."

Eli's eyes glaze over, running his fingers over the sequins like a villain pets a cat. Her fingers twitch to rescue the fabric from his dirty hands. "I don't like him," he says.

"So, you've said," she mutters. She stares at Eli's face, and how his coffee-colored eyes look hazy. "Are you drunk right now?"

Eli doesn't answer, but his eyes refocus. "That's also none of your business."

"It is my business if you make a fool of yourself in front of Alec again." She pokes him in the chest.

"Who cares? He creeps me out."

"He's nice to me."

"When he's not running from you," Eli says, snidely.

"That only happened once!"

"He hasn't even called you. How the hell are you supposed to get me into his house? Come on, Az, you say you don't want to feel like a hooker but *if* he's not gay—"

"He's not."

"—then he wants one thing from you," he continues as if she hasn't spoken. "As soon as he gets your number, I guarantee he'll be calling at 4am for a hookup and then drop you. You're too naïve to work that to your advantage like I do before they realize I'm trash."

"He doesn't have a phone!" she yells. Alec's better than that, she's sure of it. *She* is the instigator between them, not the other way around.

Eli stares at her with a pitying expression. She fists her hands on her hips and releases her anger in three steadying breaths. Eli doesn't respond to anger well; he gets quiet when she snaps. Then the conversations are over, and she's stuck doing whatever she railed against in the first place. She tries to appeal to his selfish side. "Look, let me work on Alec. He's got that giant house with no one in it but him. And apparently he needs a new dealer."

He shivers before looking back at Azzie. "I won't say no to it, but something about him puts me off. Go with James, James is easy. At least until my Raleigh guy hands pays off and we don't have to do this until next semester."

"What if I can get Alec to invite us over? He doesn't need to like me long, just long enough for you guys to get in."

Azzie holds her breath while Eli considers it, her heart pounding in her chest. She doesn't need his agreement—not really. All she needs is a few more days to tie up the loose ends and make her clean getaway. Once the bow is tied, Eli will be off her tail, and whatever chaos brews in Lonetree, Asheville, or the entirety of North Carolina won't matter anymore.

She'll be somewhere far away. Somewhere new. Somewhere with Alec.

"You meet James too," he says. "I already laid the groundwork with him and I'm not letting my time go to waste. Get Alec to open up so the boys and I can recon and then *maybe* I'll drop the James play."

"Fine," she agrees. She holds up the dress. "But do I *have* to wear this?"

Chapter 12

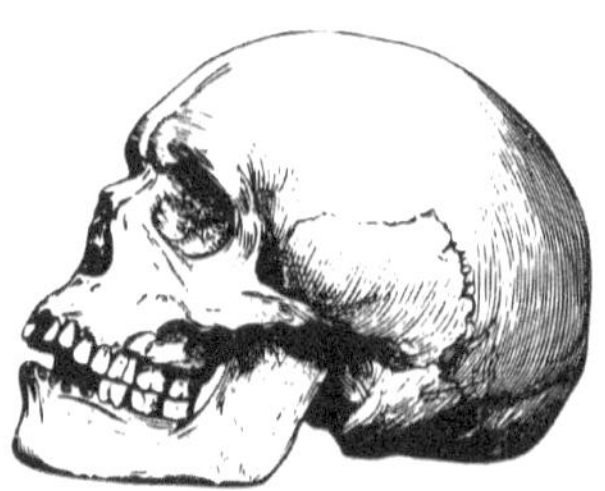

ALEC AND MICHAEL FIND another party, this one at a sprawling manor house near the university in Asheville. Judging from the mingling scents of musk, soap, and stale beer, several men must share the space. Still, the location is far better than his prior hunting grounds here; at least these occupants seem to follow a rudimentary cleaning regimen.

Michael claims the center of the largest living area not occupied by dancers, sinking into a rust-colored upholstered chair like a king taking his throne. His green eyes sparkle as he surveys the crowded room, his presence magnetic. With a casual wave, he beckons women and men alike toward him, a god demanding fealty and admiration.

Alec stands nearby, his lean frame clad in all black again, the color sharpening the glimmer of his icy blue eyes. Yet tonight, Michael, resplendent in a deep green suit that perfectly matches his sparkling gaze, draws all the attention. Before entering the manor, Alec had made Michael promise to blend in while Alec focused on finishing his hunt and gathering information about Eli. Michael's sharklike grin and his promise—qualified by the ominous "I'll do nothing *too* destructive"—had already set Alec on edge. The beginnings of a headache pulsed at the base of his skull, something his frozen body shouldn't be able to create.

Less than an hour into the revelry, the party has turned raucous. Michael lounges with two women on his lap, one draped over each leg, running his fingers along their faces. Alec, standing just behind his sire, monitors Michael's antics, fully aware the wraith could devolve into chaos at any moment. Michael keeps up a barrage of questions, asking Alec to read the emotions of partygoers until he can twist those feelings in an unpleasant, but otherwise harmless, way. Alec, however, grows weary. Sensing the darker energy characteristic of Eli, Alec leaves Michael to his debauchery, determined to find his prey—and *no one else*.

He locates them in another open living area. The faded couches and chairs have been shoved against the paneled walls to clear a makeshift dance floor. Music blasts from a bulky plastic contraption near the fireplace, the beat rattling the windows.

Azalea stands along the far wall, next to Eli. Her outfit—something bold and striking in crimson red—makes Alec falter. It clings to her form, hugging her curves and accentuating her generous bust and as revealing as an undergarment, but closer inspection reveals skin-toned fabric covering her arms and legs. The illusion of immodesty is deliberate, a design that leaves just enough to the imagination. Her hair is swept into a tight bun, save for two loose tendrils framing her face. She looks stunning, a vision of allure, and tonight, others seem to notice. Unlike the first party, where she was dismissed, here she commands attention.

He can just pick out Azalea's out her voice, slightly too loud, rising above her brother's lower, harsher tones. Eli gestures sharply, his hands hovering near her neck. Even without reaching out with his gift, Alec senses the annoyance and frustration swirling between them. When Eli grips her shoulders, Alec clenches his fists, every instinct urging him to step in and intervene. But Azalea holds her ground, her expression pinched. When her shoulders finally slump, Eli motions for another young man to join them, shoving Azalea into the stranger's arms.

Alec bites the inside of his cheek and digs his nails into his palms to anchor himself. He watches as Azalea and the boy take to the floor. The boy must be a new university student given the thick scent of self-consciousness and ambition hovering around him. Alec tracks their every step, noting the boy's hands stay awkwardly away from Azalea's body. Relief settles heavily in Alec's chest.

As the song progresses, Azalea's gaze shifts and finds his. Her face brightens, her lips curving into a radiant smile. Alec nods curtly in response, ignoring the faint thrill that courses through him at her expression. He tells himself it's only coincidence that their paths crossed again. He has no other reason to be here.

He's never more thankful wraith gifts don't work on other wraiths, or Michael would have noticed Alec's want of her seeping from the edges of Alec's caution and control.

Michael's sudden presence over Alec's shoulder interrupts his steady, focused observation. "New prey?" Michael murmurs, his sharp green eyes fixed on Azalea.

Alec tips his head slightly toward the far wall where Eli now stands, flanked by two other men, passing around a hand-rolled cigarette. "Still her brother," Alec replies evenly, his tone devoid of emotion, though his hands twitch behind his back.

Michael's speculative gaze lingers on Azalea. A flicker of something feral, hungry, gleams in his expression as he drags his eyes up and down her figure. "Then she's the one you cannot read. I see why she distracted you," he says, a touch of amusement curling his voice. "Do you also hunt for something other than souls, Alesandro?" His voice is pitched low, but the insinuation is clear.

Alec turns his frown toward Michael, his voice cold as stone. "That is your game, not mine."

"Only because you are the most controlled wraith we've had in the family." Michael's smirk deepens, his teeth glinting under the dim light. "If our kind had monks, I've no doubt you'd take vows."

"Lucky for us all," Alec retorts with a biting edge, "we have no monks. Else you'd be one of the top blasphemers, vying for the Council's punishment."

Michael laughs and several heads turn. "Would you hunt me, dearest? Use your honed rover skills to keep me from breaking any of those pesky Rules?"

Alec remains silent; Michael would enjoy his discomfort too much for him to respond.

The music fades, and Alec watches as Azalea leans close to her dance partner, her breath stirring the boy's unruly hair as she whispers something. Alec's fingers twitch involuntarily. The boy turns red and sprints off into another room, leaving Azalea free to lock eyes with Alec. Her gaze lingers, and then, with a purposefully measured stride, she moves toward him.

"I don't believe you would," Michael says beside him, voice dripping with smug amusement, "given what I imagine you'd like to do with that girl. My Alesandro, finally seeking his own pleasure." He chuckles darkly, his emerald eyes shamelessly following Azalea's figure. "You do have a type. It shouldn't surprise me that a broken human who thinks quoting literature is a redeeming personality trait struck your fancy. You always were my soft boy."

The insults—both to Azalea and himself—land with Michael's usual venom, but they still rankle. Alec draws a breath, choosing his words with care. If Michael suspects the truth of his feelings, the consequences would be severe. "She hasn't 'struck my fancy,'" he replies curtly, his tone clipped. Then a realization pierces through his irritation. "Wait, you can read her?"

Michael claps him hard on the back. "No matter, she's here now and I have my own game tonight."

"You're here!" Azalea cries when she makes it across the room. Her face is flushed and strands of damp hair curl beside her cheeks. "This is why you need a phone!" she continues breathlessly, standing close enough that he can see the light sheen of sweat on her forehead. "If I'd known you were coming, I wouldn't have fought with Eli about it."

"It's something to consider," he says, sliding a look to at Michael. But Michael's gaze focuses on Azalea's dress rather than their conversation. Bile rises in Alec's stomach as Michael grasps her hand and brings it to his lips.

"I'm Michael, beautiful. Lovely to meet you as Alex has told me *so* much about you. But he left out your most favorable assets." Michael speaks directly to her chest. Azalea wrenches her hand away and rubs it on the fabric over her stomach.

"Alex?" She addresses Alec alone.

"One of his many nicknames," Michael answers in his stead, waving a hand, clearly forgetting Alec's specific epithet. "I grew up with him, you see. Perhaps I could tell you about it later, just the two of us."

Alec clenches his fists to avoid vivisecting Michael in the parlor.

But to his secret delight, Azalea grins crookedly at Alec, ignoring Michael. "So, I can be Azalea and not Azzie, but you're Alec or Alex... which is short for?"

The boy from before rejoins them with two red plastic cups in his hand filled with cheap smelling liquor, saving Alec from responding with a lie. "For you, milady." He bows while handing Azalea a cup, spilling the liquor on his fabric shoes. Azalea's crooked smile disappears.

"Alec, Alec's friend, this is James. He's a freshman at the university." She speaks through her teeth. "He met my brother at a *bookstore* in Hendersonville and invited us both tonight."

James sticks out his hand, which neither Michael nor Alec takes. With a trembling cough, James drops it back to his side. "You guys members of Zeta? I'm thinking of rushing. I'm a legacy." He motions around the room. "The place is pretty sweet during the day."

Michael drags a finger lazily up James' arm. "Quite sweet. We are merely visitors to this place, in search of sustenance and respite. Perhaps you can give me a tour?"

James hesitates, his expression flickering between confusion and fascination before he exhales sharply and nods. Without another word, he leads Michael out of the room. As Michael disappears around the corner, he glances back at Alec and winks, his smirk both mischievous and knowing.

Azalea steps closer, drawing Alec's attention away from Michael's antics. "I really am glad you're here," she says, her voice softer now.

Her eagerness buffets at him and a small kernel of something like hope takes root in the space in his chest where he holds his souls.

"It's been a day since we saw each other," he replies, his tone neutral.

"What a romantic," she teases, the corners of her lips quirking upward. "How'd you find out about this party? Eli had to wrangle special invitations."

"Where did your brother go?" Alec asks. He works to keep his hands from shaking. "I would like to speak with him."

She hooks her thumb over her shoulder. "I think he's lighting up somewhere. If you're hoping for a meaningful conversation, you've missed your window. It won't be as bad as two weeks ago, but still, I'd keep expectations low." Her grin widens as she tilts her head. "Now, should I ask if you to dance before you run off again, or do you want to make a break for the door now?"

He closes his eyes, inhaling deeply to steady himself. When he opens them, her smile has dimmed, her teasing replaced by a flicker of uncertainty. He surprises both of them by extending a hand. As he leads her to the dance area, her happiness unfurls around them, sweet and sharp like sea salt, curling into the edges of his consciousness.

The song's fast rhythm keeps Azalea bouncing on her feet, her unrestrained energy drawing Alec's gaze briefly before he forces his attention skyward, trying to focus on the intricate patterns of the ceiling instead of the other parts of her bouncing. Minutes slip by as the singer's crooning fades into a slower instrumental section.

"I hope Michael didn't upset you," Alec says, raising his voice to be heard over the music.

She shakes her head in time to the music. "It's fine. Who is he, anyway?"

"He's... something like a brother," he replies carefully. "I stay with him when I'm away from the Rockton House."

"Oh," Azalea peers up at him with interest. "No other family?"

"Something like that."

"Must be nice," she shouts back, panting as the beat increases.

He clears his throat, a faint wryness creeping into his tone. "Had I a brother like yours, I might agree with you."

Her movement stills, and she swipes the back of her hand over her glistening forehead. Without a word, she steps out of the throng, heading toward a nearby bench. Alec follows helplessly, hovering above her as she sits and fans her flushed cheeks.

"Man, I am out of shape," she groans, leaning back slightly. Her chest rises and falls under the snug fabric of her dress, catching Alec's attention for a fleeting moment before he pulls his gaze away. "What were you saying?"

"I believe I was commenting on your brother," Alec replies, his voice steady, though his hands twitch at his sides.

Her face hardens, and she crosses her arms. "Are you that hard up for a hit? There're plenty of guys here who have a side hustle if you're desperate."

Alec furrows his brow, confused by the sharp turn in conversation. "I have business I must attend to before I leave, with—"

"You still need to have that party," she interrupts.

The topic change is jarring. He reaches out with his gift to gauge her emotions but is met with the same maddening block. All he can sense is eagerness tinged with guilt. It's an unusual combination, smelling like burnt caramel.

Alec hesitates. "It would take ages to prepare for guests. There are rooms filled with heirlooms, all of which would need cataloging and dusting." He keeps Rockton House like a mausoleum because he has no use for any niceties like kitchen equipment, bedding, and comfortable furniture. But the idea of spending more time with Azalea creates a warmth in his stomach.

Her eyes light up as though he's agreed outright. She grabs his hand and tugs him toward a hallway. "That's okay," she says, glancing back with a grin. "You and I will get it ready before you leave town, as long as it takes. Just the two of us."

"I don't know that I need help before I leave," he protests weakly, his voice barely audible over the rush of her enthusiasm.

Ignoring him, Azalea pulls him into a dining room. It's dim and mostly empty, save for Eli perched on the edge of a long table, a cigarette dangling lazily from his fingers. Another young man sits close, their knees knocking together as they share the smoke.

"Guess what?" she asks the pair. The men eye her seemingly without recognition. Azalea huffs and jabs a blunt nail in Eli's arm. "Alec here is planning on having a party."

"I'm not sure—" Alec starts.

"And I'm going to help him get the place ready. Clean up, organize those packed rooms. We'll need your help after. Way after. Meaning I definitely don't have time for James..." Her words trail off while Eli and the boy blink up at her.

"Whoa," Eli mutters. The other boy ducks his forehead to Eli's shoulder and laughs. Eli giggles before taking another long puff from the cigarette.

Azalea's eyes dart to the door before she sighs. "Give me the keys. I'm taking us home before you light something on fire again."

Eli blinks at her.

"Keys!" she barks.

He swipes at the air twice. With a growl, she digs her hands into Eli and the stranger's pockets. Her hands are empty when she turns back to Alec with an embarrassed look on her face. "I'll be dealing with this for a while. Meet me tomorrow at the library around noon? We can plan the party and figure out how long we have before you leave."

Alec recognizes the dismissal for what it is and haltingly leaves the room.

How had he let that happen?

He stalks back to Michael, anger steadily increasing to cover for the confusion stirring in his gut. He just agreed to entertain humans at his home. And he had his prey within his sights *while incapacitated* and he didn't even try to take Eli's soul. He acted more like a tamed pet for Azalea than the hardened hunter he was. And, aside from her forcefulness, he liked it.

"Michael," Alec hisses. Michael extricates himself from his harem of admirers, which includes a red-faced James on his lap. Alec is un-surprised, Michael can convince a man dying of thirst to pour out his last drop of water.

"I believe I have found several delectable swains with which to entertain myself for the evening," Michael purrs.

Alec glowers. With no prey in sight, the wraith will take all his ire. "Blending in doesn't include deflowering half the attendees."

"*Deflowering* them? Had you my gift, you'd know that—" Alec grasps his shoulder and yanks him towards the door, cutting off whatever declaration Michael planned to make about his little harem. Michael laughs and lets Alec rip him away, kissing his fingers and waving at the humans watching him leave. Several pout and one starts to cry.

Once they breach the door, he turns to Alec and loses the charming expression. His eyes flash and with a sinister voice, he spits out, "If you wish for us to blend in, you will release me now."

Panting from anger rather than fatigue, Alec releases his hold.

"To your estate, Alesandro," Michael seethes. "Now."

Chapter 13

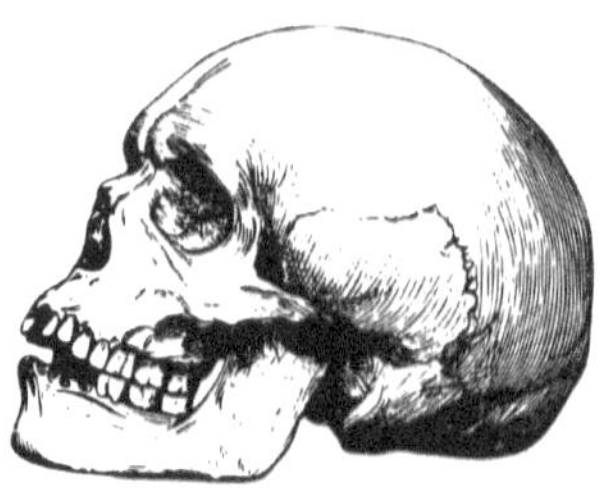

Back at Rockton, both wraiths stand at opposite ends of the library, the room colder now, despite the low crackle of the fireplace. Alec stands rigid, his back straight, his fists trembling at his sides. The misplaced anger and resentment Alec feels about the party, his failings in taking Eli's soul and weakness toward Azalea, are now solely focused on Michael. His sire's wanton behavior is an easier target than confronting his own apparent flaws.

Across the room, Michael appears relaxed, his green eyes gleaming with the satisfaction of having hit a nerve. The firelight plays off his rings, casting glints of light onto the bookshelves and walls, but there's nothing warm about his expression.

Michael speaks first, his voice razor-edged. "I give you a significant amount of latitude, Alesandro, because we are friends—and because I've known you for nearly two millennia. But don't mistake my tolerance for ignorance. I am your sire and your teacher, no matter how little respect you deign to give me."

Alec's jaw tightens. "That wasn't disrespect, Michael. It was about avoiding the risk of exposure."

Michael scoffs, a sharp, dismissive sound. "Exposure? I would have charmed them to forget anything unseemly and left you to maintain your precious veneer of respectability while you hunted."

"I'm not worried about respectability," Alec denies, the tension between them rising. "It is about preserving the integrity of the hunt."

"The integrity of the hunt," Michael repeats with a dark chuckle. "You make it sound like some sacred rite instead of the act it truly is—taking what we need to survive. Grab a human, steal the soul, and do your brooding amongst your family instead of in this human hovel. It doesn't need to be a production. You could have your pick of souls were you not so rigid in your choices. Azalea would last you some time."

Alec's control snaps. In a blur of movement, he crosses the room and grabs Michael by the collar, his voice a low snarl. "You. Will. Not. Touch. Her." Alec punctuates each word with a snarl.

"I was right, then? You like the girl with the books?" Michael says mildly, appearing unfazed at the unhinged wraith panting in his face. "You aren't running a willing soul gambit, are you? You're a strategist, Alesandro, but not that canny and you'd end up drained for your trouble."

Alec releases Michael abruptly. The cautionary tale Michael had once told him after Cassius' death resurfaces unbidden, a warning cloaked in mockery. There were stories that if a human *gives* a wraith their soul, it will last forever, with the giver living as long as the soul lasts. But no one has ever been *willingly* gifted and kept a soul.

Selina, a wraith who dared to love a human, believed the human's promise of willingly *gifting* her his soul. But the man lied, gambling on a chance at immortality. Selina's trust unraveled into betrayal, and the soulsickness that followed nearly ended her. She survived only through a fiery retaliation, but the cost was exile. Cast from the family, she was condemned to linger in the human realm, her strength depleted, her eternity reduced to aimless survival. Rules were Rules, after all. Michael had delivered the story with a cutting smile, a reminder and a warning: any attempt at eternity with a human outside of conversion, whether by deception or *love*, was foolhardy.

That was before Azalea. She isn't deceitful. She isn't manipulative. She is... *good*.

Alec bites the inside of his cheek to keep from blurting out his weakness. "It's not about the girl," he says, the words firm but hollow. "Her soul is too pure to give to a wraith. I simply don't want to undermine the cover I've created, not until I can finish the hunt."

"Not about the girl," Michael scoffs. "This is the second time in as many days you have lied to me. But I'll indulge your secrets—out of affection, mind you. Indeed, it is a testament to my fondness for you that I will not punish you for your outburst and manhandling of my person." He smooths down his collar as his smirk widens, infuriatingly confident. "But my original point stands: pick a soul, whichever you want, steal it and come home. We could travel back together by this time tomorrow and spend some time together at last. The Historian told me the renovations below Bath are progressing nicely. I would suggest a visit."

Alec's stomach twists. Would that he could. But consistency keeps him tethered. His choice—Eli—is already made. If he wavers now, what next? Breaking the Rules? He shakes his head. "I've chosen my prey. Changing now would diminish the integrity of—"

"Yes, yes. The integrity of the hunt. I heard you the first time." Michael rubs his temples, his rings clacking together like tiny bells. "Fates, Alesandro, you cannot have it both ways. You cannot behave like a human when you're a wraith, using the Rules as an excuse to keep you from living your second life. You should embrace the superiority I gave you, not allow it to be a shackle tightening around your neck."

Alec bristles, his voice cutting. "I took what you taught me and applied it the best way I could. Behaving differently will break the Rules."

Michael turns his fiery eyes to the dim ring on Alec's fingers. "No, you *choose* to behave this way and have convinced yourself it will further the Rules at the expense of your own happiness. You let the emotions you feel from humans conceal you to what you are." He waves his hand around the room. "You choose to put on this—this *costume* of humanity and pretend it furthers the Rules. You choose to return to this same estate and pretend for a time that you're not a wraith. You attend parties with humans, talk with them, dance with them, even reveal your chosen name. You wear their habits like armor against your true nature."

Alec scowls. "Look in the mirror, Michael. If I've a costume, yours is a permanent harlequin mask. At least I act with some *respectability* towards humanity, instead of spending my time sowing chaos and debauchery."

Michael's grin vanishes, his face twisting into something darker. "That is the entire point. The things we can do, the things *you* could do, if you'd let yourself. You must live this life, rather than allowing the Rules to shackle you to your misery."

Alec turns away, staring into the mirror across the room. Its surface ripples faintly. "Without the Rules, what am I?" he asks quietly, his fists clenched at his sides. "They've kept me grounded when nothing else could."

Michael tilts his head, his voice softer now. "What will it take, Alesandro, for you to see that your happiness cannot be found within the Rules?"

"That kind of talk skirts close to a Rule break, Michael," Alec hisses, the pricking turning into sharp knives stabbing something deep within. "And my chosen name is Alec!"

"Don't threaten me with your poor interpretations of this life," Michael says before tossing himself into one of the dusty chairs. He sounds defeated now. "Had I realized the man who captivated me would be overcome with guilt and believe the gift I gave him was merely a burden, I would have rethought your conversion."

Alec flinches, hiding his reaction behind a hardened glare. "Though you may consider me a failure to the race, I am the right hand of the Council, Michael."

"You mistake me," Michael starts, but Alec interrupts.

"I understand precisely. It's you who doesn't understand—you've never understood how I lived this life. I live how I know best, in furtherance of the Rules you taught me."

"*This* is not what I taught you," Michael says, jerking his arms to gesture to the decrepit library. "You're so irritatingly fixed on your own principles and your own definition of what the Rules mean you forget the entire reason for them—to be a damned wraith."

Alec exhales slowly, the anger draining from him, replaced by an ache he can't name. "You know why I choose the souls I do, why I hunt the way I do. I am living as I know best."

"You are lying to me or to yourself, my friend. If that were true, you would hunt like a wraith, even if you only steal from your murderers and thieves. You would ignore your quasi-morals and the guilt inherent in your essence. You would stop mooning over those you consider too good for you. You would have stolen a soul tonight and had no regrets. You would be happy with this life!"

Alec walks back to the mirror, turning away from Michael's piercing gaze. "We're talking in circles, now. None of this is the point."

"Then what is the point?" Michael demands. "You called me here for a reason. I am not so vain as to assume you truly missed my company after your latest seventy-year absence."

Alec clenches his fists. "I felt conflicted," he says to the mirror. "I wanted you to remind me of who we were, what I am."

Michael moved closer, turning Alec towards him, his eyes dancing. He grabs Alec's face, his burly hands curling around his neck, Michael's many rings pressing against Alec's hairline. Alec can't remember seeing such sincerity in Michael's face before, not in their thousands of years of acquaintance. "There's your weakness, dearest. You are a wraith. No matter how you try to interpret the Rules, no matter whether you follow them, no matter whether you never take another soul, you will always be a wraith. Make that enough."

Alec's throat tightens. "What if I want more?" The words burble out of him before he can stop them. Michael's regret in turning him aside, he is never more aware of the existence Michael gave him.

Michael's green eyes gleam with something close to tenderness. "Then I will do what I've always done and help you."

Chapter 14

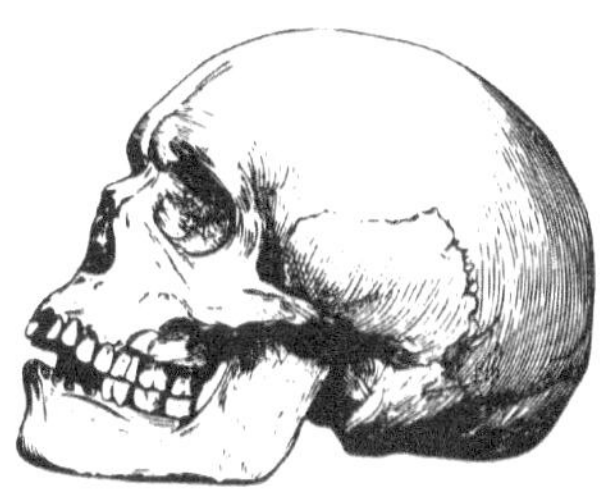

ALEC CONVINCES MICHAEL TO leave the next morning. If Alec avoids Azalea and takes Eli's soul immediately, there will be no need for his—likely chaotic—intervention. Azalea will be safe from him and the family, and he can bury the memory of her beneath the weight of the Rules. He'll return to his routine, endlessly chasing a purpose that will keep him from looking too closely at himself.

Just before dawn, as Michael prepares to step through the mirror, he grasps Alec's hand tightly. His expression is unusually serious, his green eyes narrowing. "That costume I mentioned? It's only ever that—a costume. It will never fit right, and it will never be permanent. You're a wraith, Alec. Your empathic abilities may make you feel more deeply, but that doesn't change what you are. You need to accept that, and soon. You don't have the luxury of time now." He strokes a finger over Alec's ring, the same one he'd given Alec centuries ago.

Alec stares down at the ring, twisting his lips. "I know, Michael. I'll focus on the Rules and do what I must."

Michael frowns, his thumb brushing over the edge of Alec's knuckles. "Your happiness is all I've wanted for you."

"Happiness is a weakness," Alec replies, his voice resigned.

"It doesn't have to be. Think of the fun I have."

Alec does—but Michael's brand of happiness, steeped in mayhem and indulgence, isn't what Alec wants.

Silence stretches between them until Michael nods sharply. "You need a break, dearest. You're long overdue for a century of happiness—*eighty* years, at least. Find a soul to steal, and I'll handle everything else. I'll remove your distractions and give you the peace you need."

"Don't kill her," Alec blurts, the words tumbling out before he can stop them. He exhales sharply, steadying his voice. "You needn't do anything," he clarifies, releasing a panicked breath. "Please, Michael—I'll steal the brother's soul and we can spend time together like old time's sake." And both he and Michael will forget about Azalea.

Michael grins, though it looks a little shaky. "We'll see. You worry about finding a soul while I put certain things in motion."

Before Alec can discourage him further, Michael barrels through the mirror.

Alec wears a hole in the library's carpet until it's late enough for Eli to rise. He must steal the soul before Michael does *whatever* Michael plans to do. *I'll remove your distractions*, Michael said. The image of Azalea's face fades into Lucia's sun-weathered features which morphs into Cassius' bronzed visage.

When the clock strikes eleven, Alec sprints to the field that leads to the one-lane road. His instincts guide him, sharpening as he follows the path past broken buildings littered with trash. The road snakes through low mountains, the trees rising in layered ridges, each row darker than the last. As it's still somewhat early, morning fog curls off the greenery like ghostly smoke. It has an otherworldly quality that doesn't match the impoverished housing conditions, a brighter version of the wraith world.

The path narrows as he approaches a cluster of derelict buildings. The scent of human emotions—frustration, irritation, and the faint edge of sibling affection—grows stronger.

He follows the scent of the sister's annoyance until he approaches a smaller paneled home. Trees surround the building, but it looks more like a villain's squalid hideout than any charming cottage in the woods. The clapboard sides are dingy and yellowed, attacked on all sides by weeds that spring up past his knees. Parked in the grass is a rusted vehicle older than any of the children. It reminds Alec of an old hideout he and Michael had used during a hunt for rogue wraiths: a one-room hovel, barely standing and utterly devoid of care.

A screen door opens and snaps shut, bringing out one of the younger sisters. Clara perhaps, or Cassandra.

"Whad'ya bring us?" the girl asks when she sees him, her mouth pursed and thoughts greedy. Before Alec responds, Azalea's sharp emotions bleed into him. She opens the ripped screen and steps outside.

"Cass, who're you talking to?"

He knows the moment she sees him as embarrassment leaches from her, engulfing him in its strength.

"What are you doing here?" Her voice is sharp and accusatory. She stomps from the house and crosses in front of him, facing away from the dilapidated home. She flushes as she bends her head to wipe the long strands of blonde hair into her face. "We're supposed to be meeting at the library."

He twists the ring around his finger. "Is your brother here?" He knows Eli isn't, he hasn't picked up on it, but her discomfort vexes him. For her safety, he must find the brother and soon. His absence will remove her troubled expression.

"No," she growls.

They stand in a charged silence, Cassandra watching with undisguised interest as she drops into the dirt by the door. Azalea's cheeks remain flushed, her face bright against the dull backdrop of the house. Alec struggles to keep his focus, but her presence disarms him. It's as though Michael's visit had never happened. The costume is back, tailored to fit him.

"Two birds," he offers, hoping she understands.

Azalea studies him, her expression unreadable. Finally, she turns to her sister. "Go back inside."

Cassandra stands and stomps her foot. "You're not in charge of me." Azalea stares back with a stormy expression until Cassandra looks away. "Ugh, so lame," Cassandra mutters. "Can I go to Mark's?"

"As long as you're back by dinner. I need you here while I go to the hospital."

With a loud grumble, Cassandra stalks off into the forest, the sound of her footsteps fading into the trees. Azalea exhales, her face slowly losing its redness, the tension in her shoulders easing.

Chapter 15

ALEC SHOWING UP IS the rotten icing on top of the moldy cake of Azzie's day. Eli is getting trashed and Dad—Dad can rot, for all she cares. They both can, for putting her through this.

She convinced Eli that she didn't need to chase after James, who she last saw moping after Alec's creepy friend left, she dragged Eli home only to find Dad passed out in a puddle of his own sick. Springing into action, she roused Eli just enough to help haul their unconscious dad to the back of the family truck. Ambulances weren't an option—not with the cost, and not when none would bother coming out here.

Rolling Dad into the truck bed, she silently thanked God, or whoever, that Cass and Phoebe were rebellious enough to stay at their boyfriends' homes, and that Clara could sleep through anything. Eli quit helping the second Dad hit the truck, mumbling promises to clean up the mess and concoct an excuse for their absence. Hours later, after the Asheville hospital pumped Dad's stomach, she returned to find Eli gone, vomit still on the floor, and fallout from the ordeal waiting for her. None of the girls seemed upset—either too used to Dad's benders or too wrapped up in teenage selfishness to care. And Eli? He never grew out of that phase. Eli is still in that stage, after all.

With an audible sigh, she lets loose the ball of tension in her gut at seeing Alec. She didn't want him to see her house. Before everything fell apart—before she transferred from Wretford Academy to the Lonetree school district—she had school friends who dropped her once they realized the depth of her family's poverty. Asheville's high property values and the private university meant most of her classmates were children of university professors or graduates who loved the scenery so much they made the green space their home. Children were mean, and anything that made their peers different was unacceptable.

But Alec is her chance, and she silently prays his wealth and privilege won't drive him away.

"Sorry for snapping," she says, squaring her shoulders. "It's been a rough morning, and you surprised me."

Alec's face is kind. "I heard you mention something about the hospital. Are you well?"

"It's my dad," she explains, careful to keep the details vague. "Liver problems." Alec doesn't need to know the full extent of her family's dysfunction. He's already met Eli, and that's enough.

"I am sorry to hear that," he replies, sounding sincere. The remaining tension bleeds from her.

"So, you came to see my brother—bird number one. What's bird number two?" She reaches for his hand, interlacing their fingers, hoping he can't sense her desperation.

"I wanted to express my regrets and apologize. We cannot host an event at Rockton." He looks defeated and Azzie squeezes their conjoined hands. His ring cuts into her palm, but she doesn't pull away.

"That's okay," she replies quickly. Eli might flip, but she doesn't care. The event wasn't the point—spending time with Alec was, so he'd like her enough to take her with him whenever he leaves. "You and I could hang out instead. You never said how long you were staying."

"I find more and more reasons to stay," he mutters, drawing them close together.

"But the exact date is...." She leans closer, almost nose to nose.

"I need to see your brother first," he says abruptly, stepping back and folding his hands behind him.

Azzie exhales heavily. If buying weed from her brother is what it takes, so be it. "If you have to see him, he's supposed to be at Jimmy's today, if he's not still in Raleigh," she says, unable to hide the edge in her voice. She recalls Eli's poorly worded text—*got a thig dont bother me*—and marvels, not for the first time, at how he managed better grades than her senior year. "One of Eli's high school friends works there mornings. Sometimes he lets Eli drink for free," she adds. "He never passes that up."

Alec takes a step backward and half-bows. "I will search for him there."

"You sure? I don't think it's your scene. It's sleazy. Like, 'watch your wallet or your throat' sleazy." She gestures bitterly toward her rundown double wide. "And for me to say it's gross? That means something."

Alec grins faintly. "I imagine I shall be fine."

Chapter 16

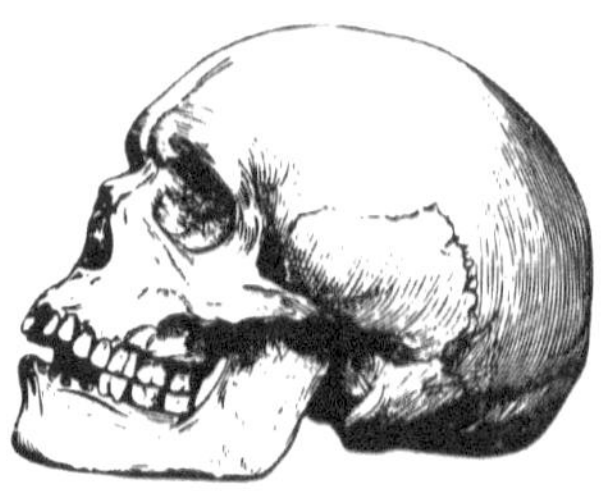

Azalea refuses to abandon him on his search for Eli, insisting she's his best chance to find him. Though Alec doubts it, he doesn't argue. One more hour in her presence can't be as risky as he imagines. Alec cut off Michael's fun the night before; he'd bet all the gold in his accounts that Michael's likely too busy indulging in his usual debauchery to bother interfering.

They take her family's vehicle, which emits smoke from the hood and clanking noises beneath their feet. The thirty-minute drive stretches in tense silence as her emotions swirl—desperation ebbing into concern. The thought of what stealing Eli's soul will do to her weighs on Alec, a feeling he neither wants nor understands.

A large neon "Jimmy's Bar" lights the derelict building. Crimped steel covers the exterior in a rainbow of colors, showing both the age of the locale and the lack of care in its upkeep from the owners.

The interior is as dank as the exterior, the air thick with the scent of stale beer and mildew. Dust clings to every surface, and decay creeps from the ceilings and corners. Wooden benches along the walls are worn smooth, and the stools at the rusted steel bar are bent and mismatched. Alec spins his dimming ring, the fading color a stark reminder of his urgency. If only he'd come *here* before meeting Eli. Before meeting Azalea.

Azalea leans against the bar, shouting for someone. Alec stalks beside her, his hand involuntarily moving to graze the small of her back.

He aborts the gesture, clenching his hands at his side. He can't afford any more delay.

A lanky man with pockmarked skin and ripped clothing lopes from the back room. Azalea leans subtly into Alec, her back just brushing his chest. He catches no fear from her, but her unreadable nature keeps him vigilant. No human will harm her—not while he's here. He can guarantee that at least, before he abandons town again.

"Looking good, Az." The man's voice is surprisingly deep for his thin frame. He stares at the proximity between her and Alec. Jealousy falls off him like water out of a bucket, deep and fast and smelling of mildew. One side of Alec's lips ticks upward.

"Is he here?" Azalea's tone is sharp, but she presses herself back into Alec. Alec uses all his strength to keep his eyes open and stop himself from groaning as the affection that bursts out from her is dizzying.

"Got here an hour ago," the bartender says stiffly. Alec senses the brother is nearby, but his emotions are a jumble.

"And he apparently went to Raleigh and back this morning. What the hell," Azalea mutters.

The bartender shrugs. "Heard Hendersonville myself."

"More hiding," she says, shaking her head. "Whatever. So where is he, Sam?"

Sam drops his gaze to the floor. "He's busy."

"It's 11:00 a.m. on a Sunday and this place is dead. There's no way he's too busy to see me." She gestures towards the opening Sam came through, which Alec assumes leads to back offices or a kitchen. "He's back there, I'm guessing?" She starts around the bar, but Sam skitters in front of her, blocking the door to the back.

"Can't do that, Az," he grunts.

"Yes, you can. Or Alec'll make you." She shoves Sam's shoulder. He steps aside reluctantly, muttering under his breath as Alec prowls past him. Alec can't resist baring his teeth, a predator's smile, just to watch Sam shrink back.

The doorway leads to a narrow hallway with two open doors. Alec senses Eli's presence to the left and gestures for Azalea to follow. Whatever comes next, he tells himself, will only further the hunt. Yet the weight in his chest says otherwise.

Chapter 17

Azzie finds Eli crouched in a corner, leaning against a stack of six-packs, blood running from his nose and his right eye pressed closed. His uninjured eye locks on her, glassy but alert.

"Azalea!" he slurs and struggles to rise. She hurries to his side, a flush rising on her cheeks.

"What happened?" she demands, pushing him back down and scanning the floor for something to clean the blood. "Handkerchief?" she asks Alec, who hovers silently by the door. He shakes his head, visibly confused.

"You're a relic of the 1800s, and you don't have a handkerchief?" she groans. Alec stiffens as Sam slips past him, handing her a stained bar towel.

"Is this the 'thing' you were doing today?" she asks Eli while dabbing at the blood smeared across his mouth. She doesn't mention that he'd abandoned her with Dad, not because of Eli's pitiable state but because Alec didn't need to know the specifics.

Eli gurgles incoherently, and she presses the white cloth closer to his nose. "Came after," he forces out. "Got stuff to think about."

"What the hell happened?" she snaps, directing her question at Sam, since Eli is clearly useless.

"So many drinks," Eli groans below her.

"Too many drinks," Sam echoes gruffly. "Got a hell of a tab, Az. Boss wasn't happy. Says he needed a little motivation to pay or else he'd call the cops."

Azzie bites her lip. That's better than what she worried had happened, afraid the closed-minded people who practically lived at Jimmy's figured out the things Eli wants kept secret. But Eli's criminal history is another issue, and will blow up everything for him, personal and occupational. Given the right information, getting the police involved could take Eli out of commission for years.

"What happened to taking care of things?" she says, glaring at Sam and then Eli.

Sam shrugs. "He covered a few drinks, yeah. But Eli don't know when to stop pushing."

"You're telling me," she says, scowling at her brother. "I thought you had *plans*, real ones, that don't involve dissolving any remaining brain cells in alcohol."

Eli struggles to grin, his teeth covered in blood. "I do," he slurs. "Drinks help me think. Need a clear head."

She wipes the blood from his teeth as Alec shifts in the door, spinning that ring on his finger. His face is calm, but the tension radiates off him, and she knows he's piecing together things she's tried so hard to hide. Between Dad's hospital visit and Eli's latest stunt, the last thing she wants is Alec seeing how broken her family is. Alec can read between the lines—'liver problems' wasn't a great code for alcoholism after all.

The shame curdles in her gut. She loves her family, but they've drained her dry. Maybe she'll just leave herself *without* Alec. Eli and the girls will be fine, she's nothing more than a crutch for them. They can be independent just like her. There was always a chance—

"I'll cover the cost of his charges," Alec says, his deep voice slicing through her spiraling thoughts. His words make her freeze. Even he looks surprised by what he's said.

"You sure 'bout that? You don't even know how much," Sam says with a furrowed brow.

Alec quirks his lips. "I can manage whatever the cost."

Shrugging, Sam leaves the room, presumably tally up the damage. Azalea stands, abandoning Eli to face Alec. She stares at him, torn between gratitude and frustration.

"You don't need to do that," she says. She loves her brother, but the consequences he wreaks are his own.

"I wanted to."

"Don't like him, not 'posed to be around him," Eli groans from the floor.

"Shut up!" Azzie snaps. She grabs Alec's hands and clutches them tight. "Thanks, but are you sure? I can take care of him." She's been doing it all her life, after all. One more time won't kill her.

"It's no trouble. I... enjoy helping you." It sounds like a question.

She looks down at their joined hands, his ring appearing more of a sick brown color than the deep amber she first saw. She swipes her thumb over the strange gem, the brown flickering to an eerie black. "And the part where this benefits Eli more?"

"I'd rather ignore that part."

She gives a soft laugh. "Will you not think about it by helping me drag him to the truck?"

Chapter 18

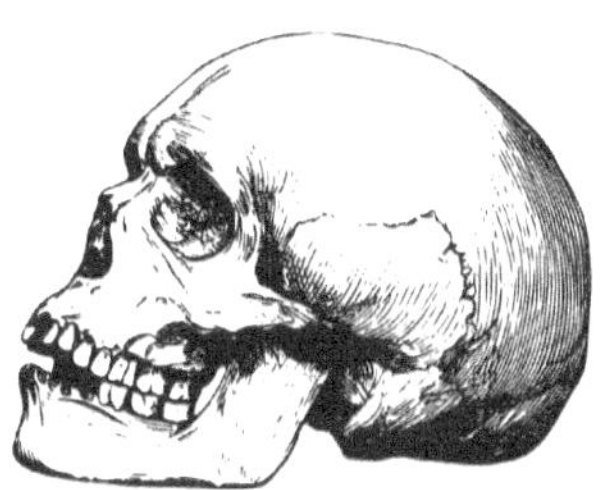

ALEC STORMS INTO ROCKTON House, his voice thundering. "Godfrey!"

The diminutive man peeks out from behind the staircase. "Yes, sir?"

"Get me paper," Alec shouts as he stalks into the library. The protectiveness he'd felt when Azalea appeared distraught hasn't dissipated. When she'd looked at him, the panic and shame rolling off her had been palpable, and something deep within him had demanded that he fix it.

Not out of duty. Not even out of guilt. Because it mattered to him that she felt safe.

And when he succeeded, when she smiled at him—that smile. No one smiles at him like that. Lust and manipulation are all he'd ever seen from the family. Even Michael's amusement was often tainted by ulterior motives. But Azalea's smile held no such shadows. It shone with something pure, something real, and it was his doing.

The sensation warms him even now, like a torch carried into the deepest winter. It's new, a gift as foreign as it is precious. To help her, to be the source of her comfort and joy, offers him something he never thought possible: redemption. *She* will be his century of happiness, though Michael surely didn't anticipate this when he suggested it.

As he waits for Godfrey, Alec paces to the bookcase, pulling out his journal. His trembling fingers trace the bold ink of the first entry:

Never show weakness, he'd written in black ink. It was the first lesson Michael taught him, the foundation of the Teachings. Weakness of mind, body, or soul would destroy a wraith faster than copper.

But what of heart?

Azalea embodied weakness. His feelings for her were a crack in his carefully built armor. And yet, Michael had assured him that happiness could be found within the Rules. What if Azalea was his happiness? What if his love for her wasn't a crack but a foundation for something new? Hugging the journal to his chest, he clings to the faint hope that Michael's suggestion of happiness doesn't have to mean chaos. He could keep her close and still honor the Rules.

Godfrey shuffles into the library holding several leaves of paper and various pen nibs. Unable to wait a moment longer, Alec snatches the items from Godfrey's quivering hands, causing the man to squeal and scamper out of Alec's reach.

Alec ignores Godfrey as he scribbles out a letter to his sire, his normally precise script unsteady. His hands tremble, the dullness of his ring a constant reminder of his failure. He'd waited too long to take Eli's soul. Now, he had no choice—he must pick another. Michael had been right about one thing: Alec didn't need to be so rigid in his choices. He could still adhere to the Rules *and* keep Azalea, if only for her fleeting human lifespan. But he needed to act with haste.

He holds his hand aloft, studying the ring. Its sickly, muddy hue hovers dangerously close to black, a warning he cannot ignore. To-morrow, he'll steal a soul. Once the issue with Michael is resolved and Azalea is safe, he'll make things right. She'll smile at him again. Maybe she'll let him hold her. The thought sends a flicker of warmth through him, and he clings to it like a lifeline.

Behind him, Godfrey peers over his shoulder, his beady eyes scanning the letter. Alec doesn't care, nor does he dwell on the odd tinge of excitement wafting from his manservant. Presumably, Godfrey is pleased that his master might have found some semblance of happiness.

The thought lingers, fragile but persistent. Happiness. Something he'd long thought forbidden. But perhaps, just perhaps, he could grasp it—if only for a fleeting moment. For her human lifetime.

The letter to Michael is brief: Alec has reconsidered his advice, intends to hunt another soul, and does not need Michael's help. There *may* be a part about Michael owing him this for Alec's past infatuations, but there isn't time to write another.

Alec pauses before adding the addendum *not* to kill Azalea, just in case that clarification is needed. He could never guess with Michael.

The letter disappears into the mirror with a toss, leaving Alec staring at his reflection. Michael *would* owe him this one indulgence. He's owed Alec for centuries.

Alec sets up his alchemy kit, his movements mechanical until Godfrey's reedy voice interrupts.

"You're leaving with her?"

Alec doesn't even glace up, adding dandelion to a pinch of sage until the two melt into the flakes of silver. "No. We will stay here. Azalea may wish to travel, but this will remain our home for as long as she lives."

Godfrey's emotions sour, the bitterness tangible. He slinks off to his quarters without another word. Alec knows what troubles him—it's the same thought plaguing Alec. Unless she gave him her soul, a request he would never make, she'd die long before him. But that brief time together would have to be enough.

Alec spends hours over the kit, creating a healing elixir from scratch. With no recipe to guide him, his mind must sense what's needed, and the elixir almost forms itself. He mixes it three times, to confirm it won't worsen the problem. For how aggregable she seems, Azalea wouldn't appreciate the accidental murder of her father. She's not a wraith, after all.

When the acrid smell of Godfrey's burned dinner wafts through the library, Alec finishes, creating a tonic for Azalea's father that should rid him of his liver issues forever. With a twist of his lips, he bursts from the house, sprinting towards the only hospital in the area.

It's only a few miles away, a red-brick monolith, quiet in the early hours. He arrives to a vacant parking lot, letting out a breath. Giving a sick human an unknown concoction would call for attention, meaning the emptier the building the better. He lurks outside for a soul that feels like Eli and Azalea's, using as little of his gift as he can to avoid the ring burning out prematurely.

Luck takes him to the father's room, where the man sleeps alone in a sanitized room, his emotions fuzzy and sluggish. Various wires creep from the man's clothing, connecting to machines that beep and trill. The scent of decay and disinfectant almost calms Alec, as the smell of injury and atrophy is familiar. For a brief instant, Alec considers stealing the man's soul. Without his aid, the man surely had only a few years left. His soul wouldn't be missed. Alec shakes himself of the thought. That's the monster in him struggling to claw its way out.

After he confirms no one is outside, Alec unstops the seal of the vial and tips the contents down the man's throat, watching with eager eyes. The healing will begin within hours, and he'll tell Azalea every-thing—what he is, what he's done. She'll smile at him again, perhaps even—

"Alec?"

He turns, schooling his face to greet his siren while he pockets the empty vial. "Good evening, Azalea."

"What are you doing here?" She crosses the room to stand closer to her father. Her expression is tight, brows furrowed.

He glances at his ring, dull and threatening, before clasping his shaking hands behind his back. "You mentioned your father was ill. I wanted to pay my respects."

She traces the wire connected to her father's right wrist. "Respects are for the dead and the good. He's neither, but he's still my Dad, so thanks for coming."

This is his moment, his opening to confess. He tries to force out the words twice before saying, "Was that another quote?"

She gives a rueful smile. "No, that was me." She perches on the edge of her father's bed by his feet and motions Alec to the chair nearby. "It was probably mean, but I'm not feeling that nice after everything today."

She's too far away for him to touch, and the distance prickles at his skin.

"Thanks for being there," she says, still watching her father. "You got a crash course in Cross family drama."

"I'm—I was glad to be there for you," he admits. "And I'd like to share some of the Gravely history with you, if you'd let me."

Her crooked smile appears as she gestures around the room. "I'm free now."

He nods, his gaze dropping to his ring as he prepares for the confession. It will breach the Second Rule, yes, but the First Rule demands honesty. He steadies himself, ready to face whatever reaction she might have.

A noise at the door interrupts him. A pale woman in teal scrubs enters, dragging a cart behind her.

"Visiting hours are over, Ms. Cross," the woman says briskly. "I need to change his catheter and check his IV line, so you'd best just come back tomorrow."

Both Azalea and Alec stand. The other woman stares at Alec until her face mottles red. Alec doesn't need to read her to know she finds him attractive. "And who is this?" she asks, voice turning breathy.

Azalea marches to Alec's side and grabs his hand. "My partner," she announces, pulling him out of the room before the nurse can ask anything more.

He can almost feel his unbeating heart pounding; she already wants to choose him. That's more than he's ever had.

Azalea keeps her grip on his hand as they descend the stairs and exit into the darkened parking lot. Only when they're outside does she release him.

"Sorry about that," she mumbles, embarrassment coming off her in waves. "I was trying not to outright lie, and partner could mean something else. But she was definitely going to ask you out."

The impulse to touch her overtakes him, and he reaches for her. She lets him, and he strokes her thick hips, sliding his hands to the small of her back until she's wrapped in his trembling arms. Her embarrassment shifts into excitement, tinged with something brighter.

"That's—that's fine," he says, voice low. "It dovetails into the conversation I wish to have. I—I've told this to no one before."

Before he can continue, a beep from her chest interrupts. She pulls out the same small device from her shirt, and the buzzing sensation under his skin flares again. Her excitement dims as the scent of discomfort caresses the surrounding air.

"It's Eli," she grimaces, shoving the plastic back between her breasts. "Can we finish this tomorrow?"

His shaking isn't any worse, but he inspects the ring and its sickly color. "Tomorrow. But I cannot wait any longer."

"Are you leaving tomorrow?"

"No," he says, *not if you can accept what I am.* "There are simply things I must tell you and I cannot wait." *Eighty* years of relaxation, Michael claimed he needed, that's her lifespan. For her, he would risk that time. She is his tether, his hope, his humanity. Even if it's irrational. Even if it can't last.

Her lips thin as her citrusy excitement bubbles, infusing with an oily undercurrent of nervousness. Suddenly, she presses into his arms, winding hers around his neck and pulling down his face. Their lips touch, magic in human form.

Her mouth presses against his as she runs her fingers through the hair above the nape of his neck. He holds himself from melting into her, from letting his baser, wraith, instincts reign.

When she pulls back, her lips are red and glistening. "Tomorrow? Ten a.m. at the big field?"

He nods, touching his fingers to his own lips.

Tomorrow, he can wait until tomorrow. After all, he's the one with eternity in front of him.

Chapter 19

THAT WAS SPECTACULAR. AMAZING. Thrilling. Azzie needs a thesaurus to list every word for *holy freaking wow*. She can't stop smiling on the drive home. If she hadn't needed to find Eli, she might have climbed Alec like a tree.

Before the kiss, she assumed Alec was slightly shy and inexperienced. He didn't *look* it, not with those eyes and the smolder. But with how chaste he behaved—how he shook and leaned in like a cat craving affection every time she touched him screamed nerves and unfamiliar with intimacy.

But he kissed like it was the easiest thing he's ever done. He kissed like he thought she held the answer to every question he'd ever had, like the meaning of the universe was in her lips. Not that she's *that* experienced either, but she knows there was something special in that kiss.

She parks the pickup on the open grass in front of their double-wide as Eli leans against the screen door with a full bottle cradled in his arms. She slams the truck door, the feelings from the kiss seeping out with every stomping step towards him.

"What are you doing?"

Eli peers up at her and frowns. "Don't get mad. I just need to think." He tips the bottle into his mouth.

"Are you kidding me? We *just* got your tab paid off today. Dad's in the hospital for alcohol *overdose*." Her voice rises with every word. "At least Dad got thirty years out of his liver before he started trashing it. You'll be lucky to get to twenty!"

Eli just stares up at her.

"Never mind," she says. "I don't care. I don't care why you texted and ruined my evening, and I *definitely* don't care what you do. Get out of the way. I'm going to bed, and you can drink yourself to an early grave."

Eli takes another large sip and swallows with his eyes closed. "I think I'll do it. I need another day because it's a huge decision but—" He lolls his head from side to side. "It makes sense."

"Do what?" She balls her fists onto her hips and kicks at his legs, but he doesn't budge.

"It's going to mean some changes," he says, swaying slightly. "But it'll be good for us. For you."

"Oh, shut up. You're not doing anything for anyone but yourself. And that's fine by me. I've got my own plans and they involve getting the hell out of this place and away from you."

Eli drops the bottle. It shatters at their feet, glass crunching as he kneels in front of her, liquor pooling on the ground. "Wait—just give me a few days. I'll explain everything."

The impulse to worry about him flickers through her but she kills it. "No."

"Goddamn it, Az." Tears glint in the corner of his eyes. The sight tightens something in her gut. He has nothing to cry about. He's the one who causes her problems. He's the one who left her to deal with Dad, who took her away from Alec.

"I'm doing it for both of us!" he finishes, sniffling.

She scowls down at him. "Don't even pretend you're even thinking about me. Whatever you're doing, you're doing for you. And that's fine. I'm doing the same."

With a sharp kick to his legs, she steps around him and goes inside. Whatever Alec tells her tomorrow won't matter. She just needs to get away.

Chapter 20

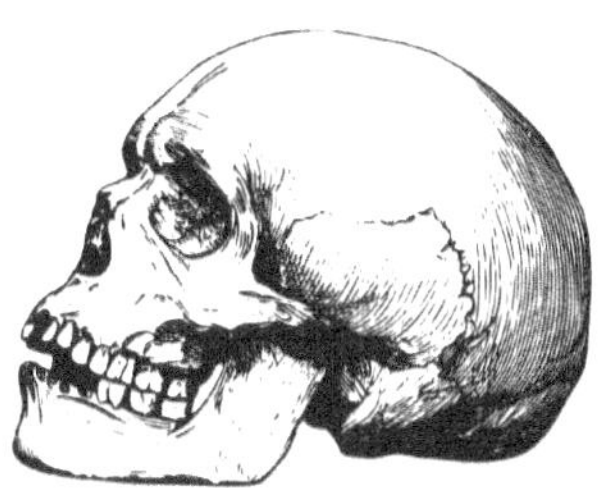

Alec waits in the empty field just after daybreak, his hands trembling from a mix of excitement and fatigue. The faint light of dawn casts long shadows over the dewy grass, but his focus is on the horizon, where he hopes to see Azalea's familiar silhouette. His ring is nearly drained of color, the dull sheen a constant reminder of how precariously close he is to failure. But none of that matters. Not now. Not when he's about to see her.

His plan is fragile, but it's all he has: confess everything, hope she understands, and then find a soul before the tavern opens. It's reckless, irrational even, but she's worth it.

It's absurd how deeply she's woven herself into his existence. Weeks ago, he didn't know her name. Now, she feels like the most vital part of him, the tether holding him to the faintest shred of humanity. He knows it's dangerous to feel this way, knows how fleeting human lifespans are and how precarious her situation remains. But none of that stops the warmth that spreads through him at the thought of her smile.

His trembling hands slip into his pockets as he paces, his thoughts racing. He's chosen a green button-down and gray trousers—a nod to his own preferences and a subtle homage to her. The green reminds him of that shirt she wore when they met, and the gray of the pants that clung to her curves. The outfit is a small, ridiculous gesture, but he clings to it like a talisman.

He sees her before he senses her, walking across the field with her hands buried in her jeans pockets. When she spots him, she runs, barreling into him with such force he almost stumbles. Only his hidden strength keeps them upright.

"Hey!" she exclaims, beaming. "God, am I glad to see you. Let's get out of the sun."

He wonders what the etiquette is to kissing her in broad daylight. She grabs his shaking hand, leading him back into town to, he hopes, a quiet place to speak.

He loves her. And things will be okay. She and her brother are safe, Michael knows to yield. He'll prove his love and find another soul before any reactions occur. But he must take care with what he shares. Lucia's shrieks aren't the only screams that haunt his thoughts. Azalea would *never* choose him if she knew exactly what it meant to be a wraith.

He's still deciding what to say when a sharp wave of sour anger and melancholy crashes over him.

"Is—is everything alright?" he asks.

"We should go on a trip!" Her brown eyes widen as she nods repeatedly. "Yes. Yes! Let's do that. You said you were leaving soon, so let's just do it. Let's go."

"I—I haven't decided if I'm leaving yet," he answers, grasping for something to say while his head reels at the abruptness of her subject change. He must reveal his shameful secret and let her accept him before tethering her to him, whether that be abroad or at Rockton in hiding. "Should—should you not stay here for your family?"

The smile he now knows is a ruse falls, and the taint of bitterness drifts from her. "They're fine. Eli's Eli, and Dad's better. Like, *completely*. Yesterday they were talking about liver transplants and today, he's got the organs of a teetotaler. The doctors can't explain it."

There's his opening. "Perhaps it was magic."

She laughs, loud and sharp, masking a scoff. "Sure. And I'll follow a white rabbit and end up a heroine in a new world while I'm at it."

He twists his lips at the anger in her tone. "Do you not believe in magic?"

She snorts. "There's no such thing as magic. If there were, my fairy godmother would have shown up years ago. Fantasy is just that—fantasy. Nothing good comes from pretending or losing sight of the reality of this life."

"But what—"

"Plus, magic is never innocent. Even the fairytales we grew up in were all about murder, and mayhem. We've sanitized the stories for children but all it does is lead to an inevitable letdown when they realize that life sucks. No one is coming to save you. You save yourself, if you can, using whatever advantages you can latch on to." The words tumble out of her without allowing a breath, her eyes darkening, wetness at their corners. When she finishes, she shakes her head, as if shaking out an unpleasant thought.

She isn't wrong. Most magical gifts are used for nefarious purposes. Most tonics in his arsenal are poisons or hallucinogens. His own kind are an exemplary example of how violent magic can be. He wishes he could read her better to understand why she sounds so bitter. He lacks Michael's gift of presight and can only guess at the difficult past she and his sire alluded to. She must have clawed herself up to the happiness and life she had now. "You have strong opinions about this," he says softly, slowly coming to a troubling realization.

She sighs and wraps her arm around his, pulling their conjoined hands closer to her. "I told you, fantasy is my genre of choice, meaning I know how absurd the idea of a perfect 'white knight' is. But that idea was seductive to a kid, you know? Someone would vanish Mom's cancer, someone would conjure Dad's job back, we'd find a magic treasure to pay the bills. But nothing happened, no one fixed anything. I had to make things better for myself. I'm the only one I can count on one hundred percent of the time." She nods, as if confirming something before looking up into his eyes. "Anyway, where did we land on us leaving?"

The words won't come. He can't tell her what he is. Even if he abandons roving and remains in Rockton for her lifespan, he still steals souls and devastates lives. He wouldn't be a 'fix' for her either, but something to tear her down. Michael was right—the costume will never become real.

Was it only yesterday that he realized he could have her?

"I must go," he whispers, his voice breaking as he withdraws from her grasp. And he flees as fast as his weakening body will allow.

Chapter 21

Then

"MS. CROSS, THANK YOU for meeting me. I'll provide you a pass back to English when we're done." The stern voice of Mrs. Malachi broke the silence as she motioned toward the chair in front of her sparse desk. Azzie, freshly eighteen and in her final year of high school, dropped into the chair with a huff.

Mrs. Malachi opened a thin file, its contents spilling onto the desk. Adjusting her glasses, she leaned back, arms crossed. "Do you know why I called you here?"

Azzie frowned. "I figured you were meeting with all the seniors about their plans."

"Indeed," Mrs. Malachi said, perusing the file. "But I wanted to meet with you specifically because I see you wasting your talents and heading down a path you might not recover from."

Azzie shifted uncomfortably. She'd never had an issue with Mrs. Malachi before, unlike Eli, who seemed to live in the woman's office. He'd described her as "an old lady with a stick up her butt." But during assemblies, Mrs. Malachi sounded like the teachers from the fancy private school Azzie had attended before their transfer—a stark reminder of what she'd lost.

Mrs. Malachi didn't answer. "Did you know Mr. Cross's grades for the prior semester bested yours by nearly two full letters?"

Azzie shot upright. That didn't make sense. She practically had to force Eli to do his homework, and even then, he barely finished it.

Mrs. Malachi nodded. "Yes. In speaking with your teachers, it seems he has maintained a heightened focus during classes while you have your head in the clouds."

"I'm not trying to zone out," Azzie said quickly. "It's just like my mind can't grasp onto anything."

Mrs. Malachi's sharp gaze swept over her. "In different circumstances, I'd recommend a prescription to help you focus. But we both know your brother would likely sell it."

Azzie slumped, heat creeping up her neck.

"What are your plans after graduation?" Mrs. Malachi asked bluntly.

"I'm not sure," Azzie admitted. "My whole family's here and like you said, my grades are slipping." She didn't need to say it; her GPA wasn't high enough to secure the scholarship she'd need to attend the private university in Asheville, There was no way she'd get away from the shackles of her family.

Mrs. Malachi closed the file in front of her. "You enjoy reading, do you not?"

Azzie nodded. "I've got a part-time job at the library. It doesn't pay, but I get to bring home more books for longer," she added.

"Perhaps you would be suited to become a librarian in one of the renowned libraries upstate."

Azzie looked down, her hopes tethered to the floor.

Mrs. Malachi sighed. "Or you could stay local. Our librarian will need to retire, eventually. To be a librarian, though, you need a degree. I've filled out a scholarship application for you. It's for first-generation students at the state program in Raleigh. Write a strong essay, and with my recommendation, you're a shoo-in."

"I don't..." Azzie faltered, unsure of what to say.

"Do something for yourself, Ms. Cross, without worrying about your family. 'The purpose of life is to live it, to taste experience to the utmost, to reach out eagerly and without fear for newer and richer experience.'" She removed her glasses, rubbing the bridge of her nose. "It is not to let that silver-tongued brother of yours drag you down."

Azzie knew she was right, but it felt impossible. "Did you come up with that, ma'am?"

Mrs. Malachi offered a rare wry smile. "That's Eleanor Roosevelt, Ms. Cross. She didn't let personal concerns—like her husband's infidelity—hold her back."

Chapter 22

THE OLD PICKUP SPUTTERS to a stop in front of Rockton House, its creaks and groans echoing the state of her mood. The house matches the truck perfectly—weathered, tired, and bearing the scars of a hard life. Thick vines crawl up the dark stone, threatening to consume the place, and vicious looking weeds slither over sprigs of dead cuttings, giving the entire place a funereal aura. With her mood, she belongs here too, a piece of decay blending into the backdrop.

After Alec sprinted away—again—leaving her stunned and fuming, Azzie stomped home to grab the truck. Dad was still in the hospital, Eli was passed out in a post-bender haze, and the girls were out or asleep. No one was around to ask questions, which was good because she didn't feel like answering.

She wipes at her face as she parks. She should've walked the fifteen miles here—it might've given her time to cool off. But her temper is still blazing.

Alec is like a glacier: beautiful and mysterious, but cold, hiding most of himself beneath the surface, and prone to cracking off pieces that leave devastation in their wake. And this morning, he cracked off a piece of her.

She thought he liked her. She *knows* she likes him, not just for the escape he offers, but because of *him*. That kiss—oh, God, that kiss. It was light dancing on her skin, fire in her veins. She knows now what Hemingway meant about kissing goodbye versus kissing goodnight.

She didn't want that kiss to be their goodbye. Not unless they kiss off Lonetree together.

But awkward Azzie strikes again. Maybe their conversation got a little deep into her insecurities and cynicism, but certainly didn't call for him leaving.

Again.

The risk that Alec will slam the door in her face weighs on her, but still she trudges to the ancient wooden door. With a steadying breath, she lifts the tarnished door-knocker and raps sharply.

No answer.

After waiting five minutes, she slumps to the ground, leaning her elbows on her knees and cradling her head in her hands. Alec isn't her white knight. But the conversation that morning and her fight with Eli further confirmed that she's prepared to do what it takes to get out of Lonetree. Help in the form of a handsome crush is the best opportunity she's ever had. That she likes him makes it doubly great.

Although she could do without the eighteenth-century melodrama. Having him flee from her twice isn't as dramatic and poignant in real life as it is in the books. Instead, it's incredibly annoying.

The door creaks open, and she scrambles to her feet, wiping her sweaty palms on her jeans. Instead of Alec, a wiry, middle-aged man with beady eyes and a hooked nose peers out, looking startled. He tugs at his frayed blond hair like a kid thumbing a stuffed animal for comfort. "May—may I help you?"

"Yes, hello. I'm Azzie, Azalea, he calls me. Well, not just him, it's my name." She takes another breath. "Is Alec here?"

The man quivers his elongated neck, which might be his version of a nod.

"Can I see him?"

He gives another not-quite nod before he steps away, cowering out of sight but leaving the door open.

"Guess I'll find him myself," she mutters.

The entryway is cavernous, with a dual staircase and multiple doors leading off in every direction. Dust floats through the stale air, catching the grimy light filtering through dingy windows. The place reeks of neglect, but even under the grime, Rockton House screams wealth.

It's a far cry from her double-wide, where no staircase exists, let alone two.

She turns left, following instinct, and steps into a library with a barely lit fireplace at the far end. Russet stained curtains cover tall windows and block any other light from entering the room. Dusty books spill from the walls and creep up to the ceiling. She recognizes none of them, each hardbound in leather or cloth and faded. In different circumstances, she'd be Belle. But Alec—her brooding Beast—is already handsome, and so far, far from hers.

"What are you doing here?" Alec's voice sounds from deeper into the room, closer to the fireplace.

She shuffles towards it and the threadbare upholstered chair sitting catty corner to the flames. Alec perches there, a leather book in his lap, hands clenched on the arms on the chair, his face half in shadow.

"I wanted to talk to you," she says as calmly as she can. If she can stay calm in the face of Eli's temper tantrums, she can avoid shouting at Alec for acting like an overdramatic child. Alec and Eli have that in common. She kills the desire to roll her eyes at them both.

"I didn't want to speak with you," Alec growls, leaning back and engulfing himself in shadow. Only the flickers of the fire allow her to see the flashes of his blue eyes.

"Well, tough," she snaps, crossing her arms. "Sometimes we don't get what we want. Like me—I wanted a nice day with you, to finish our conversation, but instead, you ditched me. Again. First at the party, now in the middle of the street."

He winces, and she bites back a triumphant smirk.

"I must end our friendship," he says, the nail of his ring finger scratching the cover of the book in his lap. "I will leave Asheville soon. I have one remaining piece of business I will take care of this afternoon, then I will depart."

Rocks sink into her gut. She hadn't played games with Alec, not like the kind Eli expected. This was real for her. Alec isn't just an opportunity—he's *hers*.

"So, that's it?" she says, voice shaking. "We have some great times, a killer kiss, and then you leave without even saying goodbye?"

His hands grip the arms of the chair, knuckles white. "I bid you farewell this morning."

"No, you didn't! You just left mid-sentence." She balls her fists on her hips. "I thought things were going well with us. Well enough that you wouldn't up and leave."

Alec stands, the book falling to the floor with a soft thump as he crosses to the dying fireplace. "I—I believed the same. The issue is not my feelings for you."

"What is it then?" Regret and grief dance inside her, at losing the opportunity to leave her hellish life, at losing her chance to experience life out of Lonetree with Alec, at losing the first boy who liked her. She laughs bitterly. "God, you're breaking up with me and we're hardly dating. I thought we *had* something."

"You have no idea," he breathes.

Her fingers graze his back, and he ducks his head like a skittish colt. "I'm listening," she breathes.

"I have never known someone quite like you," he whispers, turning to face her. "You're so good, but approachable, someone who makes me believe humanity is attainable. All I want is to make you happy."

The rocks turn to butterflies and take flight in Azzie's stomach. She intertwines their hands, relieved he lets her, relieved she still has a chance.

"But wants and obligations differ, Azalea. I was kidding myself to believe I could seek my happiness with you."

He withdraws to run his hands roughly through his curling hair. "You are the most beguiling creature I have ever beheld. But I would taint your goodness, your innocence, and respectability. I must go, Azalea. It is impossible for me to have you and you me. I would bring you nothing but pain." He recoils towards the fireplace with a hand on his forehead, like a maiden who needed a fainting couch.

If this weren't so important to her, Azzie would laugh at how utterly *asinine* this was.

"What kind of cheap melodrama are we living in, Alec?" she spits. "You can't have me, and I can't have you because, what—you've got low self-esteem? That you would somehow taint me because I'm such a good person? God, if you knew what was running through my head half the time, you'd realize how wrong you are." She clenches her fists to keep from shaking him. "I am so sick and tired of people thinking they can decide my life for me. And I keep letting them! But not this time. Suck it up and realize that *every* relationship can hurt."

"No," he sighs.

She wants to kick over his chair, but she releases a slow breath instead. "Give us a try. We'll leave together wherever you want to go. You and me. You'll show me your demons and I'll show you mine." She strokes his arm, but he flinches.

"No," he repeats, stronger now. "This cannot be. You cannot fathom what I am."

"Then tell me and maybe I will," she says, glaring at him.

"Monsters are real, Azalea," he whispers. "And one stands before you."

If things had been different—if Eli hadn't upset her the night before, if Dad hadn't promised the drinking was over, if the girls were younger—Azzie would have stopped trying, and gone back home to her usual life, letting everyone walk all over her and force her into taking care of their needs.

But things were changing—she doesn't feel tethered to Eli, Dad is better, the girls can take care of themselves. She won't let another person try to live her life for her, by making decisions she didn't agree with. That includes Alec. She wants him, melodrama and all, and he can deal with his insecurities with her by his side. She tightens her grip, refusing to let go. "Don't be a dick, Alec. I know monsters. You're not one of them."

"You know nothing. You would hate me," he says, his shoulders slumping. His glossy hair hides his face from her, but something glistens in his eyes.

Like when Eli does it, the possibility of tears doesn't sway her. Her eyes pinch in the corners. "How about you let me decide how I feel?"

But he jerks away. "I will not suffer this any longer."

"Don't walk away from me again," she bites out.

But he's gone.

She stands in the empty room, chest heaving, anger and despair battling for control. "Aggravating, ridiculous boy," she mutters, scrubbing her hands over her face.

She doesn't know what to do now.

Chapter 23

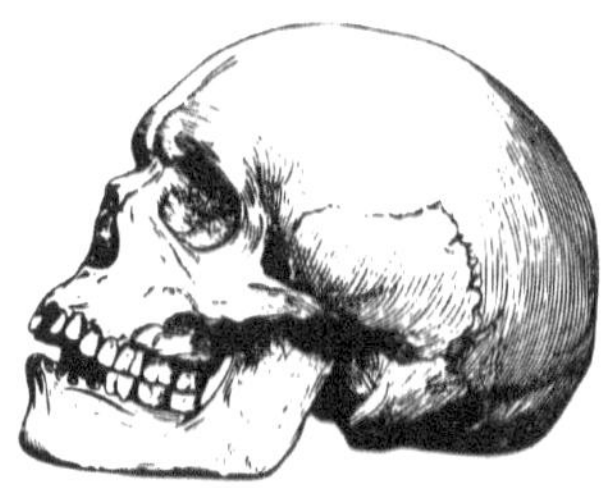

IT WAS AGONY WALKING away from her. She could tear into Alec's chest with her bare hands to rip out his heart and it would hurt less than turning from her again. But he must; he can't ruin her.

His second life is full of 'can'ts': can't break the Rules, can't show weakness, can't fall in love, can't be close to humans, can't be a human, can't can't can't. At least, in this, he has some semblance of control. His pushing her away is not simply a 'can't,' but a 'won't.' He refuses to bring her down with him.

Her appearance kick starts his trek to Jimmy's Bar. After deserting her that morning, he returned to Rockton House to lick his wounds and wait until the tavern had enough patrons for him to choose from. Once he arrived home, he squirreled up in the library and passed out as the ring turned black. Only her prompt arrival kept him from letting himself succumb to any further side effects of soulsickness. Godfrey was skittish enough without entering the library to find Alec's comatose body.

Sluggishly, he heads to Jimmy's Bar, taking him a half hour when it should have taken less than five minutes. Rockton House is on the east side of town while Jimmy's is outside to the west, meaning he passes the field that leads to Azalea's house. When he does, he clenches his fists hard enough that blood pools into his palms and drips onto the road like violent breadcrumbs.

The crescent-shaped wounds don't heal before he arrives at Jimmy's. His soulsickness is worse than he imagined. He trudges around to the rear of the building, empty save a dumpster and littered with broken glass. The weeds hit his knees and drag along the fabric of his woolen trousers. The memory of Azalea, outside her home, with grass tall enough to kiss her legs, swoops through his mind.

Is he doomed to think of her in everything? The unending trek toward oblivion never seemed longer.

Perhaps he should lie down and let whatever happens happen.

Michael will find him at some point. Not soon, given the letter he wrote. But Michael will come, he always does.

The sound of a bottle hitting the ground rouses him from that turbulent series of thoughts. An older man with graying hair and unwashed clothes stumbles outside. He sneers at Alec before dropping his trousers and urinating in the grass only feet away. The rage missing from Alec for the past few days trickles through his body. He measures the man's soul. He receives impressions of this man in the bar, the emotions greedy and disturbing. Alec's eyes flash and the color in the ring winks in and out.

When the man pulls up his trousers, Alec pounces. In less than a blink, he holds the man aloft by his neck. He crushes the leathery skin there until the man's soul detaches and slips into Alec. Given the age of the man, death will beckon him soon, but Alec doesn't have the luxury of seeking a longer lasting soul. It won't be enough but will last him several years.

Long enough, he hopes, *to forget Azalea.*

Chapter 24

Azzie drives straight from Rockton House to Jimmy's, her knuckles white against the steering wheel. Sam's working again—an afternoon shift this time—and she plans to take advantage of Eli's empty tab. She's never been much of a drinker; that's always been Eli's thing. But Eli always said drinking clears his head. Maybe it'll clear hers enough to figure out her next move.

Anger churns under the surface the entire drive and follows her into the bar, propelling her onto a rickety stool. She likes anger—it's a better companion than sadness or loneliness. Since turning eighteen, it's been easier to call up irritation than tears. Odd, considering Eli seems to do the opposite.

Sam kicks to attention the second she sits down, less jumpy than when she'd been here last. *God, was that only yesterday?*

She drums her fingers on the steel bar top as she peruses the choices. *What does one drink when mourning lost opportunities and chances?* Her dad drinks a cheap vodka swill that smells like turpentine. He doesn't care much about taste, as long as it's bargain priced and gets him drunk. And Eli will drink anything he can. Last night he chugged bourbon.

"Whiskey," she barks at Sam.

Sam crosses his arms over his skinny chest. "You had whiskey before?"

She wilts under his stare, confidence deflating. "Wine cooler."

"Not so sure about this, Az," Sam's slow voice squeaks out his censure.

"Luckily, I didn't ask you," she says frowning. Sam continues staring at her, and she knows it isn't because she's underage. "I'm at a bar, you're a bartender, tend to the bar and get me a drink."

"Tendin' bar means I listen too, if you wanted."

His face looks so earnest she can't help but release the remaining anger along with her bravado. She drops her head on the bar top and speaks to the steel. "Alec broke up with me," she admits. "He pre-broke up with me. God, we're not even *dating* and he still broke up with me."

"Idiot," he grunts, dropping a glass of water next to her face.

She huffs and turns her cheek on the steel, letting her eyes track out into the near empty bar. An older guy with scraggly hair sits in one of the back booths and lifts his drink while wagging his tongue in her direction. She closes her eyes. "Yeah, I already know. 'Lonetree trash,' 'Eli's weird sister.' I just thought he'd see what I want to see in the mirror, not what everyone else does."

Sam growls, low and deep. "Him. He's the idiot."

Her throat tightens, but she keeps her head down. "You ever feel like you're meant for something better, but life keeps holding you back? Like the chance is there, just out of reach?"

"Who says?" Sam asks, his tone sharp. She lifts her head, confused. "Who says it's outta reach?" he repeats.

"Well, Alec was my chance. You know Eli, I'll never get out without something like—"

"So, some fancy boy dropped you, big deal," Sam scoffs. "You got arms, legs, a brain. Think they just handed me this job? No, I had to work for it. Applied and proved myself."

Sam's gaze is fierce, but he doesn't understand the shackles Eli and the others have on her. It's more than just poverty and lacking opportunity weighing her down. Until she leaves, her hands will never be free to unlock the chains. Still, his words settle uncomfortably. "But getting out of Lonetree feels impossible—"

Sam raps his knuckles on the bar, cutting her off. "Knock it off, Az. I've watched you let Eli drag you down too long. You can't say the chance is gone if you never even reach for it. You looking for jobs outta town? Applying to schools? Or just whinin' and lettin' stuff happen to you?"

"You're right," she mutters, groaning as she presses her forehead to the bar. She'd thought the same thing earlier in Alec's decayed library. A fire had been lit under her, but she'd let it smolder out again. Not this time. "This isn't over."

"Damn right," Sam says, nodding his head sharply. "Apply and prove yourself, don't give up, do something for yourself for once. You'll get outta town in no time."

Apply and do something for herself for a chance, well she tried. She needs money and connections to try again. There's always James, who Eli said might swing her way. Maybe she could create a genuine friendship with him, not just to gather information. Maybe he'd invite her to more parties where she could make a better first impression on the new kids until she finds ones willing to let her tag along when they leave.

Or maybe she'll take the truck and drive until she's alone for the first time in her life. The thought sends a shiver down her spine, but Sam's eyes stay steady on her, and she pushes the scheming aside. "Thanks, Sam," she says. "You're a great guy."

He reddens and busies himself bussing out a nonexistent spot on the bar. "Drink your water."

The door creaks open, and someone plops onto the stool beside her. Azzie flicks her gaze to the newcomer—a woman with heavy rouge on her cheeks and blue eyeshadow smudged across her drooping lids.

"Sammy boy," the woman rasps, her voice scratchy. "Whiskey."

Sam's already pouring before she finishes speaking, sliding a glass of amber liquid across the bar. Azzie narrows her eyes but doesn't comment as he avoids her gaze, hiding a small smile.

"Place is looking good, Sammy," the woman says, gulping down the glass and slamming it on the bar. Sam pours another shot before the glass lands. "Get outta my sight, Donald," she yells to the old man in the back. He stands, cups his crotch, and saunters towards the back door.

"Boss had me sweep out the dust," Sam says. "Says we should start doing it once a month. Add to the 'ambiance.'" He hooks his fingers into air quotes and stumbles over the word.

The woman laughs until she wheezes. Azzie attempts to slide farther away from her. "Not this dump," the woman says, taking another sip. She grins at Sam, a lipstick stain showing on her teeth. "Saw the prettiest man out front. *That* adds to the ambiance."

Azzie looks between the woman and Sam. "What kind of pretty?"

"Oh, a fancy piece too good for this hole, that's for sure. He looked like the cover of one of my romances—all tall, dark, and handsome. Dressed nice too, like a lawyer. Or a classy magician," she amends, waving a hand over her chest. "All that green."

There aren't too many people that fit that description. At least, not who'd have heard of Jimmy's. "Where'd he go?"

The woman points towards the door the old man just stepped through. "Saw him walking towards the back."

Azzie stands and drains the water while Sam scowls. "Az..." he warns.

"Like you said, it's not over." She marches towards the back door.

Chapter 25

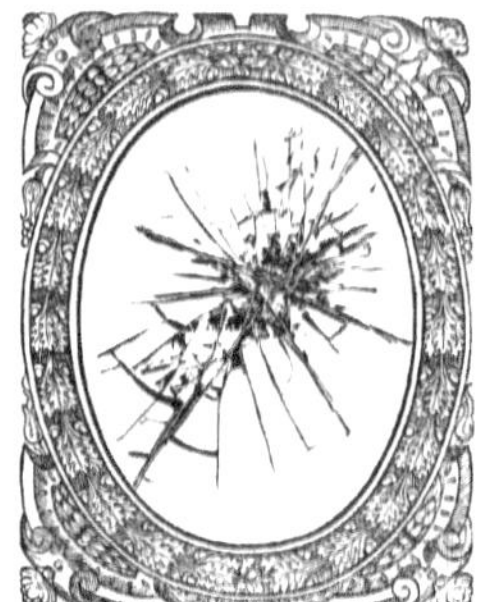

He sits on the ratty sofa in the living area and pulls his blond fringe in front of his eyes. He's hungover and moth-eaten curtains don't keep out any of the sun. He reaches under the couch to grab one of his hidden liquor bottles. He's thought about the opportunity presented to him long enough.

He'll do it as soon as possible. He can't deal with Alec any more than he has to.

The consequences if he's discovered would aren't ideal as that Alec has an alarming strength. He struggles to control his shiver as he remembers the dark look in Alec's weird blue eyes every time they interact. It's like Alec thinks he's the better man between them. But that was stupid.

Now, the potential *benefits*...

It'll be a win-win. He'll get what he needs, and Alec will be taken care of. Hopefully she'll be fine, but she doesn't really matter. He tips the neck of the brown bottle, spilling the cheap liquor down his throat.

It's like that phrase, killing two birds with one stone. It he's lucky, one dead bird will definitely be Alec.

Chapter 26

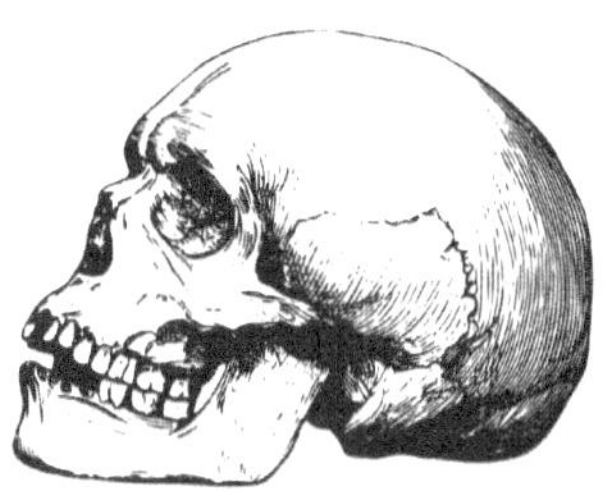

THE STOLEN SOUL SLOTS snugly into Alec's chest, and euphoria surges through him, momentarily banishing the weight of his existence. For a fleeting instant, he feels invincible—ready to sprint for miles, duel a wraith twice his size, or even... *kiss* Azalea. But the rush fades quickly. The soul is weak, a dim ember compared to the infernos he's consumed before. Still, the ring on his finger gleams as color seeps back into the jewel, signaling the ebb of his soulsickness and the return of his faculties.

The past few weeks play back in his mind, hazy and distorted. Soulsickness *had* crept in, twisting his thoughts and magnifying his doubts. It had driven him to sabotage the one thing he wanted most. He'd let her skepticism—her dismissal of magic—strike deeper than it should have. In his warped state, he'd taken it as a rejection of him, not just of the impossible.

Fates, he'd been a fool. He'd thrown away the fragile, human lifetime they might have shared because of his poisoned thoughts. Worse, he'd let himself believe she would falter, that her light would dim under the weight of his life. He had abandoned her, choosing the cowardice of retreat over the courage to face what they could have been together.

Even so, his soulsick mind had stumbled onto one truth: pining for her from the shadows, enduring centuries without her, would destroy him. He had to try, to hope she could see something in him worth salvaging. Yes, being with her might breach the Rules, but living without her would hollow him in ways no punishment ever could.

In some twisted way, he'd done exactly what Michael had always advised: removed the temptation. Michael's solution to weakness was always eradication. Alec had followed his sire's philosophy in the most cowardly, bloodless way possible. He'd left her. But Michael didn't understand. Destroying Azalea—whether by snatching her soul or severing their bond—wouldn't save Alec. It would break him. She wasn't just a temptation to be overcome; she was the tether that kept him from becoming the very monster he feared. Without her, he would be that creature again—a beast, ruled by hunger and hatred.

He could not add a third name to his list.

The rancid breath of the man crumpled at his feet pulls him from his reverie. Alec releases his grip, letting the man slump lifelessly to the ground. The absence of his soul will render him hollow but functional, unnoticed in a place like Jimmy's Bar. Alec wipes his hands on his trousers, weighing his next move. He needs to find Azalea, to apologize and explain. But not with the theatrics and melodrama that plagued his earlier attempts. This time, he would let her decide—her way, her terms.

Her image floods his mind. From the start, Azalea had drawn him in, her resilience shining through the burdens she carried. She wasn't perfect—far from it—but that raw determination, that refusal to surrender to the weight of her circumstances, captivated him. Unlike the countless souls he'd encountered, hers wasn't tainted by hatred or corruption. It was vibrant, flawed, and achingly human. And when she looked at him as though he could be other than a monster, it unraveled him entirely.

That was the truth Michael couldn't grasp. Alec wasn't eradicating weakness; he was clinging to it. Azalea wasn't just a fleeting temptation—she was his salvation. She made him believe he could rise above his monstrous nature, that he might yet be something more than his sins.

The dim hum of the bar draws him back to the present. He crouches, shifting the hollow man's position to avoid immediate discovery, then rises. There's no room for hesitation now.

"What are you doing?"

The sharp question sends a rare jolt of surprise through him. He spins to find Azalea, her arms crossed and her face set in fiery determination. She looks radiant, anger etched onto her expression and hair wild. But the rasping resentment in her voice pummels him like a tidal wave of fury. She crosses her arms around her chest, reminding him of battling with a livid and wrathful wraith.

No, that's unkind. She's like a vengeful goddess, beautiful and terrible.

"Azalea, I—I was just thinking of you," he stammers. "I planned to come find you."

She cranes her neck to inspect the old man behind him. "Did you get into a fight? You know, what? No. I don't care. Someone said you might be out here and unless you're willing to apologize for being a jerk, I'm not listening to another word from your mouth."

"I am sorry," Alec offers, voice low and contrite. "I shouldn't have walked away from you. Or shouted."

"Shouldn't have walked away from me *three* times," she mutters, but still she stepped closer. "You can't do stuff like that anymore; I'm not going to stand for it. You hear?"

He nods, relieved when she lets him intertwine their fingers. Her touch steadies him, though he senses her skepticism lingering.

"When you said you were a monster, does that mean you like beating up old men in the middle of the day?" Her tone is curious rather than accusatory, but the question twists something inside him. With a vile-souled brother like Eli, she must be accustomed to violence. That thought creates a pinching behind his eyes.

The man groans and shuffles inside, leaving them alone. Azalea peers up at him. "Did you actually beat him up?"

"No," he says. His addled mind had it right—he must tell her what he is, but only enough to allow her an informed choice to stay with him. The Rules are still a yoke around his neck. He might not survive it if it were another Lucia situation, though Michael would gleefully help him if he asked. "Though the *monstrous* part of me must be explained, should you let me."

Her expression flattens, unreadable with no emotions leaking from her either, but she doesn't pull away. "As long as you don't panic and run off after."

Muscles he didn't know he was tensing release at her agreement. But they tighten anew as he struggles to force out the most incriminating words he's ever said to a human. "It's more likely you'll wish to run from me, Azalea. I'm a—a wraith."

He's never said that out loud to a human before, he never needed to.

"A wraith," she repeats.

His eyes flit around them to confirm no family are nearby to hear his damning speech before he continues, "I'm an immortal being kept alive only through souls of humans. We are destroyers of lives."

Silence stretches between them before she steps back, shaking her head. "I thought you were serious for a second. But this—this is just a game, right? Push Azzie until she finally gets some self-respect." She stomps toward the bar, but Alec blocks her path with preternatural speed.

"Holy what!" she screeches.

"I told you, I'm a wraith," he insists. "I used my speed to stop you just now. And I stole that man's soul."

Something skitters over her expression, but he can't recognize it. Finally she cocks her head and demands, "Show me something else."

He hesitates. Choosing the lesser Rule break to stay with her didn't mean he was free to break them intentionally *and* casually. He'd already confessed the worst of it. But... revealing a little more of his secrets wouldn't hurt, not with what's at stake. With a sigh, he sprints across the street and back, faster than her eyes can track.

She rolls her eyes. "You're fast. You could secretly be an Olympic level athlete. That doesn't tell me anything."

"I—I can also read emotions and the essence of someone's soul," he whispers. "It is called being an empathic wraith."

Her voice rises, tinging with panic. "Excuse you! What a complete invasion of privacy!"

He attempts to step closer, but she steps backward in counterpoint. "I can't read your emotions in full," he explains quickly. "That's one reason you intrigued me in the beginning."

"How *comforting*." She folds her arms and thins her lips. "And that's assuming I believe you."

"If you'd let me," he says, clearing his throat. When he speaks again, he keeps his voice low and soft. "I can only get powerful emotions from you, only when you feel something with your entire being. I don't feel your more normal emotions. If you'd let me, I could try to show you?"

She stares at him with pinched lips for longer than he likes, not when he can't read her and this conversation taking so much from him. Finally, she nods. "Prove it then."

Gusting out a relieved breath, he faces the road and field, with her at his back. "Think of something that you feel strongly about," he requests. "Something that makes you embarrassed, angered, melancholic, or the like."

One by one, the emotions wash over him, culminating in a wave of citrusy lust so potent it almost knocks him to his knees. He turns to her, his voice a hoarse whisper. "Lust."

It's intoxicating. He's felt it before, both directed at him and around him, but it caresses something deep inside him when it comes from her. He turns, and she laughs.

"So maybe I believe you," Azalea says, her tone lighter than the weight of the moment. "Oh my God—is this why you got all weird about that magic talk this morning? If I'd known you were *magic,* I wouldn't have gone so hard on it." She strides toward him and slugs his shoulder. "But I still have questions. Is this why you're not staying in Asheville?"

"Yes," Alec admits, eyes on the ground. "I came to take a soul and return to my duties as a wraith." He keeps his words measured, offering only enough to explain himself without risking another breach of the Rules. When he dares to meet her gaze again, her pupils are darker, her expression unreadable.

"Do you—have you killed people?" she asks, her voice quieter now.

"You saw that man walk away under his own power. I don't kill those whose souls I take." He slumps his shoulders. She needs to know enough to choose him. "But I *have* killed men and wraiths alike."

"Does it hurt them, when you take their souls?"

"No. But it leaves them hollow. A husk, without wants or desires. I hunt the worst of humanity—their loss is nothing, and no one cares to discovery why." It's the justification he offers to the Council, the one they accept without question, thinking it reduced the chances for discovery. But his true reason is more complex. "I choose the vile ones to balance what I do willingly."

She crosses her arms over her chest. "That's noble of you."

He wants to let her believe it, but the truth claws at him. "I—I try. But it's survival, Azalea. Without their souls, I'd wither away. It's not about altruism, just—balance."

She looks at her feet. "I need a minute," she says.

He twists away from her to give her the semblance of privacy.

Alec turns away, giving her space while his mind spirals. Every second feels endless, his stomach churning as he waits. When he finally glances back, she's sitting with her head in her hands, trembling.

"Azalea—" he starts, anguish thickening his voice. He steps toward her, but she raises a hand to halt him, the other shielding her face. A muffled sound escapes her lips, but it's impossible to read her through the turmoil clouding his thoughts.

He staggers back. It's Lucia all over again. Only worse, because Azalea matters so much more. At least now she knows, he tells himself. At least he won't spend eternity wondering *what if.*

Then she lifts her head, her crooked grin shining through suppressed laughter.

"Azalea," he repeats, bewildered. She beckons him to her and winds her arms around his neck, pulling him close.

"That's what you get for putting me through so much drama." She kisses his jaw. "You said you pick the awful guys and no one's different afterward. I won't judge you for doing whatever you have to do to survive."

He bends to her, their lips brushing twice before he tucks her head under his chin. Relief floods him. He hasn't told her everything—not about choosing Eli, not about the Rules or the strain secrecy will place on them—but for now, it's enough. She hasn't run.

She pulls back to meet his eyes, her own sharp and searching. "You meant it, didn't you? When you called yourself a monster."

The fragile happiness in his chest collapses, landing heavy in his stomach. "I am," he whispers.

"For a self-proclaimed monster," she says with a smirk, "you're *really* broody."

He laughs, something tinted with hysteria and not humor, and lays his head on top of hers to nuzzle her soft hair. "Would you believe you're not the first to say so?"

"Actually, yes," she says, leaning back to brush her fingers through his hair. "But don't worry—broody works for you. Makes you mysterious."

"Mysterious?" he echoes, tilting his head.

"And melodramatic," she adds with a grin. "But save that for someone else. You may be my walking fantasy book, but we don't need to add 'daytime soap' to it."

"I'll do my best," he murmurs, his tone softening. He tightens his hold on her for a moment before stepping back. "But I can't make any promises."

"Figures," she says with a roll of her eyes, but there's warmth behind her words. "Guess I'll just have to stick around and keep you in check."

His heart stutters at her choice of words—*stick around.* "I'll hold you to that," he says, his voice barely above a whisper.

She grins, tapping a finger against his chest. "But I'm not here to fix your whole *tragic monster aesthetic.* That's on you."

He laughs, and for the first time in centuries, Alec feels something dangerously close to hope.

Chapter 27

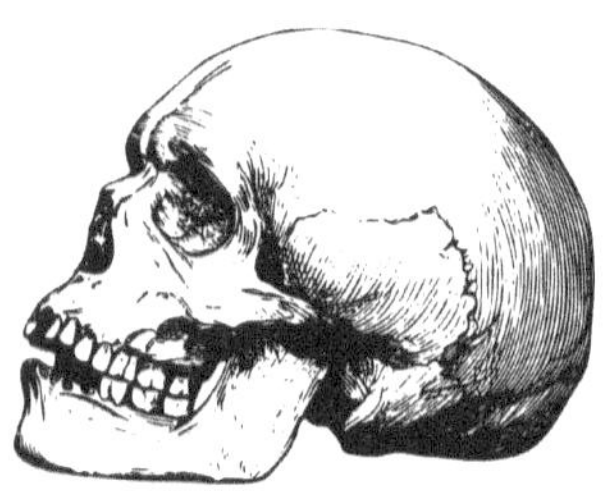

Azalea reaches for him the moment he closes the door to his chambers. Few humans had ever stepped inside, only the Godfrey family in their centuries of servitude. But when Azalea asked to see his room, he couldn't deny her.

The room boasts a bed the first Godfrey purchased, who didn't understand the type of master he tied himself and his family to. It was unused and the lace linens and canopy are grayed with age. Azalea doesn't seem to care.

Her hands grab at his collar and spread down his chest, sending jolts of want through him with each dance of her fingers. Like the lust he sensed from her an hour before, the full weight of her desire leaves him unsteady and rather woozy. It's been centuries since Alec was with another, but the ache for her floods him as though no time passed.

"I haven't forgiven you yet," she says, letting her hands curl around his neck and play with his hair.

"That is," he shivers, "understandable. We should... discuss this."

"Agreed," she says coyly, tugging him closer. "But later."

She pulls him forward by his shirt until they're pressed against the edge of the bed. Her fingers deftly work the buttons of his shirt, but his mouth finds her jawline, her neck, her ear, before capturing her lips again. It's better than he remembered.

Centuries-old memories flash in his mind. He recalls the nervous fumbling of his first human encounter in his mortal life—a brief and awkward affair. The girl, a neighbor, took pity on him and took him to her bed when he hit the age of maturity for his people, after all the eligible girls rejected his suits. He was nervous and didn't know where his limbs went or how to maneuver with two people on the straw pallet. It was over sooner than they both expected, and the girl never spoke of it again.

As a wraith, he slept with hundreds. But his dalliances with humans ended after a single mistake: losing control in the throes of passion. His vessel was full, he'd not need souls for ages, but as his pleasure crested, his hand slipped to the man's throat. He felt the familiar tingle as the soul left the man's body, which wasted into the air when it couldn't slot inside his chest or sink into his ring. It was a lost life, a meaningless theft. The memory of that wasted life ended his dalliances, leaving him celibate for centuries.

Before he notices, Azalea gets his shirt open and pushes it off his shoulders, running her nails over his skin, sending shivers through his body. That memory will stay a memory. He's older now, and more controlled. He can contain himself.

His hand slides under her thin shirt, but they don't break apart long enough to remove it. With a quick tug, he tears the fabric open, the printed design warping as it splits in two. Azalea pulls back, glancing down at her torso. His eyes follow hers, flickering between her black satin underthings and the smooth skin below.

"Was I too rough?" His voice is low, his fingers flexing as if to restrain them.

She shakes her head. "Just my favorite shirt."

He nuzzles her neck to keep his hands away, letting himself smell the freshness of her skin. "Mine is the green one." He kisses the dips in her collarbone and allows his hands to wander to the softness of her stomach. "You wore it when we first met."

"Romantic of you," she gasps, tugging on his dark hair, the sensation of her lust spiraling around him like smoke, a cranberry wine scented haze. "I'll have to remember and *not* wear it the next time we do this. I don't have enough shirts to spare them."

She pulls his mouth back to hers, their bodies pressed together, her skin soft beneath his hands. His palms skim her sides before trailing up her spine to cup the back of her neck. The flutter of her pulse under his touch is too familiar—too close to the sensation of stealing a soul.

He sucks in a breath, dragging himself away and steadying himself against the wall across the room. Azalea tumbles backward onto the bed, a cloud of dust puffing into the air as she coughs and waves it away.

His restraint almost failed him.

"Everything okay?" She leans back on the bed, shirt still ripped, breasts enveloped in a dark satin. He clenches his fists to keep from reaching for her.

"That was a mistake."

Chapter 28

AZZIE PULLS THE TORN halves of her shirt together, her fingers trembling slightly as she works to gather her thoughts. She hadn't planned on jumping Alec the moment they arrived at Rockton House, but the way he had shown her around with that quiet, amazed expression on his face—like every creaking floorboard and dusty window held a story just for her—had melted her resolve. How could she not kiss him? And once she kissed him, how could she not want more?

If things were different, Eli would've loved poking around this place. But Eli wasn't on her mind anymore. She was thinking about herself now. She wasn't going to let life just happen to her anymore, like Sam said. And until she figured out what that looked like, letting herself get swept up by a handsome immortal being who stared at her like she hung the stars felt like a solid start.

The man—creature?—in question looks downright miserable, lips pressed into a thin line, eyes squeezed shut like he's hoping the universe will swallow him whole. He's the one who ripped away and let her tumble backward onto the musty bed, so why does he look like the wounded party? Unfocused anger still simmers along the edges of her subconscious, but she breathes deep and thinks of how she handles Eli when he's in his snits.

"I'm going to give you a minute to explain yourself before I flip out," she says, keeping her tone low and even. "Because we just got over your whole 'we can't be together' insecurities, and you telling me this is 'a mistake' is absolutely not an acceptable outcome to tonight's dating experience."

He appears at her side, taking a split heartbeat to cross the room. If she wasn't somewhat turned on, it would have been terrifying. "That I wish to be with you is not the issue," he says roughly. The certainty in his voice makes her release the two sides of her shirt and lean backward again. "I have leapt off the cliff already, I cannot claw my way back to the edge."

Her brows furrow. "Is this a modesty thing?" She sits up and covers her mouth with her hands. "Oh my god. You're a virgin! That explains the 1800s speech patterns and how skittish you are. That's okay, we'll go slow."

His scowl deepens, and she struggles not to giggle. With his hair tousled from her fingers and his posture bristling, he looks like an indignant bird. "That is not the issue," he snaps. "I have lain with women. And men. While I haven't had a romantic connection in—"

"Okay, okay, you're a god among mortals, wraiths, whatever," she interrupts with a laugh, trying to squash the flicker of jealousy clawing at her. She's not going to compare her own meager experience to whatever centuries-long list he might have. "So, if that's not it, what's the problem?"

He stares down at her from the foot of the bed before pressing the heels of his palms over his eyes. "I won't be able to control myself."

"Like before? With the shirt-ripping?" She gestures to her chest. "It might've been my favorite, but it was old and cheap. And, for the record, it was hot."

His gaze flicks to hers and his expression is pained. "It's happened before when I laid with a human. I am afraid I will be so overcome that I will inadvertently..." He flaps a hand at her torso.

"What?" she prompts. "Hurt me?"

His eyes go wide, and he shakes his head fiercely. "Never. I would never hurt you. But your neck—" He swallows hard, his Adam's apple bobbing. "That is how I—"

"Suck out someone's soul?"

He looks more devastated than ever. "Yes. I've avoided physical gratification for quite a long time to limit the possibility."

Azzie lets the words sink in. The absurdity of the situation—her sitting on a dusty antique bed in a haunted mansion, arguing with an immortal about his fear of sucking out her soul in a moment of passion—would've made her laugh if his expression weren't so heartbroken.

She scoots back until she's lying flat and pats the bed beside her. "Come lie down next to me," she says gently. "I promise I won't jump you again."

He hesitates, his dark brows drawn tight, before sighing and joining her. He lowers himself carefully, as if afraid even the slightest touch might shatter the precarious truce between them. She rolls onto her side, wrapping her arms loosely around him, tucking her head against his shoulder.

His body is thin with a wiry strength in his arms and the set of his shoulders. A small smattering of black hair dusts his chest, and a dark line of it trails from his navel to disappear under his waistband. He's slimmer than her, which, combined with his lean muscles, makes him a less than ideal pillow, but he's a handsome man, making comfort her secondary concern. She runs her fingers over his chest. It's thrilling that such a powerful and attractive being wants her. It's doing wonders for her self-esteem.

"Please," he whispers. "Your feelings are—I am struggling to control myself and my reactions."

Reason number two she needs to hide her emotions from him. She allows her mind to move from lust to the contentedness of two people holding each other. "Do you have to worry about control with other wraiths?" she asks.

He stiffens against her. "No, not for that reason," he says. "Laying with a member of the family is considerably different."

She lifts her head, narrowing her eyes. "Family?"

"Not in the way you're thinking," he clarifies quickly. "We're connected by species, not blood. A unified community under the same Rules."

She relaxes back onto his trim chest. "And how's it different?"

"Violence and deceit are typical. It's more game playing and only for the ultimate physical release. I don't like those games," he finishes quietly.

She nods into his armpit. Eli picked a bad mark once, one that didn't care about who was with him, so long as someone was getting him off. He didn't go for Azzie's attempts at friendship to gain information on his parents' assets and tried to force a blowjob. Eli knocked his teeth out.

She rubs small circles over Alec's stomach. "We won't do anything that both of us want to do," she says. "But we can figure this out. I mean, what's the worst thing that could happen if you accidentally sucked out my soul?"

He lifts his head to stare at her with shocked eyes. "You would be soulless and lose your humanity, all your goodness, your desires, your worries."

She shrugs, feigning nonchalance. "Like you," she says. The idea doesn't seem so bad. If losing her humanity got rid of that pesky voice she called 'guilt and expectation,' sign her up.

His expression hardens. "No. I'm a wraith. It's different."

"Then make me a wraith," she suggests, her tone light but her mind churning.

"I couldn't do that." He sounds slightly scandalized.

She burrows into his shoulder. She said it carelessly, but hearing it aloud makes her realize it *is* a phenomenal idea. It'll certainly get her out of here. She'll have all the connections she needs. And if she's immortal, the worries of her family won't matter. In a century, she wouldn't *remember* the things that bothered her now. It isn't just a phenomenal idea, it's a *perfect* idea.

"Why not?" She kisses him lightly on the neck.

His fingers tighten against the bed. "We are a vile society," he says. "We value only two things: obeying the Rules and slaking our thirst—for souls, for pleasure, for violence. It is a terrible life to lead."

"'There is nothing either good or bad, but thinking makes it so,'" she quotes. She can handle what he described.

He huffs a soft, reluctant laugh. "Indeed. And much like Denmark, to me, even as a warden, the family is a prison."

She snorts into his neck. "I thought you weren't a reader."

"My interest in Shakespeare was punished centuries ago," he says, the corners of his lips twitching. "But some of the bard's words stayed with me."

"You really are a romantic," she teases, ignoring the statement about punishment. She needs more information about that world to unpack that, but the knowledge won't deter her now that she's set her mind to conversion.

He doesn't respond, just tugs lightly on a strand of her hair, his sigh heavy with something between resignation and contentment.

She closes her eyes, exhilarating in the knowledge that such a powerful being wants her. "But you haven't convinced me that being a wraith is an unacceptable life choice."

"You're too good for the family," he says, his voice firm. "It would snuff out your goodness."

I'm not all that good. She buries the thought, saying, "You're a wraith and you're not terrible."

He shakes his head, jostling her. "Compared to you? I am, and I am the least vicious. I would not wish that life on you."

"And if I decided I did?"

His expression turns grim. "You'd have better luck convincing a stranger to convert you than me."

"Will I meet any strangers?" She keeps her tone light and breathes slowly, hopeful her emotions are weak enough that he can't sense them.

"Never."

She doesn't miss the finality in his voice, but she won't let it deter her. For now, she tucks herself closer against him, letting the warmth of his body and the steadiness of his heartbeat lull her into a fragile calm.

Chapter 29

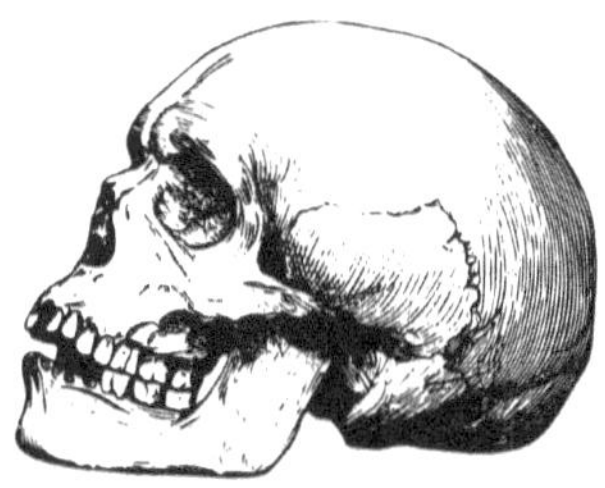

AZALEA DRIVES AWAY JUST as the sun disappears below the horizon, the rumble of her truck fading into the distance. Alec stands in the doorway of Rockton, watching her go, his chest tightening with conflicting emotions. She's wearing his shirt—the one with the odd smiling face she'd identified as a band logo. The sight of it on her, something so mundane yet so intimately his, feels like a claim he never thought he'd have. He would give her anything, except the one thing she just asked for: conversion.

The hours they spent together had been as easy as breathing, but the specter of her demands had lingered, unspoken and heavy. She wants him to change her, or she wants them to leave this place. Both options are impossible, yet the idea of denying her feels like tearing a piece of himself away.

He remains in the doorway, his eyes following the dust trail her truck leaves in its wake. She'd waved to him before disappearing down the road, and the image of her hand raised in farewell lingers in his mind. She makes him believe he could be more than what he is, that he could deserve something as fleeting and beautiful as her smile.

Though his feelings for her are born of weeks rather than years, and yet they burn brighter than anything he's felt in centuries. He tries to rationalize it: her humanity, her light, the way she looks at him like he's someone worth saving. She's a fragile, flawed human, and he's a creature of darkness. Yet the thought of her not being part of his existence is unbearable.

When he finally retreats inside, the memory of her warmth still clings to him, both a comfort and a torment. He nearly skips to his chambers, lying back on the bed where they'd curled together. Her scent lingers in the sheets, a blend of salt and earth and something uniquely hers. He imagines a future where she stays, where they share Rockton's hollow halls and create something that feels like a home. He has enough money to keep them comfortable for the rest of her life. Jimmy's Bar will provide the necessary miscreants to hunt. The Council will leave him alone once he explains he's taking advantage of their allotted 'leisure time,' given he acted as their rover more than ten times over the required allotment during this millennium.

He knows it's foolish. She's human, and humans die. If they *want* to remain entwined longer than her lifetime, the obvious solution was asking her for her soul. The possibility was a twin sword of agony and hope—he didn't know that it would work, he didn't know that she'd be willing, he didn't know how continued exposure to the family and their wickedness would affect her.

His thoughts spiral until a knock at the door pulls him from his reverie.

"Come in," he calls, sitting upright.

Godfrey edges into the room, his hands twisted nervously together. The servant smells of fear and unease, but Alec barely registers it in his current haze of elation and worry.

"Sir, your friend... Michael... just left," Godfrey stammers.

Alec bolts to his feet, icy dread crashing over him. "Why didn't you call for me?"

Godfrey is at least an inch taller than Alec, but he quakes when Alec nears. There's sweat on Godfrey's brow, turning the skin below his straw blond hair the color of dirty water. Alec reads his emotions and is buffeted by fear, revulsion, and expectation. Depending on Michael's mood, and whether he wanted to seduce or unnerve Godfrey when he arrived, those emotions aren't a surprise.

"There wasn't time," Godfrey whines, apologetic.

"And? Did he leave a message?"

Godfrey nods, his beady eyes ticking up quickly before dropping back to the floor. "He says he was handling your problem and was ignoring your note."

The blood drains from Alec's face. He'd been foolish to think Michael would listen, even for a moment. Michael thrives on chaos, and Alec's note had practically invited it. His heart clenches as Godfrey hesitates, his discomfort intensifying.

"There's more," Godfrey says, his voice trembling. "He mentioned the girl... Azalea. He said her name. And I got the feeling... he'd return for her unless you both left Rockton."

Images of Michael's smirking face, his dismissive words, and the careless chaos he'd wreaked over centuries flash through Alec's mind. His demand that Michael not touch Azalea, his shaky handwriting in the note—these were tantamount to painting a target on her back. His options with Azalea are sinking into the depths of the sea, weighed down by danger, never to rise again.

His decision is made in an instant. "Get me a traveling bag and a pickaxe," Alec commands.

Godfrey bobs his head and scurries off as Alec strides to the library. There's no time to deliberate. If Michael has set his sights on Azalea, staying here is not an option. Conversion is out of the question—he will not damn her to this existence. And asking for her soul... no. That path is fraught with uncertainties and risks he cannot afford. The only option left is to take her and run, leaving everything else behind. That's the only way to save her.

Godfrey returns, burdened with the tools Alec requested. Alec takes the bag and begins gathering essentials, tossing in books, papers, and vials from his alchemy kit. He pauses at his journal, running his fingers over its embossed cover. The Rules have guided him for centuries, and though he won't renounce them, he must live within their gray spaces now. He hands the journal to Godfrey, who slips it into the bag's side pocket. With less care, Alec rips the remaining books from their places until he can bring the ax down onto the wood. He repeats the motion twice until the ancient bookshelves splinter and he can claw them from the wall. His hands shake and a sliver gouges the back of his hand. Pain blossoms from the wound, but not enough to hinder him. It will heal before too long, anyway. With his soulsickness cured, only magic can cause permanent harm now.

The blood runs down his fingers, catching in the bands of his ring which he wipes on his shirt. He lifts the ax again, hitting the stone wall hidden behind the many shelves, until it crumbles. When the dust clears, Alec pulls out a box buried behind the wall, one full of gold pieces he never deposited. He fills the bag Godfrey provided with as much gold as it can hold. The remaining pieces he hands to Godfrey, who startles to the point of dropping them.

"I may never return to this place," Alec says, his voice heavy with finality. "Thank you, Godfrey. You and your family have served me well. Take care of Rockton. Perhaps you'll give it the care I could not."

Alec spares one last glance at the library, its derelict grandeur a testament to centuries of neglect. His gaze stops on the mirror. With a resounding crash, the glass shatters, shards scattering like starlight across the floor. The path back to the wraith family is severed, at least for now.

Turning from the destruction, Alec hefts the bag and strides into the night. It's time to find Azalea and leave Rockton behind—for good.

Chapter 30

Azzie curls up on the tattered sofa in their cramped living room-kitchen, pulling her knees to her chest. The sofa and the comfy armchair are two of the few things they hadn't sold when they moved from their family home. Her sisters are asleep in their shared room, a small space waiting for her to scrunch in next to Clara. Eli, who usually crashes on the floor, is out doing God knows what. He left the truck behind, but that doesn't help her guess where he might be—not that she cares.

She stares at the cracked ceiling. Sleep is impossible. Too much happened in the last forty-eight hours, and half of it can only be a dream. But one thing remains clear: what she screamed at Eli was still true—she needed to get out, and away.

It surprises her, when she thinks about it now, how little guilt she feels about possibly taking off and leaving her family behind. Maybe that's because she knows Dad is a brand-new man, all because of Alec's magic, meaning the girls will be taken care of, and Eli's an adult who can handle himself. But a niggling thought tells her that isn't it.

She pulls out her cell phone. *If only Alec had a phone.* He promised to visit when the sun comes up, and they'll make a final decision on what their options are. She wanted to decide right then, with the main option being 'leave Lonetree.' She'll suffocate if she stays. The second option is 'convert her.' And those options aren't mutually exclusive either. Maybe they aren't *options* either. If Alec is one of the best examples of the species, she'll be a great wraith.

A sharp knock at the door snaps her out of her thoughts. Heart racing, she grabs the crowbar from under the couch, gripping it tightly as she inches toward the door.

Her grip loosens when she opens it to find Alec standing on the other side, a large satchel slung over his shoulder. The dim light from the living area catches his face, illuminating his sharp features and making his eyes flash like embers. She can't believe she never realized he wasn't human.

"Come in," she says, waving him inside with the crowbar. "I was just thinking about you." She tucks the crowbar back under the couch and flops onto the sofa. "Have you slept? Do wraiths even sleep?"

Alec doesn't answer. His gaze darts over the room, scanning the shadows before locking onto her. His face is tense, his eyes aflame. "Has he already come?" he demands, his voice sharp.

"Has who come?" she asks, frowning.

"Michael," he hisses. "Has he threatened you?"

It takes her a moment to place the name. "You mean your friend from the Zeta party?" Her brow furrows as she takes in his appearance. "Wait—are you bleeding?"

He ignores the question, instead sweeping his gaze over the room and then behind him. "We need to leave."

She stands with a gasping grin. "Awesome! That's exactly what I was going to suggest. Where are we going and when? Soon I hope." She grabs her knapsack from its place by the door and dumps out the books into a haphazard pile. She won't need them outside of Lonetree.

"Right now," Alec says, his voice tight. "And wherever we can hide from Michael."

"Okay, let me pack," she says. "How are we getting wherever we're getting—car, plane, boat?"

He tilts his head, and she rolls her eyes. "I don't have your wraith speed, so we'll need something else. I'm certainly not walking if we don't have to. We'll take the pickup."

"Will your family not need it?"

"Eli takes it across state lines pretty regularly. It's my turn now." She ambles to the back of the trailer to her shared room and lowers her voice. "Why are we hiding from your friend?"

He flicks his gaze to the ground and exhales shakily. "I cannot tell you everything, except that Michael will look for us and he cannot catch us." He looks back up at her with pained eyes. "You must be quick and prepared to leave your former life entirely."

She slings her bag over her shoulder, biting back another smile. For once, everything feels like it's moving in the right direction.

Chapter 31

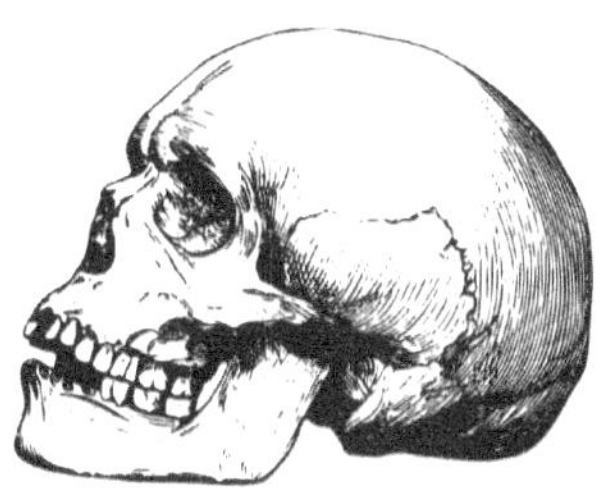

IT TAKES AZALEA LONGER to pack up the remnants of her life than it took Alec. He struggles to hide his restlessness because he understands she's leaving her home, and thus has more to manage, and his true home is spread out across the realm.

At least, it used to be. Alec's actions in absconding with Azalea most likely mean he must avoid the family until she passes on, else he'll be punished and she'll be killed.

Azalea leaves a note for her family on the buzzing refrigerator, her pen moving with sharp, determined strokes. She doesn't share the contents with him, and he doesn't ask. The vinegar-tinged entitlement radiating from her as she writes makes him uneasy, but his worry for her safety compels him to ignore it.

By the time she pulls the pickup onto the main road out of town, dawn has broken, painting the horizon with faint streaks of gold and pink. She insisted on driving, dismissing his argument that his age made him capable of handling anything. Her skepticism grew sharper after questioning his experience with human technology and finding it lacking. Instead, he's relegated to navigating, tracing a finger along the creases of an old map. It's a small mercy, as he hasn't told her—nor fully decided—where they're going. He needs somewhere far from Michael, far from the family, and far from danger.

The drive is uncomfortable, not because of the companionship but because of the reasons for their flight and the prickling sensation under his skin, one that began the moment he slid inside her aged vehicle.

Hours pass, the scenery shifting from forested hills to stretches of flat, open road. He spends the time with his journal balanced on his knees, jotting fragmented plans and possible destinations. His pen hovers over Eli's name as he considers whether his original prey remains a viable option.

Azalea's voice crashes through the silence, startling him. His hand jerks, the nib scratching out Eli's name in an uneven line. He closes the journal hastily, turning to her with wide eyes.

"What?" he asks, his tone sharper than intended.

She glances at him sideways, one hand steady on the wheel. "Where are we going, Mr. fancy-wraith man? North is all I can get from the directions you're giving me. New York? D.C.? Philadelphia?"

"The Amanas," he answers, intentionally marking through Eli's name this time with trembling fingers. "I hunted a wraith nearby in the 1900s. It seemed a peaceful place to rest."

She gapes at him. "The Amanas—the Amana Colonies, you mean? Why the hell are we going there?"

"It's quiet and safe."

"And, at best, a lateral step from the Asheville metroplex," she says, scowling. "I'm not going from Lonetree to the *Amanas.*"

"Michael is a reveler by nature," he explains quietly. "We need somewhere small, with limited or no debauchery or entertainment. The Amana are pastoral people. Michael would find no satisfaction there, making it a haven."

"I think they have a tourist business," she argues. "And there are no uninteresting places, only uninteresting people."

He suppresses a retort about how that logic could apply to her resistance. "Michael wouldn't agree with that sentiment," he says instead.

"Well, it's a bastardization of a G. K. Chesterton quote. But the sentiment is the same. If Michael is the partier you say he is, he could find 'satisfaction' anywhere. Eli certainly did in our small town," she adds petulantly. "Who is to say we're safe anywhere? We might as well go somewhere like New York or D.C. It's much bigger so we could hide easier. I've never been to either, and they always sounded fun. Better than *Iowa*."

"Absolutely not," he growls. "There are large portals in those locales and our cities just below them. We would have no chance to hide from others there."

"Oh." The mood in the pickup wilts and disappointment fills the cabin. "Are we hiding from other wraiths too?"

He hesitates. The threat isn't immediate—only Michael knows about Azalea, and the family doesn't yet know about Alec's weakness. But Michael's reputation for gossip with his lovers makes the situation precarious. "Not yet," he admits cautiously.

Her gaze sharpens, emotions slipping away like a shield she's raising. "How many wraiths are we talking about?"

"Of those who could be after us? I've no idea. It's difficult to estimate how many wraiths exist at a time. But any of the non-exiled could take up the mantle of the Council's whims. That leaves a number of over two thousand but less than five thousand family-members we may need to avoid."

"And they're hanging out in one of those portals in New York or somewhere?"

Alec wets his lips. The Second Rule runs through his head, a constant reminder of his treachery to his kind, the risk to Azalea and his failure to follow the Rules that he swore to abide and protect. Their conversation veers into dangerous territory. He promised himself he'd only share enough to keep her safe, as anything more is a Rule break that could bring them both pain. He sits ramrod straight to hide the tremor in his frame. "If they are not in a human civilization, they are somewhere in our dimension."

"Which is?"

"Underground," he says through gritted teeth, the confession pulled from him by her relentless curiosity. Hoping to divert her, he adds, "We access it through mirrors."

"Like Alice in Wonderland," she says. Her mood brightens and the citrus scent of delight fills the car.

He seizes the chance to steer the conversation away from wraith secrets. "Perhaps Lewis Carroll was a wraith," he suggests as one corner of his mouth tips upward.

"Really?"

"No," he admits. "Our world is nothing like that which Mr. Carroll described. Although, there was an uproar in the community when his books were published. I was sent to confirm whether any Rules had been broken and punish the transgressors." He curls his lips, remembering the conversation with the man and recounting the trip to the Council. "Mr. Carroll simply had an active imagination."

She laughs a little. "When do you think I'll get to visit the wraith world?"

The question shakes him from his trip through his memories as a rover, the least bloody story being the one he shared. "Never," he says, the finality in his tone leaving no room for argument.

Chapter 32

AZZIE TRIES PRYING MORE answers from Alec, but he shuts down, muttering something about it being "difficult to change a millennium of habits in one day." Of course, he won't explain what *that* means, leaving her alone with her thoughts. An ember of annoyance sparks in her gut, fanned by every unanswered question.

His silence forces her to stay in her own brain, somewhere she'd rather avoid. She doesn't want to think about how pissed Eli will be when he learns she left. It serves him right though—she told him she had plans, and here she is doing them, and he can hang. If Eli wanted to stop her, she left him a little something to make sure he wouldn't try. It had felt borderline wrong but now it feels more generous than he deserves. Nothing is going to hold her back.

The pickup lasts until somewhere outside Davenport before sputtering to its death. Eli's constant trips must have run the engine into the ground. When the highway clears, they hoof it back to a gas station they passed a few miles back. Alec doesn't complain, but Azzie grumbles inwardly the entire way. Part of leaving Lonetree should have meant no longer needing to walk everywhere.

The gas station attendant points them to a used car lot two miles west. Alec suggests they walk the rest of the way to the Amanas instead. It takes several explanations before he understands she can't walk a hundred miles, and certainly not in twenty minutes like he could. Even the extra two miles to the car lot is pushing it.

When they reach the lot an hour and a half later, Azzie's feet are screaming. The lot is closed for the night, and she leans heavily against the chain-link fence, swiping sweat from her forehead. The annoyance simmering in her gut threatens to boil over.

"Do you have a preference?" Alec's smooth voice says beside her. He's bent at the knee like he plans to jump the fence.

Her eyes widen. "It's closed."

"That's no concern of mine. I can pick out a vehicle, leave the requisite payment, and we'll be on our way."

"But you don't have the keys," she sputters. "You'd have to break a window and figure out where they're kept *and* which goes with which car, *and* you didn't exchange enough cash. You can't just leave gold."

He doesn't appear to care.

"I'm exhausted and starving," she whines, her legs buckling as she slides to the ground. Normally, guilt or self-consciousness would temper her attitude, but not today. She'd hopped into the truck twelve hours ago based on vague warnings of "danger" and "must leave now." She feels justified.

He frowns at her. "Did the sustenance at the last stop not sate your hunger?"

She groans, clutching at her stomach dramatically. "It was gas station food. Even with my family's budget, we still got something more than snacks."

Alec presses his fingers to the bridge of his nose, visibly agitated. He's been on edge all day—glancing over his shoulder, scanning empty fields, and clutching his ring like someone might snatch it. Whatever danger he's obsessing over, he won't tell her about it, which leaves her sympathy running thin. Still, she sidles up to him, sliding a hand down his side before slipping under his arm. He, annoyingly, still smells fresh, like black pepper and rain, despite the long walk.

"I saw a hotel two blocks back that had a restaurant attached," she says. "We can stay there for the night and be back here when this place opens."

He gazes down at her with flint-like eyes. Azzie flashes her teeth at him and struggles to keep her thoughts calm and content to avoid broadcasting the undercurrent of annoyance and frustration bubbling within her.

"Apparently I can deny you nothing," he says.
Her smile dims. They both know that isn't true.

Chapter 33

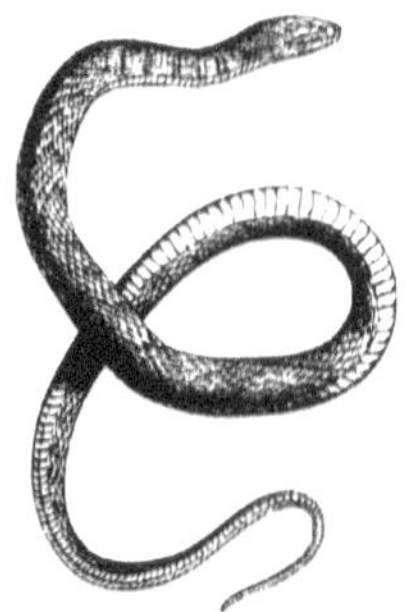

MICHAEL SITS IN ANOTHER high-rise office suite he swindled away from an elderly gentleman who used it as a meeting place for his younger mistresses. It is a clever ploy, a well-appointed office that appears professional until lights are flipped and furniture turned. The leather sofa they're sitting on only needs three turns for it to pop out into a sumptuous looking bed. Michael isn't positive that the older man changed the red silk sheets before Michael sent him on his way, but the uncertainty adds a grotesque allure to his seduction.

Eli rests with his hands fisted together in his lap, foot tapping against the caramel carpet below him. Bruises mar his angelic visage, deep purple blemishes trailing from his left eye to his nose. The memory of Eli's encounter leaches from him as Michael uses his wraith gift to learn it. If not for the damn Rules, Michael would find the human who blighted his toy and dole out justice.

Instead, Michael watches Eli, reviewing what he experienced at the tavern using his presight. Eli reminds him of Alesandro in some lights. But where Alesandro's village compatriots never recognized his beauty and passion, Eli flaunts it, forcing people to see and admire him. There's a confidence found in Eli's memories, an unkindness present, wrapped up in a cocoon of selfishness that brings Michael a sliver of pleasure to experience.

The confidence that drew Michael to him is gone now, as he squirms in Michael's presence. He sighs.

The mortals have no sense of patience. Though, in this case, that isn't a product of the man's own choices. He considers offering Eli a drink to help but wants his cells intact.

"Eli," Michael says, drawing out the syllables. Eli stops shaking. "As you know, things have changed since our last visit. We will need to hasten our plans, assuming you have decided."

Eli nods, moving his hands to run through his blond hair. "She's planning to leave, or something. I can tell! She's too focused on that piece of crap, Alec." Eli spits out Alec's name like a curse.

The rage frothing up in Eli's memories of Alec is amusing, partially arousing. But—such statements about Michael's 'favorite' are not to be born, something Eli knows. Michael zips to the space next to Eli in the breadth of a heartbeat, Eli's blond fringe fanning in the air he displaced. Eli doesn't appear frightened by the brief show of Michael's skills; he hasn't at each of Michael's revelations, making him decent entertainment. But first—

"Do not speak of him that way in my presence," Michael murmurs, bringing up a hand and running it through Eli's hair. Though Eli can't help it, lacking control isn't an excuse Michael accepts. "Alec is family, just as Azalea is your family." He cups the back of Eli's neck. "I want to help my family, just as you want to help yours. Will you help me?"

"Whatever you need," Eli whispers. Michael gives a sharklike grin and pulls the man's face closer to his own.

"Whatever I need," he repeats with a sigh. "Oh, love, you may regret that offer if you stay this docile for long."

Chapter 34

Azzie convinces Alec to stop at a hotel—one with a lobby and indoor hallways, not the motels with exterior doors that scream "stranger danger." She has exactly one memory of hotels: the time her mom had a conference in Raleigh before Clara was born. Dad took them on a day trip to visit her, and they met at a diner two blocks away. Azzie had never seen anything like it—high ceilings, crisp white walls that felt warm and inviting. The people staying there looked important, happy even, and for a fleeting moment, she felt the same.

Their current hotel is nothing like the hotel of her memory, but the feelings she gets are the same—chance and opportunity exist within the walls. If nothing else, it's the first step to making life far from in Lonetree.

Alec wrinkles his nose when they arrive, taking in the floral upholstery and mock plaster statue standing in the center of the reception area that depicts two wrestling bear cubs. Her lips thin as she conceals an eye roll; she's seen Rockton House—he has no right to judge the décor.

Their shared room is bigger than her room at home and she takes a running leap onto the bed farthest from the door. Alec storms over the threshold as if he's being chased, eyeing the mirrors in the room.

"We shouldn't be here," he snarls, ripping the sheets from the other bed. He hangs the sheets over the fake gilded mirror beside the tv. "One of these could be a portal."

"In Iowa?" she says, wrinkling her nose.

"Paranoia has served me well," he says, only half answering her question before stalking into the large double bathroom with the remains of the white duvet. She doesn't spare a moment thinking about how he'll cover the bathroom mirrors that are glued onto the wall. That's his problem, not hers. She still doesn't know what the danger is beyond his creepy friend following them.

Once the room is secure from possible, though unlikely, portals, she coaxes him to the hotel restaurant. It's a tacky, music-themed spot with fried food on every page of the menu. They settle into a table in the back with an unobstructed view of the door. While Azzie orders an appetizer, Alec watches the corners as if he expects someone to melt out of them. While that seems an unreasonable fear, maybe it could happen.

Not that *she'd* know because he keeps hiding information from her.

"We're still safe. This is the middle of nowhere," she soothes, resentment bleeding into her tone. She gestures at the garish decor of fake music albums and broken instruments. "From what you said, Michael wouldn't be caught dead in here."

"That is not a comforting statement," he snaps. "I understand you do not believe we are in near as much danger as we are but—"

Her lips twist. The similarities between Alec and Eli are stacking up, and she doubts either would appreciate the comparison. "I'd know what kind of danger we were in if you *explained* things to me."

"Not now," he says, pressing his fingers against his nose.

The server drops off their fried mozzarella. She shoves a stick in her mouth with narrowed eyes. After swallowing, she stands up, knocking her transparent plastic chair to the ground. "I'm going to the bathroom. When I come back, I expect us to talk like the mature and capable people we are."

"I am not a person," he says behind his fingers.

"Semantics," she hisses before stomping away to the bathroom behind the bar.

When the little door closes behind her and the latch clicks, she leans back against it and groans. She's finally doing what she's spent the last eight months thinking about, and it's as if nothing changed. When Alec admitted he was a wraith, she thought the world would open to her—travel, adventure, lacking guilt, immortality! All things she lacked in Lonetree.

She rinses her face in the trough-style sink and stares at herself in the mirror. She brushes her fingers through her hair, teasing out the tangles she normally left in. With a little water, it looks like a longer version of Eli's preferred style. There's a glint in her eyes she recognizes from Eli's face, one that focuses on her needs over others. She can almost sense the autonomy seeping in under her skin.

With one last ruffle of her hair, she marches back to Alec. A stranger stands by their table, leaning against her chair. Although the man looks nothing like Alec, pale and red-headed, he has one striking similarity—eyes that flicker like a candle.

Alec fondles his ring before looking up at her like a rabbit in a trap. *How odd*, she thinks, *that a predator can look trapped*.

She smirks at the two. "Hi, honey, did you miss me? Who's your friend?"

Chapter 35

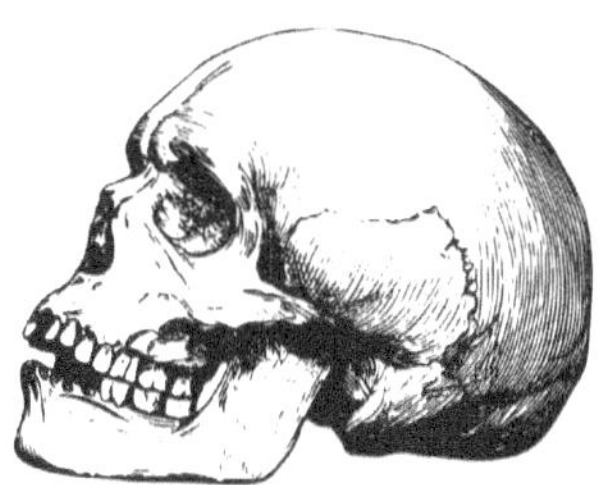

WHEN PHILIP ARRIVES, ALEC resists the overwhelming urge to sprint out of the restaurant, grab Azalea, and find a vehicle—closed lot or not. Only the knowledge of Philip and Michael's bitter rivalry keeps him seated, feigning composure. Panic, after all, is a weakness he cannot afford to reveal.

Philip perches on Alec's table, directly next to where Azalea sat only seconds before.

"Remember the Teachings," Philip whispers, his breath cold against Alec's ear. Alec clenches his teeth, refusing to flinch.

It's a small mercy that wraiths cannot use their gifts on one another. Otherwise, Philip would catch the terror spiking through Alec or the dangerous truth of his feelings for Azalea. Alec tries to recall Philip's specific gift. Whatever it is, any discovery could be disastrous.

"Follow the Rules," Alec hisses in response. The chance that Philip was working with Michael was slim, but he's still a Rule following member of the family. The risk that Philip might learn of his weakness and exploit it, to both his and Azalea's detriment, weighs heavy in his limbs.

Philip clasps Alec's shoulder, his grin wide and sharp as broken glass. "Long time no see, ya bastard. Where've you been hiding?"

"Hunting," he retorts, leaning into the practiced mask of indifference. "Why else traverse this realm?"

Philip gestures to the empty seat Azalea previously occupied. "That sweet little daisy you were just speaking with, for one."

"There is sport in that," Alec says carefully. The game of romancing a human to crush their spirits and then take their souls is popular, one Michael often enjoyed. But it burned something within Alec when good souled humans were played with, and he hadn't engaged in a millennium.

Philip chuckles again, but it's dry. "Like old times with you and that son of a bitch sire of yours."

"He taught me well," Alec says, his words clipped.

"Aye, I do. And how is Michael?" Philip growls Michael's name. Alec releases a quiet breath of relief. At least their rivalry must still exist, that means there's no chance Philip seeks them as Michael's agent.

"Sowing chaos somewhere." Alec allows a mean smirk to grace his lips, the false one he saves for speaking with the family. "Did he fail to call upon you?"

"Pull the other one," Philip grunts. "Seeing him before the next century would be too soon."

Philip's gaze slides past Alec, and a wicked grin splits his face. Alec doesn't need to look to know who's caught Philip's attention. His pulse hammers—Azalea.

"Your treat's back. Want I give her a little compulsion to ease things?" Philip offers, his tone dripping with mockery.

"I think not," he says with false nonchalance. If his heart could, it would cease beating at this very moment—if Philip can manipulate much like Michael, he may read her memories too. "It isn't much of a game if you cheat."

"We play different games," Philip says. "The take and break is more fun when they're mindlessly compliant until that last second."

"It isn't as thrilling if they don't fight you to the end," Alec argues, eyes on Azalea. Philip snorts.

"The thrill is in the fight," Alec counters, his eyes fixed on Azalea as she marches toward them.

"Hi, honey, did you miss me? Who's your friend?" Her voice is light, but Alec catches the sharp edge beneath it.

Philip's grin sharpens, his gaze dragging over Azalea in a way that makes Alec's fingers twitch. "A bold bird," Philip muses, his tone dangerously amused.

Alec stands quickly, knocking the table away. The server throws off the yeasty aroma of annoyance, but he ignores it. The longer Philip is near Azalea, the more likely they'll be discovered. "We must be off, Philip." He holds out a hand that the other wraith shakes warily. "Happy hunting."

Philip raises a single brow, his smirk unchanging. "You too."

Without another word, Alec ushers Azalea from the restaurant, his grip firm on her arm. She protests only long enough to snatch a handful of mozzarella sticks before they leave. He doesn't let go until they're locked inside their hotel room, the armoire shoved against the door. Only then does he release the tension in his bones.

But the relief is fleeting—he may have won the battle by sacrificing the war.

Alec presses his fingers to his closed eyes until spots appear. If Philip is gifted as Alec suspects—like Michael who can read someone's history—he may have read her, learning damaging information from her mind in the few seconds they interacted: Alec's weakness for her, his confession and explanation of what he was. He kept Azalea safe from Michael or any gameplay by Philip, at the loss of *his* safety. His fingers claw at his cheekbones at the realization.

Philip may know of Alec's breaches, and he'd be within his rights, indeed—his duty—to report them. The Amanas are no longer a refuge to wait out Michael—he may need to wait out Philip.

Perhaps after Azalea's... demise, he could frame it as a ploy, a tactic to make her fall harder before taking her soul. It's a lie they might believe, and no one else would think twice of his lying to her. At least he would keep his identity and life with the family that way. Else, he'd have lost her to the ravages of time *and* earned a vicious punishment for his trouble.

The thought makes him sick. He leans against the wall, dropping his hands to his side and slamming his head against the drywall until dust coats his hair.

Fates, he *is* as repulsive as he told Azalea he was. Here he is bargaining away his possible punishment after her death.

"This is supposed to be about me," the woman he loves says waspishly. *How right she is.* His sparking eyes trail to her form standing with her back to him, arms crossed around herself, the pickled scent of frustration in the air.

"You're angry with me," he says, moving towards her and shaking the evidence of his panic from his dark locks.

She spins to face him and jabs her pointer finger near his throat. "That right there. Stop that. No more reading me. It's a breach of privacy. If I want you to know how I'm feeling, I'll tell you. Deal?"

He nods, chastened, his hand aborting its movement toward her. She softens, sitting on the bed and patting the space beside her.

"We're going to talk to each other, like adults—adult people and adult wraiths, and finish our conversation from dinner. No more secrets, no more cryptic warnings. You hear me?"

He nods again, the bucket of his worries overflowing with more potential Rule breaks.

"Philip is another wraith," he begins, his voice low. "I didn't mean what I said about wanting you to hurt. You *must* believe me. I would never want you to be anything but what you are. Compulsion is not a gift I have nor one I could ever allow to be used on you."

Azalea runs a hand through her hair, a move that strikes him as achingly familiar, though he can't recall why. "I'm not mad about Philip," she says, her tone sharp but steady. "Say or do whatever you need to keep our cover. What's pissing me off is how you keep me in the dark. I need to know why we're running, what you're supposedly protecting me from—or maybe I—"

"You—you'd leave?" His voice cracks, his heart clenching at the mere suggestion. Spilled water cannot return to the jug, and he's already shattered the Rules for her, risking everything he's ever known for a fleeting chance at happiness. If she were to leave now... He can't bear the thought.

"You must believe me," he pleads. "The danger is real. Do not abandon me. I would endure a thousand deaths, take any punishment given, to see you happy, to keep you safe—if only you stay."

She pats the bed beside her with an exasperated huff, and he's at her side in an instant. Her hands find his, gently prying open his clenched fists to intertwine their fingers.

"Okay, Mr. Melodrama, calm down," she says, her tone softening. "Let's take this in pieces. You keep going on about punishments and protecting me, but that means nothing unless I understand what's actually happening. What *we're* up against."

Her unwavering gaze pierces through his doubts, and for a moment, he feels the weight of her trust like a physical thing. It bolsters him, even as it terrifies him. He's never been trusted like this before, never been someone's anchor. The thought tightens his chest. He can't let her down.

He nods, closing his eyes as he prepares to commit himself to the path he chose. "I will explain everything."

But that's easier said than done. Alec would never convert a human, meaning he was never required to carry on the Teachings or explain the Rules. He struggles to remember how Michael explained it to him in the moments after his changing. He starts at the beginning. "I am a wraith."

Azalea drops her head backward to groan at the bland ceiling. "You told me this already. You're a wraith, you eat souls, blah blah blah. Get to the point."

"We don't *eat* souls," he says, maligned. He stares at his yellowed ring, the symbol of what he is. "You must understand, I have never shared this with another. It goes against all my instincts and the Teachings I live by."

She shifts closer, tucking herself under his arm and trailing her fingers lightly over his chest. "Then we'll go slow," she says. "Start with the 'Teachings.'"

He takes comfort from her touch and begins anew, closing his eyes and organizing his thoughts. "As a wraith, we carry on the Teachings of the Elders before us. We live by the Rules, of which there are three." His handwriting flashes behind his closed eyes. "The First Rule: Never show weakness. The Second Rule: Protect the secrecy of our kind. The Third Rule: Never betray one of our own."

She hums thoughtfully. "The Second and Third I get, but the first is ludicrous. What scale are we looking at for weakness? And who decides what's weak?"

He clears his throat. The nebulous quality of the Rules seemed typical for the family, something he'd not questioned since he was a young wraith. "The Council," he explains. "They are the governing body of our kind, responsible for enforcing the Rules and providing guidance under the Teachings. I—I spent most of my second life as a rover, carrying out their punishments for Rule breakers."

She grumbles into his chest. "I have some thoughts on these Rules."

"I've no doubt you do." He chances offering more information, so she might understand the gravity of his situation. "This discussion is a breach of the Second. But they would consider my feelings for you a breach of the First."

"Lucky me," she says as her fingers skim down to his navel and traipse across the edge of his pants. "What's the consequence for breaking those Rules?"

"Pain," he whispers. "Death or exile sometimes."

"I thought you were immortal," she says perplexed.

He swallows hard, sluicing off the thoughts of the pain that could await him, the loss that is exile. "I am functionally immortal, as long as I keep stealing souls. If I don't, I'll weaken and age to the state I'd be in had I remained human. But there are ways to harm us with magical strength and one way to kill us. The Council would send rovers after me and decide my punishment later."

Her fingers pause for a moment before resuming their path. "So you're like a vampire—broody and immortal, needing something from humans to survive."

"An apt comparison," he concedes. "In your people's folklore, we are more of a cross-between the fictional vampire and ghoul. We have magical gifts after conversion to aid in hunting souls. We haven't died but remain in the condition we were in when we were converted." It's an incredibly painful process that Alec can't recall with specificity, the act occurring thousands of years ago. It involves the removal and reconfiguration of a human's body. The Historian would know, not that Alec can call upon him to ask, not that Azalea will ever need to know the specifics.

She lifts her head, eyes sparkling. "You're a walking fantasy novel. So—no vampires or ghouls, but are there other creatures that are real?"

"There are," he admits. "Wraiths are ruling class, with the lesser beings below."

"And humans? Where do we rank in this hierarchy?"

"They aren't included," he says softly. "You're a food source."

She stiffens, pulling away, but his arms tighten around her reflexively. His body acts on instinct, hoping to hold her long enough for her to forget his loathsome truths.

"Calm down," she says, wiggling until she's more comfortable. "I'm not going anywhere. I must be pretty special if humans are just food to you."

"You are."

Her lips curl into a smile against his neck and her wiggling increases. The teasing feeling migrates south, a temptation he must resist. With reluctance, he releases her to sit beside her on the bed.

"We can't," he reminds her, letting his ardor cool.

She huffs in frustration. "Fine. So, let me get this straight—you falling for me and telling me what you are means you've broken two Rules, and now the Council is after you?"

"No," he corrects. "The Council doesn't know. But if Philip learned anything damning, they might soon."

"But that just happen—"

"Michael seeks us, and he's as far away from the Council as one could be, given his own flouting of the Rules. But he's responsible for teaching me and guiding me through the Rules. He will do what he can to help me."

"Then why are we running from him?" Azalea asks with raised brows. "If he's going to help you, we should just go find him. He'll probably be somewhere better than the Amanas."

He closes his eyes to avoid the eager expression on her face. "You don't understand. He will attempt to help me in following the Rules—Rules he taught me and Rules he knows I cherished. Rules I have broken. In his mind, the only way he could conceive of protecting me is by removing the temptation of you entirely."

Her expression shifts, the realization dawning on her. "By 'remove,' you mean—"

"Yes," he says, his voice a broken whisper.

After all, that's Michael's modus operandi. And wraiths don't change.

Chapter 36

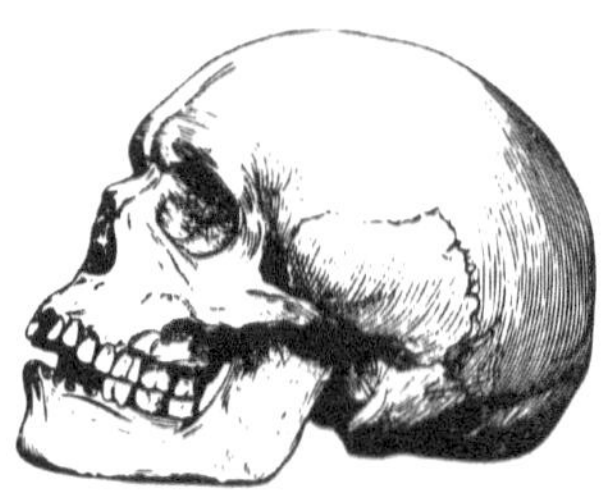

Morning finds Alec pacing the cramped hotel room, waiting for the first light of dawn and the opening of the car dealership. For hours, he's been planning: they'll hide in the Amanas, avoid attention, and bide their time until Michael's interest wanes and he can gauge the extent of Philip's gift. Perhaps they'll remain hidden there for the entirety of Azalea's life.

Azalea nodded off soon after their conversation and plotting, and he spent the smallest hours watching her sleep. She lies on her back, her blonde hair splayed across the pillow, her body melded into the colored sheets. He grabs his own hand to keep from trying to caressing her soft skin.

"That's a little creepy," she mumbles, her smoky voice thick with sleep. Her eyes flutter open. "How long have you been watching me? Actually, forget it. I don't want to know."

He sits beside her, shoving his hands into his lap to keep them from trembling. With a tired sigh, she opens her arms, and he falls into her embrace without hesitation.

"You're like a wiggly little puppy," she teases, her fingers tangling gently in his hair. "Always wanting to be near me and touched."

"I'm unused to physical contact that isn't painful or destructive," he murmurs into the warm crook of her neck. "Aside from other wraiths—who are incapable of softness—I've only touched others to steal their souls or deliver punishment. To touch you, to be touched by you, in kindness... it's a revelation."

This is why he can't give her up, Rule break or no.

Something smug sparks in her as she strokes his back with lazy fingers. "Who would've thought Azalea Cross could turn a strong, touch-starved, immortal wraith into a cuddly mess with a little light petting?"

His body stiffens slightly when her tone shifts, teasing laced with intent. "You know," she says, "if you're so worried about Michael hurting me and the Council punishing you, the easiest solution is to convert me."

He withdraws from her arms. "I've told you; I can't do that." Pain and exile are acceptable consequences to keeping her humanity intact; he'd deserve them both if he tried anything else.

Her brow arches as she props herself up on an elbow. "So, what's the plan then? Just run forever?"

"No," he says, the soothing sensations from her touch vanishing. "In time, he'll give up and go back to his debauchery. At that point, you and I will be settled in a province so small and dull he'll never find us."

She stares at him wide-eyed. "I just left one shit-hole town, Alec. I'm not going to another one, especially for someone as awful as Michael."

"Do you think you are the only one sacrificing? I am giving up my home, my family, *everything* I am for you for your lifetime," he says, scowling. "Living a quiet life with you in hiding is our best hope in staying together and safe."

She sits up, the blanket pooling around her waist and offering him the skin on her shoulders below her loose shirt. "I didn't ask you to sacrifice all that. That's on you."

"I simply wish to keep you safe."

Azalea tosses herself back on the bed. "And I'm saying, I'm willing to do whatever it takes, which includes becoming a wraith. I think I'd like it."

"You're wrong," he mutters, the words pained and final. But the sincerity in her tone tugs at him, forcing him to consider the unthinkable. "Thank you," he adds, his voice softening. "For being willing. Though... there may be another way."

The trill of her phone cuts through the tension, drawing both their attention. Azalea groans, rolling over to rummage through yesterday's clothes. As she digs for the phone, Alec's mind races with the implications of what he's just said, what it could mean for both of them—and whether it's a path he's truly willing to take.

Chapter 37

It's barely seven, and Azzie's patience is already razor-thin. The sweet feelings she had when Alec snuggled up to her like some tragic, touch-starved Adonis, evaporated the moment he started his spiel about all he'd sacrificed. Doesn't he realize what she's giving up by chasing after him? She doesn't even have time to stew properly before her phone vibrates with Eli's name.

"Azalea?" His voice crackles through her cheap cell phone speaker, irritating her further. "Where are you?"

"None of your business," she hisses. "What, are you drunk and need a ride? Too bad, I took the truck."

"I'm aware," Eli says evenly. He doesn't sound angry—more resigned, which feels worse. "Annoyingly, I'm completely sober. Otherwise, I'd probably be acting like you right now. But there's stuff I need to handle, and it can't involve booze."

She smirks. Hopefully, that means he took the tip in her note.

"Good for you. Get yourself a one-day pin and stop calling." She hangs up the phone. She's never done that, but a mean sense of accomplishment suffuses her when she does.

"Is everything alright?" Alec asks as her phone rings again.

She answers it with a terse, "What?"

"Come home," Eli says. "You leaving messed up everything. There are things you don't understand, and you *really* need to come home so we can get this done together."

"No," she spits. "I'm finally doing something for myself. You, Dad, and everyone else can deal with it."

Alec watches her with those bright flint-like eyes. She rolls hers in response and mimes something rude at the phone.

"Azalea, Az, listen to me. Listen to how responsible I'm being. Isn't that weird? Isn't it weird that *I'm* the reliable one? This isn't you, Az. I mean, you took the truck!"

"Damn right, I took the truck." Her cheeks flush hot as anger bubbles beneath her skin. "I *am* acting like you for once," she snarls. "I'm doing whatever I want, whenever I want it, however I want it without regard for anyone else."

"Goddamn it," Eli says. His voice raises. "Yes—you are. That's the point! You're acting like me and I'm acting like you! Michael warned me to hurry, but I thought we had more time—"

"Michael?" Her voice sharpens, her gaze snapping to Alec. "Alec's friend Michael?" Even saying the name makes her stomach churn—she dislikes even the thought of him.

"What? Yes, Alec's friend."

Alec stands, his body going rigid as his expression hardens into something icy and focused.

"Is he with you?" she asks. An unwelcome shiver of fear lances through her.

"No. He went home to figure out how we fix your screwup—"

She doesn't let him finish, slamming the phone shut and flinging it across the room. It lands with a dull thud against the carpet, but the act does nothing to dislodge the knot forming in her gut.

"What did he say?" Alec's voice is taut, like a wire pulled too tight.

"He's—he's been hanging out with Michael."

Chapter 38

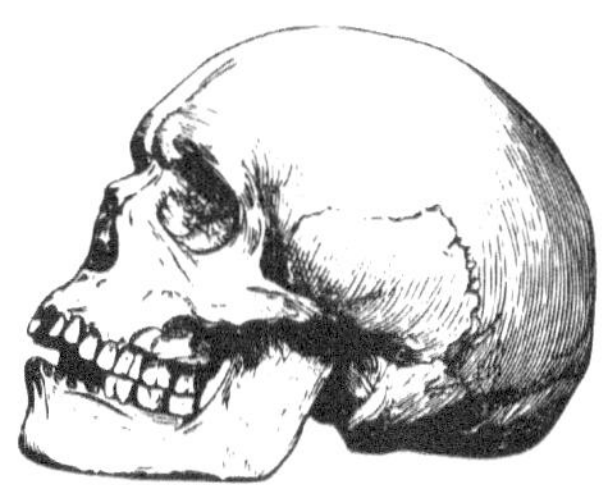

SHOCK SPILLS OUT OF Azalea like water overflowing a basin, overtaking the acrid anger she'd been radiating moments before. The scents of her emotions switch faster than an oar slices through a stream.

"What if I wasn't the target, but Eli was?" she asks, her eyes wide. One corner of her mouth twitches upward, only to collapse into a frown.

Alec shakes his head. "No, that makes little sense. Michael is determined to help me, how would targeting Eli do so?" Even as he says it, he can't ignore how well it fits Michael's love for twisted games and layered revenge. Targeting Eli might be Michael's way of finishing Alec's hunt while sending a message about Alec's weakness.

Azalea nods to herself, her breathing steadying as she processes. "I'm betting he's already done it."

Alec rubs her wrists to give her the comfort she once showed him. "You believe Michael has already stolen Eli's soul? Based on what evidence?"

She pulls her hands free, counting on her fingers. "One, Eli said Michael already went home. Why would he leave if he hadn't taken Eli's soul? If Eli wasn't the target, Michael would still be out here looking for us. Two, Eli's been acting weird—he actually said he was being 'responsible,' like me, which is so not him. Three, we're twins. I just have this feeling. We have to find Michael."

"None of those reasons convince me that Eli is the target or that we should compromise your safety," he retorts. A soulless Eli could only help Azalea, with or without Michael's threats. Alec counts on his own trembling fingers, nearly shaking the ring from his hand. "One, Michael is a liar—it's what wraiths do. Two, a soulless person doesn't become better; they become less—less vile, less aggressive, less driven. Three, feelings lie."

She crosses her arms with a pout. "A soulless Eli acting less selfish *could* mean better. How do you know it's not a possibility?"

He gapes at her. The memory of the depth of depravity within Eli's soul remains with him. There is no chance that losing it would *give* Eli the humanity he lacks. It would make him nothing. "Because he no longer has a *soul*. He'd be empty—neither good nor bad. What else could happen?"

Her chin lifts defiantly. "You don't have a soul, right? And you're not some mindless husk."

He covers his face with his hands, muffling his words. After the night before, she knows much about him and the family, but in the broad world of knowledge, so little. "Physically, I have had lots of souls," he says, though the one he has will surely run out simply due to stress. "But no, I'm unsure what happened to my original soul. We are not human—our souls don't guide us. We behave the way we do because of what we are, not because of our souls."

Her eyes narrow. "You don't have a soul, but you're still trying to protect me and act responsibly. Why couldn't Eli be doing the same?"

"You cannot subscribe human sensibilities to me," he replies. "You have your humanity, your *soul*, to guide you and confirm you're making the right choices. I have none of that. I may not be a merciless monster at this moment, but I carried on that way for centuries, like the rest of my brethren. It was only in the last thousand years that I gained a sense of perspective. And it began to protect the Rules, given my commitment to enforce them. Acting like a typical wraith draws attention." Though the realization that he was loathsome began much earlier, when he realized he couldn't burn out his regrets with death.

"You're telling me the *only* reason you're not snatching my soul and going crazy-face soul-snatcher is because you want to avoid attention?"

"Of course not! I also care for you." His eyes fall. Guilt carried him for centuries too.

"There you go." She folds her arms triumphantly. "Eli's soul is gone, and instead of being empty, he's thinking about someone other than himself for once. Because he cares for me."

He clenches his fists until his knuckles ache and the bands of his ring imprint against his skin. Not since Michael attempted to convince oil-covered partiers that the best game involved *fire* had he experienced a more ludicrous conversation. And there, the chosen plan to extinguish the fire was dunking the guests in vats of wine rather than water. "Then we should leave him be."

"We can't just give in and *let* Michael win." She tosses her hands skyward. "Hell, why is Michael even bothering with Eli?"

The fight drains from Alec, his shoulders slumping under the weight of her accusations and his own guilt. "I think I know. I chose Eli as my prey." He lowers his head. "I should have told you sooner—"

Azalea sits beside him, and he flinches, bracing for anger. But instead of a storm of emotion, she remains calm. "You were going to take Eli's soul?" she asks. When he nods, she chuckles. "Well, that explains your obsession with finding him."

"I am sorry, Azalea," he says, his voice raw. "I'll understand if you no longer wish to be with me romantically, but please don't leave. I can't guarantee your safety if you do."

She places a hand on his thigh and leans her head against his shoulder. "I'm not planning on leaving."

His heart, though unbeating, feels heavy. He rests his head atop hers. "I told you I was a monster."

"Well, the *human* thing would be to fix your mistake," she mutters.

"How do I do that?"

"Take me to Michael," she says, as if it is obvious.

At the thought, he lifts his head to stare at the covered mirror, imagining Michael might appear at any second. When no licentious wraith claws from behind the cloth, he leans back into her. "How would that fix my mistake? If you're the target, I'm delivering you to him on a metaphorical silver platter. If Eli was the target, Michael already stole his soul according to you, and we can do nothing."

She pulls away to frown at him. "There's no way to give someone their soul back? Not even to try?"

"Of course not," he answers automatically, flexing his fists. It brings his attention to his ring. She catches the movement as he studies it.

"What?" She grabs his hand and pokes the light amber jewel. He struggles to restrain a shudder. "What made your face look like that? Your ring?"

He covers it protectively. "It's a manifestation of our soul vessel, a talisman."

Her eyes gleam. "The souls are tied to the talisman? Then we destroy it. What kind does Michael have?"

"A pocket watch," he says, musing over the possibility. There's no guarantee destroying the talisman would restore the soul, but it might.

She stands again to pack up the few items she removed from her satchel. "There we go. We destroy it and get my brother's soul back."

He twists the ring around his finger while he shakes his head. "It may do nothing; it may simply anger Michael further. And it assumes he has your brother's soul already."

"It's our best option. Worst-case scenario, we've surprised him," she says in a distracted tone, pulling out various pieces of clothing and repacking them into her threadbare bag.

"Worst-case scenario," Alec growls, "you're dead."

"No, listen," she says, pulling out his favorite green shirt and swapping it for the one she slept in the night before. "He expects you to be running from him. If we go to him, we'll have the upper hand. He can't do anything to me while you're there, you told me you're the best enforcer. And if he took Eli's soul, we could get it back or make him pay for doing it."

"This is absurd." He presses his palms into his eyes, the pressure a poor substitute for calming his frayed nerves. "You cannot seriously believe—"

"You have to fix this," she says, scowling. "If you hadn't chosen his soul and made us run, he'd be safe. We have to do this."

His head drops to his chest. Guilt still carries him. "But—we cannot guess where he is."

A sly smile spreads across her lips. "Eli said he went home. I assume that means the wraith world. You must know where he lives."

His nails bite harder into his palms. Without a true mirror in Rockton, Michael's whereabouts can be narrowed down, but the danger is astronomical. By fixing the problem, he may make it much worse. "There are many places he could call home, making this the very definition of a fool's errand."

"What's the closest one to Rockton House?"

"Underneath Chicago," he says through gritted teeth.

Chapter 39

At Azzie's insistence—and her not-so-subtle reminder that Alec had vowed to 'deny her nothing'—they plan to visit the wraith realm. It's underhanded and duplicitous, something Eli would do, but she's determined to get there and be converted somehow. That it might save her brother is an inadvertent perk, but it's enough to convince the guilt-ridden Alec to take her.

Guilt is a powerful motivator, and she's finally in the position of using it against someone rather than having it used against her.

Regardless, with or without a soul, Eli would be fine. Or, if he's not, he isn't her problem anymore.

She explains the plan to Alec as they snuggle on the hotel bed before checking out. They'll go to the wraith city, Selessen, as Alec called it, and find Michael. Alec will distract him while she steals the pocket watch. She watched Eli pilfer trinkets from the Lonetree convenience store enough, she's sure the skills will transfer. If Michael has Eli's soul, they'll bargain the watch back for it and for never bothering the two again. If he doesn't, they'll do the same thing just without the soul swap. Either way, she won't need to hide in some tiny town.

But all of that is a smokescreen for the actual plan, which remains hidden deep inside, below thoughts of travel and adventure and emotions Alec might discover. After she proves she can handle the wraith realm and the dangers of being a wraith, she'll convince Alec to convert her. Then, she can put Eli and the rest of her past life out of her mind—where they belong. She'll have control over her own life—circumstances, wealth, and family won't be able to hold her down anymore.

Before they check out of the hotel, Alec retrieves what looks like a child's chemistry set from his bag. She watches with fascination as he carefully mixes powders and liquids, creating four vials in varying colors—two yellow, one black, and one a pale teal.

Curiosity gets the better of her, and she picks up a small container of red dust that smells like how funerals feel. Alec snatches it from her hands with a frown. "Be careful. That can melt skin." He places it gingerly back into its pocket and continues packing up his concoctions.

She motions to the set. "What is all this?"

He hesitates before answering, "It—it is an alchemy set."

Her eyebrows shoot up. "Like, turning lead into gold? That explains the coins." She files that bit of knowledge away for later. If alchemy is real, she's learning it the moment she gets the chance.

"Yes. Although I thought humans were unaware of such feats of nature," he mutters, avoiding her gaze.

"We don't. It's like a legend." She grins and attempts to snag the kit again, but he shoves it into his bag before she touches it. "Can I make something?" she asks, half-joking but hopeful.

His eyes flash. "It is... not something I may share."

She crosses her arms and smirks. "Is this one of those Rules? I thought you'd decided to screw the Rules since you, you know, wanted to screw me."

His expression twists in a mix of offense and embarrassment. "What I feel for you transcends physical pleasure. Indeed, I—"

"Calm down," she huffs. "It was a joke. You get the gist though."

"I suppose, though your increased use of bawdy humor is a surprise." He stares down at the vials, still looking flustered. "And to consistently and repeatedly take active steps to breach the Rules is—more difficult than I thought. I intended to breach them only as much as I must."

She softens her stance, sensing she's pushed enough for now. "How about baby steps, like last night? You let me in a little at a time, and I'll be... sensitive to your internal struggle."

His shoulders relax, and a shy smile graces his lips. She beams back, savoring the moment. If her high school classmates could see her now—with her handsome, socially awkward, centuries-old wraith who hung on her every word—they'd never believe it.

"First baby step. Tell me what's in the vials at least?" She smiles through clenched teeth.

Conflict runs over his face before he nods again, this one more determined. "Insurance," he says.

She suppresses a groan. "Okay, a bigger step than that."

He hesitates, but after a moment's pause, he picks them up and explains. "The yellow is insurance for you. The black, for both of us, but only in a worst case scenario. And the teal..." He trails off, rubbing a thumb along the smooth glass. "The teal is insurance against Michael."

Chapter 40

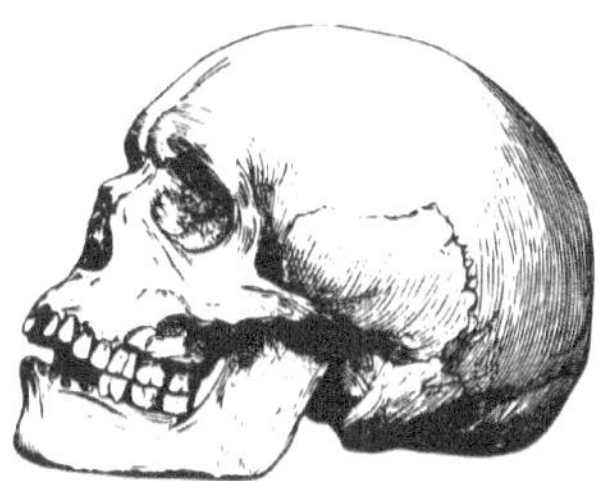

As soon as Alec finishes packing his alchemical creations, they purchase a new vehicle and drive the short distance from Davenport to Chicago. Although he will never convert Azalea, he can't help but wonder how much easier the journey would be if she had supernatural speed. Perhaps if he had carried her the twenty-minute sprint to the Amanas the night before, they wouldn't now be sitting on the cusp of Selessen and all the dangers it will bring. Hindsight, however, is a cruel master.

Azalea might have a quote that fit the occasion, but she remains focused on devouring 'deep-dish pizza.'

He watches Azalea eat to keep his mind off the teal elixir, which would do more than break a Rule. It would be more than choosing the lesser of two weaknesses, like when he chose Azalea.

He's rehearsed the justification for it countless times: if Michael poses too great a threat to Azalea, Alec will use it. But the cost isn't just a breach of the Rules; it's the annihilation of everything he's clung to for centuries. The elixir isn't just a weapon—it's a reckoning. Would that exile be bearable with Azalea at his side? Or would he lose her too, the truth of his monstrousness finally breaking whatever connection they've built?

He clenches his jaw and pushes the thoughts away. The poison is a last resort, locked behind the fragile dam of his will. For now, he focuses on her. She's a radiant, living thing, charming in her uninhibited delight over something as simple as pizza. She's utterly herself, and yet there's a surety in her now that wasn't there before. Her confidence increased and waffling emotions vanished the moment they left Lonetree, a change he isn't sure he can attribute to himself. Her increased composure, coupled with his desire to please her and 'fix what he broke,' are why he resignedly agreed to travel to Chicago.

She had been enthralled by the city, just as she now is by the pizza. But her enchantment with the idea of Selessen leaves him uneasy. If he had his way, they would be hiding in the pastoral safety of the Amanas, not venturing into the lion's den. Relationships between humans and wraiths always end in devastation, and keeping her shielded from his kind feels like the only way they stand a chance.

"Once we reach our destination, you must do everything I say," he says as she finishes her food. "No talking out of turn or causing scenes. That tongue of yours may get us in trouble."

She bites her lip around a grin. "You didn't mind my tongue two days ago."

If Alec's blood flowed, his cheeks would heat. "I mean it," he says, forcing his lips to remain a flat line. "One wrong move and you are as good as destroyed."

Azalea appears to sober. "I get it. How will I fit in with your kind? Someone only needs to read me, and they'll realize I'm human, right?" She wipes her hands on some provided tissue. "We should talk about you turning me again."

"No." His answer is quick.

"I mean it," she echoes in his serious tone. "It's dangerous and I'm okay with being changed—"

"I am not, Azalea. That won't happen. I will not turn you." He presses his fingers over his eyes tightly. "This is dangerous enough and I am not willing to lose you."

"You wouldn't *lose* me," she mutters to the table.

"I could," he says, eyes opening wide. "I could lose the you that you are. Your entire humanity gone." He snaps his fingers for emphasis.

"You don't know that—"

"Even the best person, when the ramifications of mortality no longer affect them, can change. Mortal laws won't apply to you, only the Council's. As a bastion of goodness with unlimited time, I can only *imagine* your altruistic goals. You wish to reduce homelessness and poverty? Make gold or steal it. No one will stop you from using it how you'd like if you keep your otherworldliness hidden. You want to lessen crime, protect people? After a century, killing would-be criminals sounds quite reasonable. As a human, you have choices, with consequences—societal, legal, spiritual, physical—that we don't."

Her expression pinches. "Then what the hell was that spiel last night about these Rules and how awful they are, and how terrible things could be for you if you don't follow them? That's no different."

"It's entirely different," he says, voice raising for emphasis. "Those Rules exist to keep us strong, to keep us powerful over those lesser than us, not to keep us moral. It took me centuries to understand that, and to realize the gift we lack." He closes his eyes again. "We haven't even *considered* the physical reactions. What if your body can't survive the change? Not everyone can and I can't lose you so soon."

Her anger grazes him, and he falters. "You're angry that I want to protect you?" he asks.

She lifts her head to stare at him with narrowed eyes. "You promised you wouldn't read me."

"I did nothing intentionally. I can't help that I catch what you broadcast. I can only involuntarily pick up your strongest emotions," he says. "Which leads me to my question: *what* in this conversation made you this angry?"

She deflates, staring back at the table, but the anger remains potent in the surrounding air. "I guess I'm just stressed."

That he can understand. The entire endeavor is a nightmare, and they've done nothing yet. He places palm up on the table and asks her to take it.

She does but not without rolling her eyes. "I'm trying to be helpful," she says, sounding petulant, "because someone could realize I'm not a wraith."

Alec drops her hand with regret and busies himself opening his satchel and pulling out the yellow elixir he created that morning. He passes it over to her.

She rolls it in her palm before holding it up to the light. It looks like sunshine in a bottle, ironic given its normal uses. "My 'insurance?'"

"This avoids the need for conversion. It's a tonic that should hide your true state for a time. Wraiths use it as a recreational drug. It acts to enhance the souls we've collected, heightening our skills and behaviors."

"Like overclocking a computer."

He holds out his hand for the vial, but she keeps it firm in her grasp. The sugary eagerness on her face scents the surrounding air, but he refrains from commenting to avoid another argument. "I'm unfamiliar with the reference. In a human, it should enhance your own soul, making it appear that you are carrying more than one, which is common for wraiths."

Although *he* carries only one, which will fade within years. But no one could look in his eyes and think he's anything other than a wraith. "If nothing else, it should buy us enough time to flee from anyone asking questions."

"How long does it last?"

"It will wear off after about four hours." She hands it back with a sigh and he replaces in his satchel for safekeeping. "I will dose it to you only when necessary."

The plan is dangerous, reckless, and teetering on the edge of disaster. Yet, as she flashes him a small, confident smile, he knows he'll do whatever it takes to keep her safe. Even if it means breaking every Rule.

Chapter 41

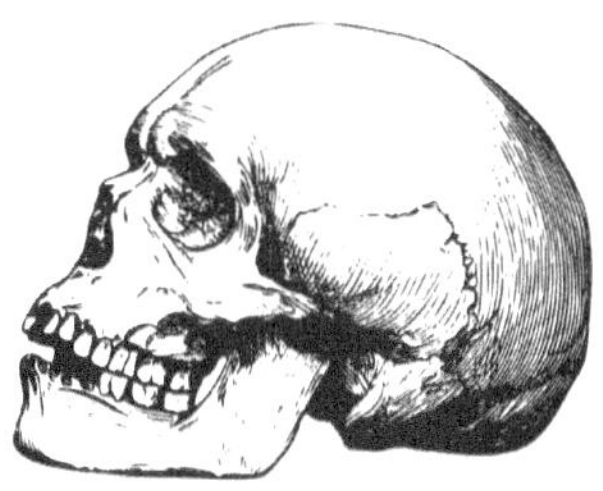

Azalea convinces him to visit one more location before they travel to Selessen, dragging him to an enormous park bustling with life. The midday sun casts long shadows over the manicured grass, and humans roam freely, laughing and snapping photos. Alec stays close, his eyes darting to every shadow and corner, while Azalea strides ahead, fearless and enchanted.

She pauses at two towering fountains, their carved faces spitting arcs of water that shimmer in the light. Tourists crowd around, some tossing coins, others simply staring in awe. Azalea grins, leaning over the fountain's edge to catch a closer look at the intricate stonework. Alec watches her indulgently, though his attention drifts to a gleaming, mirror-like structure in the distance.

The strange monument reflects the sunlight in a way that prickles at his skin. It's unlike anything he's seen in the human realm, the smooth surface eerily similar to the portals found in wraith cities. Those portals act as grand switchboards, connecting their subterranean world to countless destinations.

"I've heard it's called the Bean," Azalea says when she notices his gaze. "I think it's named the Cloud Gate, but—"

"Oh, that's clever," he says, suppressing a slight laugh. "I had heard rumblings but never knew someone was idiotic enough to try it."

She furrows her brows. "What are you talking about?"

"The Cloud Gate is an actual gate—a portal to Selessen," he explains, his tone laced with both amusement and irritation. "The Council mentioned it to me twenty years ago. One of our own had the audacity to create a portal disguised as a human art installation. They instructed me to prepare for swift punishment should it expose our existence. I hadn't heard of it since and assumed the project was abandoned."

"That's how we're getting there? That's awesome," she says, dragging him from the fountain towers towards the reflective structure. Her arm slips around his waist as she glances up at him. "How does it work?"

Wary of the nearby tourists who may eavesdrop, he leans closer and whispers in her ear. "Mirrors are our portals, as you know. True mirrors are keyed to accept travel to any other true mirror by touching a talisman to it. I could stand in my home and appear in any mirror in the world, both above and below, so long as it is also a keyed mirror. Other reflective surfaces or first-surface mirrors, like the Cloud Gate, can only be keyed to travel to one destination. I know of one portal here in Chicago to Selessen. *This* is new."

"Is that how you knew Michael would go to Chicago?" she whispers.

He nods. "There are only a few portals to wraith cities in North America. Unless Michael acquires his own mirror, he must use the public portals to get to and from the Asheville area. The next closest first-surface mirror is under Montreal, but takes an additional hour of travel. Other than the mirror I destroyed before we left, the closest above-ground true mirror Michael could use to travel anywhere is in Mexico City."

"Why there?"

"Wraiths have a long history, which meant we had an entire world to explore. Mexico City, as it is now named, is the oldest capital city in North America and it caught our interest such that we created our own city beneath it, Martalk."

They are almost at the portal now. "You say that like you were there," Azalea whispers.

He flits his gaze to her before returning to study the large mirror-like surface in front of him. "I wasn't exaggerating when I spoke of my years. My first life ended before the Roman Republic became an Empire."

She remains quiet as he moves them into position. After eyeing the open space around them, he taps his ring to the surface of the structure and feels the telltale 'give' on the surface that confirms its portal status.

"I've never heard of a human traveling by mirror before," he says, narrowing his gaze at the tourists nearby. "Keep ahold of me for as long as you can and walk through first. I may need to push you through, to get the speed necessary to avoid detection. Then, I'll follow."

Azalea squares her shoulders and takes his hand, lacing their fingers together. "Let's do this."

A momentary gap in the crowd opens, and Alec moves them into position. He presses his ring against the portal, whispering a silent prayer to the Fates. And then he pushes.

Chapter 42

AZZIE LANDS HARD ON her back in the dirt, groaning as an unnatural shudder ripples through her body. It's like she's been dunked through a waterfall of pudding—gloopy, heavy, and gross. Worse still is the metallic film lingering on her skin and the tinny taste clinging to her teeth, as if she'd been chewing on aluminum. Behind her looms a tarnished, carnival-funhouse version of the Cloud Gate, dulled and streaked with grime.

Alec offers his hand, pulling her to her feet. His fingers brush lightly down her sides as he assesses her condition. "All limbs still attached," she says, running her tongue over her teeth to dispel the taste. "Though I could use a mint."

"I am thankful that it worked," he says, exhaling deeply. "We have conquered the first hurdle. Onto the next in this foolhardy plan."

Ignoring his brooding tone, she dusts off the dirt clinging to her knees and runs her fingers through her hair, rearranging it until it resembles the style she perfected yesterday. Probably even better now. Eli would be envious. "Do I take that tonic now?" she asks casually.

Alec shakes his head. "I've no idea how long we may be here. I intend to ration it."

She stretches, pushing off the last of the side effects from mirror travel. When she does, she gets her first look at the underground realm.

It's bleak. A desert of sorts, complete with heat prickling her skin and a lazy wind kicking up spirals of dust. If her face hadn't already met the dirt moments ago, the gritty breeze would've plastered it onto her sweat-slicked skin. The landscape is dotted with strange, jagged plants—red and gray sticks stabbing out of the ground like frozen shards of ice. Everything carries a layer of grime, as if the entire realm needs a thorough dusting. No wonder Alec's Rockton House felt like a gothic mildew pit.

The worst part is the "sky," though she isn't sure it qualifies as one. It stretches high above, black as pitch, with smoky tendrils swirling through it like storm clouds. If she doesn't focus too hard on it, it almost looks like a metallic ceiling, oppressive and impenetrable. The surroundings are barely illuminated by orange and blue lights dotting the horizon. They look like murky flames flickering behind smudged glass.

The whole place reminds her of one of those surrealist paintings from an old library art book. Add some melting clocks, and it could pass for Dali's fever dream. She was never a fan of surrealism—reality is bad enough without extra embellishments.

Azzie turns to ask Alec whether all cities are as barren, but he's fidgeting in alarm, his eyes searching the horizon.

"Come," he says, his tone clipped. "I have a contact nearby who may know where Michael is. It's a twenty-minute walk from here. We must hurry before someone else attempts to use the portal."

She inspects the flames nearby and suppresses a shiver. The glow looks more sinister than they did when she face planted a few minutes ago. "Twenty minutes for you, or twenty minutes for me?"

"For you. For me, an instant," he says, twisting his lips. "After last night, I am more cognizant of your human limitations."

She rolls her eyes but keeps her thoughts to herself. Reminding him she wouldn't *have* those limitations if he converted her isn't worth starting a fight—not when she's so close to achieving her goal.

As they walk, Alec's demeanor shifts, his jaw tightening and shoulders stiffening as if he's pulling on an ill-fitting mask. It reminds her of when they first met, back when he was stiff and unreadable, before his façade cracked. Passing a patch of those jagged stick-plants, she asks about his change in attitude.

"I am known here as a rover and enforcer," he says, his tone formal. "I must wear…" He hesitates, searching for the word. "A costume, so as not to arouse suspicion."

With his gaze on her, she restrains herself from rolling her eyes a second time. He's an immortal being with immeasurable power acting like his life is the worst. Aside from the dismal surroundings wraiths lived in and an intense government system, his life still seems great. The independence is certainly something valuable.

After some time, a shack emerges from the barren landscape, nestled among the stick-plants. It's about twice the size of Jimmy's Bar, with rotting wood slats for walls and windows covered by newspapers and filthy cloth. From afar, it looks completely abandoned.

"Is that where your contact is?" she asks skeptically.

"Yes, he runs the trading post."

"And this is your biggest city?" She waves vaguely at the desolate surroundings. If this is what Alec thinks of as grandeur, no wonder he found Lonetree tolerable. She's definitely finding them better accommodations when they return topside with her gold coins—after he inevitably converts her.

"It is one of our larger ones in North America, but not the largest overall." He stares at her and the shack and a look of understanding passes over his face. "This Post is on the outskirts. Consider this the Jimmy's Bar to the more illustrious Asheville. The rest of the city is that way," he explains, pointing behind them.

She barely keeps from groaning. Either sensing her frustration, which she desperately needs to stop him from doing, or expecting it, he continues, "I thought it safest to avoid larger crowds where possible."

"Will we get to go somewhere else? If I wanted the 'Jimmy's Bar' of Selessen, I could've stayed in Iowa. Or Lonetree."

He shakes his head as he rummages through his bag and pulls out the yellow vial. "We cannot afford to delay any longer. Drink this."

She snatches the vial with pursed lips. Even here, she's not fully in charge of her choices. Complaining, however, risks Alec deciding to abandon the plan entirely, so she tilts her head back and downs the elixir like Eli takes a shot.

"Oh." She blinks, a smile blooming across her face. "That's nice. Like honey or pound cake."

"It *is* an aphrodisiac. It wouldn't do to gag on it as that could ruin whatever amorous mood you were in." He starts walking again. "That should take effect in a few minutes. We will need to be careful about how long we spend here to avoid it wearing off."

She pulls out her phone and sets an alarm, tucking it back into her pocket. Her smile widens as she carefully keeps her thoughts light and neutral. Alec doesn't need to know she set the alarm for five hours instead of four, ensuring the elixir wears off while they're still here and probably in danger. It's all part of the plan.

"Problem solved," she announces brightly, following him toward the trading post. "Now, show me the wraith world."

Chapter 43

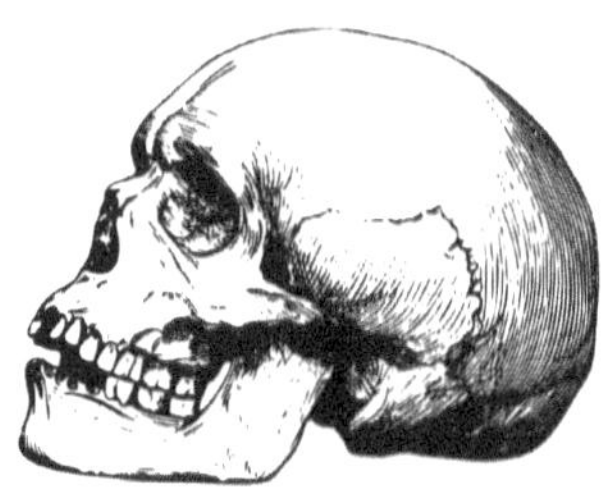

THEY ARRIVE AT THE entrance to the trading post just as the elixir takes effect. Alec pauses, watching Azalea closely for any visible signs of the change. She tucks her hair behind her ears and ducks her head, a small, self-conscious gesture that feels at odds with her recent confidence. Out of habit, he reads her—just for a moment—and is overwhelmed by an emotional torrent.

A flood of panic, guilt, wonder, self-consciousness, worry, and anticipation crashes into him, so potent that he staggers back. It's not like the times he tried to read her before, when her emotions were faint and hidden, requiring significant effort to glean even a fragment. This time, her feelings surge toward him unbidden, a deluge impossible to ignore.

He presses a hand to his chest to steady himself.

"Are you okay?" Azalea reaches for him, her expression pinched.

"I apologize, Azalea," he says, gasping. "I was curious as to the effects of the elixir and attempted to view your soul. Your feelings nearly pummeled me." She withdraws as he scrambles to take her hand again. He can't bear if she's angry with him for inadvertently breaking his promise. "I had no intention of reading you, I swear."

She pulls on a strand of her hair, her voice soft. "I believe you. We'll figure out how to stop that from happening later." Her eyes, wide and vulnerable, glance up at him through her lashes.

He laces their fingers together, grounding himself in her touch. "Are you feeling alright after ingesting the elixir?" he asks carefully.

"I'm okay," she says, her smile tremulous but genuine. "I don't know how to explain it. Whatever I was feeling, it's just... more. Like me, but better—whole."

That makes sense. Adding the illusion of a second soul to someone as pure as Azalea would amplify her essence. He gestures toward her chest. "May I?"

"Read my souls? Go ahead," she says, standing taller and straightening her shoulders.

Alec exhales slowly before focusing on the space where her soul resides. Last time, it had been difficult to locate, almost obscured. Now, it's clear, but something is still wrong. Her soul still reads as singular—whole, not plural as it should after the elixir's effects. Worse, it's changed. No longer pristine, it feels dulled, more typical, like any random human's he might encounter.

He frowns. "It reads as though you still have only one. And it's... altered. Are you sure you're feeling alright?"

She shrugs. "Yeah, I feel fine."

He purses his lips, glancing at the Sumerian inscription on the threshold of the trading post. A worry for later. For now, they must press on and survive this. And he pulls her towards another place where no human had been before: the Selessen Trading Post #2.

The air inside hits like a physical blow—thick with the stench of sulfur and the din of raised voices. The room sprawls before them, tables and merchandise packed in tight rows, the distinction between bodies and goods blurred in the haze of activity. Traders bark at potential buyers, their voices tangling into an unintelligible roar. If one isn't careful, the press of bodies could pull them under, like a riptide.

"Are all these wraiths?" Azalea whispers, her gaze fixed on a serpent-like creature slithering nearby. The creature coils itself around a pole, its forked tongue flicking as it speaks with a wolfish being behind the table.

Alec tightens his hold on her arm, his voice low. "Not all. Just as I can travel to your realm, other beings can travel here." He gestures subtly toward the serpent and the wolf as they haggle over a bolt of silver cloth. "Many of these are lesser creatures, not wraiths."

"You live together here?" Azalea's eyes widen with fascination. He steps closer to shield her from view. That curious look on her face could draw the wrong kind of attention.

"They may live here, or in your realm. These are a few of the lesser species I mentioned yesterday that wraiths dominate," he says as they pass something with a human head and torso but goat limbs. "Be wary. Michael cannot manipulate other wraiths, but his magic could corrupt any of these beings." That thought renews his purpose for being in the Post and he drags Azalea to the back of the room.

As they move through the maze of tables and creatures, she suddenly halts, planting her feet before a table piled with azure and black jewels. "Sorry," she says, her voice tinged with confusion. "I felt like I had to stop here, like I couldn't go further without looking."

Alec's brows knit as he glances around. Compulsion. The thought spikes his chest with unease. Such magic is trivial but common—used to influence lesser beings into stopping, staring, buying. That someone might use it here, where creatures of varying power mingle, is dangerous. Just as wraiths can't use their gifts on the highest creatures on the hierarchy, themselves, lesser creatures can't either. But that still leaves other creatures and those lower in power as fair game. All it would take is one creature to realize Azalea wasn't acting under her own power, a human. Then the floodwaters would rise.

The hawker, a short androgynous creature with tepid green skin, a shock of white hair, and grey marble eyes lopes towards Azalea from behind their table. They grab her hand and yank her towards their level. "Yes, yes, so pretty, so nice. Perfect for lady."

Azalea wretches her hand back as Alec steps forward, catching the hawker's arm in a vice-like grip. "Know your place," he growls, baring his teeth. The hawker cowers, releasing Azalea's hand to hug themselves.

"No harm, no harm," they croon, flashing a grin filled with jagged teeth. "Lady has troubles. Necklace hides them."

"She has no such troubles, nor does she need your cheap parlor magic." Alec's voice is sharp.

Azalea speaks at the same time. "What do you mean hide them?" Her cheeks flush as their voices overlap.

The hawker's gaze lingers on Azalea, studying her face too intently. "Yes, troubles. Necklace hides them. No one sees but me."

Alec's hand itches to strike, to reinforce the violent reputation he's cultivated, but Azalea pinches his side. "Don't," she whispers. "They're just doing their job."

He exhales through his nose, suppressing his rising anger. She doesn't understand the danger. He settles for glaring at the hawker, who slinks back to their table, muttering apologies and dispelling the compulsion with her distance.

"Do you have troubles?" he asks Azalea as they walk away.

She shrugs, running her finger along a rough-hewn table. "I'm an eighteen-year-old girl trying to save my twin brother's soul, avoid being murdered by my boyfriend's creepy immortal friend, and figure out my life after leaving home for the first time. What do you think?"

He attempts to smile reassuringly and pulls her closer. They travel down the row and come upon a wall that seems to grow as they approach it. With a knock, cracks of light appear, forming a doorway. The door swings inward, and Alec leads Azalea into the brightly lit room beyond.

The room is bright, natural light invading every corner even though it is windowless. Gerald, an overweight wraith, greets them. His mismatched attire—a long white shirt emblazoned with *Island Hoppers* over obscenely tight pants—feels jarringly out of place in Selessen.

"Remember the Teachings," Gerald says, bowing.

"Follow the Rules," Alec replies stiffly.

"It's good to see you, my boy," Gerald exclaims, his round face breaking into a broad grin. "What brings you here?" He ducks his head almost reflexively. "Whatever the problem, I saw nothing."

Alec struggles not to snort at Gerald's predictable evasion. Gerald had perfected his peculiar strategy of dealing with trouble by closing his eyes to it—literally. Alec vividly recalls interviews from centuries past when Gerald sat with his eyes shut tight, pretending ignorance of any Rule breaking in his post. Odd strategies for an odd wraith.

"Settle down, Gerald," Alec says, gesturing to Azalea as she steps to his side. "I'm not here on rover business. I'm on leave." He pauses for effect. "Gerald, meet Azalea, my newest convert and pupil. Azalea, this is Gerald, proprietor of Post #2."

Pretending Azalea had already been converted wasn't a foolproof strategy, but necessary. Nothing about their trip to Selessen could withstand scrutiny. Alec's only consolation was knowing that Gerald's gift, telekinesis, posed no threat to their ruse.

"A pleasure, milady," Gerald says with an exaggerated bow, his bald head gleaming under the bright light. He takes Azalea's hand, kisses it twice, and beams at her blushing reaction. "Thank the Fates you were converted young. Imagine eternity with the problems of age. Awful, awful business."

He turns to Alec. "But did I hear you right—you say turned her?" At Alec's curt nod, Gerald beams. "You needed a young one, to fix your clothes and make you hip." He leans towards Azalea. "Did you know he still wears roving clothes on his off hours? Looks like an extra in that *Braveheart* movie. Only dressed normal when he needed to hunt topside."

Azalea's crooked smile tugs at the corners of her lips while Alec scowls, though the words bite deeper than they should. He'd avoided human trends intentionally, a defense against the very weakness that brought him here.

"There's no need to succumb to the frivolities of human society," Alec retorts sharply. "As you well know, too much time in the human realm and their fads can lead—"

"To breaking the Rules," Gerald finishes with a wave of his hand. "Yes, yes, I know. But some of those human inventions are dead useful." He pulls a small plastic square from his desk and waves it in the air. "Like this. I send a message, and my guards get it instantly. Hurts a bit, but still."

"You could also fly notes through the air, *without* the risk of breaking the First Rule," Alec says.

Azalea tilts her head, peering at the device. "That's a pager. I've never seen one in real life."

"Do you use something better?" Gerald asks, his curiosity gleaming. Azalea fishes her cell phone from her satchel and holds it up as it buzzes. Gerald reaches for it, but Alec swats his hand away.

"We're not here to discuss human inventions," Alec says.

Gerald heaves an overdramatic sigh and slumps down behind a table covered in junk. "If you're not here to harass my customers or engage in polite conversation, then how can I help you?"

"We're looking for Michael," Azalea says, slipping her hand into Alec's and lacing their fingers together. His jaw tightens, and he hopes the desk hides her affectionate gesture from Gerald's sharp gaze.

"Haven't seen him since the last time you stole one of my paying customers," Gerald says, interlacing his fingers over his stomach.

"That 'customer' was a lesser creature selling poisonous tablets to wraiths masquerading as relaxants," Alec snaps.

"To be fair, none of the buyers who ate them were stressed afterward," Gerald says with a shrug. "They were shriveled into nothing. That must count for something."

Alec fixes him with a pointed glare. Gerald looks away, feigning a pout.

"Gerald," Alec tries again. "I must find Michael. I simply need a direction, or some tip where we may find him. I believe he was coming to Selessen."

"What do you need him for?" Gerald asks, his tone light but his gaze sharp.

"That is none of your business," Alec says.

"To meet me," Azalea interjects, her tone bright. "Now that I'm part of the family. He's like my... grandwraith."

Gerald's jaw drops before he erupts into booming laughter, his belly shaking as the sound echoes through the room. "Grandwraith! That's funny, that is. Alec could use someone quick."

Gerald's laughter subsides into chuckles as he leans toward Azalea. "Michael's a riot but a bit too kinky for him. Though considering how cozy you two are, maybe you're the kinky ones—what with Alec being your dadwraith."

Azalea's hand slips from Alec's as he scowls, irritation rippling across his face. "We aren't related," he says, his voice tight. "That's not how it works. I am neither her father nor a father figure. And frankly, it's none of your business."

Gerald chuckles again, pulling out his pager with a wince. He taps it and leans back in his chair, gesturing to the two empty seats across from him. "I've sent a request for a report. I'll let you know when I get it. But in return, I have a few questions of my own."

Chapter 44

AZZIE SITS STIFFLY, KEEPING her hands folded in her lap as Gerald prattles on about human culture. He's been fixated on *Magnum P.I.* for at least five minutes, recounting plot points with an enthusiasm that makes Alec's shoulders visibly tense.

Azzie needs the distraction, as the elixir brought back the guilt that oozed out when they left Lonetree. She hates how it churns and bubbles. Still, Gerald's ramblings offer a welcome distraction from the sinking weight of her lies, her hidden alarm, and her real reasons for being in Selessen.

"You're a regular Higgins," Gerald quips, throwing a playful jab at Alec after explaining the premise of the show.

Alec's glare smolders, his displeasure radiating like heat. "This discussion of human entertainment is dangerously close to a breach of the Second Rule," he mutters, his voice low and sharp.

"Loosen up, my boy," Gerald replies with a laugh. He waggles his eyebrows at Azzie, then launches into an impromptu impersonation of the titular detective.

Alec shifts uncomfortably, and his eyes find hers, a question in his gaze. Azzie shrugs, helpless. She didn't have cable after she was seven, and the library didn't stock TV shows—only old movies. She picks a benign question to change the subject, hoping to ease Alec's tension and distract herself from her twisting thoughts.

"Err—how's business?"

Gerald laughs, dropping the hand he was using as a pretend mustache. "If this is how you dig into my affairs, you'd best let Alec do it. He's a bit more subtle."

Azzie forces a smile, though it feels tight on her face. She imagines Alec scolding her later, his voice low and disappointed. "I'm just curious," she says lightly. "I don't know much about the, uh, family yet."

Gerald rubs a dirty hand under his chin. "How long have you been one of us?"

"Only a day," Azzie blurts before Alec can answer. Alec tenses at her statement, looking like he could light Gerald on fire with the force of his scowl.

"A day," Gerald repeats slowly, his gaze sharpening. "And you've recovered already?"

Azzie falters, her mind racing for an answer. "Just lucky, I guess," she says with a weak laugh, glancing at Alec for backup. He glares silently, his disapproval palpable.

Gerald inspects at her with an expression she can't place before he chuckling. "Lucky indeed." He slaps the table and shifts in his chair. "Well, there's been a bit of drama lately. Calm yourself, my boy, nothing that the Council's not knowing about," he says, reassuring Alec with a wave of his hand, though Alec hadn't moved. "Been a spot of trouble brewing with the others, the so-called lesser creatures. Council's been setting their price margins lower and there's talk of restricting their magics more."

Azzie looks to Alec for clarification. "Do you recall the Teachings on the hierarchy?" he asks quietly. "Gerald speaks of the lesser species, the ones wraiths control. The Council regulates their magic to ensure secrecy and prevent breaches."

"Or because they're scared of what the others can do," Gerald counters, his tone sour.

"That's close to a breach, Gerald," Alec warns, sliding his eyes over Gerald's shirt. "Particularly after your interest in human culture."

Gerald's expression is unimpressed. "I think we can have a few secrets amongst us, especially in front of the newly converted."

Alec stiffens, curling his hands into fists until Azzie takes them. "We're at an accord," he says begrudgingly.

"It's no secret that the Council's short-sighted," Gerald retorts. "If the others revolt, how long do you think the family's secrets will hold?"

Azzie leans forward. "Why would they revolt?"

Gerald gives her a pitying look. "Because they're treated like second-class citizens, stamped as 'lesser' just because they don't hunt like us. But they've got their own magic, and they're getting sick of being told how to use it."

"But how does that affect your business?" Azzie asks.

"They're my friends," Gerald says simply, like it's the most natural thing in the world.

"And there are only two Trading Posts left in Selessen," Alec interjects, his tone clipped. "If the lower creatures decide it's no longer in their best interest to set up shop here, Gerald's business would flounder."

"That's not fair, Alec," Gerald says, putting on a wounded expression as though Alec had insulted his character. "Wraith needs to eat."

"You physically do not," Alec says dryly.

A beep sounds from the pager and both Alec and Gerald's frustrated expressions clear. He peers at the tiny screen and stands. "Got something on Michael. Be back soon."

And just like that, he's gone, leaving Azzie alone with Alec in the cramped, overbright office.

Alec slumps into his chair, though even slouched, he looks like someone carved him from stone. His elbows rest on his knees, and he presses his palms into his eyes like he's trying to block out the world.

"You don't really think other magical beings are second-class citizens, do you?" Azzie asks. She knows what it's like to be under someone's thumb.

"It's the truth," Alec mutters, not looking at her. "Wraiths are the ruling class. That's how it is." His voice is firm, but there's a flicker of something in his tone—doubt, maybe. He finally lifts his gaze to meet hers, his eyes flashing with that strange, unearthly light. "I still believe in the Rules. I must. I must continue to believe in the work I've done for our society. My lapse doesn't change that."

She bites her tongue at the word *lapse*. Part of her wants to lash out, remind him she isn't some mistake to regret. But the elixir still hums softly in her veins, tempering her darker instincts. The larger part of her, understands how difficult it must be for him to reconcile his past with what they're doing now.

"It's not a lapse to realize what you knew was wrong," she says gently, placing a hand on his back. His muscles are rigid under her touch. "It's a valid choice to recognize that the Rules are garbage." He flinches slightly, but she doesn't stop. "No, I mean it. The Rules meant you had to reign over others when that hierarchy is bogus. The Rules meant you couldn't share who you are, your life, with the person you care about." Her hand moves in slow, deliberate circles over the cotton of his t-shirt. "That's me, by the way."

Alec exhales sharply, and for a moment, she thinks she hears the ghost of a laugh.

"It's hard to give that up," she continues, her voice softer now. "You're going to second-guess yourself. You're going to have to choose again and again, every day. All you can do is trust yourself."

The words sting even as she says them. She thinks of the lies she told, the alarms she set, her relentless focus on being converted. She doesn't trust herself, not fully. If this is how conversion feels—if this fleeting clarity and guilt are what she'd carry with countless souls in her chest, instead of just the echo of more with the elixir in her veins—could she handle it? Or would it stretch her until she breaks?

Alec shifts away, displacing her hand. "I make the choice every second I'm with you," he says, his voice low but firm. "I have no regrets." His gaze flicks to hers, his eyes softer now. "You've been certain of your decision to leave your family and join me, without hesitation or doubt. That strength is something to admire."

Her stomach twists. She thinks of Eli, of the betrayal she left behind, of how single-minded she's been in pursuing her goal. Before the elixir, it had all seemed so clear, so easy. Now, the weight of her actions presses down on her, unrelenting.

She's saved from responding by Gerald's return. He bustles into the room, his expression triumphant. "Got something. A hawker's got information but won't leave their table."

Alec stands immediately, his posture snapping back into its usual controlled form. He strides toward the door but pauses, turning back to her. "Will you be alright in here alone?" he asks, his voice laced with concern.

For a moment, he's nothing but a dark silhouette against the harsh light of the doorway. Something about his stance—his presence—makes her chest tighten. He's a shadow—all dark, like Lucifer bearing down on her. She blinks—no, that was Eli. Alec is the angel Gabriel, guarding and offering her promises.

Alec waits for her answer, squinting at her in concern. He's felt her emotions again, most likely.

"I'll be fine," she says, her voice steady even as her hands tremble in her lap.

Alec waits a beat longer before following Gerald out, the door clicking shut behind them. The room feels suffocatingly bright without him. She presses her palms to her face, taking a shaky breath.

"'Will all great Neptune's ocean wash this blood clean from my hand?'" she says to the empty room.

Alec would recognize that quote. Eli might too. *They'll understand guilt*, she thinks. Alec especially, with his thousand years of bloody history. Eli might, buried under his bravado, if she got him drunk. Her fingers claw at her neck, as though she could drag the elixir out of her bloodstream by force and banish the feelings it stirred up.

"Pretty words. Necklace helps," says a rasping voice from nearby.

Azzie jolts upright, the chair screeching as she stumbles back against the desk. Her heart pounds as her vision doubles. When it clears, she sees the hawker—a creature of unsettling green skin and black, unblinking eyes—standing exactly where no one had been a moment before.

"How did you get in here?" she demands, her voice sharp. Her gaze darts to the closed door. It's still shut.

The hawker cocks their head, blinking slowly. "Necklace for Lady," they say, holding up a strand of beads in their long, three-fingered hand. The necklace gleams, turquoise stones threaded along one side, meeting at a black bar of stone in the middle.

Her hand twitches toward it instinctively, like Sleeping Beauty to the spindle. At the last moment, she yanks it back. "What's it for?"

"To hide troubles," the hawker replies. "Lady's feelings and soul too open. Alby's necklace will help."

"You can tell?" she asks before she can stop herself. Her voice wavers.

Alby tilts their head further, the movement eerie. "Elixir almost gone, but feelings remain. He will see, he will know."

A sick feeling churns in her stomach. Alec. If he realizes the full extent of what she's been hiding, what she's been planning, it'll be over. Everything will unravel.

"What does Lady want?" Alby asks.

"Freedom." The word slips out before she can stop it, as if Alby has reeled it out of her mouth like a fish on a line. And it's true—freedom is all she's ever wanted. Freedom to make her own choices, to put herself first without guilt, to finally become the person Lonetree wouldn't let her be.

"This helps," Alby says, raising the necklace higher. The turquoise beads catch the light, shimmering like something magical, something powerful. It's beautiful—nicer than anything she's ever owned.

"I don't have anything to pay for it," she says, even as her fingers itch to take it.

Alby shrugs, a jerking, unnatural motion. "Lady stopped wraith. Alby gives for favor."

Her brows furrow. "You'll give it to me because I stopped Alec earlier? To repay a favor?"

Alby pulls the necklace slightly closer to their chest, sharp teeth flashing in a grin. "No. Favor is now. Alby finds Lady for stopping wraith. Lady keeps necklace for favor."

Azzie hesitates. The need to hide her emotions wars with her caution. She's survived this far by staying wary, by not jumping at every shiny thing. "I've read too many stories about deals like this. Next thing I know, you'll be asking for my firstborn."

Alby's grin widens, showing an alarming number of jagged teeth. "No children come from wraiths. Silly Lady."

Her stomach drops. She's outed herself. Her pulse roars in her ears as she forces a nervous laugh. "Right, of course. No kids for me, what with me being a wraith and all. Still, I can't agree to some undefined favor."

Alby pauses, considering her with those unreadable black eyes. Then, slowly, they extend the necklace again. "Gift for Lady. But if Alby asks for future help, perhaps Lady gives favor then. Lady's choice."

It's more than fair—almost suspiciously so. But her hands are shaking, and her mind is racing, and she takes the necklace before she can overthink it. The beads are cool against her skin, and for a moment, everything stills. She realizes, belatedly, that it could be cursed or enchanted, that Alec warned her about items like this. She opens her mouth to ask Alby more, but before she opens her mouth, the hawker's grin grows impossibly wide, and it disappears into thin air.

She stares at the empty space where it stood, her heart pounding, tightening her grip on the necklace.

Chapter 45

Eli lounges awkwardly on the neon-colored pillows, surrounded by a decor so aggressively sixties it makes his head spin. Tufted cushions of every fluorescent color dot the floor while rainbow tapestries hang on the walls. The patterns on them are abstract, chaotic, but if there's a story in the threads, the moral is clear: have an orgy.

He rubs his hand over the back of his neck, the lingering slimy sensation of the mirror portal still clinging to his skin. After the disastrous call with Azzie, Michael had dragged him to an old-timey trunk. Instead of explaining, Michael had muttered something about "rising trading prices," then told Eli to close his eyes.

Eli had begrudgingly agreed, and they'd stepped into the trunk. It had been disorienting—like standing on glass—and then a *tink* sounded and he'd dropped straight through, landing on the pillows with a dull *thump*. Of course, Michael landed like a cat, smug and unruffled.

"That was better than the whooshing," Eli grumbles, remembering the last time Michael had carried him—*bridal style*, no less. "But you could've warned me the damn door was on the ceiling."

There is a simmering anger in his gut that was missing during the past few days. It covers the embarrassment that Michael saw him fumble. The last few hours, he's felt everything stronger, but anger overcomes it all.

Michael ruffles his now apple red hair. "That's less fun."

"So, this is your sex den?" he deadpans, glaring up at the mirror on the ceiling.

Michael laughs. "One reason you are such a diversion, dearest. Nothing phases you."

Eli rolls his eyes and shifts to sit cross-legged on the pillows. "You're supposed to be explaining what's going on with Azzie while I'm not acting like a total bitch. Clock's ticking, right?"

He wishes he had a drink.

Michael smirks, reclining back on his elbows as his sharp green eyes glint in the dim light. "With what I expect Alec to have done, and Azalea's reaction to them, I'd have thought you'd discarded the paltry emotions of 'worry' and 'concern' by now." His fingers trail lazily over Eli's knee, and Eli bats them away.

He bats Michael's hands away. "I'm not worried; I'm pissed," Eli snaps. "Plus, I knew things were bad, but getting a mirror view of that selfishness makes me nauseous. With Azzie's acting like this, we need to find her to stop the whiplash I'm getting and finish the plan."

Michael ignores him, his hand creeping higher, now brushing against Eli's thigh. "Ah, anger—an emotion I both expect and enjoy."

Eli exhales sharply, pulling on his hair in frustration. "You never stop, do you?" Not that Eli's in much of a rush to stop him. The man is built like some kind of dark-skinned Hercules, a fact that complicates Eli's usual self-perception as the most attractive person in any room.

"I don't know whether I want to fight you or fu—." Eli cut himself off with pursed lips. There isn't time for that.

"More emotions I like," Michael purrs.

"Business first," Eli growls, shoving Michael's hand away. His irritation simmers, his earlier embarrassment replaced with a familiar anger that feels like coming home. "We don't have time for your games."

Michael sighs theatrically, flopping back onto the pillows. "Taskmaster."

"You like it," Eli retorts, growling.

Michael's grin turns predatory. "True. Though I must admit, your submission yesterday had its charms. But to business, as you insist." He sighs as though put upon. "Now that Alec and your Azalea have gone off together, my plan may need... adjustment. I trust you'll be willing?"

Eli's anger flares at the mention of Alec, the sanctimonious wraith who ruined everything without even realizing it. "That dick—"

Michael's hand shoots out, gripping Eli's neck—not tight, but enough to make his point. Eli scowls up at him, refusing to flinch. Michael's grin returns, sharp as ever.

"What have I said about insulting my Alec?"

Eli remains silent, continuing to glare and jutting out his chin in defiance. Michael sighs again and returns to lounging next to Eli's now prone form.

"I suppose I'll have to delay explaining everything until you're properly chastised for your cheek," Michael says, his tone light but laced with a promise.

Eli raises an eyebrow, considering. *Maybe we have time.* Though Michael jokes about liking the sudden bouts of submission Eli keeps experiencing, he knows Michael prefers Eli reckless and hotheaded. That's how Eli prefers himself too. "Guess so."

Michael's grin widens as his hand slides upward, lifting the edge of Eli's shirt. His breath is warm against Eli's skin as he murmurs, "Ah, as the deviant Sade once said, 'It is always by way of pain one arrives at pleasure.'"

Eli snorts, thumping Michael's arm. "You sound like my sister, spouting quotes. Not exactly what I want to think about right now."

Michael's grin turns wicked. "Oh, give me an hour, darling, and I'll have you quoting verses that would make your sister blush." He tugs Eli's shirt higher. "We'll start with one I learned this century..."

Eli groans, letting his head fall back onto the pillows. "Speed it up. We don't have all day, considering the way she's been acting."

Michael's teeth scrape lightly against Eli's hip. "Impatient as always. Very well, pet. Take notes."

And then, with his rich, low voice, Michael begins to recite. "'Please master can I have your thighs bare to my eyes; please master can I take off your clothes below your chair; please master can I kiss your ankles and soul...'"

Chapter 46

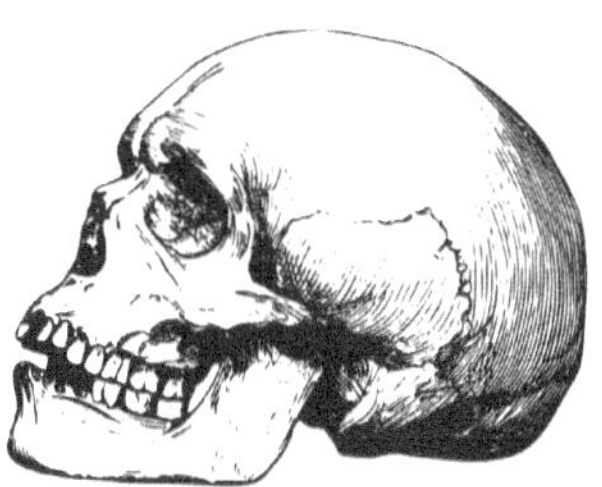

WHEN ALEC RETURNS TO Gerald's office, Azalea is leaning against the desk, her expression odd. She shoves her hands into her pockets the moment she sees him, but there's no outward distress, no rush of emotions radiating from her like usual. It's unsettling, but he cannot dwell on it. His anger overrides everything else.

"He was here," Alec growls. His voice is tight, barely contained. "He was here and left with a true mirror!"

Although he knows he'll pay for it later, he doesn't let Azalea linger or question him, instead grasping her hand and pulling her back through the trading floor. He can't speak, as he fears he will take out his frustration on her.

It takes an hour to reach the car parked in Chicago, an hour of her compliant silence trailing behind him, an hour of the suffocating knowledge that this entire venture was reckless. A gamble. And it had gained him nothing except confirmation of what he already feared: Michael could be anywhere. He had risked Azalea's life and humanity for nothing.

With that information, Azalea *must* agree that any wraith civilization is too risky and abandon her decision to seek Michael. Her brother is a lost cause and Alec will find some other way to fix his mistake.

As they settle into the car, Alec's tension reaches its peak. His nails dig into the dashboard, ripping through the fabric and exposing the foam beneath. He doesn't care. Anger courses through him, sharp and bitter.

Azalea's hand lands on his shoulder, light but grounding. "Better now?" she asks softly.

Her voice and touch cut through his spiraling rage. He exhales through his teeth and forces himself to release the dashboard, staring at the damaged interior. "I'm fine," he mutters, patting her fingers where they rest on his arm. "You must see now that the best course is to avoid the wraith realm entirely. We must continue to the Amanas as planned."

She furrows her brow. "I thought Michael could go anywhere with a true mirror."

"Only to another spelled mirror," Alec explains, his eyes closing briefly. He's exhausted. "I cannot imagine we'd find one in the Amanas. But every moment we remain in Chicago is another moment at risk."

"And my brother?"

Alec winces, ducking his head. "We're out of options," he says, guilt threading through his tone. "I'm sorry, Azalea. I've caused you so much trouble. Perhaps it would've been better if we'd never met—or if I hadn't given in to my weakness for you."

"Hey," she snaps, poking his arm sharply enough that his eyes fly open. "Don't say that. We'll figure this out."

Before he can respond, she leans forward and kisses him. The suddenness of it steals his breath, and the rage and melancholy coursing through him are replaced by something softer: relief and the overwhelming desire to hold her close. Lightly, delicately, with more control than he thought himself capable of, he slides a hand around the back of her neck, deepening the kiss.

Her hands rest on his chest, not pulling him closer, not pushing him away, simply anchoring him. Their timing is off, their movements awkward, but it doesn't matter. There's a gentleness in her touch he's never experienced, as though she fears he might vanish if she presses too hard. He allows himself to exhale against her, a silent promise that he isn't going anywhere.

A sudden beeping breaks the moment. Alec jolts, alarmed, but Azalea pulls her cell phone from beneath her shirt. The buzzing rattles against his heightened senses, making his teeth ache. She silences it with a few button presses and tosses the device into the backseat. Then, with a mischievous glint in her eye, she leaps at him.

All gentleness vanishes. Her mouth presses against his and she grabs his neck as pleasure sweeps over him. He tightens his arms around her, pulling her closer. A gasp from her breaks them apart but doesn't slow her. Instead, she hops into his lap, placing her legs on either side of his knees. "We'll move to the backseat eventually," she says, her voice low and breath labored. He shivers at the implication in her tone.

She kisses him again, moving from his lips to the column of his throat. The pleasure races through him with each touch on his skin. She lays little kisses against his neck before lightly biting on his Adam's apple. It feels good, but like something he shouldn't want. Gritting his teeth, he pushes her away with more force than intended. She lands against the broken passenger door, her lip catching briefly between her teeth, glinting against the red and wet skin.

"That was..." His voice is hoarse, the words sticking in his throat.

"Fun," she finishes, brushing her hair out of her face.

"Too rough," he corrects, though his pulse still races.

She huffs and crosses her arms around her middle. "Says the guy who ripped my shirt open, but sure, me giving you some love nips is 'rough.'"

Alec stares at the stained bench seat. "I thought you understood my concerns about coupling."

Silence stretches between them, and he risks a look up at her. She looks puzzled, but the frustration is still present in her enthralling brown eyes.

"What if you—" She points her finger at him, eyes narrowing at his expression. "Don't give me that look. You don't know what I'm going to say."

He winces but lets her continue.

"What if you fill up on souls?" she suggests, waggling her eyebrows in a way that makes his lips twitch despite himself. "Then your vessel, or whatever, will be full, and you won't worry about accidentally taking mine."

He tilts his head, considering her logic. It's true, being "full" had made his last feeding a waste, but the thought of her witnessing such a moment creates goosebumps that skitter over his skin. Visiting Se-lessen was bad enough.

"I won't think differently of you," she says. His brow furrows as he meets her gaze. "It's an educated guess. You're self-flagellating about me seeing you take a soul. But I want to see it. I'll have to *some* time." Her hand drifts to his thigh, her fingers tracing the fabric of his trousers. "Unless you plan on withering away," she adds lightly.

No, he doesn't, but he has thought little past 'remove Azalea from danger,' and 'hide from the family' in the past twenty-four hours. "I didn't, but I also didn't intend to subject you to that part of my life."

Her expectant expression doesn't falter. "Aren't you still trying to make up for Eli?"

He rubs a hand over his face. The balancing act of keeping her safe, keeping her pure, and staying true to his principles feels more impossible by the second. "It hasn't worked before," he admits quietly, remembering what led to his celibacy. "But for you, I'm willing to try."

She smiles, but something about it feels off—too sharp, too know-ing. It would fit well on Michael's face.

Chapter 47

Azzie almost vibrates with excitement. The necklace, now tucked discreetly into her bra, works wonders—its calming effect smoothing over the turmoil she felt in Selessen. The elixir's side effects are gone, and with them, the gnawing guilt that had threatened to choke her. She feels like herself again. Better, even. And Alec is close to breaking and converting her. She can feel it.

She tries to convince him to grab a random person off the street as soon as they park near the Field Museum. People mill around everywhere—tourists, locals, easy marks. But Alec hesitates, his expression pained as she points out potential targets. He argues they could find a suitable soul on the drive to the Amanas, but she knows that's just an excuse. Eli's name becomes her trump card, and when she brings him up, Alec reluctantly agrees to search the area. She's not ready to surrender to life in the Amanas yet. Without Alec's active participation in her plans, she'll need to rely on his passive compliance.

The sun dips low as they wander toward the harbor next to the Field Museum and the aquarium. It's a cliché, thinking the docks might attract the dregs of society in modern times, but Alec doesn't comment, so she doesn't either.

The harbor is nearly deserted except for a handful of people waiting for a late-night concert. Alec stops them near a takeout spot between the venue and the public beach, studying the crowd with the focus of a predator sizing up prey. He shakes his head at every potential target.

"No one depraved enough?" she asks, her patience thinning. Being a wraith is supposed to be more exciting than stalking people from afar.

"Not yet."

She huffs, folding her arms. "Seriously, why don't you just pick one at random?"

He finally looks at her, his gaze dark. "I've told you. I only choose the vile, to remove some of your world's blights. It is my only opportunity for penance."

Another fifteen minutes pass, and he shakes his head again. "There is no one. This was folly. I can't *fathom* why I agreed to this."

Before he can retreat to the car, she steps in front of him, blocking his view. Her hands run over his chest, the soft fabric of his shirt sliding beneath her fingers. She leans in, just enough to catch his eyes drifting to the neckline of her shirt, where the necklace lies hidden but her skin is on full display. Men, wraiths—it doesn't matter. Eli had always said they're all the same when you know what they want.

"You could snack a little," she says, her voice soft and coaxing. "Like, you take a little sip from lots of people to fill up, and then fill me up," she says, channeling Eli. She's taking a page from his book—doing what she wanted without regard for consequences is one lesson he inadvertently taught her. Freedom, she's learned, doesn't just come from throwing off shackles—it comes from tossing shame to the wind.

His gaze travels to her face before straying back to the t-shirt. "That is theoretically possible, I suppose."

"Everyone's a little sinful," she coaxes.

His expression hardens, though his eyes betray him, burning with conflict. "You aren't," he says firmly. "Indeed, I am seconds from returning to the car and hiding you away from this."

She bites her lip, holding back a laugh. How did someone so repressed end up with her? "Please, Alec. I want to see it."

He stares at her for a long moment, then at the ring on his finger. The hesitation in his eyes clears, replaced by steely resolve. "I sense someone," he says finally, peering past her shoulder. "Stay behind me. We must hurry—I won't have you around such filth for long."

"Whatever you want." *Whatever he needs to get what I want*, she adds silently.

He moves like a shadow, his sparking eyes glinting in the fading light. She follows as he leads them behind the concert venue to a cluster of dumpsters. Between them stands a skeletal woman with stringy blond hair leaning against the wall.

"What did she do to make her evil enough for you?" Azzie asks.

"I can only guess based on her emotions and soul," he replies quietly. "But I've had limited time to read her."

Before she can blink, Alec is next to the woman. Azzie watches as the woman murmurs something and runs her finger from Alec's clavicle to his beltline. Oddly, she feels no jealousy—only curiosity. The necklace must be working.

Alec leans forward, his hand wrapping around the woman's throat in what looks like an intimate embrace. A moment later, he's back at Azzie's side. The woman remains upright, though her movements are sluggish, her balance unsteady.

In Alec, the difference is immediate. His breathing is ragged, his eyes glowing with a light that seems to consume the space between them. He prowls closer, his slim chest brushing against hers with every inhale. Heat flares in her stomach, her body responding to the hunger in his gaze. Smirking, she grips his hips and leans in, nuzzling the spot on his clavicle the junkie had touched moments ago.

"Playtime?" she murmurs, her voice dripping with suggestion.

Alec groans low in his throat, his restraint fraying. His arms tighten around her as he leans down, his breath hot against her ear. "Vehicle. Now."

Chapter 48

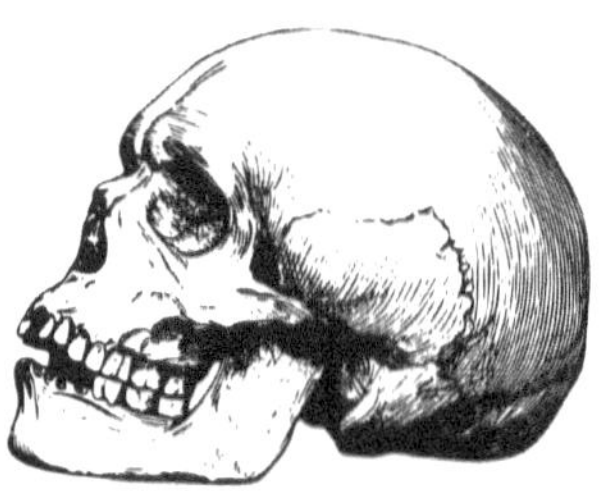

ALEC MOVES WITH WRAITH speed, slipping them into the backseat before the euphoria from the soul wanes. He presses Azalea onto the worn cushions, stooping over her to ensure he hasn't hurt her in his haste. Her quick grin and the way she hooks her arms around his neck, fingers digging into his scalp, confirm she's unharmed. She pulls him down, her lips meeting his in a kiss so fervent it makes his breath stutter.

The cramped space forces him to hunch over her, his larger frame enveloping her. She tilts her head to deepen the kiss, her lips moving against his with an intensity that sends sparks through him. When his head accidentally knocks against the cold metal door, he ignores the jarring buzz in favor of the warmth beneath him. Her hands travel to the nape of his neck, anchoring him to her.

"You're so powerful," she murmurs against his lips, her voice thick with admiration. Her words stir something primal in him. She's a contradiction, this mortal woman—pure but fierce, fragile yet unyielding. She shouldn't want this. She shouldn't want him. But she does.

His hands drift to her hips, fingers hesitating for a moment before they slide her tight pants down to her thighs. Her skin is soft beneath his touch, and he kneads it instinctively, earning a gasp as her hips buck against him. He pulls back, dragging his face along her neck, brushing his lips over her jawline, savoring every reaction she gives him.

This isn't where they should be. She deserves silk sheets and moonlight, not a dingy car with stained floorboards. But Azalea—always defiant, always impatient—smirks and sits up. In one swift motion, she pulls her shirt over her head, bundling it and tossing it aside. She leans back, her chest pushed forward, the curves of her body framed in alluring black fabric. Her confidence is electric, her anticipation sparking through the air between them.

His gaze roams over her, lingering on the shadows and dips of her body before settling on her face. Mischief and desire light up her eyes, but there's a softness there too, something unguarded that catches him off guard. She flushes under his stare, her lips quirking in a teasing smile.

"This is what you want," he says, his voice rough. It doesn't sound like a question, but it is.

He doesn't ask lightly. Not after Cassius. Not after the centuries when consent was implied or manipulated, when he never had to question. But with Azalea, it's different. It has to be. She's choosing this, choosing *him*, and he must know that it's truly what she wants. A monster doesn't deserve such certainty, but he needs it from her.

For him, the answer is yes. Though the euphoria is waning, he still wants her. He thinks he might always want her.

With an impatient huff, Azalea slinks to sit on his lap in answer, wrapping her legs back around his waist, hooking her ankles together anchor her on him. The position is new, he's never had a lover take control. She reaches between them, unbuttoning his pants as he succumbs to her strong fingers. Finally, she rocks them together until he fully sheathes inside her. He groans, the sound more like a growl as his hands grip her hips, while she gasps, wrapping her arms around his back.

He continues rocking into her until her head falls back, hitting the backside of the headrest. The long and soft line of her body unearthed desires he's not felt in centuries. Her mouth drops open while her eyes slide closed and he sees the flutter of her pulse against her delicate, human, frail neck. Her eyes snap open with renewed intensity as she tears her hands from behind him, clutching his own and placing them around her neck in a replica of what she saw him do minutes prior.

He rests his fingers against her throat and squeezes in time with her pulse. Her eyes close again with a hum. His mouth falls open, his head tipped back. He's the most aroused he's ever been. The tandem feelings of power and helplessness thrum through him—the knowledge that she, his soft human, takes command in rocking into him—the knowledge that he, a dangerous creature, holds his control tight against the fragile skin of her throat. One wrong move and he would destroy her humanity. Pleasure builds, better than he remembers, something he can't name as anything but "good" and "right" and "joy," something that threatens to spill from him at any second. Fire licks at his low back and rises, caressing every part of him and ending with a white hot flare of bliss where she connects with him. His hips stutter as he bites off a groan, and Azalea gasps sharply against the tight grip of his hands around her throat.

Panic floods him in fear that he missed the familiar tingle of her soul leaving her body. He rips his hands from her just in time for her to claw at his shoulders while she captures her own release.

When they finish, a trickle of remorse seeps into Alec, coiling tightly around the fleeting euphoria. He clenches his fists at his sides, his jaw locking as he watches Azalea hop off him with a breathless laugh. She radiates satisfaction, her cheeks flushed, her movements languid.

"Are you alright?" he asks, his voice rougher than intended. He studies her with an appraising eye, seeking any sign he might have hurt her or, worse, taken something from her he couldn't return.

"That was so much better than I thought it would be," she says, each word emphasized by a deep breath. She wiggles in her seat."... You did?"

He nods stiffly, unclenching his fists and glancing down at his hands as though they'd betray some sign of his momentary loss of control. Wraiths cannot procreate, and their bodies function in stasis, yet he knows he did. Fates, he *did*. And while the act itself hadn't harmed her, the risk was too great to repeat. Relief at her apparent wholeness wars with the guilt of his indulgence, the fear of how close he'd come to disaster.

"I loved that thing at the end, with my throat," Azalea says, oblivious to his internal struggle. She flashes a mischievous smile. "Kind of thought you might convert me for a second there—that was the rush that did it for me."

"It was too close," he mutters, his voice tight.

She shrugs, brushing slick strands of hair from her face, unashamed as she leans against the opposite window. The glow of her satisfaction almost eclipses the words that follow. "I liked it. You did too." Her lips curve into a knowing smirk. "And that power you must feel all the time? I can see why wraiths want to hide it—not everyone deserves that."

"It is not a matter of deserving," he replies quietly, his gaze fixed on the creases in the leather seat. "It's akin to a curse."

Her laughter rings out, rich and unbothered. "I'm betting not everyone agrees with you." She stretches languidly, her arms arching back as far as the cramped space allows, and the soft curves of her body stir a flicker of arousal within him. He suppresses it immediately, crushing the spark before it can ignite again.

"You just need to relax," she teases, her tone light, as if they hadn't just brushed against the edge of something dangerous. She tilts her head, her grin still firmly in place. "So, what did you want to do now?"

Alec exhales sharply, dragging a hand down his face. What he *wants* to do and what he *should* do are two entirely different things.

Chapter 49

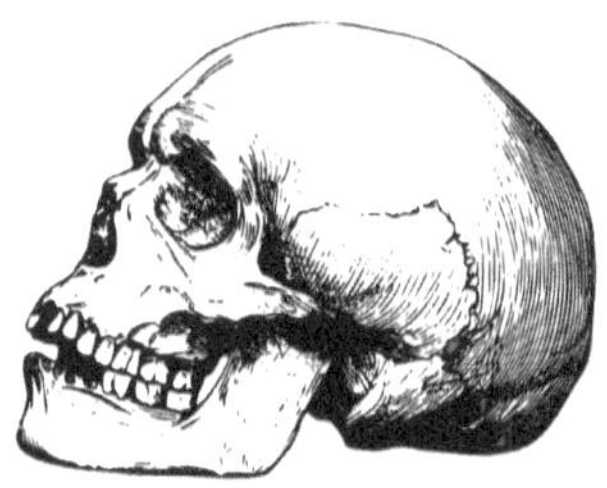

ALEC SITS RIGID IN the passenger seat, Azalea munching on fried potatoes, her free hand gripping the wheel. The small car hums steadily as they drive out of Chicago and toward the Amanas. Evening falls, casting long shadows across the highway they'd traversed that morning.

Azalea had offered to let him drive, but he declined, retreating into a quiet, uneasy haze. The allure of driving was gone, replaced by discomfort and restlessness. He had come far too close to losing control earlier, and her indifference—or worse, enthusiasm—toward the danger unsettled him deeply. He needs to get her away from all of it: Selessen, Michael, and the looming threat of the family.

He exhales heavily and pulls his journal from his bag, his hand brushing against the cold glass of the teal vial. The sight of it taunts him.

"What is that, anyway?" Azalea asks, her tone light as if they were discussing the weather. "Insurance for Michael, you said?"

"It is a poison," he admits, voice low. He braces for her censure, expecting her to recoil from him. First, she'd seen him take a soul; now she'd know he's plotting murder. Breaking the Third Rule to use it feels like a betrayal of everything he stands for—but Michael has left him no choice. He can't have regrets, or else they'll drown him.

"Oh," she says casually, her tone devoid of judgment. "So, poison's how wraiths die then?"

Alec tucks the vial away and flips his journal open, his movements stiff. "Copper," he corrects. "We can be wounded through magic or brute strength, but we heal almost instantly. Copper undoes that stasis. Touching it burns us. Too much... would kill."

"And the vial?"

"It's a poison composed of copper." His grip tightens on the journal as he imagines the gruesome consequences of using it. The thought of inflicting that on Michael is repugnant, but it's a necessary evil. He hates how it gnaws at his principles, how it feels like renouncing his identity entirely.

She looks at the bag before turning gaze back to the dark road. "What a weird form of kryptonite."

He clears his throat as he replaces the journal. "I have no experience with that mineral. To my knowledge only copper harms us."

She snickers, tapping his shoulder with her knuckles. "It's not real. It's from comics, I don't know, I never read them. Like iron for fairies or silver for werewolves. Everyone's got a weakness, right?"

His brow furrows. "Iron for fairies is an outdated myth. Pure cold iron is no longer produced. And there are no such things as werewolves."

"But there *are* fairies?" Her eyes brighten with genuine delight. "Awesome."

Alec softens despite himself. "Yes, though their magic has been bound for centuries."

They lapse into silence until she perks up again. "Is that why you're so bad at using human technology? Because of the copper in it?"

He shakes his head. "I was unaware copper was prevalent. Wraiths avoid technology because it's beneath us."

She scoffs. "Beneath you? That's ignorant. Humans might not have magic, but we've got brains. You can run fast and do alchemy, sure, but we've got cars, planes, and the internet. And don't get me started on communication."

"We can speak to each other through spelled mirrors," he says.

She snorts. "And you'd have to lug one of those around. Even my crappy flip phone is portable." She pulls it out of her pocket and tosses it to him. "This is much more convenient."

He catches it gingerly. The plastic feels odd, tingling faintly against his skin. The image on the screen has changed since the last time—no longer a smiling Azalea with a friend but a photograph of a red amaranth. He isn't sure of the flower's meaning, but the choice unsettles him.

"Does it hurt?" Azalea watches him with a curious expression. He shakes his head. "It's got copper in it," she explains. "I just remembered. So does the car."

He flips the phone over. Like the first few times he was near the phone, the tingling is unpleasant but feels nothing like the stabbing pain that comes from touching raw copper. The revelation explains why sitting in the vehicle causes him discomfort as well. The layers of the plastic in the phone must protect him somehow. When it pings, he returns it to her in case the copper inside is reacting to him.

Azalea opens it and presses it to her ear with a groan. "I'm too relaxed to deal with you right now, Eli. Stop calling."

Alec straightens. Has she abandoned her mission to save her brother? Only hours earlier, she'd been adamant about risking life and limb on the mere *suspicion* that Eli needed help. Perhaps his willingness to steal a soul for her—and their coupling—had shifted her priorities.

Her sudden bark of laughter startles him. "It's gross when I have sex but not you? Hypocrite. How'd you even know?" She leans back, glancing at Alec with a smirk before focusing back on the road. "This is why I left, Eli. It was always the Eli show, featuring Azalea."

She pauses, then raises her voice. "No, the reason I'm *angrier* is because I'm finally out from under your thumb, and you can't stand it. Newsflash, Eli: I'm done being your backup plan. I've got some ideas of my own now." She grins wickedly at Alec, before speaking back into the device. "Have you checked out that little tip I left you?"

Her smirk falters as she listens, then her face twists into a scowl. "Oh, screw Michael. If the cops don't deal with you, maybe he will." With a sharp snap, she slams the phone shut and hurls it at Alec's feet.

He flinches as the phone skids across the floorboards. "Is everything alright?"

"It's fine," she snaps. "Except he's still cozying up to Michael."

He'll never correct his mistake in choosing Eli for prey at this rate. He can only hope Michael loses interest soon and Azalea forgives him for his part in it. "Did he say Michael was still hunting us?"

She shrugs. "I'd guess he still is, considering he's got Eli trying to convince me to go home to 'show me everything in person.'"

Alec stares out at the dark road, unease prickling at his skin. "Should I assume your final declaration means you've abandoned your quest to save him?"

Her silence stretches, and he takes it as agreement. "That's wise. After some time, we'll find a new sanctuary—perhaps one of your choosing."

"How magnanimous of you," she mutters. In a louder voice, she says, "At least Eli's handled now, either by Michael or my surprise."

"What surprise?"

She gives him that sharp, unpleasant grin again. It's an expression he didn't like on Michael and hates on her.

"I tipped off the cops about Eli." Her tone makes it sound reasonable, but Alec knows it is anything but. "Told them he's been stealing from you. He should get a visit from the boys in blue any time now, if he hasn't already. That'll stop him from bothering me."

His skin feels as though he's still touching the phone. "Why would you do that? What happened to 'he's important' and we must save him?"

"Oh, like you liked him? Were you two going to be best friends? You planning to invite him to the Amanas, and we'll all share a town-house?"

That wasn't the point. "I'd be remiss not to mention that is an incredible breach of my privacy—"

"It's not like they wouldn't catch him if he actually stole from you," she says. "But a night in jail would have done him some good."

"—but your actions towards your brother are both baffling and irreconcilable," he says, as if she hasn't spoken. "I knew he frustrated you, and I certainly detest the man. But I believed you cared for his wellbeing. You asked that I save him to make up for choosing him as prey."

"I changed my mind," she says flippantly.

"When—then or now? You left the note before leaving Lonetree. But it was only this morning you demanded we risk traveling to Selessen and now want his punishment. Why did we spend an entire day on a fruitless errand that could have *killed* you if you actively intended on some manner of harm befalling him?"

She smirks. "Two birds, remember? You can't blame me for taking advantage of the opportunity to get into Selessen."

His fingers twitch as he restrains tearing at his hair in agitation. "What happened to you, Azalea? The woman I met, one whose soul is filled with light and joy, would not so readily abandon her family and blithely disregard my concerns. That woman cared for her family and had not a vicious bone in her body. The woman *this morning* wanted to save her brother, not send him to his gaoler!"

She laughs, a callous sound. "Don't be a hypocrite, Alec. Eli was looking at a few nights in jail, maybe some long-term deserved consequences, with or without a soul. At least I didn't create a poison for him."

"I'm the monster, Azalea," he responds with a growl. "You don't have that excuse."

Her only response is to toss her phone out the window, its faint clatter on the pavement echoing in the silence that follows. They don't speak again for the rest of the drive.

Chapter 50

Then

ALEC HAD WALKED THIS path countless times in his human life, but not once since his conversion. Yet, a week after Cassius's untimely death, he found himself back here, treading the worn trail that circled the crystal-clear lake. The familiarity struck him with every step. He could almost hear his sister's teasing voice echoing over the water, chiding him to do all the chores while she splashed and played. At the time, her taunts had grated on him, but now he would give anything to hear her laugh again. That longing was why he'd returned—to remember, to mourn, and perhaps, foolishly, to feel some fragment of his old self again.

The trail curved around a bend, opening up a breathtaking view of the mountain that towered over their village. It stretched skyward, claiming its space alongside the gods. The sight churned a familiar ache in his stomach. As a child, he'd felt dwarfed by its size, a tiny, insignificant speck in its shadow. Now, as a wraith, he knew the truth: he, and all his kind, were still insignificant.

A gnarled tree stood sentinel by the path, unchanged in the decades since he'd last walked this way. Beyond it, a modest circular hut came into view, its roof still covered in pink-tipped heather. Outside, a young woman sat braiding flowers, two children crawling at her feet. Her black hair, longer than Alec remembered, was styled like the crown she wove. She worked with a quiet, practiced ease, her soul radiating contentment and fulfillment. Alec felt its purity, unblemished by guilt or malice. He sighed softly. She hadn't moved on to her husband's kin-group as tradition dictated but stayed here with their mother. He wondered if that choice had been influenced by his disappearance, though he knew better than to dwell on such thoughts.

He smiled faintly as she placed the completed crown on the elder child's head. The boy, no older than six, beamed and tilted his head to admire his new adornment, chattering excitedly. Alec felt a warmth he hadn't known in years, the guilt threatening to drown him ebbing slightly at the sight of their simple happiness.

The hut's door creaked open, and an older woman emerged. Alec froze. His mother. Her hair, now white, was styled like her daughter's, and her frail frame seemed to shrink in the doorway. She moved slowly, leaning on the wooden frame for support, but her eyes were sharp, full of the same determination he remembered.

"Mother," his sister said, leaping to her feet and easing the children aside. "You must rest. You shouldn't be up."

The older woman waved her off with a teasing smile. "Daughter, you forget—I am still your mother. You may have children of your own, but you'll always mind me."

Their gentle bickering sent a pang through Alec's chest. He closed his eyes, trying to imprint the moment into his memory. He'd never been good enough for their village, always falling short in the eyes of others, but he had been happy enough. He could almost imagine standing beside his mother now, guiding her back inside. But the woman in his mind, like the real one before him, would have waved him off too.

"I want to see the mountain again," his mother said, gesturing to the peaks that loomed in the distance. "While I still can."

Alec's breath caught. This was his last chance. There would be no seeing her again after death, no redemption for his cowardice. He stepped forward, determined to bridge the gap between them. Surely, just this once, he could be allowed this weakness.

Before he could take another step, the hairs on the back of his neck rose. He stilled. Another wraith was near.

In an instant, Michael appeared behind him, his grip firm as he cuffed Alec lightly on the head and dragged him back from the familiar scene.

"Alesandro," Michael hissed, his voice low with warning. "We've discussed this. You cannot be here. There is nothing for you here."

Alec lowered his gaze to the ground, sand shifting beneath his feet. When Michael had converted him, he'd framed it as salvation from a dull, lonely life. But more often than not, Alec wondered if it would have been kinder to take his soul or end his life outright. Surely it would have been less painful than drip-drip-drip of regret like water beating down rocks.

"I know," Alec muttered. "But I wanted to see her. Just once more."

Michael pinched the bridge of his nose, exhaling sharply. "You're playing a dangerous game. This would break not one but two Rules. I've told you before—there are ways to bend them, but what you're doing here? It's reckless, and I can't protect you if you keep making these choices."

"It couldn't hurt," Alec insisted quietly, daring to look up. "Just to let her know I'm safe. To say goodbye." His gaze returned to his mother, the weight of his longing pulling him forward. "I should have done it before. Maybe even—"

The slap was sudden, sharp. Alec's cheek burned as he staggered slightly.

"Damnit, Alesandro," Michael growled. "Have you forgotten the Teachings so soon? Revealing yourself would bring them nothing but pain. You'd hurt them, Alec. And it would destroy you."

Alec stared at the ground, his fists clenched. "It's already destroying me."

Michael's expression softened, and he placed a hand on Alec's cheek, covering the sting. "They would hate you," he murmured. "If they saw you as you are now. You'd be nothing but a monster to them."

Alec's gaze lingered on his mother and sister for another long moment, memorizing the curve of their faces, the warmth of their laughter. Then, slowly, Michael began pulling him away.

"You still have me," Michael said, his tone light but his words heavy with finality. "And the family. You must have realized by now—only monsters can care for wraiths."

Chapter 51

Azzie sets them up in a small hotel near the main Amana colony. It's five to midnight when they arrive, and even in the dark, the place radiates cleanliness and care. The room is tiny, furnished with light woods and floral patterns. Azzie from a few years ago, Azzie from a few months ago, hell—Azzie from last night would have *loved* it. A quaint little escape, far from the monotony of Lonetree. But now, after everything she's seen and done, the charm feels stifling. Quaint isn't enough. Humanity isn't enough. Not anymore.

Alec sulks on the drive, and when they arrive, he gives her those puppy-dog eyes that make her want to laugh. Or scream. She suppresses an eye roll and plants a quick goodnight kiss on his cheek. It seems to placate him enough for her to slip into bed without further conversation. He doesn't argue or push her, which is good because she doesn't have the energy for him right now. She may have shocked him on the drive, but she's not apologizing for her evolving mind. In fact, she's downright proud of it—she isn't a damsel and Alec won't be saving her, much like Eli can't lock her in a tower. Alec will understand that someday. And if he doesn't, she'll figure that out. Freedom comes in all forms.

She curls into the queen-sized bed, pulling the crisp sheets over her shoulders, and hides the necklace pooling at her throat. Today changed everything. It clarified her path. Tomorrow, she'll make it happen.

Azzie wakes to the feeling of Alec's gaze on her. He's sitting across the room, his face carefully neutral, though his shoulders are tense. She stretches languidly, brushing the sleep from her eyes, and reaches for her green shirt.

"Did you have plans for today?" she asks casually, keeping her back to him as she pulls the shirt over her head.

"To lie low and avoid possible exposure," he says.

She claws her fingers through her hair until the strands are tangle-free. When she finishes, she saunters towards him and strokes her hands down his chest. It still surprises her that this lithe hipster-looking body holds so much power. She can only imagine how much she'd have. "You should relax like we talked about. Take everything off and take a bath or shower. Wraiths can shower, right? You don't melt or anything?"

"We don't melt. We also don't need to clean, but I've heard it done."

She drags her fingers from his chest, migrating downward "There you go. Go take a shower."

He furrows his brow but doesn't outright disagree. "Why would I do that?"

She curls her lips. "You're giving up the Rules, that means acting more humanlike. Humans stand in the shower, or bathe, to relax."

His frown deepens. "I haven't abandoned the Rules."

"Of course not. Just the ones that mean you hook up with a human, tell me everything I want to know about wraiths, and have copper poison for Michael. Those Rules?"

He closes his eyes, pinching the bridge of his nose. She grins. He's like a skittish lamb sometimes, so unsure, so self-contained. It reminds her of her past self. It's almost sweet. But growth comes quickly, and he needs to catch up.

"Let me help," she says, tugging at the hem of his shirt. He hesitates for a long moment before lifting his arms. Piece by piece, she undresses him, the reluctant compliance in his movements making her smile. Finally, she gestures to his ring. "That too."

He stares at her, his fingers twitching toward the band. "Why?"

"Part of letting go," she says lightly. "You can put it back on after. For now, you're human. Showers are human."

He exhales sharply but slides the ring off, placing it carefully into his bag. "What will you do while I shower?"

"I'll grab breakfast," she says, glancing toward the window. If not for the necklace, she doesn't know how she'd pull this off. "No point sitting here waiting on you. Since you don't eat."

"Would you need to drive?" He clenches his fists again, running his thumb over his bare ring finger.

"It's fine. I'll be safe," she assures.

"I worry about you taking the car."

She affects an anguished look, one she saw Eli make each time she called him on his games. "Do you not trust me?"

"With everything," he murmurs.

It's a lie, but she doesn't call him on it. Lies are the foundation of her day, after all. "I want to check out the sights without having to walk everywhere."

He reaches out for her but aborts the movement when his eyes land on his empty finger. "I apologize, Azalea. I didn't realize your distaste for walking. You appeared to do it regularly in Lonetree and the surroundings here are more charming than your hometown," he says.

"It's not my hometown," she snaps. She inhales deeply. She can stay calm for a few more minutes until he's ensconced in the bathroom. "That's why I want to drive. I prefer to enjoy the grandeur of nature from the other side of a closed window. In this case, a *car* window."

His shoulders are taut, breath gusting out of him in deep pants. But he melts into her when she steps up to him, her arms winding around his hips and coming to rest on his slim back. His interest rouses against her thigh, but she doesn't have time for that now.

"Look, I'll go explore a little and get breakfast, you go relax in the shower." She kisses his neck right under his ear. "Maybe I can convince you to relax with me later."

He shivers and releases her, frowning. "We can discuss that," he says. She pecks him on the lips and points towards the bathroom.

The bathroom door clicks shut, and the sound of running water begins. Azzie doesn't hesitate. She grabs the car keys from the nightstand and rummages through his bag until her fingers close around the ring. It's heavier than she expected, the gem bisected with a line and inscribed with Latin she can't fully read. Something about life and death, and Domination.

She slips half of the ring back into his bag and slides the other onto her thumb. Admiring the way it feels, the way it gleams in the faint light of the room, she grins. Without looking back, she heads for the car.

Chapter 52

ELI SITS SLUMPED ON the floor of Michael's bizarre, suffocating den, his back pressed against the cool glass of the mirror that brought him here. It's been over an hour since Michael vanished, leaving him stranded in the technicolor nightmare of neon pillows and scandalous tapestries. He's tugging at his dirty blond hair, lank and lifeless now, a far cry from the artful tousle he used to maintain with pride. Every move feels sluggish, as though the oppressive air of this place weighs him down.

The rippling sound of the mirror draws his gaze upward. Michael spills into the room in a flash of motion, landing with a graceful bow that makes Eli's stomach churn. His blue hair brushes the ground before he straightens, grinning like the Cheshire Cat.

"Decided traveling through mirrors was too normal so you added in acrobatics?" Eli motions to the new mirror hiding behind one of the curtained walls. He's learned a lot in the past few days.

Michael smirks. "Life's too short to do things *normally*."

"Not for you," Eli whispers.

Michael slinks to his knees and crawls over to him, grabbing the back of Eli's neck with his big hands. "What mood did I find you in, dearest?"

Eli shrugs, his shoulder brushing against Michael's arm. "Trying not to feel anything. Just waiting for it all to be over."

Michael's hands tighten briefly, and his emerald eyes flash with something unreadable. "Not long now. We'll find her, and I'll fix everything she's ruined." His voice is sharp, but there's an edge of something else—perhaps regret, though Eli doubts it's for him.

Michael avoids mentioning Alec, which is fine with Eli.

Eli sighs. "What next?"

Michael's mood shifts instantly, brightening as he gestures toward the other mirror. "A trip, my darling. I've a co-conspirator to see, and I'd hate to leave you here alone again. Shall we?"

Eli hesitates, his instincts screaming at him to run back to Lonetree, to whatever normalcy might still exist there. But he doesn't move. The allure of the wraith world has faded, replaced by a bone-deep weariness. Everything about it—Michael, the mirrors, the endless scheming—grates on him. All he wants is to go back home to their dull, predictable lives without being touched by the supernatural. He blames Azzie for those thoughts.

It *is* her fault. And it's also her fault that he follows.

The mirror deposits them in what looks like a dank cellar. The stale scent of earth clings to the air, and the flickering light of a single candle casts long, eerie shadows across the packed dirt walls and ceiling. Eli slumps against the mirror, already regretting the journey.

Michael strides forward to greet the room's other occupant, a petite woman draped in nothing but her own hair and a mantle of scars that glint faintly in the candlelight. Even in the gloom, Eli can tell she's beautiful, her sharp features exuding a quiet menace. Her gaze locks onto him, piercing and unnerving, even as Michael kisses her cheek and lets his hands roam her bare hip. When she looks away to kiss Michael on the lips, the bottom drops out of Eli's stomach.

"This one's jealous," she says. "I didn't think that was your type." Even her deep voice is alluring, like a lounge singer.

Michael sighs theatrically, glancing back at Eli. "Yes, it's frustrating. But with your help, I hope to have it handled."

The woman sneers, her eyes raking over Eli like he's an insect. "He's distracting."

Michael sighs again. "You must accept it for now. I certainly am."

The woman tugs Michael toward a wooden door that looks as flimsy as a fence. "Let me show you the war room. He can stay here."

Michael grins, and Eli curls lower until his back bows against the glass mirror behind him. He's surprised he hadn't toppled to the ground to curl up in his own insecurities.

Michael casts Eli a tired smile over his shoulder. "Be patient, sweetheart. I imagine that's easier for you now."

The door creaks shut behind them, leaving Eli alone in the dimly lit room. He slides down to the floor, his back curving under the weight of his own misery. In the two days since Az left, he's become someone he doesn't recognize—dull, sad, directionless. He hates it. He wants to be angry, reckless, alive again. But all he feels is a hollow ache.

He pulls hard on his hair before crawling over to the door, too uncomfortable to even stand. He'll tell Michael how much he wants to go back home and for everything to be back to normal. Michael might listen this time.

As he reaches the door, he hears voices through the thin wood. He freezes.

"He will hate you for this," the woman says, her tone sharp.

Michael's laugh follows, low and tired. "No, love. In centuries, he'll thank me."

Eli stays rooted to the spot, unable to move.

Chapter 53

Azzie barrels into Chicago in just under three hours, her foot pressed firmly on the gas the entire way. The storm that chased her from Iowa City to Illinois—a thunderous beast of rain and dark skies—would've terrified her once. But now? The slick roads and howling wind are nothing. She has a mission, a goal, and nothing will stop her. Not the storm. Not the car. Not Alec.

Especially not Alec.

She doesn't know how long she has until he figures out she lied. He'll find the ring missing, and the yellow vial too, and he'll know. He's clever—too clever sometimes—and he'll guess where she's going. To Selessen. To take what she needs.

He's hers, she knows that much. It doesn't matter that she lied to him or left him behind. Somehow, he's imprinted on her, his presence wound tightly around her soul. The thought makes her snort as she wrenches open the car door, stepping out into the city. Her flats squelch against the wet pavement, but she doesn't care. Alec is only a piece of her puzzle. There's more to her than him, and it's time to chase what she really wants. That's what her entire trip is about: focusing on her own needs for once. Not Eli's, not Alec's.

And what she wants is simple: *freedom*. Freedom from Eli's drama. Freedom from Alec's rules. Freedom to become something bigger, something stronger. The idea of being converted beats in her brain like a second heartbeat, as if it's been there all along, written in ink so permanent it can't be scrubbed away. She doesn't question it. Why would she? The pull is undeniable.

She knows she'll find what she's looking for in Selessen. Gerald likes her. She can convince him. All she has to do is get through the Cloud Gate.

The storm breaks over Chicago just as she reaches the park. Rain lashes against her face, cold and stinging, but it doesn't slow her down. She races across the wet concrete, her flats slipping with every step. Around her, tourists flee for cover, but she doesn't stop. She's almost there. Her chest heaves as she skids to a halt in front of the Cloud Gate, its metallic surface gleaming like a beacon in the rain.

The ring on her finger feels heavy, the weight of it grounding her. She presses her hand to the mirror, and the surface ripples beneath her touch. With a grin of triumph, she steps forward, her right foot plunging through the portal. The sensation is strange—like walking through pudding—but she doesn't falter. The rest of her follows, the cool, otherworldly pull dragging her forward.

Then something catches her by the collar and yanks her back.

The force is brutal, snapping her out of the mirror and sending her sprawling onto the wet pavement. Her shirt rips as she spins around, scrambling to her feet. She already knows who it is.

There stands a panting Alec, one arm holding her oversized and half-shredded shirt, with eyes like a lit flame.

Chapter 54

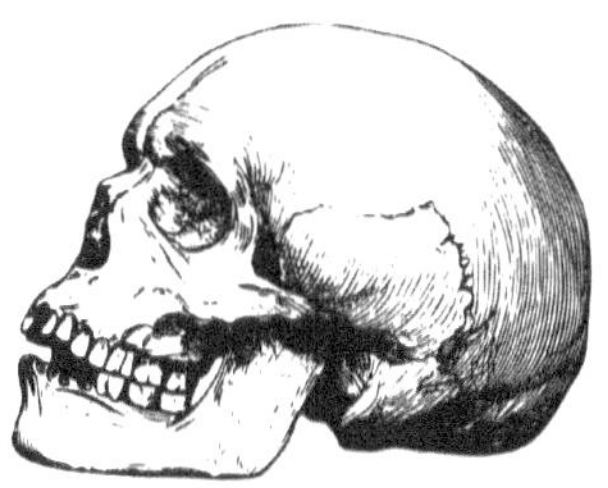

ARRIVING IN THE AMANAS should let him breathe without dread for the first time in days. He's done everything right this time—no trace for Michael to follow, no mirrors nearby to expose them, and a place secluded enough to keep Azalea safe from both wraiths and herself. But as he sits on the edge of the bed, elbows on his knees and head in his hands, the familiar dread returns.

Azalea is becoming nearly unrecognizable. The woman he met—charming, sweet, with a light so radiant it pierced through his eternal darkness—is vanishing before his eyes. In her place stands someone consumed by a selfish, single-mindedness that rivals the worst of his kind. He doesn't want to believe it, but her choices scream louder than her smile. He hadn't seen it coming, hadn't realized how far she'd slipped until now.

He's a fool for not seeing it sooner. The signs were there—her defiance in Selessen, the way her gaze lingers on wraiths as though they're something to aspire to. But Alec isn't ready to let go. He can't. That light she carried—no matter how dim it's become—is the closest he's felt to humanity in centuries. If there's a chance to guide her back, to protect her from the abyss she's skirting, he must take it.

When she suggests he take a moment for himself, he's wary but moved. Her request feels like a fragment of the Azalea he met, the one who saw him as more than a monster. Azalea has been his tether to humanity, the proof that he isn't beyond redemption. If she thinks something as simple as a shower could help, he'll try. It's the least he can do to show her he still trusts her, even as she's pulling away.

But by the time he notices his ring and the vial are missing, she's already gone.

The realization strikes like a physical blow, leaving him reeling. The ring, the vial—they're not just objects. They're symbols of everything he's tried to balance: the Rules, his feelings for her, the fragile thread connecting him to the wraith family and his humanity. She's torn that balance apart with a reckless abandon he never expected from her. His chest tightens as anger, fear, and betrayal collide in a storm of emotions. She knows what those items mean to him, knows the cost of her actions.

But more than the anger, there's a deep, aching sadness. He thought he could keep her safe, that he could protect her from the darkness he inhabits. Instead, he's brought her closer to it, let it seep into her soul. And now she's slipping away, chasing the very thing he fears most for her.

Alec rises from the bed, his movements mechanical as he reaches for his coat. He can't waste time wallowing in regret. She's out there, vulnerable and unprotected, walking straight into the jaws of danger. He's made too many mistakes already, but he won't let this be another. Whatever it takes, he'll bring her back. Even if it means shattering himself to do it.

He searches for her on foot, moving swiftly through the Amanas, his bare finger a constant reminder of her betrayal. Each step feels heavier than the last as weariness pools in his bones, dragging him down. She's taken more than his belongings—she's stolen his trust, his hope. But he can't abandon her. Not yet. Not ever.

The sprint to Chicago takes an hour, every second spent stewing in his anger and despair. By the time he reaches the Cloud Gate, he sees her—a streak of desperation and defiance—pressing through the mirror, the puddle-like surface rippling around her.

Before she can disappear entirely, he grabs her by the collar and yanks her back.

Her shirt tears as she stumbles out of the portal, spinning to face him with wide, startled eyes. Rain pounds around them, soaking her hair and plastering it to her face. She glares at him, her defiance sharp enough to cut through the storm. He stands there, his hand still clenched in the wet fabric of her shirt, panting from exertion. His anger ebbs; instead, he is simply tired. But words fail him.

Instead, he extends his hand, palm up. His silent demand is clear.

With a huff, she pulls the stolen items from her pocket and slaps them into his hand. The ring slides together easily, the two halves snapping into place with a satisfying click. The vial, however, he lets fall to the ground, where it shatters in a pool of gold liquid that swirls away with the rain.

"You're impossible," she spits, crossing her arms over her chest and jutting her chin out. The shiver that ripples through her body doesn't escape his notice, nor does the exhaustion that tugs at the corners of her mouth.

Before he can respond, a scroll shoots out from the mirror, hitting the wet pavement at his feet. The sight of Michael's elegant script sends a fresh wave of unease through him. He snatches it up and unrolls it, his hand shaking as he reads.

The girl's quite troublesome, isn't she? Of course, I can help if you meet me in Martalk tonight, dearest. Do not make me find you.

The paper crumples in his fist as the weight of his failure crashes down on him. He thought he'd outrun Michael. He's wrong.

"Can we get out of the rain?" Azalea says, drawing his attention to the damnable woman.

He grabs her wrist without a word, pulling her under the awning of a nearby building. Her wet shirt clings to her, the torn fabric revealing more than he cares for anyone to see. She leans back against the paper-covered wall, crossing her arms again.

"Alright, go ahead and lecture me," she says, closing her eyes and dropping her head back.

There's a metallic taste in his mouth. He must have bitten through his tongue. He spits the blood onto the ground. "That's all you have to say for yourself?"

She shrugs, the nonchalance in her posture igniting something dangerous in him. "I only did it because you won't convert me."

His voice rises, sharp and biting. "So, because I refuse, you try to get it on your own? Did you think Gerald would welcome you? Instead of using you to barter a better position for himself? Do you even understand how dangerous this was?"

Her smirk is maddening. "Maybe."

"Did you think some nice wraith, like me, would take you in and convert you? Someone less monstrous?" Alec stalks toward her, bending until their faces are inches apart. "Do you know why we don't convert people like you? Because you're the best kind of food—pure, naïve, and too docile for your own good." He studies her unconcerned expression. The Azalea he met two weeks ago would have panicked over spilled iced cream; this one might poison it.

"At least you *were* docile," he mutters, shaking his head. "You *were* kind. At the bare minimum, you weren't so duplicitous! Something's changed you, Azalea."

"It's called growing a spine, Alec. Maybe *you* need one," she says, jutting out her chin. "And fine—I shouldn't have lied or taken your stuff, but you need to stop acting like conversion isn't the end game here."

"You shouldn't have," he agrees, his voice straining for calm. "You shouldn't have lied to me. You shouldn't have stolen my ring. You shouldn't have driven three hours from safety." His voice rises until he's shouting. "You should not have tried to enter a wraith city as a human while Michael is after you!" He brandishes the parchment. "What if this had been him and not a note? He could've walked through that mirror instead of tossing this. He knows we're here now!"

She bares her teeth. "But he didn't. For all he knows, that note hit the ground."

"That isn't how it works! It would refuse to deliver unless I was within a certain range of a mirror," he says. "He's narrowed down our location much further than either of us should be comfortable with!"

"I'll say it again—you know we wouldn't have any of these problems if you just converted me," she says through clenched teeth. "You wouldn't have to explain this stuff to me, and Michael wouldn't be a threat if I was one of you. That's why I took the ring!"

"With circumstances as they are," he growls, "you will stay human for the entirety of our relationship. A relationship that shortens with each action you take."

"And of *course,* you get to make that decision," she says, rolling her eyes. "That isn't a relationship, that's a dictatorship. You're as bad as Eli."

She could have stricken him, and it would have hurt less. He presses his palms to his eyes, willing himself not to crumble. "I'm not trying to control you; I'm trying to protect you. My life is darkness, Azalea. You're the only light in it. I can't let that light be snuffed out by me."

"I won't make you better," she growls. He nearly recoils at the ferocity in her tone. "I might be naïve, but I'm not dense. I'm not your ticket to getting humanity back, or whatever it is you're wanting. You'll never be human again, but I *can* be one of you."

Alec opens his mouth, praying the Fates will grant him something—anything—to salvage this moment. But before he can speak, a voice comes from behind him.

"Hello, Alesandro."

The blood that is ever stagnant in his veins burns.

Chapter 55

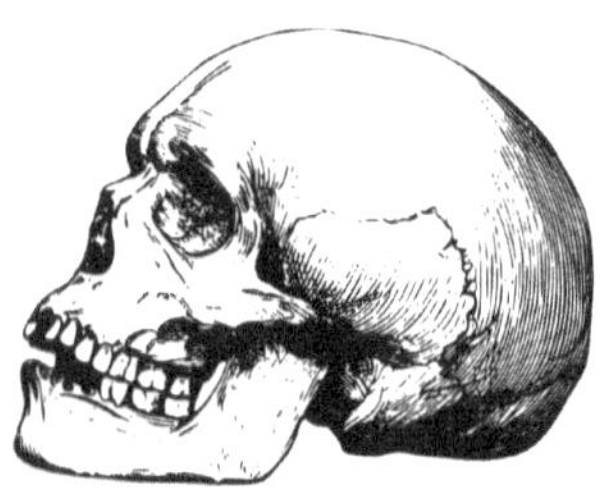

It isn't Michael. He knows that within an instant of hearing the first syllable from the wraith's mouth. But Gunval is a threat by himself, and he isn't alone. Myra and Agnes hang off Gunval's thick arms, vipers in humanlike form.

Azalea shuffles closer to Alec, finally showing some self-preservation at last. He shifts the traveling bag to rest between his feet. Two vials and his strength are all that stand between them and disaster. He recalls that Gunval is empathic like himself but doesn't remember if Myra or Agnes can read Azalea's thoughts or memories. Regardless, all three will have measured Azalea's soul and take any sign of affection as an invitation to strike.

Gunval is Alec's opposite in all things. A foot taller, inches broader, and brawny, Gunval was a raider in his human life, a member of an elite that demanded respect. He still expects that deference in his second life. His silk tunics and golden arm rings trail up his hairy forearms, his blond braids connecting neatly to a trimmed beard. The lines in his face suggest an elder's wisdom, but Alec has centuries on him.

Another wraith converted Gunval for his ruthlessness and indiscriminate killing. Alec exiled Gunval's sire for an unrelated Rule break long ago, leaving the family burdened with Gunval for a thousand years.

Alec and Gunval clashed early when Alec pushed the Council to curb human torture to avoid exposing their existence. Though Alec argued it was pragmatic, he suspects Gunval and Michael saw the deeper, personal reasons. The Council agreed with Alec and Gunval never forgave him of that.

Alec shifts Azalea behind him and starts to recite the customary greeting. Before the first syllable leaves his mouth, she elbows him and presses back to his side. Gunval's smile turns feral.

"Remember the Teachings," Gunval drawls, his gaze dragging down Azalea's wet form. Rain has plastered her ripped shirt to her body, emphasizing every soft, curving line. Myra and Agnes, two waiflike brunettes who travel with Gunval and act as both his lovers and entourage, sniff disdainfully at Gunval's obvious interest.

Panic and fury seize Alec. This is far worse than meeting Philip. Philip follows the Rules, and any infraction would involve the Council. Gunval, with his hatred for Alec, has no need to involve anyone. He could act on his own whims here and now. And Myra and Agnes, while frail in appearance, are ferocious killers, known for stalking and overpowering their prey together. Alec could possibly overpower Gunval and his entourage, but not while protecting Azalea.

Too much time passes without Alec speaking, and Gunval's eyes narrow as Myra and Agnes edge forward. "Follow the Rules," Alec rasps, his voice tight. He mutters to Azalea, "Wait by the car."

She inclines her head, staring at the three predators but refusing to move.

"What brings you to Selessen, Alesandro?" Myra titters, her baby-like voice grating.

"Playing," he quips, repeating his approach with Philip.

Myra and Agnes relax their stances slightly, but Gunval's leering continues. Azalea squares her shoulders, pushing her chest forward and displaying more supple skin. Alec feels her defiance in every motion.

"Alec's converting me," Azalea announces. Thunder booms overhead, a fitting omen. Alec's nails bite into his palms. Her words are lunacy, reckless idiocy, and yet they're said with such certainty that for a moment, he's stunned into silence.

"Is he now?" Gunval stalks toward her, extending a hand. Alec tenses, preparing to intervene, but Azalea allows Gunval to take her palm. He bows over it, his lips brushing her skin as Alec's entire body coils, ready to strike. A desperate plan flickers through his mind—attack Gunval, create a distraction, hope she runs fast enough.

"You'll make a welcome addition to the family, pet," Gunval purrs, his tone mocking but not hostile. Lightning flashes, illuminating the faint scar on his cheek from the time the Council had Alec punish him with a copper rod.

Alec sucks in a breath. He must have misheard but no—Gunval is smiling somewhat sincerely, even if it the expression would fit on a hissing cat. Myra and Agnes' expressions are blank but not hostile. Gunval straightens to smirk at Alec. He still holds her hand, and she doesn't yank it back like she did with Michael. "Where did you find her?"

"At a party," Alec lies, his voice carefully casual. Michael's crumpled note burns in his pocket.

"A wonderful party," Gunval says, leering at Azalea again. "She has the darkest soul of any human I've come across. And only half." He kisses her palm a second time while Azalea cocks her head in question. "I've not seen a human with half a soul. Were you that vicious you burned the good parts away?"

Alec's stomach plummets. Azalea doesn't react, save for a curling smirk. "I've lived a life," she says, chuckling darkly.

"Indeed, you have," Gunval murmurs, releasing her hand and snapping his fingers. Myra and Agnes wind their arms around his. "Come find me when he's done it. As you can see, I share very well." He growls a farewell to Alec before stalking away toward the Cloud Gate.

Azalea turns back to Alec, laughter bubbling from her lips. "Too pure to be a wraith, huh?"

Chapter 56

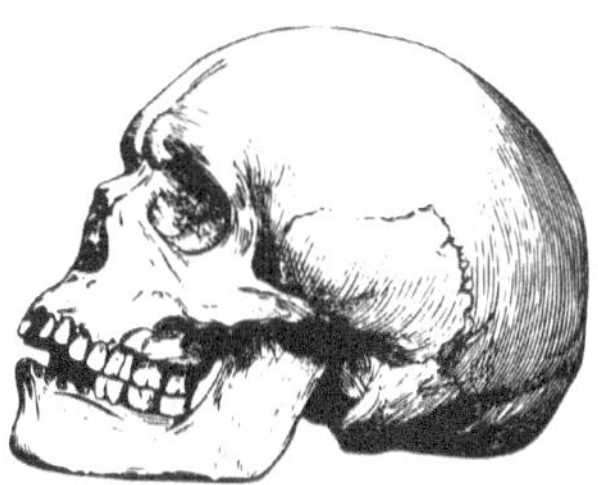

GUNVAL IS RIGHT, WHICH is not a phrase Alec has ever uttered or thought before. Michael somehow knows as well. As soon as Gunval and his lackeys disappeared through the portal, Alec reads her soul a third time.

It's identical to Eli's when Alec first met him—half gone, rotting with infection. The revelation feels like a physical wound, one that bleeds sluggishly and twinges with every beat of his stagnant heart. All his efforts to protect her humanity, every step taken to preserve the virtuous, good person she was—gone. Alec knows he didn't misread her when they met. Something drastic has changed in their three-week association. And the only new variable is him.

She was right—he'll never regain his humanity, and somehow, he's leaching out hers.

Defeated, he lets her lead him to a nearby restaurant without complaint. No other wraiths would question their acquaintance now, not after reading her soul. Even Michael might forgive him his lapse. Michael might even convert her as she so desperately desires.

At least then one of them would be happy.

The restaurant she chooses exudes luxury. It's sparsely lit with dark walls that accent with white linen-covered tables tucked into semi-private alcoves. Sleek wooden benches nestle under the tables, each capped by an unobtrusive candle centerpiece and gauzy white curtains. The entire room reeks of decadence and Alec scents more than one couple taking advantage of the flowing wine and closed curtains.

At Azalea's sharp demand, the hostess guides them to an open alcove. Once seated, a server appears, and Azalea orders. When the server leaves curtain swishes closed, Alec turns his gaze to the half-souled woman he loves. She stares back unabashed.

"Is the pouting because of the stealing, or the half soul thing?" she asks.

He slumps in his chair, pinching his eyes closed. "How cavalier you sound. We've learned your soul has darkened at an alarming rate and only just escaped from an encounter I was sure would end your life. Had I recognized that my continued presence would affect you thusly—"

He feels her shift in her seat. When he opens his eyes, she's frowning. How long has it been since he saw her smile, instead of that cold, Michael-like smirk?

"We're not done," she says, firm. "We're sticking together. We're not going back to Lonetree."

It's little comfort that she still desires him. "We won't return," he says, letting his hands fall to the table. But he doesn't know what they should do now. Even if Michael is in Martalk, his note confirms he will continue chasing them. And Alec also doesn't know if Gunval will seek them, or Michael, to meet Azalea again. He can't convert her, that's clear. "Not while Michael is still at large, and not while Gunval may remember you."

Azalea nods, appeased. "He seemed cool."

Alec sucks in a breath through clenched teeth. "He would have gutted you and let his minions ravage your corpse had your soul not already been corrupted."

She wrinkles her nose. "Lucky for me then."

He fists his hands until his knuckles lose color. "It wasn't lucky. It was reckless. We've both been reckless." He releases his fists and ducks his head. "I find myself at a loss now. I let you bring yourself to such risks."

"You didn't *let*—"

"I should never have agreed to take you to Selessen. Perhaps then your mind wouldn't have been tempted." He ducks his head, guilt pressing down on him. "I have acted contrary to every instinct since we met. I hunted in front of you, I took advantage of you in the euphoria-filled aftermath... any of these things could have tainted your soul. It's no wonder all of them together changed you."

The server returns with warm bread, and Azalea grabs a roll without concern. "So, my soul isn't as 'good' as it was when we met. Big deal. Changing is the whole point of being human."

"But my presence caused it," he says, voice cracking. "You were so pure and all I have done is show you the underbelly of society. My actions have done nothing but corrupt you."

"Please," she scoffs, tearing into the bread. "Every choice I've made, I've made knowingly. I wanted to go to Selessen, so we did. I wanted you to hunt, so we did. I took your ring because I wanted to. If my soul paid the price for those choices, that's a consequence I accepted. I have no regrets." Her gaze sharpens. "Well, I might have felt like something was off was when I drank the elixir. But the upside is we will both agree on what happens next."

He presses his palms to his eyes, shaking his head as if to dislodge her words. "Not again—"

"You'll convert me," she says without pausing. Her tone makes it sound as if she thinks it's obvious, but his tongue wants roll to the roof of his mouth at the demand.

"Gunval thinks you will, meaning it's the safest choice," she explains. "It'd certainly hide me from Michael. Plus, I've got less of a soul than I did when we met, right? Part of a soul is better than no soul." She thumps her clean hand on her chest. "Lock it in there now before it disappears." He growls when she has the gall to roll her eyes at him. "It's just practical," she says, shrugging.

"Gunval is an insect who can be crushed beneath my boot. Given time and preparation, I can remove him as a threat. I don't care about whatever you told Gunval," he snarls. "The same can be says for Michael," he adds as an afterthought, remembering his reasons for the vial.

"Further, your pragmatism at 'locking it in' ignores that I would have to *destroy* who you are. If this is how you behave with half a soul, I can't imagine how you'll be as a wraith." His mouth sets into a sneer.

She attempts to interrupt, but he speaks over her. "I would lose the Azalea we know entirely."

She laughs, the sound bitter. "According to you, that Azalea vanished the moment we met. You should have expected it. 'He who fights with monsters might take care lest he thereby become a monster. And if you gaze long into an abyss, the abyss also gazes into you.'"

He slams his hands on the table, drawing curious glances from nearby patrons. "Don't patronize me with quotes. You have fought nothing—you've *welcomed* the abyss," he says, waving a hand at her. "Evidenced by the deterioration that has been wrought. You have put us at continued risks, demanded I change you and blithely disregarded the consequences of your actions beginning, I'm only realizing, as far back as when I told you what I am."

She drops the bread and squares her shoulders, baring her teeth at him in a replica of a smile. How had he not recognized the change in her? That expression isn't new. The betrayal of her brother can't have been the first sign.

"I'm not ignoring them," she retorts. "It's just inevitable. For such an old being, it's ridiculous how naïve you are."

"And yet as I told you before, the naivety lives within you," he growls back. "You ignore the damage the change could do to you, assuming you survive it. You treat my entire existence as if it is a game you want to play."

"It is," she says, staring down at her bread with no sign that this conversation is as gut wrenching for her as it is for him. "We're all playing a game and wraiths are the clear winners. Who wouldn't want to join the elites?"

"I wouldn't," he hisses, the truth of his shame and hatred burbling from him to spill out over the table. "No one *sane* would choose this life, to willfully, willingly, destroy the souls of humans."

"You're only saying that because you've in it already and get to hold the keys. You use your gifts and get to keep that handy-dandy immortality by sucking out souls. And you'll never stop because you don't want to lose those advantages over your poor human food sources." She smirks at him. "Sure, you may feel guilty about doing it, but you'll take advantage of it at the expense of those who aren't wraiths. I bet if someone asked you to turn back to being human *right now,* you'd say no."

"I would—"

"And let's not forget how you balked at the lesser creatures wanting more power."

He startles. "What does that have to—that's irrelevant. During that same conversation, you told me it would be honorable to abandon the Rules and make the right choice. I assumed that meant *leaving* the depravity, not adding to its numbers."

She rolls her eyes, tossing her hair over her shoulder. "Please. You're not giving up the Rules, you're just hiding from them until I'm not around to tempt you anymore."

He reaches for the traveling bag sitting between them, yanking out the journal, his physical manifestation of the Rules, and brandishing it in her face. "Is that what it would take? If I renounce everything, if I exile myself for eternity, on the hope that we'll have a happy human lifetime together, would that satisfy you enough that you'll stop this madness?"

"No. You *know* what would satisfy me."

The journal falls from his hands, the spine hitting the table and the pages opening on their own. Words stare up at him, memories of his past life staining his missing soul. The idea of human happiness was nothing but a fantasy. "Where did it go wrong?"

He asks it of himself, but Azalea answers.

"I lost half my soul, unless you forgot," she says with a twist of her lips.

Chapter 57

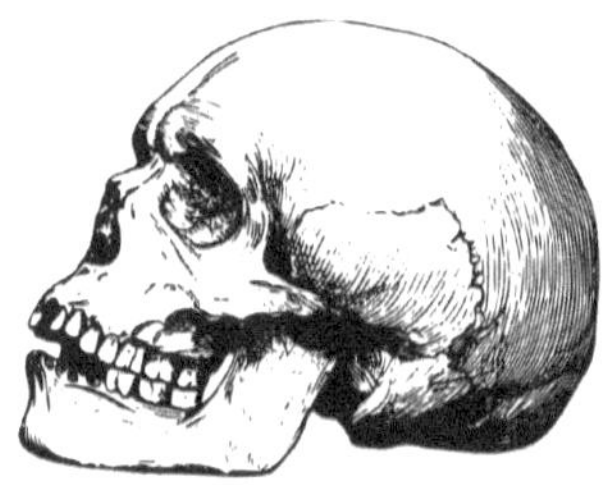

Conversion isn't the only choice for them. Desperation demands compromise.

There's one other way, a veritable last resort, one Alec hardly considered because it meant Azalea would spend more time with the family. But that didn't matter now. It's there, within the journal, one page after he'd written his choice of Eli, one line that marks the possibility of it, something Alec's heart had teased as a prospect when he experienced soulsickness: a gifted soul.

Azalea's half-souled status and audacity make the idea tenuous at best, but it could buy time and preserve what remained of her soul. It was a chance to stop her from slipping further, to avoid losing her entirely. Yet Alec couldn't rush into it like he had when he took her to the Amanas. Recklessness had led them here. This time, he needed to proceed with care.

He needs to ask Selina. She was the only wraith Alec knew who had loved a human and attempted the process. It hadn't worked for her, but Alec always suspected the failure stemmed from either a lack of true love or something flawed within the human. Selina could confirm whether Alec's relationship with Azalea had changed her and, more importantly, whether Azalea gifting her soul to him was even a possibility.

He knows where Selina lives—tracking the exiled was a habit born of necessity. Based on all reports, she lives a quiet life alone in a shack in Eastern Europe. His greatest obstacle is traveling there.

"Don't consider it bribery," Azalea says as they step into a bank in Milwaukee.

When he mentioned the need to travel, her brown eyes lit with a mischievous gleam, and her now-devious mind immediately provided a solution. Overcome by the allure of Europe, she'd agreed to return to the Amanas to rest and collect their things before driving here at sunrise. Along the way, they stopped only once—to buy her a new phone, a purchase she insisted was essential for the trip. Alec, unable to disappoint her further, relented and bought whatever she wanted.

"How is it not bribery when we are giving them a significant sum of gold to expedite a process that provides paperwork falsely stating we're citizens of some island?" he asks, his skepticism evident.

She shrugs, eyes fixed on her phone's bright screen. "That makes it fraud, not bribery. Maybe there's some overlap, I don't know—I wasn't really into legal procedurals when we had cable. Anyway, you shouldn't be so judgmental about another society's rules given how much you hate your own. If this is how they dole out citizenship, who are we to question it?" She raises her head and smirks at the tellers ahead of them. "We shouldn't say all this too loud though, just in case."

Before he can respond, she plants a light air kiss near his cheek and swans toward the counter. She returns much sooner than expected, her movements brisk and efficient.

"All that's left is for you to sign the wire verification," she whispers, practically bouncing on her heels. "They'll get the money this afternoon, and our passports will arrive tomorrow. Don't say anything to the teller if he asks." A giggle bubbles out as she grins up at him. "This is so cool!"

The teller asks nothing, merely pointing to where Alec needs to sign. With each signature, Azalea's smile grows wider, the crookedness he adores reappearing. His own faintly echoes hers. Perhaps this plan has merit. If Selina can identify what went wrong and confirm a gifted soul might work—

"And that's that," Azalea says, snatching the signed documents and sliding them back to the teller.

She leans in close, her breath warm against his ear. "I gave them the address of a fancy downtown hotel, so we'd better get a room."

And she grabs his hand, pulling him from the bank and into the bright morning light.

Chapter 58

Having half a soul *rocks*, Azzie decides, especially when it means a night at a fancy hotel and a free trip to Europe. The hotel she picks in Milwaukee is the most decadent in the city. There's a ceiling mural in the lobby, paintings lining the walls, and a marble staircase winding past ballrooms she can't resist exploring. The guest room is no less impressive—silk sheets on a massive pillow-top bed and a jacuzzi tub big enough to swim in.

When she wakes on those luxurious sheets the next morning, she briefly considers convincing Alec to stay a few more days. Only the thrill of the journey ahead keeps her from suggesting it.

The small Caribbean island she'd read about in an old issue of *Time* delivers as promised, even if their prices increased in the ten years since publication. Their "growth fund" accepts Alec's half-million-dollar donation without batting an eye, and expedited passports arrive the next day. Alec didn't even flinch at the price. He claims they're meeting a friend in Europe who can help "fix" her.

Not that she *needs* fixing. But if it gets her farther from Lonetree, she won't complain. Wraiths are immortal beings, so the friend must live somewhere pleasing, even if it's in a rundown mansion like Alec's. She assumes it's only Alec's guilt complex keeps him in squalor, the same guilt she floundered in until snapping up that necklace. She's met enough wraiths now to recognize that is a special Alec trait. Garish as he was, Michael at least looks wealthy, so she figures Alec's other friend is too. Wraiths can make *gold*, for God's sake.

Wealth does open doors, she thinks as she stares at the pharmacy photo of herself in the green booklet claiming her dual citizenship.

By the time they're boarding a plane—tickets purchased in cash—her excitement hasn't dimmed. It's her first flight, and though Alec refuses to divulge their destination, the promise of adventure in Europe keeps her simmering anger at a low boil.

Alec doesn't fare as well. He shivers and winces throughout the flight, his reaction to the copper in the plane's construction making him look miserable. She tries distracting him at first, but eventually gives up when he closes his eyes and broods. She makes a mental note to solve the copper issue after she's converted—something practical that will help her, Alec, and any other wraith worth her time. So far, that's a short list.

Their first-class cabin from New York to London more than makes up for his sulking. Complimentary snacks, celebrity treatment, and no one caring about her old clothes or ratty hair? She snaps photos of herself with a virgin mimosa, and even a few of them together, a memento of their first real trip together. She considers sending one to the barista at *The Baroque Bibliophile,* just to rub it in her face.

They land in London close to 1 a.m., just as her excitement fades. Alec, still brooding, drags her onto a smaller plane headed to somewhere called Kosice, Slovakia.

It's not her first or second choice, but when they disembark and Alec leads her into the town center, her spirits lift. Even at dawn, Kosice looks like a fairy tale—rainbow-colored gothic buildings, delicate streetlamps, and a tiny canal cutting through cobblestone streets. It's charming and well worth abandoning the United States for.

But when she suggests finding a hotel to rest, Alec insists they have one more leg of the journey. Begrudgingly, she helps him buy bus tickets to a place several hours away called Gordamara.

He isn't as affected by the copper in the bus and instead of flinching and digging his fingernails into his thighs, he remains silent at her side and watching her with gloomy eyes. Her new phone allows her to ignore his melancholic expressions.

After all, it's not like it's *her* fault she lost half her soul.

Then, the worst happens. The bus dumps them in a field that is too reminiscent of Lonetree for her liking and gives way to the most rundown place she'd ever seen.

Gordamara is nothing but a few dozen shacks crowded around the main street where the bus left them. It's dirt poor, and Azzie knows poor. The shacks appear to double as both stores on the bottom and homes at the top, but no windows display anything recognizable for purchase. Just beyond them is a trash filled road that leads off into the distance, where Alec frog marches Azzie as soon as they arrive. She considers planting her feet and standing her ground, but he's powerful enough to carry her. She scuffs her feet on the ground as she follows him, kicking up dirt and who knows what else.

Eyes watch them from broken windows and openings in thresholds that may at one point have had doors but have since rotted out. A few blocks down the street, Alec finally slows. In front of them stands a wooden building that looks like a poorly made shed, the sides not flush and the roof dipping in the center. It makes her family home in Lonetree look like a glamorous vacation spot.

"Tell me you didn't ruin our first vacation by taking us here," she says.

Alec doesn't meet her eyes. "I believe this place holds the answers we seek."

She plants her feet, crossing her arms. "The only answer you need is to the question 'will I convert Azzie today or tomorrow?' Because that's our only option unless you want me leaking out my soul the rest of my life. There is nothing you could learn here that we couldn't learn in a hotel back in Kosice."

"There is another option," he says quietly, "but I'm not sure it will work. It—it may do nothing."

They've been traveling for almost twenty hours, and she's too tired for his usual brooding. "Spit it out then so I can sleep."

"There is lore that a human may gift their soul, and we may share it," he explains softly. "You would gain immortality, and I—I would no longer need to hunt. The monstrousness inherent in wraiths would no longer apply to us."

"And we had to come to a landfill to do that?" she asks, huffing out a frustrated laugh.

"No, I—I don't know that it will work. It—it must be willing. My contact may know."

Her expression is flat. "What part of my actions lately made you think I *wouldn't* be willing?"

"Subtlety is lost on you both," an unfamiliar voice drawls.

Azzie and Alec whirl toward the source, where a woman leans in the doorway of a shack. Her sharp smile gleams in the dim light.

The depth of her voice rivals Azzie's own, though that's where the similarities end. The other woman is tall and waiflike, with tar black hair reaching her waist. Her golden skin is mottled, like someone threw a vat of acid on her, making it a kaleidoscope of metallic colors. Alec's eyes trail over her, but Azalea can't tell if he's staring because of her marked skin or because of how much is on display. She's barely dressed and, even with her burned skin, holds herself with a confidence that would make the old Azzie insecure and jealous.

That's one of the many unintended benefits of having only half a soul.

The woman smirks. "Get inside," she orders. Her dark eyes flare as they land on Azzie. "You first, Azalea. Then you, Alesandro."

Chapter 59

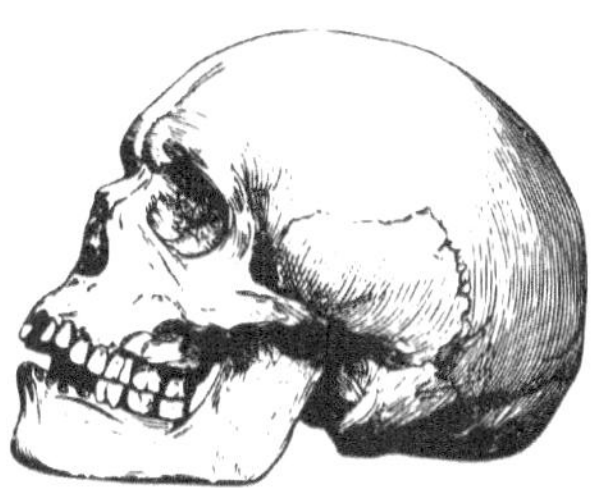

AZALEA STOPS SPEAKING TO him the moment he ushers her onto the bus to Gordamara, her gaze fixed on her new cell phone. Her silence is both a relief and an irritation. She only breaks it when they reach the shack where Selina supposedly lives.

Alec stares at the dirt and dead weeds underfoot as Azalea snarls her complaints. He can't bear to see the gleam in her eye—one part defiance, one part anticipation. He explains his thoughts quietly, not wanting to alert Selina to their presence prematurely. Azalea's anger and greed, radiating off her like a toxic cloud, are worrying signs of her soul's continued decay.

Azalea doesn't share his caution. Her voice rises in exasperation. "What part of my actions lately made you think I wouldn't be willing?"

"Subtlety is lost on you both," a woman who must be Selina says from her broken wooden door.

Alec spares a moment to study her. The fire that both ravaged her body and saved her life is evident on her skin and his eyes trail over her burned flesh. Does she regret what she lost for her spurious human love?

"Get inside," she demands. "You first, Azalea. Then you, Alesandro."

The sound of his birth name startles him. Azalea doesn't react to it, stomping inside without a word. He hadn't told Selina his true name, but Selina must have pulled it from Azalea's thoughts.

"Exile breaks through many of the blocks the family pressed down upon us." Selina laughs throatily. "This is twice I've explained myself in a single week and I tire of it. Get inside."

Alec follows Azalea into the shack, resigned. At least she still seems willing to proceed—though how long that willingness will last is another question.

The interior of Selina's home is no better than the exterior, comprising one small room, bare of furnishings and any comforts save a single mat on the dirt floor. Shadows loom from the corners, darkness cloaking anything, or anyone, hiding there. Azalea scoffs upon entry, wrapping her arms around herself.

"If you're finished mentally insulting my home," Selina cuts in, dropping gracefully onto the mat, kicking up a puff of dust, "I'll explain." Her vest hangs open, and Alec averts his eyes as she chuckles. "Sweet Alesandro. I'm covered now," she purrs.

Reluctantly, Alec looks. Her long black hair and open vest shield her body, but the image does little to ease his unease. Selina's demeanor and the squalor surrounding them could be poison to Azalea's already fragile soul.

"And now you insult *me*," Selina says, her tone clipped. "My desires to help you wane with every thought."

Azalea snorts, drawing Selina's sharp gaze. "I am aware of your thoughts, human," Selina says icily. "You, who wish to be my kin, do not deserve the opportunity you've been given."

"Don't speak of her in that way," Alec growls.

Selina stands and prowls towards Alec, hair swishing against her dark nipples. "Does the right hand of the Council have an issue with how I live? That is quite hypocritical. To answer your unasked question, exile removed the blocks on my magic, meaning I am no longer limited in my skills like you." She drags her gaze up and down his form. "Which is why I know any leverage you may have against me is nonexistent because of *her*."

"If you know why we're here, stop the games and give us the answers," Alec snaps.

"I know why you *think* you're here," Selina replies with an air of smugness. "But I'll only explain in private."

"Not that waiting inside or outside is that different," Azalea says under her breath.

Selina ignores her. "As for the question rattling around in your mind, your obsession in knowing why little Azalea turned up with such a vile half soul." She runs dirty fingers over Alec's black shirt, broken fingernails like cat's claws catching on his collarbones. "Have no fear, Alesandro. It was nothing you did. Michael did it, in his way."

Alec stiffens, instinctively stepping between Selina and Azalea. Michael. Of course. But how? Michael had barely spent five minutes in Azalea's presence, and Alec had been there the entire time. Regardless, Alec may not have thrown the stone, but he directed its trajectory.

"It's amusing that you trust me to speak on willing souls but not on this," Selina says, dropping back onto her mat.

He doesn't respond, turning instead to Azalea. Gently, he tilts her face toward him, studying her. Her phone drops to her lap, and she tilts her lips into a small, crooked grin—the same grin he fell for. Michael couldn't have done this. Alec would've noticed earlier, before they left, wouldn't he?

"I do not exist merely at your leisure, Alesandro," Selina says, watching his inspection of Azalea with narrowed eyes.

"Because you're so busy," Azalea mutters, rolling her eyes. The motion catches Alec's attention. His hand trembles as it trails down her neck, brushing against a thin cord that disappears into her shirt.

"What is this?" he asks, his voice tight.

"It's a grynn stone a hawker gave her while you were in Selessen," Selina says. Azalea's mouth drops open as smirk blossoms on Selina's angular face. "Yes, human, I can read present *and* past thoughts. Would you care to antagonize me more?"

Alec's stomach churns. "What were you thinking wearing this?" he hisses, tearing the cord from her neck.

"I don't think that's any of your business," she says, crossing her arms around her chest.

His jaw works before he can force himself to respond. "Everything you do is my business when your safety is at issue."

"She obtained it to mask her emotions from you for fear you would catch onto her plot," Selina coos. Her expression is gleeful. Though his gift doesn't work on wraiths, it doesn't take magic to recognize her disdain for Azalea.

"Oh my god, shut up!" Azalea snaps, her travel-weary hair tossing as she glares down at Selina.

"What plot?" Alec asks before his heart drops into his stomach. He presses the stone against his stomach with shaking hands. "The plot to have me convert you? Or something else? Something more?"

She scowls at Selina, before turning to Alec. "No. Yes. I wanted you to convert me the entire time, it's not like I've been subtle about it. But the emotions-erasing plan was to keep you from reading me until you did."

He clutches the stone, tensing his arms so much he almost vibrates, from fear or anger, he can't tell. "What were you thinking wearing this? *This* could be what diluted your soul."

Azalea crosses her arms. "Don't blame my jewelry. She said Michael did it."

"What if the hawker lied?" His voice rises. "What if it's imbued with something else? How—how did you even pay for it?"

"The stone did nothing to her soul," Selina says, unfurling from the mat like a feline and slinking toward him.

"Did exile give you a gift for truth scrying?" Alec's tone is snide even as Selina smiles like she has a secret. She probably does.

"Leave the whelp outside and I will give you the information you need," she says.

Azalea wrinkles her nose as she tracks her gaze down Selina's lithe body. Disgust and disinterest pool off her, scenting the surrounding air. Perhaps Selina was right and the grynn stone's only purpose had been to mask Azalea's stronger emotions, as they reach for him without effort again.

"Whatever. The sooner she explains, the sooner we can leave, and the sooner I give you my soul and become a wraith," Azalea says, stomping toward the door.

Alec catches her wrist, his other hand fumbling with his ring. The interlocking bands slide apart with a metallic click, the jewel splitting in two. He presses one half into her palm, curling her fingers around it. The honey-herb scent of intrigue and confusion wafts through the fetid air.

"Don't—don't seek a mirror, please," he says quietly. "This is only if you must escape. There is a true mirror in Montreal, near the Sulpician Seminary. If something happens and a wraith finds you, run through the closest mirror with that destination in mind. And I'll find you."

Azalea holds the jewel up to the dim light, her eyes gleaming. Alec falters.

"Promise me, Azalea—promise me you will only use this if you are in danger."

Azalea's eyes flick back to Alec as she nods, then slips out of the shack. The acrid scent of eagerness lingers in her wake. Alec moves to follow, but Selina's hand clamps onto his forearm, yanking him back.

"No true harm will come to her when she is out of your sight," Selina says.

"That you qualified your promise doesn't ease my fears," Alec counters, his gaze locked on the closed door. "Why should I believe you?"

She flattens her hand and strokes it down to his palm. "Do you have a choice?"

Alec clenches his fist, cutting off her unwelcome touch. "Again, that's not a comforting response."

"It wasn't meant to be, Alesandro." She steps back, her burned lips curling into a faint smile, and motions toward the mat. She lounges on it as if she doesn't notice the dirt and dust. Alec sits stiffly beside her, back straight, muscles taut as bowstrings.

Selina chuckles, a low sound that grates in his ears. "How ironic that Alesandro, enforcer of the family's Rules, now seeks advice from an exile."

"Azalea would surely have an applicable quote for this moment," Alec says grimly. "Though whether it would console or cut would depend on which Azalea we're speaking of."

"It all comes back to her," Selina observes.

"She is everything to me," he admits softly. If Selina has been prying into his thoughts, she already knows this. Azalea is all he has left.

Selina narrows her gaze at the closed door. "You've known her for mere weeks. It was her purity that ensnared you, but that human has not a pure trait within her now."

He slumps until his bowed back presses into the dirt wall behind him. Part of his dogged determination was to refuse conceding a defeat, that he'd ruined another human just as he ruins everything. But the rest can feel her phantom fingers interlaced with his, hear her quiet laugh, smell the cranberry scent of her affection for him. "It began that way, yes," he admits. "Her humanity drew me, along with my intrigue in being unable to read her, but her effortless charm kept me returning to her until I could no longer resist."

"Effortless, I will agree with, as she appeared to put little effort in. But charm?" Selina says, sneering. "Debatable."

Alec's fists clench at the insult. "Do not speak ill of her. This may be your home, but she matters to me."

Selina tilts her head, studying him. "And what if the willing soul gambit doesn't restore her? What if it keeps her as corrupt as the worst of us?"

He's thought through the same over the past twenty-four hours. Azalea burrowed under his skin, no matter that she's stinging him like a nettle now. "I'll still be with her."

Selina sighs, leaning closer. "I've been where you are, Alesandro. I had my Ennam. Don't forsake everything for her. You aren't bound to her."

"It feels as though I am."

"That is your honor speaking," Selina says with a sharp scoff. "Not your feelings."

"Wraiths do not have honor," he mutters.

She strokes her fingers down his shoulder. "Some more than others."

He straightens, brushing her hand off. "I don't want to leave her alone too long. Tell me—can I fix her, this?"

"There is a way to give you what you seek," she says. "If you are sure this is the path you wish to take."

Alec's jaw tightens. "You have proven your skills by slipping within the crevices of my mind. Do you sense such fickleness in me?"

Selina smirks, her scarred lips twitching. "And yet, you're here, questioning."

Alec lets his head fall back against the wall with a dull thud, dirt crumbling around him. "You haven't been near the family in millennia, yet you still play their games. I assumed exile would be a wholly different life."

She slithers to stand and holds out a grimy hand. "Let me show you something."

Chapter 60

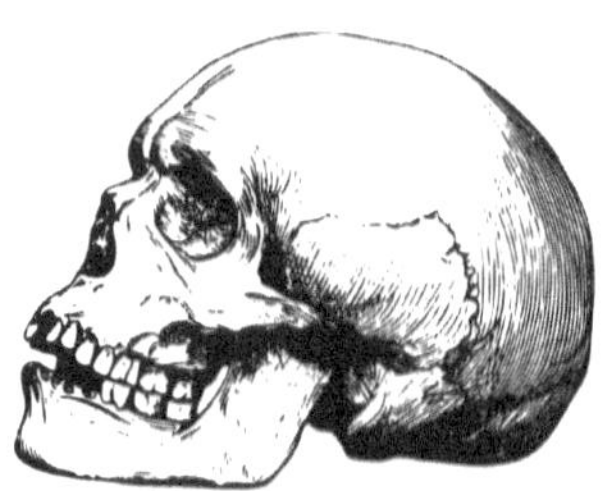

He doesn't take her hand but follows her as she lifts the mat they sat upon, revealing a hidden hole. Selina slips into the darkness below, and Alec hesitates, glancing at the shack's door. Then he steps into the void after her.

The hole leads to a labyrinth of rooms—an interconnected warren painstakingly carved out over years of exile. Selina leads him through twisting passageways, her bare feet kicking up dust. Alec's sharp eyes catch details as they pass: footprints of varying sizes in the dirt, a room filled with weaponry, another with glimmering gold, and yet another packed with copper plates that hum in his teeth.

Each room builds on a troubling conclusion. Selina hasn't been idle. She's been preparing. But for what?

Finally, they enter a small chamber lit by a single flickering candle. The walls shimmer like polished marble. Selina leans against one, flinching slightly, and Alec stays near the doorway, ready to flee.

"It looks as though you're preparing for war," he says cautiously.

Selina's teeth flash in a grin. "This is life in exile. We've been busy."

"You intend to attack—what? The Council?"

She shrugs, her vest slipping slightly to reveal more burned skin. Alec quickly averts his gaze. "Did you truly expect anything less? You put half of us in here, Alesandro. Did you think we'd sit idly by while creeping toward oblivion?"

"You were punished," he accuses. "You broke the Rules. You're lucky Council left you your lives."

"The Rules?" Selina scoffs. "You of all people, with your human burden, must understand how limiting the Rules are. Instead of recognizing the fallacy of their Rules, the Council, the *family*, forced us out of our homes, from our friends and the lives we had known, because we failed to meet the ideals defined before either of us lived our first lives." She motions to the room with a casual hand that belies the anger simmering in her expression. "We have clawed our way from the grave into which they tossed us, thrown off the dirt that buried us and are ready for our revenge."

Alec steps toward the door, his instincts screaming to leave. "I must alert—"

"Alert who? The Council? Michael?" Selina's voice cuts through his thoughts as she prowls closer. "You have nowhere to go. This," she gestures to the room, "is your future."

"No," he denies. "Azalea is my future. She will be restored, and we will live in peace, away from whatever conflict you attempt to bring. I thank you for the warning to avoid the family until you bring your foolhardy mission to its unsuccessful close." He planned stay away for the length of Azalea's human life; with a gifted soul, he can protect and hide them for the centuries until Selina and her band of rebels pursue a senseless coup. When things calm down, they'll reenter society/

Selina laughs bitterly, pressing forward to stand toe-to-toe with him, their chests brushing. "You think that human will be content to sit silently with you? I have been in her head; I know her desires. Indeed, I have walked this path. I let myself be veiled to my human lover Ennam, and his flaws."

"If you fix her as you alluded to," he snarls, "if she's returned to the woman I knew, then my life will branch from the path yours took."

"Even if she is 'fixed,' you can't go back," Selina argues. "You will have willingly accepted a human soul from one you claim to love. You considered the ultimate betrayal to protect her. Your compromises are Rule breaks, no matter how you try to disguise them. You can only choose *how* it happens, but you will be exiled at the close."

Hearing it out loud made it much more real. He clears his throat. "You don't know that."

She tosses her hair behind her shoulder, not to entice him but in frustration. Her skin slides against his chest and he shudders. "I do, Alesandro," she says, quieter now. "You must make the choice—your comrades in arms or an insignificant human. I cannot believe the Alesandro spoken of in whispers, the one ever fixed on the family would choose a human over those of us who did nothing except display some *supposed* weakness."

"You broke a Rule," Alec snarls, shoving her hard. But she remains pressed against him, her feet planted in the dirt.

"As did you," she says, breath and spittle spraying from her taunting mouth. "But my exile came from loving a worthless human. I am not blameless, but others are. Brygyd published poetry for the masses. Rawi acted as a healer. Those are not weaknesses!"

Alec scoffs and slips around her, gazing back towards the doorway that would lead him to Azalea. "And for every wraith who was exiled for things *you* consider acceptable," he growls, "another dozen were punished for the exposure they brought by murdering or torturing scores of humans. We cannot throw out the Rules because some were caught within it." They are monsters, no matter how gentle some can behave.

"Yes, we can," she roars. "Not simply for us, but for all the creatures oppressed by the Council's reign."

Alec clenches his fists until his nails scrape into the skin. "I said no, Selina."

She prowls around him to gaze into his eyes. Sincerity and anguish stare up at him. "I can accept that this choice is difficult, and you may need time to join us. But I tell you this as a former sister—you *must* abandon Azalea. Loving a human can bring nothing but pain."

His eyes flash. "I never asked your opinion. The only thing I need from you is your knowledge—tell me if giving me her soul will bring her back. Tell me if it allows me longer with her, half-souled or no. Tell me—tell me if I will spend eternity alone."

She reaches forward to run broken fingernails over his high cheekbones. He stiffens, grasping her wrists to remove them from his skin. Pain flits over her features before she appears to arrive at a decision. "Give me a moment."

She disappears into another room, leaving Alec with his racing thoughts. He presses his palms to his eyes, gripping the last thread of hope. Something buzzes under his skin, his worry perhaps. He can't sense Azalea's presence this far underground, but he's sure the solution is near. No matter what information Selina gives him, he will accept Azalea's soul, and she won't abandon him for her own selfish aims.

It's perfect. He'll make it perfect.

When Selina returns, she holds a compact bundle in her arms. Alec reaches for it, but she pulls it back, cradling it against her bare chest. "I do not believe the human will bring you happiness, but even with her—no man is an island. You cannot subsist on her alone."

"Another wraith citing verse," he says, twisting his lips. "You have that in common with Azalea. You might like her when I restore her humanity."

"I suspect I must accustom myself to her presence, regardless." She waves the bundle, wincing. "If you're sure?"

She hands it over, and he unwraps it with trembling hands. A piece of plastic drops into his palm—a cell phone, Azalea's new toy. Then a small piece of paper flutters to the ground. Alec snatches it up, dread pooling in his stomach.

It has only one line, in a neat script, one he's seen for millennia and more recently a day earlier outside the portal in Chicago.

We'll see you soon, dearest.

Chapter 61

Azzie fists her hands on her hips, Alec's ring catching on the loop of her jeans. The metal feels heavier than usual, like it knows she's betraying him just by being here. "At what point do you explain your dastardly plot?" she demands, her tone biting.

"Plot?" Michael splays his hands, his blond hair brushing his broad shoulders, the very picture of mock innocence. He tilts his head, studying her with unnerving intensity.

Azzie rolls her eyes, the gesture exaggerated. Michael's theatrics bored her when she had a full soul; now, they're just grating. "You know, the part where you reveal what you've done, why you're here, and what you want."

He chuckles softly. "That must make me the villain in your mind. And from your perspective, you believe yourself to be the hero? Your own subterfuge aside, do recall I can read your past and am *intimately* aware of each step you took that brought you to me."

"It's called self-interest," she drawls. "It makes the world go around."

"Self-interest," Michael repeats, the word dripping with disdain. "And yet, you don't wield it nearly as well as your brother. His confidence, his charm—they made his self-interest a weapon. Yours... is blunt at best."

Her fists tighten, but she forces her tone to stay flat. Eli didn't matter anymore. "Are you going to explain your plan, or do we just keep playing this little game?"

Michael leans back against the wall, his movements languid, as if he has all the time in the world. "Do you have somewhere else to be? As I recall, you came willingly," he responds mildly.

That's true. Azzie waited in the dirty street outside Selina's shack, uncomfortably reminded of the home she left, when Michael appeared beside her. Their conversation had been brief, Michael promising things Alec never would. But she kept her promise—she didn't search for a mirror but followed Michael to his home with the ring on her finger as protection.

Wherever Michael took her looks like a den of pleasure. Heavy brocade upholstery hangs on the walls, which swayed when Michael pushed them through the golden framed wall mirror. The room is dizzying, with greens, golds, reds, and purples combining in a chaotic kaleidoscope of color. Spooled silk and floor pillows cover the floor, like a pile of plush decadence. The floor pillows look unused, but the ostentatious mirror hanging on the ceiling says it's a lie, a place whose only use can be for Michael's debauchery. It isn't a room for a wraith but for a sultan with his many wives.

"I came," she says, returning her thoughts to the present, "because I thought you'd do what Alec wasn't man—wraith enough to do."

Michael's expression sharpens. "What a singularly minded creature you are. And what, precisely, do you think I'll do?"

Azalea spins to look at the uncovered mirror. She doesn't need the escape route yet; Michael might see reason, as he doesn't have the hang-ups Alec does. She fingers through her hair before turning back to him. "Convert me. Not drag me into some 'Picture of Dorian Gray' nightmare."

Michael laughs, a rich and full sound that grates on her nerves. "Does that mean I murder you before killing myself? Because *surely* you aren't comparing him to me simply because of my ageless beauty and life of hedonism. Shoddy work, love."

She sneers. "Reading human literature, Michael? How pedestrian. Shall I alert the Council at the next meeting?"

"We are all weak," he says, suddenly serious. "That's the Council's greatest fallacy. I have a weakness for human delights to overcome boredom. You have a weakness in your lack of self-worth, which you hide in spewing quotes to make yourself seem smart and aloof, hoping no one will call out your fraud."

She stiffens before dropping on one of the floor pillows. "It's not fraud," she says under her breath, staring down at the ring. The Latin words stare back, with only two she understands. *Non vita—not life.* Alec must have kept the half about 'not death' this time.

"Perhaps not fraud, but it provided you a cover of self-assurance that you were 'better' than everyone else you knew, when you knew, deep down, you were not." He tosses himself onto a pillow beside her, his blond hair spilling over a jewel toned throw pillow. "You quoted literature your peers had never heard and would never confirm whether what you were saying was applicable or appropriate. It made you feel smart."

"That's not why I did it," she grouses. It's not the *only* reason, at least.

"Not the sole reason but your stated reason—that literature allows you to experience the world without leaving your own home, that it was your only alternative until you can 'create quotes' of your own—is not the *true* one. That's buried in your psyche. It's why you desire to be converted, to gain the power you're lacking."

Azzie's jaw tightens. "Enough with the armchair psychology. Alec will be here in any minute. He'll take care of you, then I'll give him my soul and get immortality that way. You're only hurting your own chances of avoiding pain," she finishes with a simpering smile.

Michael leans forward, shuffling on a sequined pillow and resting his head on his hand. He looks the picture of ease and comfort. She wants to kick him. "Let me guess, the self-confidence started waning around age sixteen and became a crushing weight when you turned eighteen, which is when you first realized you needed to get away from it all."

The smirk falls. "Where the *hell* would you come up with that?"

Michael runs a finger over the hem of another pillow, leering up at her. "Your brother is quite chatty when the right pressure is applied."

Any embarrassment vanishes when he mentions Eli again. A tensed thought wants to ask if Eli's okay, but she buries it. "*Of course*, Eli would try to say something bad about me. I thought you were reading my mind, like that other wraith did." She smirks back at him. "Newsflash: Eli isn't the most reliable narrator."

"I cannot read your mind, only your past," he says. "But I know you. I've seen your past and, yes, have spoken to Eli at length about you. In fact, I just left him."

That buried feeling unclenches, but her focus remains fixed on her own needs. Michael smirks, as if he knows.

"From Eli," he continues, "I know his confidence soared at sixteen and was an oft-relied upon crutch at eighteen. He felt he could do no wrong."

"He couldn't," Azzie grumbles. "He did whatever he wanted with no consequences while I had to be the dependable one and didn't get any slack."

"I'm familiar with Eli's conflicts, ones that were deflected and hidden to fester and bubble. But it is *yours* that brought *you* to me."

She snorts. "Does that mean the wordplay is over? Or is this when we get into the threats?"

He appears pleased. "Are you always this outspoken or is this from the half soul you carry?"

"Always," she snaps. "I'm also damned practical, soul or no."

Michael leans closer, his smile predatory. "And the practical solution to my absconding with you and chasing you around the globe is to… convert you?"

"Yes, then your weird protective instincts about Alec abandoning the Rules can fade away," she explains. "You can stop chasing us and we can move on together." Then, everyone gets what they want. She can't understand why Alec can't see the benefits to her plan.

Michael ignores her, staring down at the pillows instead. "Your recklessness is admirable, I suppose. That's what originally interested me in your brother, though it isn't as attractive in your half. But I do so love a selfish and chaotic soul. The lack of self-preservation shouldn't be a surprise, but will need handling," he muses. She gets the impression he isn't speaking to her.

Azzie snaps her fingers until his gaze refocuses on her. "Glad that's settled. Convert me. I'm ready whenever you are."

Michael hops to his feet, surprisingly nimble for a man his size, and positions himself by the mirror. His frame fills the space, effectively blocking her only known escape route. The move is calculated, but it doesn't scare her. *Reckless*, he'd called her. Eli had been the reckless one between the twins, maybe that's what Michael meant by her half.

"My primary goal," Michael begins, his voice low and deliberate, "indeed, my only goal until I met your brother, is advancing Alec's happiness. Since meeting you, however, he has become... quite unhappy with the life he lived. While that unhappiness didn't spring from the earth overnight, it flowered too quickly to grow without fertilizer." His emerald eyes flash, his smile razor-sharp. "You are that fertilizer. So, tell me—why would converting you as you are fix the sadness within him?"

She doesn't miss a beat. "He can't be weak if I'm not a weakness. Make me a wraith, and the liability I pose disappears."

He leans against the wall and frowns. "I am well past caring about the Rules and their implications. Tell me why *you* would make him happy if I converted you as we stand here today."

She lifts one shoulder. "He loves me."

Michael's sharp laugh echoes through the room. "Alec loves the pure-souled human ideal he *thinks* he met," he counters, his gaze sweeping over her. He lingers on her scuffed shoes, his lips curling in disgust. "That is not you."

She shrugs again, unbothered by his judgment. "He'll get over it. In a few hundred years, me differing from he thought won't matter. He'll still have me around and I'll get what I want too. Win-win."

Michael's piercing eyes hold hers, searching for something, and then he speaks again, his voice softer but no less cutting. "Do you care for him? Or is this just an endgame for you—a path to immortality?"

She fights the urge to roll her eyes. Of course, she cares for Alec. Why else would she have followed him across continents, put up with his endless brooding, or endured Michael's games? She wouldn't have gone through all this trouble if she didn't care. And yet... wasn't the endgame always part of it?

Michael growls, his voice slicing through her thoughts. "No. Don't lie to yourself. I see the wheels turning in your head, Azalea. I can't read your current thoughts, but your past? It's written in bold. I see your preoccupation with Alec's wealth, with the opportunity he represents. Think back—think to those moments before you accepted the grynn stone. To when you met him. You spoke with him, shared confidences, danced."

She exhales sharply but humors him, if only because he'll convert her when she's finished—or Alec will swoop in and save the day. Either way, she'll get what she wants. Closing her eyes, she dredges up the memories he's asking for.

It's not a long review of their history, but the highlights make her heart beat faster. That first moment when she kissed Alec, and for the first time, the world didn't feel so suffocating. When he promised to help Eli, despite clearly hating the idea. When he didn't flinch at her rundown house or Eli's drunken outbursts. When he visited her father at the hospital. When he smiled shyly and compared her to a flower.

Her chest tightens, and her hand presses against her shirt, the fabric bunching under her palm. "Yes, there's a part of me that—that knows," she says, her voice quieter than she intended. "I could've ditched him earlier. I don't need him anymore, but I didn't." Her eyes snap open, defiance returning. "But I don't love him at the expense of myself. I'm not sacrificing my needs for the sake of someone else ever again."

Michael's lips twitch into a humorless smile. "There's that missing self-preservation again, dearest," he purrs. "But your honesty, while typically dull, is refreshing in this moment."

Before she can form a retort, he moves. One moment he's leaning against the wall, relaxed as ever, and the next he's towering over her, his presence suffocating. The ring on her finger burns cold, useless against his strength.

"I know I love Alec," Michael murmurs, his voice a low growl, the words dripping with something darker than love. "I love him as I have not loved another. Which is why I also know he will 'get over' what I intend to do."

Azzie doesn't even have time to scream before he lunges. If she survives this, Alec will kill her.

Chapter 62

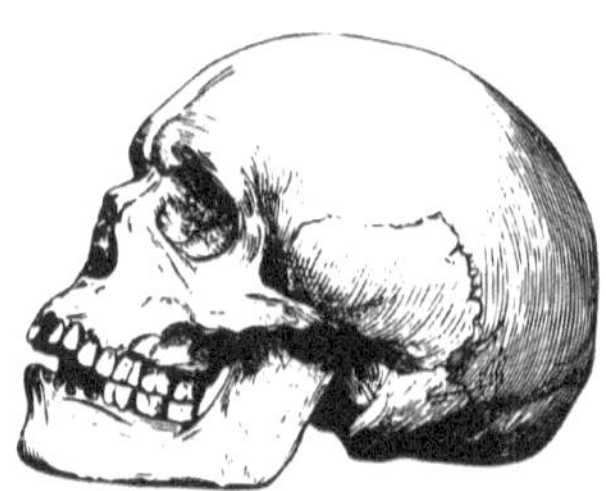

Selina's muscular legs swing as Alec propels her up the dirt wall by her neck. She smiles down at him, stroking her hands up to his shoulders. From a distance, they might appear like lovers in an embrace. The thought churns his stomach.

"Where's a mirror?" Alec snarls, tightening his grip around her burned throat. His fingers dig into her scarred flesh, and yet she has the gall to arch an eyebrow and curl her lips into a mocking smile. She points to her mouth, a silent invitation.

He bares his teeth in disgust and releases her, though his arms cage her in. "Talk," he growls.

"In the next room," she rasps, her voice rough, "but it doesn't go to Michael."

A low growl rumbles in Alec's throat. He doesn't have time for her games. Azalea's life is at stake, and Selina's cryptic taunts are wasting what little time remains. "Where's the one that *does*?"

Selina's laughter is soft but cuts like glass. "The willing soul gambit wouldn't have worked the way you imagined," she says, her burned lips curving wider. "She has *half* a soul, Alec. How could you share that? She is broken enough as it is. A quarter soul each? You'd both shatter."

Her words strike like a dagger to the heart. His grip tightens on her shoulders, his fingers trembling. "And you let me believe it might—for what? Your sick amusement?"

She tilts her head, unflinching despite his anger. Her hands drift back to his chest, a mockery of tenderness, until he slams her shoulders into the wall again. The impact rattles the room, but Selina doesn't stop smiling. If anything, it grows wider, more unhinged.

"You should leave," she purrs, her tone maddeningly calm. "You have more time than you think, silly boy, but not enough to waste searching my halls. The mirror in the next room will take you where you need to be."

Alec's pulse pounds in his ears. He wants to end her, to snuff out that smug grin and silence her lies for good. But there's no time. Not for her manipulations, not for revenge. Azalea is waiting, and every second spent here feels like a betrayal.

"I'll kill you for this," he spits, his voice low and cold as he spins away.

"Michael will explain everything," she calls after him, her laughter echoing in the dark.

The words offer no comfort, only a deeper dread. With a roar of frustration, Alec storms into the next room. The mirror looms before him, its surface rippling like liquid silver. Without hesitation, he launches himself through it.

He tumbles out into darkness, landing on his feet in what feels like a closet. The air is stale, the space cramped, and only a thin line of light outlines the door in front of him. His heart pounds as he steadies himself.

Azalea. Whatever lies beyond this door, he'll face it. She's worth it. She *has* to be worth it.

The light spills into the closet, illuminating a familiar room.

"Hello, Alec, my boy. Remember the Teachings."

Chapter 63

Eli leans against the wall in Michael's opulent but oppressive bedroom, flipping the pocket watch open and closed with one hand. The dials move sluggishly, half the speed of a normal watch. Michael claimed that was normal, just another one of his bizarre quirks. He also said it would all be over soon.

Eli closes his eyes, letting out a shaky breath. He can only hope.

There's a stillness to the room without Michael's presence, since it's soundproofed and dampened. Michael could be in the next room, and Eli would never know. Michael said that was the point as it creates a more intensifying experience.

Michael's right, but the experience isn't comfortable—the only sounds are his heart beating, the heaviness to each breath, his pulse ticking in his neck. He wants to sit in the silly pillow room, but Michael barred him from it until he finished everything.

The new cell phone pings in his pocket, shattering the silence. Eli groans low in his throat as he retrieves it, the bright screen a jarring intrusion. He doesn't bother with a greeting when he answers. Only one person has this number.

"It's time?" His voice feels too loud in the deadened room, echoing in his own skull.

"Nearly, dearest. I need two hours to finish. Can you meet me then?" Michael's tone is smooth, unhurried, as if he's savoring every word.

"Two hours your time or mine?"

Michael sighs, a theatrical exhale. "Thank Fates you're attractive. I assumed some common sense would have latched onto you by now, but—"

"Hey, you're the one who gave me the broken watch," Eli snaps, the irritation spilling over. Michael could at least cut him some slack. Wallowing in pity and second guessing every action is new to him.

"I did, and you know why. Or did you forget how to come to me?"

Eli frowns, even though Michael can't see him. "Shove it up against the mirror and think of you," he mutters, repeating the instructions he's heard too many times.

"What a good boy you are," Michael purrs. "I must go. You know how this machine stings. But buck up, by tomorrow evening, it will all be finished."

Eli slides down the wall, letting himself sink into the plush carpet as his head thuds lightly against the wood paneling. His fingers tighten around the phone. Before Michael hangs up, the question tumbles out, unbidden. "And Az?"

Michael chuckles. "Not to worry, I will deal your sister."

A slow smile spreads across Eli's chapped lips. "Good."

Chapter 64

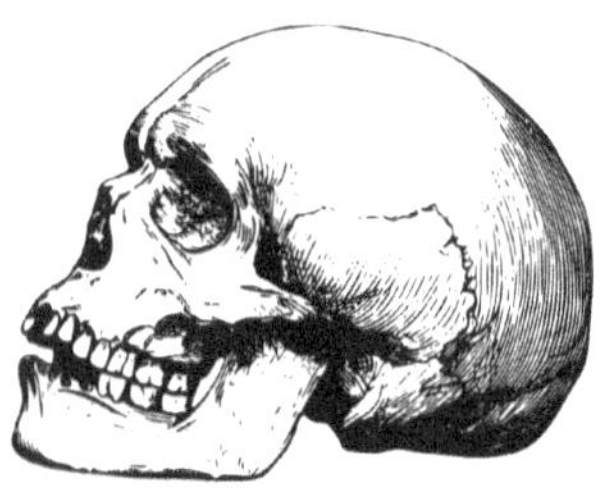

"Why do you have a direct portal to Selina's?" Alec growls.

"Better question is why you've come through it," Gerald replies lazily, seated behind his desk. His fingers, smeared with some unidentifiable grime, are laced casually over his stomach. The dismissiveness in his tone is enough to make Alec's fingers twitch toward violence.

"Never mind," Alec snarls, crossing the room in a heartbeat and leaning over the desk, his teeth bared. Muscle memory of centuries spent roving and enforcing the Rules floods back unbidden, shaping his posture, his movements. The predator he tries to suppress rises to the surface, honed and waiting. "Get me a true mirror."

Gerald, however, doesn't flinch. Instead, he chuckles, pulling a plastic device from a drawer and tapping idly on its surface. "You didn't finish the refrain. Do you still follow the Rules? We couldn't figure that out. Not to worry—I'll get you where you need to go."

A muscle ticks in Alec's jaw as he settles his hands around Gerald's thick neck. His grip tightens, pressing against the wraith's throat, though he knows it won't accomplish much. "Do you know where Azalea is?"

"I do." Gerald's grin doesn't falter.

"And you'll take me to her?" Alec's thumbs press harder, enough to elicit a coughing sound from Gerald.

"I said I'd get you there, not that I'd take you," Gerald wheezes, tilting his head in mock submission. "Mind letting me loose?"

The smugness in Gerald's tone is enough to make Alec want to squeeze harder, but he forces himself to let go, shoving away from the desk with a glare. He doesn't give Gerald the satisfaction of seeing him straighten his coat as he backs up to perch on the edge of the chair across from the desk, fists clenched and trembling with barely restrained anger. "Why are you wrapped up in Michael's schemes?"

Gerald shrugs. "I'm not. I'm working with Selina."

Alec stands so abruptly that the chair topples to the floor. His movements are sharp, a mimicry of his last visit to Gerald's office, though his fury now burns hotter. If only he'd known then how far Azalea had fallen. "Then why am I here? Where is Azalea?"

"This is about more than Michael's plans for your sweetheart," Gerald says. "We found common ground."

Alec slams his hands down on the desk, the force of the blow denting the wood. "Don't test me, Gerald. I may not be in my roving gear, but I can still gut you where you stand."

"That's exactly the point, my boy." Gerald slams his hand on the desk. "Everyone knows how you follow the Rules like a monk. If Alec, the Council's pet, can be exiled, who can't? You're a walking bit of propaganda."

The words sting more than Alec cares to admit, but he doesn't have time to dwell on them. A commotion erupts outside the room—roars and squawks that seep through the cracks of the door. Alec's head snaps toward the sound, his gaze darting around the room for an escape route. He finds none.

He turns back to Gerald, who watches him with a smug smile that sets Alec's teeth on edge. "I thought you liked Azalea," Alec hisses. "Why would you sign her death warrant to Michael for something as base as money?"

Gerald frowns as if the suggestion offends him, but before he can respond, the doors burst open, crashing against the walls. Alec moves on instinct, his hand diving into his bag for the black vial. He raises his fist to smash it to the ground.

But they're faster. Four wraiths rush into the room, and before he can release the vial, a svelte blonde—Helen, a wraith he once aided as a rover—wrestles his arm behind his back. Alec kicks out, his foot connecting with the kneecap of another wraith, who collapses with a howl. The sound is satisfying but fleeting. His grip loosens on the vial as two more wraiths slam him face-first into the wall.

He jerks his head backward, the crunch of a broken nose signaling his success. But it's not enough. A snarl forms on his lips, feral and dangerous. They deserve the darkness, the burning pain the black dust would bring when it billows out in a cloud of destruction. They all deserve it. If not for Azalea counting on him, he'd let the blackness consume him too.

Alec thrusts backward, his skull connecting with the wraiths behind him. It's enough to shove them off balance, and the vial slips from his fingers. He hears it skim the air but freezes when it doesn't shatter. Instead, Gerald catches it mid-flight, holding it aloft with an infuriating smirk.

"Can't have you getting acid flakes on my furnishings; paid a pretty penny for them," Gerald says. He toddles around his desk, straightening the thin collar on his oversized t-shirt. "Good timing, friends. Suppose he'll go straight to the Council?"

Alec's eyes pinch shut. He stops struggling, his muscles tensing with a new kind of fury. Helen yanks the ring from his finger, and the bald wraith clamps burning cuffs onto his wrists. The violent buzzing against his skin tells him they're copper, and the pain is sharp enough to draw a hiss from between his clenched teeth.

The bald wraith spins him around, slamming his head into the wood again. Blood dribbles from his nose, staining his sneering mouth. The fourth wraith—a snarling brunette—spits blood into his face, the iron tang filling his nostrils. He glares through the sting as Helen curls her lips in disdain.

"Where's the mirror?" she demands.

Gerald gestures lazily toward another closet. Alec struggles, but the cuffs bite deeper, weakening him further. As the wraiths drag him toward the entrance, Gerald clears his throat.

"There's a human saying that seems fitting," he calls after them. "Something about two birds."

Alec whips around, his vision swimming, to see Gerald give a thumbs up. Helen yanks his hair, forcing him through the mirror before he can respond.

Chapter 65

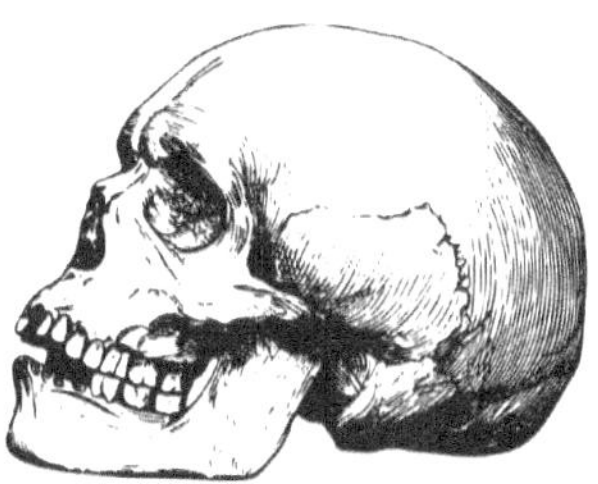

THE ROOM THEY SHOVE him into is one Alec knows too well. The judgment chamber—cavernous, cold, and unforgiving. Each detail is etched into his memory from centuries of roving assignments. After every hunt, he knelt here before the seven daises where the Council sat in judgment, perched high above him as if to look through his very soul. His hand would rest over his chest as he offered his testimony, the Accuser against the Accused, who remained shackled in the ominous copper stocks to the side.

Now, for the first time, he stands where so many had knelt under his accusations. The realization burns deep, an ember of shame and bitterness igniting in his chest. The chamber, vast enough to hold hundreds of wraiths during infamous trials, feels suffocatingly empty save for the mildew crawling up the walls and the oppressive silence. Mildew and graying moss claw their way toward the pointed ceiling, where squat balconies spiral upward, watching from the shadows. The air hangs heavy, thick with the weight of past condemnations and lessons enforced through pain and spectacle.

Perhaps his trial will be the next showpiece. If Michael is his Accuser, Alec doesn't know what that means. Had he misjudged his sire entirely? Had Michael never intended to help him at all—not to eliminate Azalea to protect Alec's secret, but to destroy Alec entirely? After what he planned—after what can be found in that vial—perhaps it is what Alec deserves.

Yet Michael isn't here. Neither is Philip, nor Gerald, nor anyone who might testify against him. Something is wrong. Something is different.

Helen shoves him to his knees, the cuffs on his wrists burning his skin. He doesn't flinch as she drives the toe of her sharp shoe into the back of his thigh. The force splits the skin along his tendons, and warmth trickles down his ankle, pooling in his socks. The other rovers laugh under their breath, their amusement sharp and cutting. He keeps his gaze ahead, staring into the hollow, condescending eyes of the Council.

"Leave us," Sanders, the current Head Councilmember, commands.

Helen kicks him one last time before she saunters out with the others, their laughter echoing until the heavy door slams shut. The sound reverberates like the tolling of a bell, sealing Alec in with the Council's scrutiny, in front of the faces he's served for nearly two millennia.

"Do you know why you are here?" Sanders asks, his black eyes narrowing with predatory focus. It was only weeks ago that Sanders pulled Alec aside and suggested he take a break from roving. Alec wonders if Sanders now regrets that suggestion—or if this was always part of a larger game. Blood drips into Alec's mouth, pooling with the bitter tang of failure. He swallows without wincing. He's had worse.

"I may have an idea," Alec replies carefully, keeping his tone respectful. The absence of an Accuser muddies his conclusions, but someone must have spoken of Azalea—Michael, Gerald, someone.

"Do you?" Kamela simpers. She's the newest member of the Council, joining when Bisa let herself languish until the remaining Councilmembers ended her. "You should tell us," she says, giggling. Her voice drips with condescension, her eyes gleaming with amusement as they rake over Alec's form. They stop on his crotch, and she widens her eyes theatrically, her lips curling into a pout. Alec has rejected her advances for over seven centuries, but her infatuation lingers like a disease. One would think his exile and likely death would cool her ardor, but Alec isn't so lucky.

"Now, Kamela," Tinder, another elder Councilmember, admonishes. "We agreed to offer Alec a boon for his years of service."

Kamela huffs, crossing her arms over her chest. The movement presses the sheer white fabric of her robe tighter against her copper skin. She smirks when she catches Alec's fleeting glance, her game transparent.

"That is correct," Sanders says. "Your Accuser has provided evidence as to your preoccupation with human society. As Tinder suggests, we will forgo a trial and release you, should you publicly renounce your weakness."

Alec straightens, the muscles in his back screaming when he does. They must not know of Azalea, or else they wouldn't be so lenient. Studying literature, like the Shakespeare he quoted to Azalea days earlier, earned him twenty years of flogging. This—this is a gift. Perhaps Selina's attempted revolt is unnecessary if they are accepting weaknesses like Alec's without pain or exile. The rovers saw Gerald's human t-shirt and didn't even comment on it. He can renounce his fascination with human culture, take the public censure, and disappear with Azalea until the fervor dies down. He can still follow the Rules while keeping her safe.

"I understand and accept your guidance," Alec says, his voice steady. "I will publicly renounce my weakness for human society."

"Bring in the girl for her execution," Sanders demands, snapping a hand.

Alec freezes, the air leaving his lungs all at once. His hands, shackled though they are, clench until his nails dig into his palms.

"Do not forget our agreement to take her soul first," Onan says, running clawed fingers down his throat. His milky blue eyes are barely visible over his pale skin. "I find myself in need of a small sup."

Alec clears his rasping throat, more blood collecting in his throat, which he swallows. "And if I don't?"

The Councilmembers narrow their eyes in unison. "Are you suggesting you have a choice?" Tinder's voice is deadly.

"I'm requesting one."

The Councilmembers' expressions darken. Tinder's chair screeches as he rises, but Sanders' raised hand halts him. When they have resettled, Sanders curls his thin lips into a vicious grin, white teeth blinding against his russet face. "Alesandro is nothing if not thoughtful. Very well. We will give you an hour to decide. But with you know there is but one answer."

Chapter 66

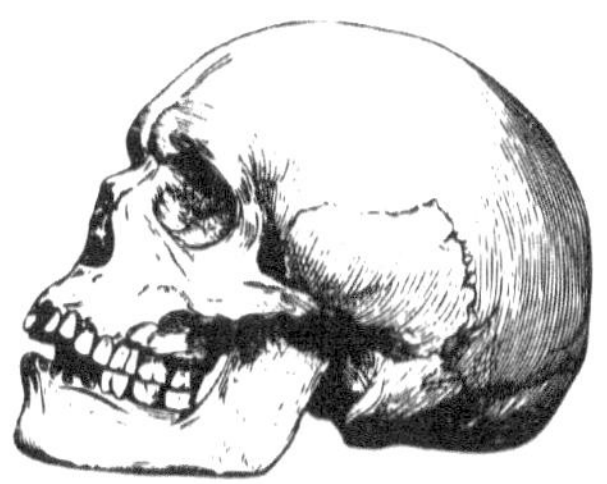

THE ROVERS DRAG HIM down the winding stone corridors and shove him into a cell. Alec had once thrown countless potential wraith criminals into this very place, a space designed to strip even the most defiant of their pride. Windowless, damp, and cold, the cell reeks of mildew and old despair. Its straw-covered floor is sticky with age and rot, and the wet stone walls glisten in the faint torchlight. Though the cell could hold six wraiths, it's empty except for him. A deliberate decision. Isolation is punishment in itself.

Helen sneers as she hurls his traveling bag at his head. Alec's hands dart up to catch it, the weight jarring his already aching wrists. The bag spills onto the filthy floor, and the teal vial rolls out, bumping gently against his scuffed shoes.

"You don't deserve the choice, traitor," Helen spits, her voice brimming with disdain. She waits for a reaction, but Alec keeps his head bowed, his expression neutral. Let her think he's broken; it costs him nothing. With a final derisive snort, she turns on her heel, and the door slams shut behind her, the echo ringing in his ears.

For a moment, he simply stares at the bag and the vial, his thoughts churning. The open door moments earlier was nothing but a taunt, and the remnants of his belongings scattered before him feel like another. Slowly, with deliberate care, Alec drags the bag onto his lap. His fingers tremble as he repacks it, each item a small piece of the life he's clawed together—and the life that now threatens to crumble entirely.

The clothes come first, their fabric still bearing faint traces of Azalea's scent, a cruel comfort. The green button-down he wipes across his bloodied nose, leaving streaks of red against the fabric. Azalea had kept the smiling shirt from their second human party, tucked into her tote bag with a triumphant grin. He remembers her insistence that he listen to the band's music on their drive from Lonetree to Davenport. The lyrics—something about how people should act—echo faintly in his mind now, their rhythm blending with the relentless buzz of the copper cuffs digging into his skin.

His gaze lands on the teal vial, and his throat tightens. He picks it up and turns it in his hand, the liquid inside gleaming faintly in the dim light. Helen didn't leave it as a kindness, but to remind him how far he fell from his place by the Council's right hand. It isn't a safeguard anymore; it's a symbol of his failure. Using it on himself is unthinkable. He doesn't deserve such an escape. He slides it beneath the clothes, burying it like a sin too heavy to confront.

Next comes the clutter of receipts: for pizza in Chicago, for the hotels they stayed at, for the magazine Azalea had insisted he read on the plane. Even half-souled, she'd tried to distract him from the copper reaction that had left him writhing in agony. It's those moments—those flickers of humanity and care—that remind him why Eli, as tainted as his soul may be, still loves his sister. Alec closes his eyes, the realization pressing down on him. Perhaps souls aren't the ultimate arbiter of worth. Perhaps humanity isn't so easily defined.

Finally, he comes to the journal. His bloodstained fingers trace the embossing on the spine as if seeking some kind of solace. He opens it without thought, the familiar pages staring back at him with the words that have guided him for centuries: the Rules. He flips through them until he finds notes from one of Michael's earliest Teachings.

The memory rises unbidden. He was sitting at the base of a cliff, staring up at peaks he'd known intimately during his human life, ones that clawed from the land to claim their space in the sky. He had taken those trails countless times, hiding from the longshoremen or simply seeking solace from the chaos below. Michael had brought him back there, two centuries into his wraithhood, lifetimes after Cassius' death. The village lay in ruins, the air thick with decay. Time had marched on, obliterating the demons of his first life. But the demons of his second threatened to drown him.

Michael's lesson wasn't about the Rules that day, but about the irreversibility of change. Water can't flow backward, he can't expect things to stay the same, that he wasn't the same—he was and will be Alesandro the wraith, not Alesandro the human.

And now he's Alec.

He exhales shakily, his back slumping against the damp wall. Both Selina and Michael saw this coming. They knew before he did that he couldn't straddle the line between wraith and human. He'd have to choose. He couldn't wear the costume of humanity and pretend it fit. Even Azalea knew it. She'd told him outright—he would never be human again, and she couldn't give him humanity.

The weight of the past three weeks crashes over him like water wearing down stone. The deception, the compromises, the laughter and smiles he'd fought to protect, her lies and betrayals, the Rules he'd clung to like a lifeline—they swirl together in a torrent of guilt and futility. He'd made a mess of everything, and humanity has never felt farther away.

But that was the point, wasn't it? It was always about choices.

Alec lets the journal slip from his hands, his head falling back against the cold stone. The cuffs hum against his wrists, a constant reminder of his constraints. He closes his eyes and breathes deeply, his chest rising and falling with the weight of finality.

He's made his choice. Now he must live—or die—with it.

Chapter 67

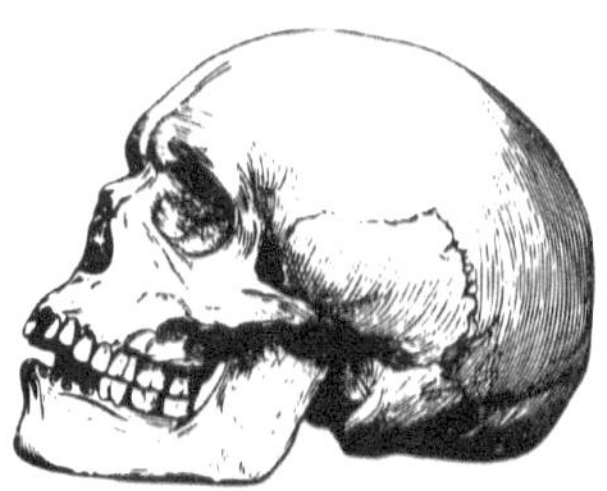

"I HOPE YOU'RE PROUD of yourself." Michael's deep voice cuts through the haze of Alec's agony, pulling him from the fog of waiting for his trial to begin. Blood still pools in his mouth from the earlier beating, after he'd refused to renounce his weakness, the copper cuffs on his wrists biting into his skin like the shackles of his mistakes. The rovers had kicked him in the gut until he coughed red, calling it a "preview" of the Council's punishment. He'd curled on the floor afterward, cradling his ribs and willing himself not to cry out.

Michael leans indolently against the open doorway of the cell, his long hair cascading like a pale waterfall over his broad shoulders. The dim candlelight washes it almost white, casting shadows across his sharp features. Alec is on his feet before he even realizes it, driven by instinct and rage. He lunges toward Michael, the pain in his stomach and wrists momentarily forgotten, only to collide with the invisible barrier that cages him. The force knocks him backward, sending a fresh jolt of pain through his already bruised body.

Two unfamiliar wraiths—guards—peer into the cell and chuckle at the spectacle. Michael's eyes flick to them, twitching slightly, but he doesn't address them. Instead, he runs his fingers along the shimmering barrier, his curiosity as apparent as his disdain.

"I've always wanted to see these in action," Michael muses, pressing his fingertips against the air. He pulls back with a hiss when the barrier bites him. "It stings! Delightful. I must incorporate these into my parties. Imagine the entertainment."

Alec growls low in his throat, the taste of blood sharp on his tongue. He spits toward Michael's feet, but the barrier sizzles, consuming even that act of defiance. "Where is Azalea?" he demands, his voice raw with fury. The bite of the barrier is nothing compared to the fire raging within him.

"No, no. I'm speaking now," Michael says, his tone languid and condescending. "We've a short while before I give my testimony, and I intend to use it lecturing you. Had I taught you better, we wouldn't be in this predicament." He makes it sound as if the two are disagreeing about which color cravat Michael should wear rather than the outcome of Alec and Azalea's lives.

Alec surges toward the barrier again, his fists slamming against its invisible wall. "When I leave this cell—"

"You'll what?" Michael interrupts with a smirk. "Poison me before collapsing under the weight of your punishment?"

Alec flinches, unable to stop himself, and Michael's smile widens.

"Ah, I see you're aware. Yes, I know all about your little plot. Azalea was most helpful in that regard." He tilts his head, his expression maddeningly smug. "Well, perhaps not directly. Her thoughts were quite helpful, though. And the things I saw! How have I never fornicated in public? Glass and steel separating you from the world, yet still... titillating. I must try it."

Alec slams his fist into the barrier again, the burn a small price for his rage. "If you've hurt her—"

"No, *you* listen," Michael growls, his voice dropping to a venomous hiss as his eyes dart toward the door. "We could have avoided all of this if you'd waited, if you hadn't been led around by that two-faced girl of yours."

"Do not speak of her that—"

"I was trying to help you!" Michael roars. He looks to the door again, lowering his own voice to a sibilant hiss. "I had it planned!"

"To *remove* my weakness," Alec snarls, his voice rising. "No matter the collateral damage. That's always been your way."

Michael's lips curl into a snarl, his earlier indolence replaced by something sharper. "Don't chastise me for doing what *you* demanded.

You came to me, groveling for help with your past mistakes, just as you did for your precious Azalea."

"Not to kill her!" Alec roars, pacing back to the barrier and slamming his hands against it again. His voice cracks, raw with fury and fear. "That's not help, Michael—it's a death sentence. I can only be thankful Godfrey warned me before you could pass your warped judgment." Alec stalks away from the barrier, running a trembling hand through his hair. "Though it doesn't matter now, does it? I will bear my punishment as I must. At least she's far from here; even you wouldn't be reckless enough to bring a human to the Council."

Michael's head tilts, the anger in his expression softening into confusion. "Wait. Godfrey?" he echoes. "Your rodent of a servant?"

Alec nods, his jaw tight. "He told me of your threat. I know everything."

Michael blinks once, then again, his lips parting slightly as if he's processing something unexpected. "Alec," he says slowly, "I don't believe I've spoken two words to Godfrey or his ilk since you buried yourself in that mausoleum you call a mansion three centuries ago. I certainly never told him I intended to kill Azalea."

Chapter 68

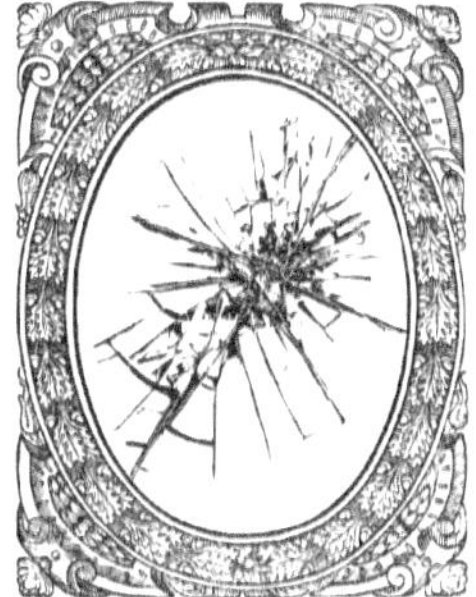

Mark Godfrey slouches on the ratty old sofa in the living room, the one he's sat on for years—first next to his dad, who droned endlessly about their immortal master, and later on his own, waiting for Alec to show up. Now, though, things are different. Now, he's lord of the manor, with no demon lurking in the shadows to haunt him or make him jump at every creak in the walls.

He runs a hand through his lank blond hair, tugging it in front of his eyes like it might shield him from the sunlight filtering through the new curtains. Moth-eaten ones were fine when Alec was around to terrorize him, but now that Mark's in charge, he upgraded. It wasn't much—just enough to keep the sun out of his eyes while he sat around and thought. The rest of Alec's gold? That was squirreled away for safekeeping. He'd need it to live comfortably for the next few decades. First things first, though—he'll get himself a butler. Maybe a decent whiskey cabinet, too.

It was just dumb luck he read Alec's notes. Just luck he paid attention when skulking around corners and eavesdropping on the demon's private conversations. A few weeks of serving Alec were enough to make it clear the guy wasn't right in the head. And then that girl—Azalea—showed up, and Alec spiraled even further. It didn't take a genius to see the opportunity. Mark wasn't about to let it pass him by.

He tips his head back, a smirk pulling at his lips. Hopefully, Alec and that green-eyed demon he's partnered with will kill each other. Problem solved, and Mark's free to live his life in peace.

His thoughts drift to that girl. She seemed nice enough, soft around the edges. Too pudgy for his taste, but she had that innocent look, the kind that made you think she didn't know what she was getting herself into. Oh well. Serves her right for trying to romance a monster. Didn't she know they were heartless? She could've done better for herself. Someone like him, maybe. If she slimmed down a bit, he could've saved her. She'd probably be real grateful, too. The gratitude he deserves.

The smirk widens as he considers it. Yeah, that's what he'll do. First, a butler. Then, maybe, some high-class company. Alec's gold is going to good use. It's about time someone appreciated him.

Chapter 69

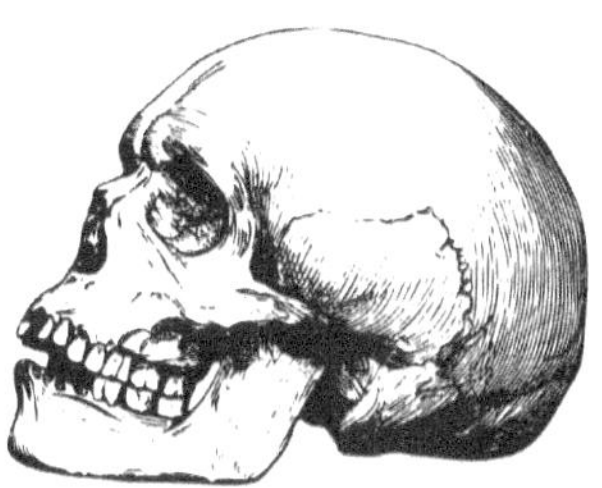

THE LOOK ON GODFREY'S face when Alec planned to stay in Rockton burns behind Alec's eyes. The taint of the man's fear and anticipation when he claimed Michael visited seeps into his pores. Michael hadn't been after them. *He had a plan*, Michael said. *He wanted Alec happy*, he said.

The familiar ache of doubt gnaws at Alec as he slides down to the dirt floor. His back scrapes against the rough stone as he tilts his head back, staring at the damp ceiling. *Fates.* Maybe soulsickness had longer lasting effects than anyone realized. If he hadn't fled Rockton so impulsively, if he'd paused to think, Azalea wouldn't be tangled in this nightmare. She'd be safe. And he wouldn't be here, awaiting the Council's judgment. He raps his head lightly against the wall, the dull pain offering no clarity.

But no. He pushes himself to his feet, brushing dirt from his trousers. Michael is to blame. For all his claims of care, for all his talk of plans, Michael had hunted them across continents and taken Azalea. Alec stalks toward the barrier, his finger raised in accusation. The shimmering energy separating him from his sire diminishes the impact, but his anger surges anyway. With Michael safely ensconced on the other side, all Alec can do is glare.

"Godfrey may have started our flight, but you continued it," Alec snarls, his voice echoing in the small cell. "You chased us around the world and kidnapped Azalea."

Michael, leaning indolently against the far wall of the cell, merely tilts his head. His hair, cascading down his broad shoulders, gleams almost white in the dim candlelight. "I chased you," he says mildly, "because you refused to stay in one place long enough for me to speak with you. What was I supposed to do? Write you a polite letter?" He mimics scribbling in the air, his tone mocking. *"'Hello, dearest. We should discuss the human you fell in love with. I've got some ideas on how to keep her. Let's hope the Council doesn't find out and punish us both. Talk soon. Love always, your sire.'* As if that wouldn't get me thrown in here with you, and then no one could mop up your messes."

Alec sneers. "And it comes back to Michael. Fates forbid if you did anything that would diminish your own lifestyle, including mopping up the mess *you* created."

Michael's smirk fades, his eyes darkening. "Don't test me, Alec. You have no idea what I would do for you."

"I've an idea," he snarls. "I've centuries of memor—did you call me Alec?"

Michael hesitates, his shoulders softening as exhaustion dims his green eyes. "Yes," he murmurs. "You told me once you preferred it. It's your chosen name, dearest."

The unexpected sincerity cuts through Alec's fury like a blade. His throat tightens. He presses his palms against the barrier, ignoring the sizzling pain as his skin reacts to the magical energy. "Michael, if you care for me as you claim—"

"I do."

"Then help me survive whatever punishment the Council plans to mete out. Bring Azalea back, unharmed and unchanged, and let us leave this life behind. You told me I couldn't find happiness within the Rules, that I can't have both. And I agree now."

Alec thinks of Azalea with her lust for adventure and books, Gerald with his 'Miami Vice,' about finding joy in the trivial things. He thinks of his friendship with Michael, one he maintained at a distance for fear too close a relationship would compromise him. He thinks of Azalea again and the possibilities she could bring him. "Being human isn't weak, it's a choice. I've made my choice, no more Rules. Help me, and let us three—you, me, and Azalea—find a life outside the family."

Michael's lashes lower, his face cast in shadow. Away from the scant light, his hair looks more yellowed blond. Like Azalea's. "We're too far down this path, dearest. I can't protect you from the punishment coming, nor can I return Azalea to you as she is or even as she was."

A vice grips his heart. "Please, Michael, please. Tell me she's safe. Tell me she is miles from the Council's reach In Martalk, or Selessen or Tellach, at *Selina's* even. That she's far from the family and in no danger."

Michael's face tightens, pain flickering in his eyes. "I can't tell you that either. She's here."

The words hit like a blow, a damning truth that reverberates through Alec's body. Rage erupts, primal and fierce. He roars, his voice shaking the walls and summoning the rovers. Six crowd outside the cell, sneering, before a seventh trips a mechanism to lower the barrier. Alec barely registers the hiss of disengaging magic before the rovers rush in, their boots crunching his traveling bag and spilling teal liquid onto the floor.

Helen and another wraith seize his arms, their nails digging into his skin as they wrench him backward. The copper cuffs burn against his wrists, but Alec doesn't struggle. His blood drips onto the dirt floor as the rovers drag him out.

"One positive to hold on to, love," Michael calls softly, his voice trembling. "It's almost over."

Chapter 70

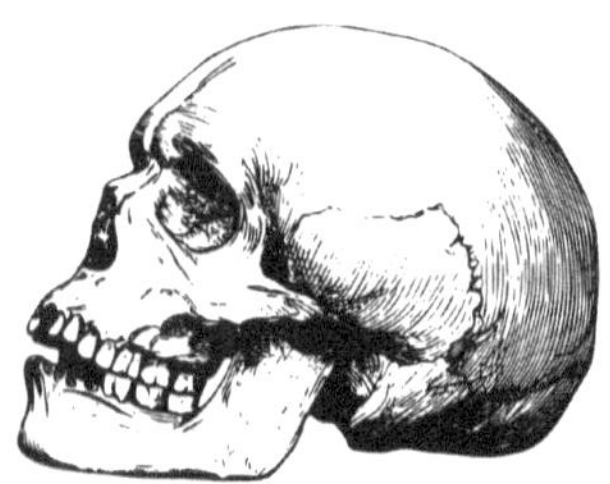

THEY STRAP ALEC TO the stocks near the side of the chamber to begin the trial. From afar, the stocks resemble a capital T or a short-headed cross. Up close, thatch marks in the wood depict a roughly carved bird. Alec's arms are splayed outward, affixed to the outspread wings with thin copper wires.

The copper stocks dig into Alec's wrists, the thin wires wrapped tight around his skin cutting deeper with each moment he struggles. He doesn't even try to shift his weight; the copper saps too much of his strength. Blood drips in slow rivulets down his forearms, pooling where the wires bite into his flesh. The poison seeps into his veins, a sickly heat that crawls through his body, leaving him lightheaded. He knows the signs. Minutes from now, he'll lose consciousness. An hour, maybe less, and he'll be dead.

After they bind him, the rovers skulk from the room. The judgment chamber looms vast and oppressive, the mildew-streaked walls seeming to lean inward, pressing him further into despair. Only Michael and the seven Councilmembers are present, their faces shadowed by the flickering torchlight. No spectators fill the balconies; there will be no grand spectacle for the family. This trial is intimate, a punishment meant to be precise and devastating.

Michael kneels before the Council's daises, his back straight and his head held high. Alec knows that posture well—it's the one Michael assumes when he intends to charm. Michael's hand taps a steady rhythm against his left pocket, the only sign of nerves betraying his carefully constructed poise.

Sanders steps forward, his black eyes locking on Alec with a disdain that seems to pierce right through him. "So begins the trial of Alesandro of Caistor," he declares, his deep voice echoing off the chamber's stone walls. "Sired by Michael of Ur. Though this trial is but a formality, Alesandro's refusal to renounce his weakness and kill the girl evidences the rot of weakness within him. Rules are Rules."

Sanders scowls in Alec's direction as the other Councilmembers hiss. He turns his black-eyed gaze back to Michael.

The Council hisses in unison, a sound that sends a chill crawling up Alec's spine. Sanders turns his gaze to Michael. "In accordance with our Rules of retribution, we demand the Accuser Michael of Ur, sired by Marduk of Nippur, offer your testimony."

Michael rises smoothly to his feet, flashing his teeth in a smile that's as practiced as it is insincere. "Esteemed and most beautiful Council," he begins, his voice honeyed and smooth. Kamela giggles, and Oman purrs his approval. "It pains me to present this testimony today. As you know, the success of Alesandro is the success of us all. If he cannot fulfill the tenets of the Rules, who among us can?"

There's more shuffling of the Councilmembers. Rhena, the eldest in appearance who was converted in her sixties after serving as a chiefess for her clan, spits into the dirt, landing inches from Alec's feet. "Watch yourself, Michael. This is not your opportunity to prance about as you would otherwise."

"What a delightful turn of phrase," Michael replies, unbothered. "I accept your counsel and the understanding that we must change depending on our needs. Alesandro showed weakness by loving a human. He allowed her to drag him to and fro as she demanded he convert her, though he adamantly refused at every turn. The only extenuating circumstance in his favor is that the human he loved is a duplicitous little minx, one whose soul is as abhorrent as—" Michael pauses for effect, letting his fiery emerald eyes sweep over the Council. "—as mine."

"Thank you, Michael," Sanders says. "You are a credit to your race. As Michael's sire and closest confidant for two thousand years, it is gratifying that you put the Rules and our demands above any... empathy... you might have for the Accused."

"Empathy would be a weakness," Michael says with a leer. "But I'll do more than that, I've an idea for punishment."

Braggan, a warrior member who rarely speaks, snorts, crossing his arms around his naked and scarred chest. "What would you suggest?"

Michael's smile widens. "Exile."

The others nod as if they expected the same. Alec closes his eyes. Exile was his best option. He'd still be free to find Azalea once he recovered from the pain.

"And emotional warfare," Michael finishes.

Alec's eyes snap open.

"Which means?" Tinder snarls. Neither Tinder nor Rhena ever liked Michael. Alec isn't sure that's in his favor now.

"Convert the girl," Michael says, smirking.

"No," Alec shouts, pulling at his restraints. The copper grips harder into his wrists and forearms. With each movement, more poison trickles through his veins.

"No!" Alec roars, thrashing against the restraints. The copper wires dig deeper, the poison spreading faster. His body weakens, but his desperation surges.

Oman tilts his head thoughtfully. "Would not stealing her soul and then killing her provide the most emotional turmoil?"

Michael shakes his hands. "Alesandro's sole goal was to keep her pure, unaware that she was already in possession of a soul as black as mine. Tearing out her soul and killing her is a temporary gain—Alesandro will feel the loss, but it will fade. *Converting* her, letting him live out his days in exile knowing that she remains with the family, corrupted and lost to him forever? That's the true punishment. It will stick to his skin as a stain that will never wash clean." Michael stands, brushing off the knees of his pants and sticking his left hand in his pocket. "You honor me by claiming I am a credit to the family. But this girl—*she* is the true credit. She reeled Alesandro in on a fishhook of affection and physical touch. She caressed his heart until she could rip it from his chest to gain what she wants. Her single-minded ambition, her deviancy, make her a proper recipient of our gifts."

"I wanted to sup," Oman whines, stroking his throat again. The lights dim in the room, or perhaps Alec is slowly losing consciousness.

Michael slides his gaze to Alec. "Let me bring her to you so you may see what a meager morsel she would be."

With a wave from Sanders, Michael prowls from the room. Alec fights the restraints, but the poison makes his movement sluggish. The lights continue darkening around him.

Michael returns, dragging an annoyed Azalea. She doesn't look hurt, but he's too far away to confirm. Her face is defiant, but she doesn't see Alec. She's too focused on the Councilmembers, her eyes scanning them with a mix of irritation and fascination.

The Councilmembers watch her like a scorpion watches a frog too slow to hop away from danger. Alec slumps against the bindings, bowing until his head rests against the crown of the bird. He should have seen this coming.

The tight gag on her mouth doesn't muffle the complaints she snarls at Michael. When Michael removes her gag, she stares unblinking at the wraiths above her.

"I can see why you believe she is an appropriate convert," Sanders rasps.

"Her history shows such pain and greed," Tinder says.

"And her emotions!" Kamela runs her hands over her copper locks, down her throat and under the edge of the fabric holding her gown together. Braggan grunts.

"Her current thoughts depict the single-mindedness of which you spoke," Rhena says, lifting her chin to stare down at Azalea. "And her soul is half gone. Indeed, Oman, this one will not serve as but an appetizer."

The last member of the Council, the longest serving, speaks. "She finds us beautiful but not fearsome." Iliana observes coldly, narrowing her eyes as Azalea stares back unabashed. "Should she not quake before us?"

"What she lacks in self-preservation she will make up in entertainment," Michael says. "Go on, tell them what you told me."

Azalea blows the frazzled blond hair from her face and flicks her gaze to Michael, who nods. "Wraiths need to focus on using human technology," she says. "They'll be able to hunt more efficiently and blend in. I've been thinking about ways to correct the deficiencies." Her emotions wash towards Alec against his will, a foul combination of entitled and smug.

His head lolls to the side. The combination smells like something, or someone, else, something he'd experienced recently. But he can't remember where.

The Council laughs, Kamela the loudest of all. "Humans are less than ants beneath our feet. Why would we deign to follow anything they do?"

"Ants that you can't live without," Azalea says, lifting her chin.

Kamela hisses like a feral cat until Sanders slashes his tattooed arm through the air. "Proud, undisciplined, overconfident. Those are wraith-like traits," Sanders says, almost licking his lips. Azalea smiles up at him, which Sanders returns, his sharp teeth glinting. "Very well, we shall convert her."

Alec straightens as the blood rushes to his ears. They're speaking again but roaring inside him drowns it out. It's as if he's underwater, somersaulting through the breaking waves, never getting a moment to claw to the surface. Time slows down, ticking in tune to the stabbing sensations in his head and heart as the poison draws further into his veins.

Michael turns his back to the Council, facing Alec. He smiles grimly as he pulls something from his pocket. It's a vial filled with something yellow. Michael says something, and the Council laughs. Alec still can't hear the words.

He rips against the binding, his heartbeat overtaking all other sounds. Odd, since it doesn't beat. *Is this what happens when a wraith dies?*

Azalea finally notices him at the edge of the half-circle stage. She furrows her brow but before she can take a step towards him, Michael tips the contents of the vial in his mouth and spins towards her to give her a swooning kiss. She claws her hands over his chest, but Michael has strength on her. He dips her until she's almost parallel to the ground.

Alec's vision dims further, the edges of his world blurring as if being swallowed by shadows. He's slipping—his body betraying him as the copper poison threads deeper into his veins.

Michael releases Azalea while the Council jeers. Azalea turns to him a second time, her eyes wide and mouth a horrified circle. She screams, that breaks through the ringing in his ears. Unfamiliar emotions lap the air, but the poison in his system muddies them.

Regret perhaps? He gives her a bloodstained smile. He understands. This is his fault, his failure, his punishment. He made his choices, and this is where they led.

"Now, dearest," Michael murmurs, his voice distorted and echoing in Alec's ears like it's coming from underwater. Michael's thick fingers, adorned with gaudy rings, press against Azalea's throat. "You'll appreciate this in time."

Azalea's scream crescendos, cutting through Alec's waning consciousness like a jagged blade. It rises and falls, raw and primal, a sound that will haunt him for the eternity he no longer wants. If he could sleep, he knows this would be his nightmare. But instead, it will become the soundtrack to the hollow existence he's consigned himself to.

Michael's hands glow faintly as the conversion rites take hold, the dark magic a sharp, oily stain on the air. Alec's muscles spasm involuntarily, his body jerking against the copper restraints as he fights to stay upright. Emotional warfare, Michael had called it. Too kind a phrase for this exquisite agony. Perhaps the poison in his veins will mercifully finish him before the full weight of it sets in.

And then, just as suddenly as it began, it's over. Michael releases Azalea, lowering her limp form to the ground with a gentleness that feels like a mockery of everything Alec just witnessed. Michael's hand lingers in her hair, smoothing it as if she were a cherished doll rather than the shattered remains of someone Alec would burn the world to save.

"Thrilling show," Sanders remarks, his voice cold and clipped, cutting through the heavy silence. "Now for our turn."

The Council stands in unison, seven figures looming above him like executioners. Their collective focus locks onto Alec, and the room seems to constrict around him, their dark power coiling in the air like a storm about to break.

Alec doesn't have the strength to brace himself. The first wave of their punishment slams into him, and it's worse than anything he's ever known. Every nerve screams, every muscle contorts, his very soul feels as if it's being unraveled thread by thread.

Azalea's scream still lingers in his ears, a phantom echo as the agony consumes him.

Chapter 71

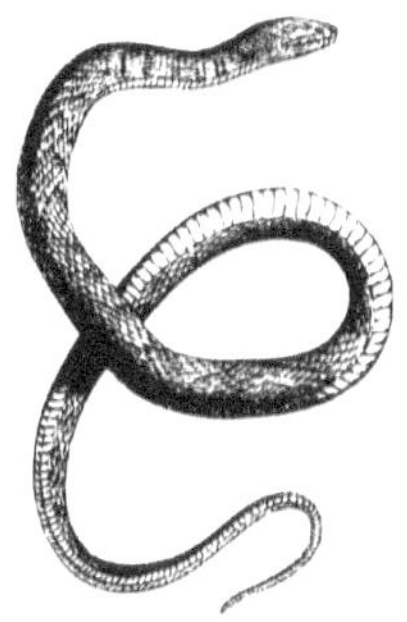

"Oh God, let me die," Azalea groans, her voice raw and uneven. Eli perches at the edge of the bed, his posture stiff, his eyes locked on his trembling sister. Alas, the week of chaos and strain she and Alec inflicted on them left Michael feeling less than sympathetic.

She's fragile, shivering from the aftereffects of conversion. Ideally, she should rest for days, perhaps a week, to let her new existence settle. But time is not a luxury they have. Gerald's whispered advice earlier that morning—detailing where the Council had dumped Alec's unconscious form—has left Michael's mind racing. There is much to do before his boy wakes.

Michael leans over her, shaking her with more force. "You can sleep when I'm finished," he growls.

Eli smothers a laugh, and Michael quirks the corner of his mouth in response. This version of Eli, with his quick humor and softer edges, has proven entertaining. Still, Michael longs for the Eli he first met, the one bursting with raw, reckless potential. This will bring him back—or it should.

Azalea's eyes flutter open, unfocused and glassy, but still flaring like the wraith she is now. Her chest rises and falls with shallow, rapid breaths as her gaze darts around the room, wild and untethered. The shivering deepens into violent shaking, and her hands fly to claw at her throat as though she can tear away the sensation gripping her.

Eli shifts closer, sliding his hands over hers with a gentleness Michael has rarely seen from him. He presses her hands to his neck, his voice low and soothing as he murmurs to her. The sound is unfamiliar coming from Eli's throat, and Michael represses a flicker of unease. That softness will be corrected soon enough.

Azalea's trembling hands tighten instinctively, her thumbs brushing the dip of Eli's collarbone. Both twins look to Michael—Eli with an odd, questioning steadiness, Azalea with wild, fractured fear. Michael allows none of his internal turmoil to touch his expression. He doesn't need them sensing the uncertainty churning inside him. He has never guided two people simultaneously unless pleasure was involved, and even then, the stakes were far lower.

Fates, he hopes it works.

"Take his soul," Michael coaxes, resting his hands atop Azalea's. His rings clink softly against hers, the half of Alec's gimmel ring on her index finger catching the dim light. Everything has led to this, and failure isn't an option. If this doesn't work—if she steals Eli's soul instead of him giving it willingly—the guilt would overwhelm them all. Except Eli, of course.

At that thought, he offers Eli the sincerest smile he has, which makes him laugh and the nervousness behind his eyes wanes. Eli keeps his focus on Michael, grounding himself, while Azalea's hands shake violently. Her breaths hitch, and then her eyes roll back, her body collapsing into the bed as her hands fall away.

Eli shudders and falls forward into Michael's waiting arms. Michael holds him, perhaps tighter than necessary, and buries his face in his hair. The scent of him—so human, so alive—floods Michael's senses. He presses a surreptitious kiss to Eli's temple, savoring the moment. If he's lucky, neither of the twins will remember.

Azalea stares, her expression frozen in horror. Her trembling hands rise to cover her mouth, and Michael's gaze flicks to the ring on her finger as it bursts with vibrant color before settling into a sharp, golden glow.

"Now you may pass out," Michael tells her, his tone almost kind as he gently strokes Eli's hair.

Whether because of his permission or not, she does.

Chapter 72

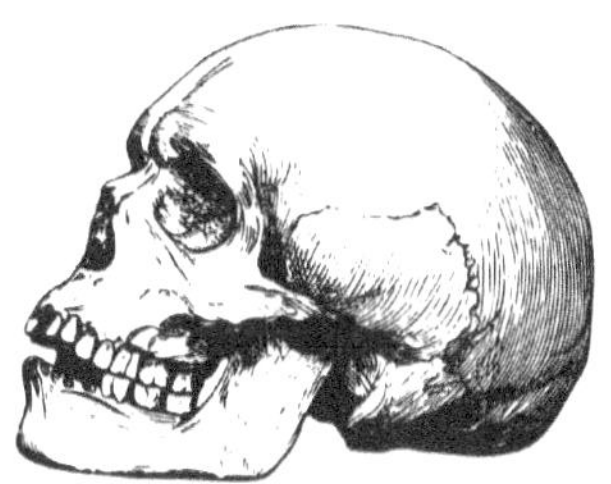

ALEC WAKES IN A room heavy with the scent of oil and damp dirt. A single, weak candle flickers above his head. The haze in his mind recedes slowly, and he pushes himself upright. The dirt floor beneath his hands feels cool and grainy, offering no comfort. He scans the dim room, but it reveals little—a cell, perhaps, judging by the oppressive atmosphere.

He receives the faint impressions of consciousnesses nearby. Wraiths. Humans. Their past thoughts race through his mind, fragmented and incomprehensible, like a shuffled deck of cards too quick to catch. He senses their emotions too, a tangled web of fear, anger, and apathy. His ability to differentiate between them fails.

This must be one of the consequences Selina mentioned, the removal of mental blocks granting him gifts beyond those he received in his second life. Useful, perhaps. But right now, all it does is overwhelm him.

A flicker of bitter realization cuts through the fog: he hasn't been abandoned in a landfill or cast into some desolate wilderness. He's still in one of the Council's cells. It seems they've decided exile and watching Azalea's humanity crumble wasn't punishment enough. That's the luck he's left with.

"Welcome back to the land of the living," Michael's voice says.

Alec reacts instinctively, surging toward the sound. He expects the bite of a barrier to throw him back, but his luck shifts—his body slams into Michael's torso, sending them both sprawling. Alec wrestles Michael to the dirt floor, straddling his chest and clamping his hands around his neck.

Michael's smirk never falters. "Who knew exile made you so amorous?" he rasps, his voice strained but teasing.

Alec growls low in his throat, the scent of Michael's confidence mingling with something sharper—nervousness. He tightens his grip, feeling the faint resistance of Michael's windpipe beneath his fingers.

"Unless the next words out of your mouth are, 'I know where Azalea is, and she's safe,' you will not speak," Alec hisses.

Michael grins wider, baring teeth that glint in the candlelight. "I know where Azalea is, and she's safe."

Relief rushes through Alec, unbidden and unwanted. He doesn't release Michael, but the storm in his chest quiets ever so slightly. "Why should I believe you?"

Michael's voice remains too casual, considering Alec's hands are still pressing against his trachea. "Did exile bring you any new gifts, dearest? Perhaps something useful?"

Alec narrows his eyes. His grip tightens further, and Michael's confidence crumbles under the weight of peppery apprehension. Alec's nose twitches at the scent, an anomaly. Michael never gets nervous.

"Where is she?" Alec repeats.

"I'm serious, dearest," Michael says, his smirk faltering at the edges. "If exile granted you new gifts, you could see for yourself what happened *and* why."

"Stop playing games," Alec snaps, his voice shaking with barely restrained fury. "Tell me where she is."

Michael holds his gaze and works his jaw. "I am, as I have been for the past month, utterly serious. Read my past."

With everything to lose, Alec does.

Chapter 73

Then

MICHAEL LEANED BACK AGAINST the headboard, his broad shoulders pressing the wrought iron filigree into the wall behind him. One hand absently drew a pattern on his bare chest. There had been a time when he railed against his conversion occurring before he'd been able to prepare his body for its immortal change. Two thousand plus years ago, his clean-shaven face had been a sign of his inadequate social standing, as vanity demanded a heavy beard to complement his rough body hair. With age came wisdom and the confidence that his innate power overcame any deficiency in his looks.

His other hand held tight to the long black hair attached to the wraith whose head was working diligently over his lap. It appeared his latest swains found nothing wanting in his body now.

"I met with that boy this morning," Michael said, loosening his grip and letting the wraith continue pleasing him without direction. "Man, I suppose."

To his disappointment, his lover pulled off and sat up, placing his hands on Michael's thighs. The bed sheet covering the Historian pooled to his waist but did nothing to hide his interest in their morning activities. Michael's own interest was still bobbing, saliva slick and decidedly not sated.

Michael frowned. "I didn't tell you to stop."

The Historian, as he was known, pouted prettily, his lips wet and slightly swollen. Though his physical body appeared a decade older than Michael's, he had only been converted three hundred years prior. The second son of wealthy parents, he'd been a dandy who couldn't, or didn't want to, find a wife. He remained immaculately perfumed and brushed even while naked on Michael's bed.

"Only yesterday you halted our play to answer a call from Alesandro and interrogated me about a human that may be immune to our gifts," the Historian whined, "then you meet with the human during our only free time and tell me whilst I am engaging you?"

"Two separate humans" Michael soothes, reaching down to tilt the Historian's chin. The Historian had provided little guidance on what could have caused Alesandro's limitations, but Michael had hedged in his questioning, never telling the Historian that Alesandro couldn't read the human to avoid any accusations of weakness.

"The first was his sister. I met with the man, Alesandro's prey, this morning on a lark," Michael explains. Gently but firmly, he placed those petite fingers back where they belonged, at the juncture of Michael's thighs. "I have little free time while on assignment for the Council, love. You know this. It's simply efficient to speak with you whilst we play to maximize our time."

The Historian made to lean back down. "I wasn't aware efficiency was the goal of today's endeavor," he muttered. His lips grazed Michael's skin before his bright brown eyes lifted upward. "If I could obtain a reprieve on your assignment, perhaps we could extend our time together?"

Michael's grin was sharklike, lips pulled taut over gleaming teeth. Although the Historian was a pleasant diversion, he clung. Michael hadn't found a lover he wanted to keep, and that included the Historian between his legs.

But Michael was an opportunist and allowed his expression to turn coy while he brushed his fingers through his temporary lover's wavy hair. "Provide the reprieve and then we can discuss further games, pet."

Satisfied, the Historian returned to his work, and Michael let his head tip back against the headboard.

"As I was saying," Michael continued, once the Historian's mouth was fully reengaged. "I met with the man. He appeared exactly Alec's type. There's a ruthlessness in his past and in his soul that I haven't seen in a human in at least a century. But when we spoke, his desires were unexpectedly generous." Michael shook his head in memory. Eli was a beautiful human and full of contradictions.

The Historian paused again. "I cannot hear you wax poetic about another while I'm attending to you. Either you focus, or you send me away."

Michael suppressed a sigh. None of his lovers ever met his exacting standards, too jealous and willfully blind to Michael's promiscuous ways, as if each one of them didn't know Michael's habits. He waves an idle hand about the bed. "Do you see the human in this room with us? Is he hiding beneath the sheets? I assumed your duties with the Council would make this an interesting topic of historical significance. The man's soul didn't match his demeanor, and his twin sister may be immune to certain gifts."

The Historian's irritating melted into intrigue. "Did you say twin?"

When Michael nodded, the Historian shifted closer, interest overtaking his earlier pique. "That's the dichotomy you found. Twins' souls are riven, split between them. The halves should be mirror images, both holding good and bad parts. But what's true in theory doesn't occur in practice."

He moved to sit in the space between Michael's knees. Michael hid his disappointment as it was his fault for the interruption. For the first time, his curiosity won over his carnal wants. When his sexual appetite finally flagged, he beckoned the Historian to continue lecturing.

"I read of one account from the Byzantine times about human twins that battled for dominance over the good and bad, rather than being complementary," he said, warming to his subject. "The elder was predisposed to the good, a near pristine half soul, while the younger held all the bad. When the younger turned to the healing arts, the elder's soul tainted. Each time the younger helped another, the elder committed a selfish act. With the elder's soul inclined for good, his terrible actions and desires were exaggerated, worse than the younger would have ever contemplated. The souls refused to split evenly and instead switched entirely."

Michael tilted his head, considering. "So if one acts against their nature..."

"It could amplify the other's traits," the Historian finished. "A literal tug-of-war."

"They share a soul," Michael repeated softly. He should have guessed that based on what he'd read of Eli's past.

Indeed, he should have listened to his own sire about the early Teachings. Then, he wouldn't have a need to further engage the possessive, and somewhat sexually deficient, Historian.

"Tell me," Michael asked, keeping his tone idle. "Do you believe these twins are the same?"

The Historian frowned. "Based on what you described, most likely. The boy has the negative half and the girl the positive, but they are battling for balance if he is attempting to behave generously. While her goodness could counteract with our gifts, that is supposition as there is no record of that. It's more likely the soul reading was flawed because the wraith looked in the wrong place. Her soul would not encompass the full space," he added, shifting to sit beside Michael, covering his nudity with the sheet. "Perhaps the girl is now fighting for control and acting counter to her normal-nature," the Historian suggested. "Her negative thoughts and actions would push him towards the positive, hence is generosity and the dichotomy you saw. Or perhaps the boy," he wrinkled his delicate nose, jealousy apparent in his gaze, "is voluntarily acting weak and good, and he cannot grasp the ruthlessness you admired in his past because it now lives in the girl."

"Can he get it back?" Michael asked. He petted the Historian's thigh and reached under the sheet. A sated lover was a talkative lover. A jealous lover rarely cooperated. The Historian shifted to allow Michael a better grip, straightening his legs.

"I suppose it's possible," the Historian murmured. "Though I don't know why you'd care," he added with another pout.

Michael leaned forward, his voice a silken thread. "Oh, love, you know me. I'm simply gathering information. The only real currency we wraiths have. That," he squeezed, and the Historian grunted, "and the games we play."

Mollified, the Historian closed his eyes. Michael held in his frustration that he was now in the subservient position. The information was needed, and if he visited Eli again, would be handy. No pun intended.

Another thought struck him, and Michael asked, "Has anyone converted a twin?"

The Historian opened his eyes, sighing. "Not to my knowledge, though the recently converted rabble could do anything and not deign to tell the Council," he said with a sniff. "With that boy, you'd have to be sure you converted the right half. Can you imagine if we brought the good twin into the family? That one is only useful as a food source."

Michael hummed, only half paying attention to both his task and the Historian. The twins presented a unique opportunity, what with Alesandro's interest in the girl.

And Michael had always been one to play the long game.

ELI GRUNTED FROM HIS position lounging on the floor beside a black leather couch. The man's nudity, shameless and comfortable, only added to the tableau of decadence.

He'd met with Eli three times before he fisted his hand in Michael's hair and crushed their mouths together. He was a perfect specimen of human—beautiful, lacking embarrassment and shame, with a soul black enough to keep Michael repeatedly interested.

Michael had originally sought him out because of boredom. If the girl intrigued Alesandro, the other could entertain Michael. If nothing else, he could explain what made the girl so interesting to Alesandro. After the Historian revealed Eli's unique half-souled status, and when Alesandro's 'intrigue' with the girl morphed to the notion that he loved her, Michael's purposes for Eli changed too. He had a plan, one that would delight Alesandro and satisfy Michael for a time.

"Move your hand up, I've got a knot," Eli ordered, his head resting on his folded arms. The plush rug under the mortal wasn't as thick as it appeared, and goosebumps erupted over Eli's skin at Michael's touch.

Michael dug his palm into Eli's lower back, eliciting another groan from him. "How demanding you are," he purred. No one had truly demanded anything of Michael in centuries. Only Alesandro defied him; outside of the Council, the rest of the family simpered at his feet, begged, or avoided him. Eli would be an excellent addition to the fold.

Michael let his gaze linger on Eli's form before dragging his hand down his spine, savoring the shiver it elicited. "I'm thinking of converting you," Michael said, petting Eli's nude backside.

Eli grunted, rolling onto his side to look up at Michael. His eyes reflected a mix of curiosity and casual indifference, a hallmark of his particular charm. "That's the best compliment I've gotten after sex," he said, sounding mocking.

Michael smirked, his lips curling just enough to show the sharp edges of his teeth. "It's no mere compliment, pet. It's a consideration."

Michael rolled to his back and directed Eli's fingers onto his stomach, letting Eli play with his muscled flesh. His lips curled as Eli took him in hand.

"Do you have no opinion on my suggestion?" Michael asked.

Eli snorted, focusing more attention on Michael's standing interest. "You'll do what you're going to do."

"Your flexibility is commendable," Michael said, his voice a purr, "though I wonder how much is from you and how much your sister."

"Keep talking about my sister and you'll never enjoy my flexibility again," Eli grumbled. "She's mad right now, probably about Dad and me, since she just took him to the hospital for some liver problem and I ditched her for you," he said, staring hard at the rug. "And considering how I'm feeling, maybe embarrassed... and ambitious?"

"Perhaps," Michael replied. Eli had been fascinated to learn his emotions and desires could contradict hers, and vice versa. Michael, of course, was more interested in Eli's emotions than Azalea's, indulging Eli's one-sided guessing game. His soul was endlessly fascinating, its murky depths a stark contrast to his sister's fading light. The interplay between their shared soul was a puzzle Michael hadn't entirely solved, but he intended to. "I imagine Alesandro sought her out the moment the sun rose this morning, searching for you," Michael added. "Which reminds me—he intends to take your soul; you should avoid him for the next few days."

"That asshole," Eli said, clenching his fingers tight around Michael's skin. Eli wasn't strong enough to harm him, but it wasn't pleasing.

"Watch yourself," Michael groaned. "Don't speak of him that way."

Eli blinked, surprised by the sudden change in tone. "I can't help it. You know that."

That was true. Azalea's affection for Alesandro had the side effect of Eli hating him. But Michael didn't care for excuses. "Which takes us back to my initial statement," Michael said. "That I'm thinking of converting you."

Eli sat up, dropping his hand while Michael pouted. "Cool it, I won't leave you hanging. Will converting keep me from clinging to her like a kid, and the up-down crap?"

Michael dragged Eli's hand back where it belonged before answering. "It should lock in your normal emotions and behavior. You'll no longer trade with your sister." He walked his fingers up Eli's trim chest. "Your base personality remains your own. But it will allow Azalea to remain the honorable half she was before you turned eighteen, while you can return to your inherent deviancy."

Eli pumped his fist hard and fast, and Michael struggled to suppress a groan. He was twenty-five hundred years old, but the man had talent. Much more than that Historian. There was a reason he visited Eli almost daily since those first few visits.

"Wanna tell me why you want to convert me?" Eli asked.

"Can't—can't I do so out of the goodness of my heart?"

Eli halted his movements, narrowing his eyes. Before Michael could growl, Eli slipped his knees on either side of Michael, straddling him. In the dawning light, he looked like a Roman iconized angel. A small part of Michael yearned for Eli's golden locks, rather than his natural pitch colored hair. Eli braced both hands on Michael's chest and scowled down at him.

"I believe it will help Alesandro," Michael admitted.

Eli sneered but refrained from voicing the disdain on his face. "How?"

"Alesandro will have his precious good-hearted Azalea."

Eli snorted. "If the point is to get him a friend, maybe you should convert someone for him instead. Maybe Az, since she wants to leave so much."

Michael brushed a strand of Eli's blond hair from his forehead. "Anyone converted could change for the worse, as your baser human needs and traits expand to supernatural levels. I don't know her well enough to how Azalea would react to losing her soul, whether her goodness would sour." He stroked his hands up Eli's thighs. "I know how you'd behave without one. It would be nice to have another that flaunts the Rules." He remembered Gunval and his ilk. "Someone agreeable that flaunts them. And one not wrapped up in guilt and insecurity." That statement applied to both Alesandro and his female swain.

Eli studied him for a long moment, his lips quirking into a faint smirk. "I'll think about it."

Michael dragged him closer, their bodies flush against each other. "Think long and hard, pet. This decision changes everything. Your second life will be entirely different from your first."

Eli nodded. "I've got a way to clear my head. I'll do that once we're finished." He shifted against Michael's thighs, his smirk reappearing. "Speaking of long and hard..."

MICHAEL LOUNGED IN HIS den in Martalk, counting the pillows strewn across the floor as though their number might yield some revelation. After their earlier conversation about conversion, Eli had departed, leaving Michael teetering on the edge of boredom so profound it felt like a punishment. He considered tearing at his hair in frustration but decided against it—the damn strands would simply reappear by morning, their usual black color mocking his efforts. Instead, he'd redyed them yellow in honor of Eli and the plan that still brewed in his mind.

He could return to the Historian, but the thought was as appealing as biting into a sour fruit. Jealousy and inadequate carnal skills weren't worth the effort, no matter how sweet the Historian's earlier sycophancy had been. The wraiths who might provide a fleeting distraction had all either bored or irritated him. As for roving assignments, he refused to take another unless demanded by the Head Councilmember himself. After all, a year ago, the Council had dared censure him for a possible Rule break—a slight Michael neither forgave nor forgot.

That very censure had reignited his loathing for the system Alesandro still defended. His love for Alesandro, steadfast and unwavering for centuries, hadn't dimmed his frustration with the boy's blind adherence to the Rules. But then, love rarely made sense. It was both a blessing and a curse, this devotion to his protégé.

At least Eli added spice to the unending monotony. His ardor and shamelessness would entertain Michael for a time. Perhaps Michael could even convince Eli to teach that humorless Historian a thing or two. Unlike most of Michael's conquests, Eli lacked jealousy and didn't harbor expectations. It was refreshing. He was an unintended benefit to Michael's unending task of cultivating Alesandro.

Still, Michael hoped Eli would decide quickly. If he agreed to conversion for Azalea's sake, the resulting emotional shift would be fascinating to observe. Azalea's half of their shared soul would no doubt flood into Eli, making him more palatable to Alesandro, while her newfound darkness would bring Azalea herself in line with Michael's tastes. A saintly Azalea held no interest for him. He'd made the mistake of engaging with someone good centuries ago—an error he had no intention of repeating.

A faint ripple in the mirror above him caught his attention, and moments later, a folded piece of parchment slipped through the surface. It floated lazily down, landing on Michael's chest.

Spots of ink marked the page, blotting around Alesandro's wobbly handwriting.

Michael,

I love her, Michael, like I've loved no one else. The others, they... they are nothing compared to her. Stop whatever you have planned. Please, I beg of you. Think of our history and our times together and let me have her, if she agrees. Let me experience time with her what I was denied with Cassius and Lucia.

I will tell her what I am and ask her to choose me, if she can accept the monster that I am. Our decades together will be short, but the time we have will be worth it. The memory of our time together will last through my eternity without her.

Do not shorten our brief time together by killing her. I could not—would not—survive it.

Michael groaned, crumpling the parchment into a tight ball before tossing it across the room. It bounced off a pillow and landed in a heap of silks. Clearly, Alesandro was overdue for a hunt. Unless "rambling melodrama" was a new feature of the boy's personality, it was time to address his mounting instability. Alesandro was his soft, maudlin boy, but not irrational.

The note, however, revealed more than Alesandro's penchant for sentimentality. It made something painfully clear: simply converting Eli and allowing Azalea to live out a mortal life wouldn't resolve anything. If Azalea died before Alesandro finished with her, his mourning would stretch across the centuries, each sigh and lament echoing through eternity. He'd held on to Cassius far too long, and that connection never even began. (And he really wasn't worth it.) And Lucia? Fates, she was no more than an idea!

Michael closed his eyes, imagining the endless whining, the maudlin grief Alesandro would undoubtedly unleash upon him.

No. That future was untenable.

Springing to his feet, Michael felt the first stirrings of excitement in days. At least, for now, he was no longer bored.

Chapter 74

Then

Michael stepped into Selina's hovel, his lips curling in disdain. The things he did for Alesandro. If only the boy hadn't run off with that troublesome girl or sent that melodramatic note swearing he'd die without her, Michael wouldn't have had to come to this pit of despair. He'd planned everything so neatly: convert Eli, trap the sordid half of their shared soul safely within him, and leave Alesandro with his untainted darling. But no, the girl's erratic descent into depravity and Alesandro's maddening unpredictability had upended it all.

Now, here he was, in Gordamara of all places, the stench of decay and despair clinging to him as he approached Selina's makeshift palace. He'd taken a mirror several villages away and sprinted through the filth-strewn streets to reach her, passing squatters gnawing on what could only be described as refuse. He wondered, not for the first time, why he bothered. If Alesandro weren't so tediously devoted to the Rules, Michael could have simply told him the plan outright and avoided all this subterfuge.

Selina's "home" was hardly a home—just a single cramped room with dirt floors, a sagging pallet, and a dim candle lamp dangling precariously from the ceiling. Though reading her was beyond his ken, he imagined he could sense her bitter history and the horrors through which she'd lived to survive in the squalor of the small town of Gordamara.

"It fits, does it not?" a whiskey-deep voice purred from the darkness. The strike of a match followed, illuminating her figure as she lit a candle. Selina lounged on threadbare pillows, her dark hair cascading over her shoulders, her posture regal despite the squalor. In this pit of despair, she was undoubtedly queen.

"Remember the Teachings," Michael's baritone swept outward, the sound crashing against the dirt walls.

"I do not follow the Teachings anymore," she responded as she placed a lit candle on the ground. "And your thoughts on my home, while amusing, are a distraction."

Michael swallowed his discomfort. He needed to be more circumspect with his thoughts if she could hear them. Her answering smile was feral. "The pain of exile breaks through many blocks, including those that limit me against the family. Tell me why you are here, Michael. I would hear it from your own lips."

Michael bowed low and focused his mind on the present, imagining his thoughts at the bottom of an endless well, one she would need to fall into without hope of clawing back out if she intended to keep reading him. "Selina, my love, can I not visit a friend?"

Selina's lips curved into a feral smile. "The family doesn't visit." Her dark eyes glittered as she took a step forward, moving so quickly it seemed the air itself bent around her. "Are you here to kill me?" Her voice was a coo, her pout as provocative as it was dangerous. "Has my time in exile finally ended?"

Michael let his gaze drift over her, taking in her burnished copper skin and scandalously tight clothing. The fire that had ravaged her in life left her scarred but striking. She wore close to nothing—scandalously tight pants and a vest that covered only what decency would require. And Michael cared not for decency. He trailed his fingers over the edge of the vest, letting it open so he could gaze more on that dusky flesh.

Her brown eyes flashed as she tipped forward to receive more of his touch. "I am not here to kill you," he said, licking his lips and bending down toward her. His lips nuzzled at her neck until and slid towards her hair. She smelled like smoke, sharp and intoxicating.

"Setting an entire civilization ablaze in your rage will leave lasting effects," she murmured, that rich voice thready and gasping.

"Tell me more." Michael licked at her earlobe. "Tell me about the willing soul gambit that brought you to this existence."

Selina shoved him back with startling strength, feathers and dust rising as he landed on her pallet. "Are we playing first?" he asked, patting his lap with a grin.

She stalked toward him, her teeth bared in a mockery of a smile. Straddling him, she gripped his hair in one hand and his chin in the other, forcing him to meet her gaze. Her black eyes burned with the weight of centuries. The color was a reminder that she was an older wraith by far, one of the first converts who at one point wielded more power than Michael could have imagined. Her nails, rough and jagged, bit into his skin, leaving red trails in their wake.

"Still Michael," she said, her voice a purr. She ran both hands through his long locks and then pulled. He pulsed upward beneath her, aching. "Still a deviant."

She leaned backward, the vest falling open to his gaze, and he moved his hands to her hips. He skimmed his hands from her hip to shoulder, her flesh pebbling. She shuddered but didn't seat herself on him or let go of the hard grip she had on his hair. The flash in her black eyes told him she was well-nourished on souls. The scent of her arousal told him she was starved otherwise. He planned to meet Eli later that day, depending on this visit, but one could never overindulge in passion.

She leaned closer, her lips brushing his ear. "Why do you want to know about the gambit?"

"I seek information for another," he admitted.

She groaned, the sound shooting to his groin, but instead of continuing, she slipped her leg off him and sat beside him on the pallet. "Is it the favorite? Alesandro."

Michael held in a startled movement. He had converted Alesandro years after her banishment; there was no reason for her to know of him or realize his regard for the boy, not unless her gift was much stronger than he knew. He said nothing, instead sighing. She laughed.

"And there is my answer, without needing to pluck it from your head. The wraith who seeks the violent service of the Council seeks a willing soul?" Her laugh turned grating and bitter.

"I hadn't realized either of us were so infamous to reach the ears of those exiled from the family," Michael said mildly.

She leaned her head back against the wall and closed her eyes. "The exiled speak of Alesandro in whispers, as the Council's weapon who brought us to our ill-favored existence, but your exploits have not changed since I was cradled within the bosom of that family. Remember, I was there when you were found alone in Ur when Nabonidus died. They could take my home, my beauty, but they cannot take my memory."

He placed a hand on her thigh and stroked it upward toward the dip of her sharp hip. "They did not take your beauty."

She shivered and batted his hand away. "Why does your Alesandro desire this information?"

Michael ran a hand through his hair, choosing his words carefully. Selina was exiled, yes, but her awareness of family affairs was unnerving. "There's a woman."

"There's always a woman," Selina scoffed, rolling her eyes. "Or a man," she added with a smirk, her fingers brushing his exposed chest.

He matched her smirk, Eli's plush lips appearing in his thoughts. "Humans can be a treat."

"And yet, too soft," she said, straddling him again. "A trade," she purred, tugging at his shirt. "For each piece of information."

He leered at her, the flames of the candle sending colors through her hair, inciting his arousal further. He shifted his hands to cover her bare breasts. "You've a head start." Hands back on her hips, he began. "Is it possible?"

Selina's eyes darkened, and her expression turned serious. His gift of reading the past was still limited to humans, unlike her own exiled consequence that allowed her to cross into his own head. Thus, it was not his gift that told him she was remembering her own human lover, the man who betrayed her, who she ultimately killed. It was the look of pained fury in her eyes.

"Theoretically, yes," she said. "A human could willingly give their soul to a wraith, sharing it for as long as the bond holds. But it's not simple." Her fingers slid underneath his shirt and pulled, buttons popping off and scattering to the dirt floor and baring his brawny chest for her.

"Why theoretical?" he asked, his voice rough as her teeth grazed his collarbone.

"A human must be broken to do it," she whispered, sucking a mark on his neck. "That is the trick. Beings splitting souls and not going mad with the constant tug and pull? You need someone who can live with only half." With effort, she pulled herself backward and looked at him, her expression serious. "If you truly want to help your boy, make him forget her."

Michael considered her words, his mind racing. It wasn't the plan he'd envisioned, but it would suffice. He moved her hands where he wanted them, his grin wicked. "You are the expert, 'lina love."

IT WAS THE FOURTH time in four days that Michael visited with Selina, as the plan he tossed into the dirt sprouted and grew. This time, the meek and self-conscious Eli joined him. Michael left him in the next room as Selina planned to show him the fruits of her years of exile. While Eli's submissiveness was pleasing for a time, Michael missed his spirit. Unlike how the trait appeared in Azalea, Eli's version of Azalea's jealousy and docility was off-putting. Much like Azalea's version of Eli's stronger traits, his assertiveness and egoism appeared poorly on her, like a rancid version of the real thing.

Michael would curse the Fates for halving twin souls, except for how helpful it was in this exact situation.

"He will hate you for this," Selina said, making Michael laugh. With his most secret thoughts walled away, she didn't know that the gifted soul wouldn't be Azalea to Alesan—Alec, but the twins to each other.

Michael chuckled. Alec had forced his hand with that pathetic letter, and now Michael was left to untangle the mess and ensure the boy's happiness. Happiness, of course, was subjective.

"No, love. In centuries, he will thank me." He already envisioned Alec's gratitude, the praise, and, of course, the inevitable gifts. A converted Azalea would be his ultimate act of generosity, securing Alesandro's happiness while giving Michael access to Eli for as long as they both desired. A win-win.

"I do not enjoy seeing another go through what I did, when Ennam betrayed his gift," Selina pouted, dropping to her knees in a room filled with weaponry. Two knives carelessly laying on the dirt ground dug into the flesh of her shins. "Humans only bring pain."

He tilted his head, letting his gaze trail over her scarred yet striking form. "I don't believe history will repeat itself," he said. He knew Alesandro better than anyone, and the boy wouldn't risk the breach if he didn't truly love her. Azalea, however, was an unknown variable. Her heart was hidden, her motives a mystery. He'd have to ask her, though at this point he was committed to the plan merely to keep Eli.

Selina slithered to her feet, her eyes glinting with suspicion. "If, as you believe, your Alesandro seeks me for the same reason you did—to learn about receiving a willing soul—it will. I told you, the gambit won't work unless the human is broken. Do you wish to saddle him with that?"

Michael hesitated for a fraction of a second before answering. "He appears to love her," he admitted, keeping his tone nonchalant. That was the most information he could allow until the deed was done.

Her hiss cut through the room, sharp and venomous. "There are easier routes to exile."

"Exile isn't the goal, 'lina love. His happiness is." Michael's voice dropped an octave, becoming a low rumble. "The willing soul gambit is the only chance he has." Though, as Selina would never guess, not in the way she assumed.

Selina laughed, the sound rasping against the dirt walls. "If he wants to keep her and her willing soul, exile is the only choice the Council will grant."

Michael didn't disagree, though he doubted exile would be the Council's sole punishment. Alec was too renowned, too important, to let off so easily. They would make an example of him. Alec would be better off converting Azalea. That, the Council might forgive—loving a human they couldn't. But Michael knew him, Alec would never convert Azalea, or anyone. The only path to survival, for both Alec and Azalea, was through Michael's plan. Conversion, exile, and a willing soul transfer. It was delicate work, requiring precision and manipulation—a game Michael had long mastered.

He moved to a spear leaning against the wall, running his hands over its shaft. "You must trust that I know what I'm doing."

Selina raised a brow, her lips quirking into a smile. "Trust? Hardly. I expect something in return." She pushed the spear aside, her fingers trailing up his shoulders to tangle in his blue hair.

Michael smirked, his hands finding her hips. "More of me? Fates, I hope to remain in such high demand after my exile."

Her laughter was dark, rolling from her chest like thunder. "Will your human allow you to share?"

He pinched the hollows at her hip. Probably, he admitted to himself, but he didn't want to share anymore. Something about that boy clawed into his skin and he didn't want Eli to let go. "He's ill. I will need to reintroduce you when he's back to his usual self."

Selina's brows raised, her amusement sharpening. "Perhaps you should have told me I had more than one lovesick wraith to handle."

Michael pouted but didn't contradict her.

She huffed a bitter laugh before dragging him to closer to the mirror. "I will guide your Alesandro to exile, but I expect him to join our cause."

Michael planted his feet, causing Selina to trip and reveal more alluring skin. "I told you, 'lina, I seek his happiness. I will not force another millstone around his neck. The Rules restrained his life enough. He deserves the choice."

She fixed her dark eyes on him. "It is quite disingenuous to speak of his choices when you control them."

Michael shrugged. Sire's privilege, more like. To Selina, he said, "Nudging in the proper direction isn't controlling."

"Then I desire the opportunity to nudge him as well."

That was compromise enough for Michael. "When he is in your home, you may make your offers. I expect you to notify me of his presence so I may collect Azalea."

She frowned but didn't question Michael's demand. "Very well. You know my feelings. Thus, what you do with his human matters not to me. I will separate him from the human and give him the choice—I will complete the exile rites privately if he joins us. If he doesn't, the Council must exile him itself."

Michael licked his lips. It would take a silver tongue to restrain the Council from further bloodletting, and it changed the last step of his plan. "Fine. I will be his Accuser. But someone else will need to alert the Council of his breaches."

"I have that handled," she said with a wry smile. "We exiled have been busy. I've an insider who will sound the alarm when you give notice."

"Who?"

She spun to the mirror leaning against the corner and pressed a hairpin to the glass.

"Where were you keeping that?" Michael asked, his curiosity piqued. Selina only smirked, her attention focused on the mirror as a figure materialized.

"Good morning, Selina," a familiar voice greeted. "Before we get to business, you'll never guess who visited me yesterday with a human in tow. Our favorite rover."

Selina's smile turned wicked as she glanced at Michael. "I have even better news, Gerald."

THE SUN CREPT SLUGGISHLY over the artificial horizon, casting a faint glow through the fake window Michael had bought on a whim. It was a gift for Eli, something to soften his fraying edges. The window was cheap, sold by a hawker in Post #2 during Michael's last visit to Gerald to finalize the steps of their plan. Eli lay beneath Michael's silk sheets, his pale skin ghostly in the dim light, a haunting reflection of the soul-tugging chaos that had engulfed them both.

It had been two days since the two had visited Selina and struck their bargain. And now, Azalea was enraging him. She had grown increasingly erratic, creating a tarnished and warped mirror version in Eli, who could hardly walk under the weight of his own neuroses. Had she not made him wait, Michael might have spared a minute to empathize. While Eli's version of Azalea's traits was distorted and magnified, Azalea's own life must have been filled with self-doubt and a need for control, explaining why she leapt off the cliff with Alec. But now Michael was bored, worried, and had to care for his sweet, troubled, love.

If Azalea's love for Alec proved false, Michael promised himself that her second life would be an eternity of misery. A little more sire's privilege.

Michael leaned against the headboard, watching as Eli shifted, his lithe body curling tighter into the plush bedding. "Have you decided, pet?" Michael murmured, stroking his fingers through Eli's tousled fringe. The softness of the gesture belied his mounting frustration.

"Whether it's me or Az who gets converted?" Eli mumbled, his voice husky with exhaustion. "Not yet. I'm afraid to decide."

Michael hummed, understanding the hesitation. Eli's last decision—to confront his sister—had coincided with Azalea and Alec's flight, throwing them all into chaos.

"I'm almost scared to say it," Eli continued, his voice cracking. "What if I'm the giver? What if me doing it makes me the good twin?"

Michael smothered a smile. The idea of Eli as the "good" twin was laughable. Even without Azalea's moral half, Eli's inherent nature was too wild, too selfish. But he humored him anyway. "I've considered that, love. The elixir Azalea took rebalanced your halves, or simulated it enough to recreate your personalities. I'll slip it to her again. Then, your deviancy will return, and she'll reclaim her honor."

She'd most likely have an immediate crisis of conscience as well, meaning he'd need to sprint to a converted Eli waiting for Azalea's gifted soul or quickly convert her before she ran back to Alec and further ruined his plans.

Eli shifted to sit beside Michael, draping himself over Michael's lap. "That's what I'm worried about. That me giving her my half of the soul does the same thing as last time."

"Do you love her?" he murmured into Eli's hair. Eli nodded. "I told you, that part of you—the base part—remains no matter how much of a soul lives within you. You may tease her, fight with her, take advantage of her, just as she may do to you—"

"Like siccing the cops on me."

"But she's your sister. You would do anything for her, much like I will do anything for my brother, despite him vexing me." Michael pressed his lips to Eli's hair, inhaling his scent. "I am still the wretched wraith I have always been; my love for Alec doesn't change that. Thus, your gift can be willing, even if you're a corrupt man."

Eli sighed heavily. "Right now, I just want my half back. Maybe go back to my trailer and... I dunno, volunteer at a soup kitchen?"

Michael laughed softly, the sound rumbling in his chest. "Benevolence. Azalea must be reaching her peak selfishness. Alec will take her to Selina soon. It's inevitable."

A soft rustle drew Michael's attention to the floor. A note had slipped through the nearby mirror, its folded edge brushing against the carpet. He leapt from the bed and snatched it up, recognizing Selina's precise script.

The words were brief but clear: It's time. Prepare the human.

Michael smiled, turning to rummage through an aged ash dresser. He retrieved two pocket watches, handpicking the pair that hummed with the energy he needed. Satisfied, he returned to Eli, who watched him with weary curiosity.

"Wonderful news, dearest," Michael said, his grin sharp and predatory. "We're nearing the end. In just a few hours, your soul will be yours again, Azalea will have her darling Alec, and you'll have an eternity to play with me."

Eli offered him a shy smile in return.

Chapter 75

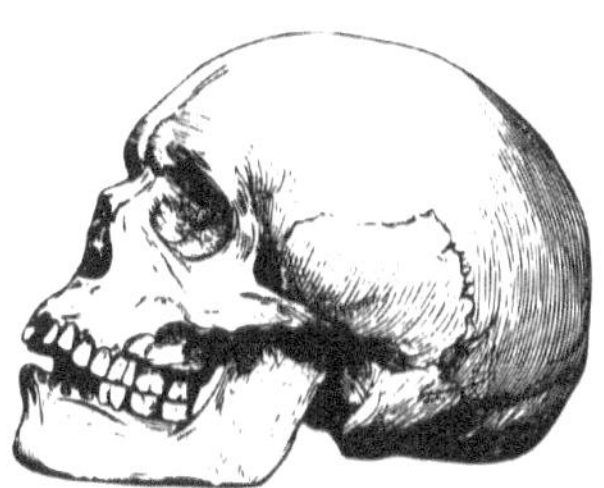

ALEC STILL SITS ON Michael's chest, his hands limp at his sides. The memories Michael forced on him swirl in his mind like a poison cloud. "Why?" The word tumbles from his lips, fractured and raw.

Michael shrugs, the motion almost throwing Alec off balance. Alec scrambles off him, instinctively reaching out to help him to his feet, though the act feels alien. Once standing, they retreat to opposite corners of the cell-like room where Alec woke, both silent, their movements unsteady. Michael rakes his fingers through his black hair, the color unfamiliar. Alec can't remember the last time he saw Michael with his natural hue—centuries ago, in the Middle Ages, perhaps.

"You saw the memories." Michael's voice is low, almost steady. "You're my brother."

Michael presses the backs of his hands to his eyes, and Alec blinks. The bittersweet scent of relief mingles with something more fragile—grief, maybe. If Alec couldn't smell it, he wouldn't believe Michael is on the verge of tears.

"But all that I planned—" Alec's voice cracks.

Michael doesn't respond. He spins toward the doorway, his shoulders taut, the air around him charged. At the threshold, he pauses, half-turning back with a smirk. It's shaky, almost fragile, as if held together by sheer will.

"I'll reap my rewards from you for centuries, dearest," Michael says. "Now, shall we call upon our twin paramours?"

Chapter 76

Azzie curls against the cold stone wall of one of Selina's basement rooms, her knees pulled tight to her chest. She hadn't seen Selina since she woke up, but it was inevitable as they were living in her underground home waiting for Alec to wake.

"I can't believe I acted that way," she murmurs, her voice barely above a whisper.

Eli sits beside her, his fingers absently twisting a lock of her hair. "We've been over this like eight times since yesterday, Az," he says, leaning his head back against the wall. "You weren't in your right mind." His gaze shifts to the mirror across the room. Their reflections stare back at them—musty-haired, red-eyed, and somber. But only Azalea's brown eyes flash in the low light. "Besides, only I can pull off Eli-style narcissism and arrogance. You shouldn't have even tried."

A reluctant twitch pulls at her lips, almost a smile. Eli's attempts at comforting her never quite land, but the fact that he tries warms her in a way she doesn't yet have words for. It's the same place in her chest where she feels the steady pulse of their shared soul, a connection both alien and familiar.

"I wonder how much of the soul-bleed will stick with us," she says, pressing a hand to her chest. "I can feel you. But also me. It's... different."

"Soul-bleed?" Eli wrinkles his nose. "Man, does immortality come with homework? Because no one warned me about this."

She chuckles softly. "I made that up. But Alec told me some things already, and you won't be able to *siphon* off me to learn it like you did senior year."

Eli elbows her in the stomach. "I know it's going to be hard, but at some point, you'll have to admit I'm the smarter twin."

She elbows him back, rolling her eyes. "The smarter twin wouldn't have kept all this a secret and let me spiral like that."

"Nope," Eli says smugly, folding his arms behind his head. "Still the smarter twin. The evil twin too. And definitely the one with the hotter boyfriend."

Her smile falters. Eli isn't evil, but she *had* been, or close enough, when she carried his half of their soul. The weight of that realization presses into her stomach. How would Alec see her now? She never abandoned him, not truly, but she browbeat him and acted like... like some grotesque parody of Eli. She glances at Eli now, a pompous smirk on his face as he probably daydreams about Michael. She could use her gifts to check, but it doesn't feel right.

She was worse than Eli. Michael and Eli had explained it: her traits twisted and warped by his half of their soul, amplifying her basest desires. Her thirst for adventure and escape had turned her into a self-centered prissy queen obsessed with immortality, while Eli had been reduced to a fearful, reclusive shadow of himself.

"Also, have you picked up on the civil war stuff?" Eli asks, straightening suddenly. "Selina and Gerald kept dropping hints, but I think Michael was going to hide us from it until we all talked. Good thing you like adventure and I like thrills, or this immortality thing might blow."

She sniffs. "From the thrill of petty thievery to a soldier in an immortal battle, you know how to live," she jokes, her voice only cracking once.

Eli bumps her shoulder, grinning at their shared reflection in the mirror. "What can I say? I'm versatile."

Their conversation is cut short by the sound of heavy footsteps in the hallway. Both of them stand, tension crackling in the air. Michael appears first, his confident swagger filling the doorway, but Alec barrels past him, his eyes locking onto Azalea. She wipes her palms on her jeans, phantom sensations of sweat clinging to her hands despite her new wraith physiology.

Michael opens his arms, and Eli struts over, the air around his head bursting with *affection-mine-arousal-playtime* without her needing to reach for it. Azalea wrinkles her nose as they leave, trying not to read too much into the feelings she senses.

Then, Alec is in front of her.

For a moment, she forgets to breathe. He looks different—leaner, sharper, like exile chiseled away at him and left only the essentials. His dark curls are mussed, his jawline more defined, and his eyes—those fiery, unrelenting blue eyes—lock onto hers. There's something flickering there, something raw and guarded but unmistakably yearning. It twists her chest into knots.

"Azalea," he rumbles, his voice like a low hum in her bones. He takes a step forward, then stops, like he's waiting for her to make the first move.

And she wants to run to him, but a voice in her head—her voice finally, the one that still doubts, the one that knows all she put everyone through—holds her back. She twists her hands together, her eyes darting to the floor.

"Are you alright?" he asks, his voice softer now, like he's afraid he'll scare her off.

She nods, wrapping her arms around herself. "I think so. Back to me, or close enough. I don't know how the soul sharing works yet. My half is mine again, but maybe I borrow Eli's sometimes. It's... confusing."

Alec exhales, his shoulders relaxing a fraction. "I understand," he murmurs. "Things are... different now."

"Yeah," she says. "Different." Different how she wanted, and different how she didn't.

The space between them feels heavy, but not unbearable. She takes a step forward, then another, until she's close enough to feel the warmth of him. She tilts her chin up, her fingers twitching at her sides. "I was *awful* to you," she blurts. "I—don't even know where to start making up for it, but I swear I—"

"Stop." His voice is gentle but firm, and he lifts a hand to her cheek. The touch is hesitant at first, as if he's afraid she'll pull away, but when she leans into it, his thumb brushes against her skin. "There's nothing to make up for. What happened wasn't your—we were both..." He shakes his head, the words stalling in his throat. "If anything, I should've realized something was wrong. But I didn't want to. I was—captivated by you."

She steps back, just enough to catch her breath. "That's the problem," she says, her voice steady despite the ache in her chest. "That wasn't me. Or it isn't me now. This soul-splitting thing is confusing."

His brows knit. "I know exactly what you are, Azalea," he says. "You're you. The rest—whatever you're figuring out, this you as a wraith—it doesn't change that."

Her eyes drop to the ring on her finger. She fumbles to twist it off, the amber band refusing to budge. "This—this is yours," she stammers, tugging harder.

Alec's hand covers hers, stopping her, his grip steady but careful. "Keep it," he says softly. "It suits you."

She looks up at him, her heart stuttering in her chest. "Can we start over?" she asks, her voice small but steady. "Not like nothing happened, because that wouldn't be fair. But... I don't want us to be stuck there either. I want—" She hesitates, the words catching in her throat. "I want us to try again. For real this time."

He studies her for a long moment, and she wonders if she's asked too much, after all she put him through. But then his lips curve into a real smile—not the brittle ones she's seen so recently, but something warmer, more honest. "We'll figure this out. Together," he says. "If you'll have me."

It's not even a question she has to consider. She throws her arms around his neck, and he stiffens for a second before pulling her in, his frame shaking, holding her like she's the only thing tethering him to the world.

His face buries in her hair, and she hears him murmur, "I'm so very sorry, Azalea."

She pulls back just enough to look at him, her heart thundering in her chest. Both have unshed tears glimmering in their eyes. She doesn't know how being a wraith works yet: sweat—not possible, tears—at the drop of a hat.

Her throat works as she tries to think of what to say. Finally, she offers a tremulous smile. "You know what they say. The course of true love never did run smooth."

He huffs a laugh, his hands twitching against her sides. He looks relieved, like it was the perfect thing to say. "The bard speaks truth."

Smiling through the tears, she rises onto her toes and kisses him. And the *happiness—yes—relief—thisisstillsogood—adoration* tumbles around them and she knows it can only be from her, that his thoughts and memories are hidden since her gifts don't work that way, but she images he feels the same way, that he still will once she makes up for everything—no matter his claims she doesn't need to—once she proves she deserves what he originally offered without expectation. When they pull apart again, Alec's smile is even brighter, steadier.

The sound of footsteps in the hallway breaks the moment, and Azzie glances toward the door. "Michael's going to barge in any second, isn't he?"

"Most likely," Alec says with a resigned sigh. "And that brother of yours, too, no doubt. I'm sure they've come up with something debauched to announce."

She laughs, the sound light and easy, as happy as she's been in years. "Well, then," she says, her smile widening, "let's make the most of this before they ruin it."

Alec's answering smile is soft, his expression open. "I intend to."

And with that, he kisses her again, the kind of kiss that feels like a promise.

As the footsteps grow louder, she smiles against his lips, her hand sliding into his. Whatever comes next—whether it's battles, the weight of immortality, the consequences of their past actions, or even Michael's meddling—they'll face it together.

And for now, that's enough.

FOR MORE

Alec, Azalea, Michael, and Eli will return in:
A BONE INTERRED.
If you'd like to stay updated on the next adventures for the four, check out my website (kmalady.com). You can also find other fun information there, including a free prequel novella for my romantic fantasy series in the Ascend Trials, and updates on other fantasy projects.